THE COST OF LIBERTY

A Novel

David Ross Cornish

ISBN: 1977783414
ISBN 13: 9781977783417
Library of Congress Control Number: 2017915507
CreateSpace Independent Publishing Platform
North Charleston, South Carolina

ACKNOWLEDGMENTS

Special thanks to my wife, Diane, and my daughter, Lindsay, for their patience during the lengthy time of research, outlining, writing, and rewriting this book. Without their support this first book in a series would never have come to fruition.

Thanks to my wife and also to numerous individuals, who read portions of this work and provided valuable thoughts, and insights: historical author William Federer; Florida state representative, physician, and attorney Dr. Julio Gonzalez; attorney Bretton Inganamort; Pastor Matt Day; Randy McLendon; attorney Tom Rhoads and attorney W. Russell Snyder. My thanks to authors Kim Cool, and the late Tate Volino, who provided advice and support pertaining to the publication of this work, and special thanks to another author, Mary Schoenecker, who reviewed and commented on a portion of this work, and gave me valuable tips regarding the publication phase. I am also grateful to attorney Sandra Wiseman and author Doug Ross. Sandra introduced me to Doug, who gave me suggestions regarding the publishing of this book and most importantly provided me with the name of my self-publisher, CreateSpace. The people of CreateSpace have been wonderful to work with, guiding and directing me through editing the manuscript and the publishing process. Additionally, I thank the Venice

Public Library for its resources that proved valuable to my research. Most of all I am grateful to God for His inspiration for this work and His guidance throughout.

Of the books consulted, I would strongly urge anyone who would like to learn more about this critical period in our nation's history to read the following for himself or herself: *The First American: The Life and Times of Benjamin Franklin*, H. W. Brands, Anchor Books—an outstanding work on the life of one of the greatest minds in history; *Patriots: The Men Who Started the American Revolution*, A. J. Langguth, Touchstone—an excellent, compelling, and captivating read; *American Sphinx: The Character of Thomas Jefferson*, Joseph J. Ellis, Vintage Books—a wonderful portrayal of the author of the Declaration of Independence and third president of the United States; *John Adams*, David McCullough, Simon and Schuster—another masterful book by one of the greatest historical writers of all time; *The First American Army: The Untold Story of George Washington and the Men Behind America's First Fight for Freedom*, Bruce Chadwick, Sourcebooks—a well-written behind-the-scenes glimpse at the men who actually won our freedom; *The Day the American Revolution Began: 19 April 1775*, William H. Hallahan, William Morrow Paperbacks—the quintessential account of that fateful day of the shot heard round the world; and *The Night the Revolution Began: The Boston Tea Party 1773*, Wesley S. Griswald, S. Greene Press—a powerful look at the events leading up to and culminating in the most important party in our nation's history.

Other books that were important to me in this endeavor are as follows: *In Pursuit of Liberty: Coming of Age in the American Revolution*, Emmy E. Werner, Potomac Books; *Patriot Battles: How the War of Independence Was Fought*, Michael Stephenson, HarperCollins; *His Excellency: George Washington*, Joseph J. Ellis, Alfred A. Knopf, a division of Random House; *Redcoats and Rebels: The American Revolution Through the Eyes of Those That Fought and Lived It*, George F. Scheer and Hugh F. Rankin, DaCapo; *The War of the Revolution*, Christopher Ward, MacMillan; *The*

Fire of Liberty, Edmund Wright, St. Martin's Press; *Founding Myths: Stories That Hide Our Patriotic Past*, Ray Raphael, New Press; *The Marketplace of Revolution: How Consumer Politics Shaped American Independence*, T. H. Breen, Oxford University Press and *Glory, Passion and Principle: The Story of Eight Remarkable Women at the Core of the American Revolution*, Melissa Lukeman Bohrer, Atria Books.

AUTHOR'S NOTE

The Cost of Liberty is a work of historical fiction. While I attempted to bring fictional characters to life in hopes that the reader could in some way identify with them and thereby better appreciate what it was really like to live in the crucible of the times that brought about the formation of this great nation, the focus of this work is the events. It was the events—some small, some monumental, lived in and, of course, shaped by men and women of different backgrounds—that helped to make the United States of America the beacon of liberty throughout the world and in a way that is unprecedented in the history of humankind. It is our liberty, that precious gift from God Himself that has been entrusted to us and that we must endeavor to protect and preserve at all costs, that provided the impetus to write this book. As mentioned in the following prologue, the hope is that we will understand the incredible sacrifices that were made to obtain that liberty and that have continued throughout our history to maintain it.

I have attempted to stick closely to the historical record, but I have taken obvious liberties with *liberty*. No headdresses were worn by the "Indians" who carried out the Boston Tea Party, though the author added one on the head of Jean Paul Pierre DuBois, believing that this was the perfect touch for his disguise. There were also some liberties taken with the character of Lydia Finch, particularly pertaining to the courting of her by James McDonnell and her being permitted to remain in Philadelphia to continue the courtship. Also the servants, particularly Judah Smith, are treated with more deference and respect by Master William Finch and his family and friends than was generally the case in colonial times, and women in general in *The Cost of Liberty* are also treated with more deference and respect and are more open about expressing opinions than most of their counterparts from colonial days. I am sure there may be other liberties, but these stand out.

I do want to make it perfectly clear that I have no ill will for the British people; indeed quite the opposite is true. I simply am attempting to portray the struggles between the colonies and the mother country as I have been able to glean them from all the sources at my disposal (see the acknowledgment section). Indeed my own ancestry is traced back to Britain. I have friends and clients who are British and hail from there. I have nothing but the utmost respect and admiration for them, and I believe that it was by God's hand (Washington referred to God's intervention as providence) that this nation was formed, in part, to later come to the aid of the mother country in the world wars of the twentieth century.

This book is in loving memory of my late father, Dr. George G. Cornish, who served in the United States Navy and United States Air Force and who had a passion for history.

This series is dedicated to all those who have sacrificed for the cause of our liberty, with special gratitude to those in the armed forces who have given so much to secure the liberties we enjoy.

PROLOGUE

When I first conceived of this book series several years ago, my primary purpose was to honor all who have sacrificed so much, in so many ways, to enable us in this country to enjoy a standard of life that is and has been second to none in world history. The thinking was that through a novel series, we could briefly step back in time and relive the monumental events that gave rise to the great American experiment as seen through the eyes of fictional as well as historical characters. It is my hope and desire that this series will be read even by those who have little interest in history. (While I have tried to be historically accurate, I have taken liberties, some more obvious than others, with the pure historical record.)

This work been created not only to express gratitude to the aforementioned but also to serve as a reminder to us all that liberty is a very precious commodity indeed and that if we do not continue to remember the great price that has been paid and is continuing to be paid to purchase and maintain it, we are almost certainly doomed to lose it. This leads me directly to the next matter, namely, the ominous and troubling events that have occurred since I first conceived of this project and began writing, events that I fear gravely threaten the future of our most precious commodity. While I am a believer in the need for government as the protector and guarantor of our liberties, it is also, in my opinion, the greatest threat to those liberties it is designed to protect. Our government exists for the individual, not the individual for the government. The alarming growth of government, with its tentacles reaching deeply into nearly every aspect of our lives, has, as its inevitable result, erosion of personal freedom. More government regulation has to, of necessity, mean less liberty. "Power corrupts and absolute power corrupts absolutely," said British Lord Acton in a letter to Bishop Mandell Creighton in 1887. No truer words were ever spoken. Yes, but ours is a democratic republic, and power in the hands of the federal government will only be used to benefit us, not to harm us, you may say. I say the founding fathers were very wary of too much power in the hands of a few (in keeping with this thought, I believe the time has come for what I have advocated for years-congressional term limits-too much time in power often leads to abuse and isolation from the people they represent). They knew that it could lead to despotism. All they had to do was to look across the Atlantic to the mother country and King George III, who directly impinged upon their freedom. Those founding fathers risked everything they had to throw off the shackles of that "benevolent monarch" and his minions in Parliament. Personal liberty is at the heart and soul of our nation, it permeates every fabric of our society, it is what separates us from all other nations and cultures, and it is why people have come to this country and continue to come. In the words of that prominent fictional character in this book, Jean Paul Pierre DuBois, "What is the cost of our most precious commodity—our liberty? I assure you, messieurs, the cost of freedom is not free—it is very high indeed—but it is worth *everything* to me. Let me say that again. It is worth *everything* to me! That is why I came to this dear country, to be free to do whatever I choose, to build a better life, the only thing that really matters." Jean Paul and many other real people of his day understood, yet we today are literally giving away that precious liberty. And what are we receiving in exchange? A proverbial "bowl of porridge"? Do we honestly believe that the government can take care of us from the cradle to the grave? No government can do that (at this date the US government is over $20 trillion in debt); the task is far too great, and if it could just partially succeed in that endeavor, it would only succeed in squelching one of the most important products of liberty that has resulted in the great economic engine that has made us the marvel and envy of the world: personal initiative. This country was founded on the notion that if we let people pursue their dreams and passions, we will all benefit. Who can deny the incredible results that have followed and have done so much for the world in which we live? Fantastic inventions—the electric lightbulb, the automobile, the engine-powered airplane, the telephone, and the phonograph, just to name a few— along with tremendous discoveries and developments in numerous fields such as medicine, architecture, and engineering.

Our founding fathers were wise men. They looked to the Almighty for insight and wisdom, and they realized that God Himself entrusted them with this precious gift of liberty. They took this entrustment very seriously, eventually creating one of the greatest documents in the history of humankind to protect and nurture that gift—the Constitution of the United States. Without that document and the proper interpretation of it, we are no different than any totalitarian regime that has ever existed.

Abraham Lincoln, sixteenth president of the United States and the Great Emancipator, had much to say about liberty and freedom and gave warnings about any attempts to stifle it:

> Don't interfere with anything in the Constitution. That must be maintained, for it is the only safeguard of our liberties.

> If there is anything that a man can do well, I say let him do it. Give him a chance.

> Our defense is in the preservation of the spirit which prizes liberty as a heritage of all men, in all lands,

everywhere. Destroy this spirit and you have planted the seeds of despotism around your own doors.

Those who deny freedom to others deserve it not for themselves and, under a just God, cannot long retain it.

Fourscore and seven years ago our fathers brought forth on this continent, a new nation, conceived in liberty and dedicated to the proposition that all men are created equal.

There are many others, but perhaps the most poignant, cogent, and ominous quote of all is this: "America will never be destroyed from the outside. If we falter and lose our freedoms, it will be because we destroyed ourselves." Lincoln knew history. Many great empires, chiefly Rome, died not from outside forces but inside. Are we destined to go the way of Rome? Is the great liberty experiment destined for the ash heap of history? I hope and pray not, for I believe that we have been and continue to be the great hope for the world and for all humankind and that God still has a purpose for us.

Recently, steps have been taken to shrink the size of government, primarily by eliminating regulations. I applaud these efforts, for I believe it is imperative to not just limit government but also eliminate unnecessary agencies, and wasteful government regulations, and spending. I firmly believe that this can be done without depriving the most vulnerable among us, who depend on government programs for support and even for survival.

You may disagree with me, and I am certain that many may vehemently disagree with me. Whether you agree or disagree is not so important; what is important is that we think deeply upon these issues and have civil discourse. I say "civil discourse" because while it is important to have strongly held beliefs and convictions, it is equally important to maintain civility when expressing them, lest we plunge into chaos.

I believe our nation and what it stands for hangs in the balance. The brave men and women who have given so much and are continuing to give so much to defend our liberties and the liberties of millions around the globe, including many yet unborn, deserve to know that their defense of our liberty is not unfounded.

I am not a politician, nor do I have political ambition. I am not a journalist, talk-show host, or commentator. I am just an average citizen who loves his country and cares deeply about its future for its sake and for the sake of the world.

I hope that you enjoy this story and that it spurns you to study, for yourself, the history of the founding of this great nation and reach your own conclusions as to just what was and what is "the cost of liberty."

1

"Mister William, Mister William," shouted Judah Smith as he burst open the front door of the Finch residence, "where are you? We have to leave right away!"

"Judah, calm down, calm down—I am in the parlor. Come here."

"Mister William, Mister William," Judah repeated, though in a more subdued, softer tone. He came to the door of the parlor to greet his master, prominent Boston merchant William Finch, who sat in a comfortable chair next to a crackling fire in the spacious yet homey room.

William, a handsome man of forty years, with light, rather straight brown hair (he eschewed wearing a powdered wig, except for special occasions), and dark-brown eyes, had a solid build and stood five feet ten and a half inches, tall for his day. He was light complexioned, had a slightly upturned nose, dimples in his cheeks, an infectious smile, and a look about him that conveyed trustworthiness. Both his parents died several years before, his father as an officer in the French and Indian War and his mother of smallpox. William's one sibling, Joseph, age thirty-seven, with strong loyalist leanings, was a newspaper owner in New York City, and while the two were close, their political differences put a strain on their relationship.

William worked his way up the ranks, working on the docks, doing manual labor, and then managing a mercantile business and eventually owning one. He and forty-two-year-old Jonathan Barnes, general-store owner from Lexington, Massachusetts, met when William was starting out. Jonathan was looking for a merchant to supply him the goods he needed to stock his new store. The two became best friends, and their families grew very close.

"Judah, come in here," William said, as he motioned his servant to enter the room. "What is the meaning of this?" William continued as Judah stepped into the parlor. "You of all my servants should know better than to burst into this house, shouting my name. I count on you to be the example for the others, and while you have been that through the years, this behavior cannot be tolerated. I may not be a typical Boston master, but I will have proper decorum and respect in this house. Do I make myself clear?"

Judah Smith, fifty years old, had been William's chief servant since William became a young merchant some thirteen years ago. Judah had been entrusted with numerous duties, including being in charge of the other half dozen Finch servants, all female. He was dark skinned with a warm, friendly face that had enough creases to convey, along with his soft but strong eyes and prematurely snow-white hair, a sense of wisdom coupled with strength, strength that showed forth despite his rather thin, wiry build. Judah had been educated by his former master, the wealthy financier Henry J. Lloyd, who, though giving Judah vast responsibilities in his household, was much more traditional about the roles of master and servant than the young, somewhat radical William Finch. Henry Lloyd had been a mentor to William, seeing a younger version of himself in the energetic, ambitious Finch. On his deathbed, Lloyd gave Judah to William, believing that the match would be a perfect one. The wise older servant and the young, brash entrepreneur. He was right; they were a perfect match, and both benefitted greatly from it.

"Yes, sir, Mister William. I am very sorry, sir; it will not happen again, I assure you, but—"

"But what? And what is all the commotion about anyway? What do you mean we have to leave right away, and why did you come home without Jonathan and Richard? Where are they?"

"That is just it, Mister William. Mister Jonathan told me to come back here, get you, and bring you to Griffin's Wharf right away—there is no time to lose."

"Judah," said William, now with a quizzical look on his face, as he was softening a bit to the plight of his chief servant, "what happened at the meeting?"

Before Judah could answer, William's lovely, petite, youngest child, sixteen-year-old Victoria, appeared at the parlor door. "Father, Judah, what is going on? I heard the front door burst open and Judah shouting your name. Is everything all right with Richard and Mr. Barnes?"

"Richard and Jonathan are fine, my dear. They sent Judah to fetch me and take me to Griffin's Wharf," said William. "Judah was just about to tell me what happened. Judah, is it all right for Victoria to hear this?"

"Miss Victoria," Judah said, acknowledging her. "Yes, sir, she may hear it."

"Good," said William, "then get on with it."

"The Old South Meeting House—it was packed when we arrived back there for the afternoon session. I stayed with the carriage as you told me to do, Mister William, while Mister Jonathan and Mister Richard headed for the meeting. I made certain to get back early, but well, there was such a big crowd that they could not even get in. After they were standing outside in the cold and rain for a long time, listening to what was going on inside, all of a sudden, there was a loud war whoop, and the people started shouting, 'Boston Harbor a teapot tonight!' and 'Hurrah for Griffin's Wharf!' Next thing I knew, the crowd streamed out of the building. Mister Jonathan and Mister Richard had to muster all their strength to move toward me. Mister Jonathan shouted at me over all the whoopin' an' hollerin', telling me to head back to the house, fetch you, Mister William, and get to Griffin's Wharf as fast as we could. They disappeared down Milk Street, being pushed and shoved along toward the wharf by the crowd. It was a sight, Mister William—a real sight to behold."

"Boston Harbor a teapot tonight!" exclaimed William, jumping out of his chair. "They are going to destroy the tea, just as I thought! Why did you not say so in the first place?" His eyes were wide open with excitement. The news quickly overshadowed his servant's indiscretion.

"I tried to, Mister William; I tried to."

"Never mind, Judah—we have got to get out of here immediately. Go get the carriage. I will be out in just a moment."

"Yes, sir, Mister William, yes, sir!" said Judah as he practically ran out of the parlor.

"Victoria, tell your mother that Judah and I are going to Griffin's Wharf and not to expect us home until late. I have a feeling that this is going to be a long night."

"Yes, Father, I will tell her. Please be careful, and tell Richard and Mr. Barnes to be careful."

"Do not worry; everyone will be fine."

Jean Paul Pierre DuBois was one of the true characters in colonial Boston. Born in Marseille, France, Jean Paul, age forty-five, immigrated, at a young age, to Montreal, Canada in New France, with his widower father, a merchant by trade. When he was nineteen, during one of several lengthy trips to Boston with his father, Jean Paul met a young woman by the name of Maggie Mae, with whom he had an affair. She became pregnant and bore his son, Francois. Though not yet ready to settle down in a committed relationship, Jean Paul, on subsequent trips to Boston, visited with Maggie and their son, until the outbreak of the French and Indian War in 1754. He fought in the war until its conclusion. His father, who also fought in the war, was captured and executed by the British. Jean Paul remained bitter toward the British, though not to the Americans, as he chose to move to Boston following the war, believing the colonies to be the next best hope for humankind. A capitalist at heart, he entered the mercantile business, taking various jobs, working for different Boston merchants. Jean Paul renewed his relationship with Maggie, who had become a tavern owner, and he became very involved in the life of his son. Despite being a bit too colorful for most members of polite Boston society, he became good friends with William Finch and subsequently with William's best friend and business customer, Jonathan Barnes. He proved to be very shrewd in business and was eventually able to open his own mercantile business as well as what was to become a popular Boston tavern, JP's, with help from Charleston, South Carolina, merchant and financier Michael Beaumont, who made frequent forays to Boston and New York. Jean Paul and subsequently the Finch and Barnes families developed close friendships with Michael, his lovely wife, Mary, and daughter, Lucy, that would have lasting benefits for all of them and for Boston.

Jean Paul was introduced to Paul Revere by William Finch. They were both of French descent. Revere's father, Apollos Rivoire, being a French immigrant, came to America on his own when he was just thirteen years old. Revere, also a French and Indian War veteran, and a very strong, swarthy thirty-eight-year-old, had built a sophisticated spy network in Boston and surrounding locales. A renowned patriot and silversmith by trade—he was widely admired for his devotion to the cause. A strong friendship developed that resulted in Revere proffering a joining of forces to Jean Paul, who had his own vast spy connections. Jean Paul was intrigued by the prospect of significantly increasing the scope and efficiency of American reconnaissance in and around the town. After working out the details, they merged their networks, and Jean Paul soon became Revere's most loyal and trusted lieutenant.

Jean Paul believed that the destruction of the tea was inevitable, given Governor Hutchinson's hard line that the duties must be paid by ships that entered Boston Harbor. He knew that Sam Adams and the Sons of Liberty, of which Jean Paul and Revere were members, would never tolerate payment of the same. Jean Paul informed Revere that he would meet him at Fort Hill along with other "Narragansett Indians."

"Monsieur Revere, a 'French Indian' from the 'Narragansett tribe' shall make an appearance tonight at Fort Hill at approximately five o'clock."

"Monsieur DuBois," said Revere, grinning at his friend and lieutenant and speaking in his best French accent, "the 'French Indian' from the 'Narragansett tribe' will meet up with the 'French Indian' from the 'North Boston tribe' tonight at Fort Hill at approximately five o'clock—good Lord willing."

"Oui, monsieur, good Lord willing."

Jean Paul applied a mixture of burnt cork and red ocher to his cheeks, forehead, and nose, spreading the copper-colored substance thoroughly all over his face, then to his ears, and lastly his neck. With his straight black hair and slightly hooked nose, he looked every bit a Narragansett Indian. He threw a shawl around his shoulders, put a feathered headband on his head, grabbed a small hatchet from his shed behind the house, and headed out to Fort Hill. Jean Paul practically bounded down the street, his excitement level at a fever pitch as he thought of this blow about to be leveled upon the king, his ministers, and Parliament. This was the moment for which he had waited for such a long time.

As he gleefully raced along toward Fort Hill, he was soon joined by others from the three groups that had assembled in other parts of town, dressing and preparing themselves, while the large crowd gathered at the Old South Meeting House to hear the final musings regarding this long-dragged-out saga. One of the groups had stopped off at the meeting house on the way to the fort. The plan, made at Faneuil Hall on December 13 at a secret session of Committees of Correspondence from several towns, was that groups taking part in the engagement would dress in homemade costumes as Indians and gather at Fort Hill after dark. There they would receive instructions and move as a body to Griffin's Wharf.

"Monsieur Revere, I must say you make a convincing 'Indian' in that outfit," said Jean Paul, with a wry smile.

"Not nearly as convincing as the 'French Indian' from the 'Narragansett tribe.' He is an 'Indian's Indian,'" Revere replied as he firmly slapped his friend on the back.

Jean Paul nearly doubled over. He wheezed as he fought to stand upright and catch his breath.

"Careful, monsieur, with slaps like that, you may knock not only the wind out of this 'French Indian' but also the copper off the face of him."

"Sorry, I sometimes forget my own strength."

"Ah, I will be fine, monsieur. I passed my first test: my headdress is still on, and so is the copper on my face. I should be good for the evening's events."

A militia officer by the name of Daniel Horne addressed the group, which now totaled approximately two hundred.

"The time has arrived for us to do our duty. We must perform that duty in the most orderly fashion. We will move out from here in groups of two, proceeding two by two to Griffin's Wharf. Once there, we will first board the *Dartmouth*. We will need to bring the chests forward into the hold, put a rope around them, and hoist them to the deck by means of a tackle. The chests are to be taken to the side of the ship and opened, then the tea dumped into the water, and the broken chests tossed over the side. Do all of this in an efficient manner, with little or no talking. We have a job to do, but we do not want to be identified. After the tea has been removed from all the ships, make sure the decks must be swept clean and all other items are put back as they were. There is to be no damage to the vessels. No tea is to be placed in anyone's pockets or cuffs. Anyone who does so will have to account to the Sons of Liberty.

"Civilians may want to join us in our little party. If they do, then let them. We will probably need their help; however, you must lead by example. They are to follow our leadership and do what we are doing, or they must be carefully and quietly removed.

"Lastly, thank all of you for your presence here tonight. Any questions?" Hearing none, Horne said, "Move out!"

The great group flowed into the street, initially two by two. That soon changed as civilians and "Indians" coming from the Old South Meeting House merged into the Fort Hill group.

"Mr. Rotch, it is good to see you, though I doubt that you have come on such a dark and dreary day to pass the time in idle conversation," said Governor Thomas Hutchinson, who was at Milton, his summer mansion, where he sometimes sought refuge during times of trial.

"Excellency," replied Francis Rotch, who, though only twenty-three years old, owned, with his brothers, the *Dartmouth,* one of three ships that arrived in Boston Harbor, carrying a load of tea. "I apologize for imposing upon you at this late hour, but I have been compelled to do so by circumstances over which I have no control. I was forced to make an official protest to the comptroller of customs that my ship had been denied passage back to London without paying the duty. I have come from a meeting at the Old South Meeting House, convened this morning, where the committee ordered me to set sail before midnight. I protested that it would bring a financial disaster to me and my family. The meeting was adjourned until I could meet with you. I have come, sir, to plead with you that you grant me a pass for my ship, since the custom house has refused clear passage."

"I will be pleased to grant a pass for the ship once it has been emptied of its contents and the duty paid, but absent that, I cannot and will not grant your request. I am duty bound as the emissary of the Crown and Parliament to enforce the law of the land regardless of the situation. Surely you must know that."

"I do, sir, and I understand, but as I said, I was forced by the committee to make this last and final appeal to you."

"Can you tell me what you think the people are going to do with the tea?"

"I suppose that they will attempt to force the ship back to England. I think they would like to see the ship be stopped by cannon fire from Castle William."

"In that event, I would be willing to offer you a letter to the admiral to ask that he give your ship and its contents protection at Castle William, should you desire to remove it there for temporary storage until cooler heads will prevail."

"Thank you, sir. I do appreciate the gesture, but I believe my ship will not be harmed. The anger and fury of the people is not directed at the ship but at the tea."

"Very well then, I believe that there is nothing that I can do for you. I wish you the best in this exceedingly difficult situation."

With that, Rotch bid the governor adieu and set out for the Old South Meeting House, riding in the dark, now without rain but with a foreboding cold wind nipping at him.

"Mr. Rotch, I am glad you made it back before we adjourned. Were you able to meet with the Governor?" asked meeting moderator, Samuel Savage, upon Rotch's return. The meeting had reconvened at 3:00 P.M. anticipating Rotch's return at that hour, but he did not arrive until nearly 6:00 P.M.

"Yes, moderator Savage. I found him at Milton."

"Did he grant you a permit?"

"Unfortunately, no. He said as an emissary of the crown and parliament, he was sworn to uphold the law. He deemed it his duty to refuse a pass until the ship qualified at the custom house."

"This was anticipated. Mr. Rotch, will you send your ship back with the tea under the present circumstances?"

'Sir, I reiterate that I will not sent the ship back to London with the tea as it would prove financial ruin for me and my family, but I will consider unloading it, if I must."

"Who knows how tea will mingle with seawater?" William Rowe, an attendee asked.

"We will soon find out!" another attendee proclaimed.

"Indeed. Not a shard of the infernal stuff must escape from the ships!" a third shouted to the delight of the crowd, bringing more cries to destroy the tea.

"Order, order—this meeting will come to order!" Savage screamed over the din in the meeting house.

"Gentlemen, Mr. Rotch is a good man. I urge you that no violence be perpetrated upon him, nor any damage be done to his ship," Dr. Thomas Young said, upon the restoration of order.

"This meeting can do nothing more to save the country," Samuel Adams said.

A war whoop went up from those assembled in the building, and then shouts of "Boston Harbor a teapot tonight!" and "Hurrah for Griffin's Wharf," as several men, dressed as Indians who were standing outside, came in.

"Order, order!" Savage again pleaded to the now very excited gathering. As order was again restored, Savage read from a prepared text. "Let the record reflect that all efforts have been made since the arrival of *Dartmouth* spanning several meetings, to avert the crisis that looms before us. However, all, unfortunately, to no avail. Tonight an unmistakable message will be sent to the king and his parliament that this tax will not be tolerated. Remember the object of our righteous indignation is the destruction of the tea, nothing else. Do your work quietly, efficiently, and in an orderly manner. Thank you all for your attendance. I now move that this meeting be adjourned."

"Is there a second to the motion?" Savage asked.

"Second," said Sam Adams.

"All in favor of the motion, signify by saying aye," Savage said.

"Aye," was heard loudly coming from the throats of all in the room and those outside. With that, the clamorous crowd pushed out into the street to the sound of howling war whoops.

Jonathan and Richard Barnes were literally being swept along with the crowd pouring out of the building down Milk Street toward Griffin's Wharf. Jonathan had just dispensed Judah Smith to fetch his master, William Finch, and bring him to the wharf with all due speed. While William had attended many of the meetings in recent weeks as the tea crisis escalated, he was unable to attend on that morning due to pressing business matters, which occupied him well into the afternoon.

The noise was deafening. "Indians," savage "Indians" from Narragansett, clothed in blankets, heads muffled, faces colored red or copper, carrying hatchets or axes and pairs of pistols, were leading the pack, howling all the way. The amazing thing was that, despite the hundreds from the meeting who followed the "Indians," no one seemed to know who they were; conveniently no one could identify them. As the "Indians" reached Hutchinson Street, they swerved off Milk and headed down Hutchinson, southeast past Fort Hill, where more of them coming from the direction of the fort merged into the crowd. The growing crowd crossed a couple of lanes as they moved inexorably onward to the wharf.

"Father, may I ask, who are these 'Indians'? Some of them sure look like Sons of Liberty I have seen before. Are they really going to destroy the tea stored in the ships at Griffin's?"

Before Jonathan could open his mouth to answer the questions, Richard posed another.

"I mean, I know that the East India Tea Company is largely to blame, but I still am unclear about the events that led up to what is happening tonight."

"Slow down, son, one question at a time," replied Jonathan. Barrel chested, Jonathan was of stout build. He stood just under five feet seven inches in height but seemed taller since he carried himself with shoulders back and chest out. He had piercing blue eyes and a broad nose. His reddish-blond hair, thick on the sides of his head, was thinning on the top. Like his best friend, William Finch, he eschewed wearing the powdered wig except for special occasions. Jonathan was a warm and caring family man with a terrific sense of humor and a deep laugh that seemed to emanate all the way from the tips of his toes. He loved his country and would do anything to support her.

"I am sorry, Father." Richard, age seventeen, was the oldest child of Jonathan and Eleanor Barnes. Jonathan removed Richard from school for a few days to bring him to Boston to assist Jonathan in stocking up with goods for the store from William Finch's supply and to attend the meeting at the Old South Meeting House. As was the custom, since the beginning of the Finch-Barnes friendship, whenever the Barneses came to town, they stayed with the Finches. Richard, a handsome, rather tall young man, was quite knowledgeable, disciplined, and focused for his age. He and Victoria Finch had practically grown up together, and while as young children they were just friends, as they matured and spent more time together, a budding relationship was developing. Richard relished every opportunity to come to Boston and spend time with her, and she eagerly anticipated each moment they could be together.

"It is all right, son; this whole situation can be difficult to understand. To address the question of the 'Indians,' you are quite right; they are not *real* Indians. No doubt, many of them are indeed Sons of Liberty, though I must admit I do not recognize anyone, what with their coverings and war paint. However, I could have sworn that one looked just like Jean Paul Pierre DuBois and another like Paul Revere," said Jonathan, with just a trace of a smile on his face, "but surely I must be mistaken."

As they conversed, they continued to be swept along, jostled by a sea of humanity moving relentlessly, much like lemmings, to the waterfront.

"As far as what they are going to do, yes, it is quite apparent from the tools they are carrying that they have every intention of destroying the tea in the ships at Griffin's Wharf, making Boston Harbor a teapot, in a manner of speaking."

"Will they not meet resistance from the British?" asked Richard, with a concerned look on his face.

"Let us hope they do not meet resistance, for everyone's sake, or it could be a terrible night. I am trusting that the Brits will actually do the right thing and let the 'Indians' go about their business. We will see soon enough, but to answer that last question of yours," Jonathan practically shouted the words to overcome the loud whooping "Indians" who were completely surrounding them, "the immediate events that led up to what is happening tonight have unfolded over the last several months, but the causes behind the events themselves have been brewing for quite some time, several years, actually. Parliament would tax the colonies, and we would resist."

"And how was that accomplished?"

"By smuggling goods into the colonies, thus avoiding the tax, and by boycotts of imported goods from the mother country. This resulted in Parliament rescinding the tax, and things would quiet down again?"

"Why did not Parliament rescind the tea tax when resistance began to grow in the colonies?"

"I believe this was more Lord North's doing than Parliament, but I think we have to go back to what precipitated the problem to answer that question."

"Which was?"

"Which was the fact that the British believed we were drinking too much illegally imported tea—tea that primarily came from Holland through the Dutch West Indies."

"And…"

"And the illegally imported tea deeply cut into the East India Tea Company's market. Now the tea company is the largest commercial company in Britain."

"Being the largest, it has much influence with the government?"

"Correct—so with the tea and other supplies sitting in warehouses and the company facing financial ruin, it appealed to Lord North for a loan and to allow it to sell its extra tea without having to pay import duties. However, Lord North would not lift the import duties. Parliament passed a law, and East India started choosing tea consignees in Boston, New York, Philadelphia, and Charleston, who had sworn loyalty to King George."

"The tea consignees received the tea instead of our merchants?"

"Precisely."

"Did not the Brits realize that this action would cause resentment?"

"Yes, almost certainly they did, but I do not think they ever anticipated that this type of a reaction would actually occur."

"Who are the tea consignees for Boston—I mean other than Richard Clarke and Sons?"

"The Hutchinsons, Faneuil, and Winslow."

"Father, should not Governor Hutchinson be supporting us? He is an American, not a Brit. How is it that he was named a tea consignee?"

"Yes, he is an American, as are all the consignees. Born here in Boston and educated at Harvard, he has served in many important positions in the city and the colony. He is our governor and should support us or, at the very least, be fair in our dealings with the mother country, but he has always been loyal to the Crown. That does not mean that he always agreed with everything the king did regarding the colonies. But when his house was destroyed eight years ago by an out-of-control vigilante mob who wrongfully thought he supported the Stamp Act, this had a major negative influence on him toward the colonies. As it concerns his becoming a tea consignee, I think it is questionable at best, inappropriate at worst, yet almost certainly due to politics and his loyalty. Nevertheless, several hundred pounds of tea were shipped in ships to Boston. One of them was the *Dartmouth*, owned by Francis Rotch and his brother, who as you know are carrying the tea for Richard Clarke and Sons."

"Mr. Rotch sure was severely questioned by the committee today."

"Yes, he was, son."

"Seems to me that he was made a scapegoat, Father. Am I wrong?"

"No, I do not think it is wrong to say that he was made a scapegoat by the committee, but he was not without culpability. He agreed to ship the tea for Richard Clarke and Sons, knowing very well that this would not meet with favor in Boston."

"Why did he keep protesting that he and his brother faced a financial disaster, and how would this occur?"

"It all has to do with the intricacies of the law. The consignees are required to pay the tea's value to underwriters in London within two months of receiving the tea, but before the shipment even reaches its destination."

"You mean before the tea is actually sold to the customers?"

"Yes."

"How can they pay for something before they have been paid themselves?"

"That, son, is the essence of their problem; many cannot. Then to make matters worse, once brought to the dock, the shipment is subject to the tea duty, and the ship, with or without the tea, cannot be sent back to where it came from unless customs officers approve. That can only happen if the duty is actually paid and if a pass is given by the governor. So you can see why the Rotches could be facing a major financial calamity. When this whole plan became known to Bostonians, along with the people involved, this crisis was ready to occur. All it took was the arrival of *Dartmouth*, on November twenty-seventh, followed by *Eleanor* and *Beaver*."

"So the committee sent Rotch to the governor to get the pass?"

"They did, but the governor would not give him one unless the duty was paid. The duty must be paid within twenty days from the arrival of the shipment, or the tea would be subject to confiscation or seizure by agents of the king."

"If the Brits would be the ones seizing the tea, why is Sam Adams so concerned?"

"Because he fears, rightly so, I believe, that the tea would eventually end up in the possession of the colonists. To let that happen would thwart the efforts to send a message to the king and his Parliament to rescind the tax. With tomorrow being the twentieth day, it was imperative to take action tonight."

"Now I understand, Father. Thank you!"

"You are welcome!"

The carriage clattered along on Milk Street as Judah exhorted the horse to pick up the pace.

"Careful, Judah, we will get there soon enough," said William as he tightened his grip on the railing next to his seat. No sooner did he make the remark than he saw a few shadowy figures in the middle of the road in front of them. "Slow down, Judah; slow down, *now*!" he yelled.

"Yes, sir, Mister William! *Whoa, whoa,* Betsy!" Judah instinctively yelled as he tugged hard on the reins. The mare slowed but nearly ran into the backs of stragglers of the huge crowd heading to Griffin's Wharf.

The stragglers parted to let the carriage through as a man who was almost hit screamed, "Watch it, Mister! What were you thinking? You could have killed me!"

"Very sorry, sir, but we thought everyone who was going to the wharf would already be there by now. We did not anticipate stragglers walking down the middle of the street at this hour," replied William loudly as the carriage passed by the man, who was waving his arms in disgust as Judah turned down Hutchinson Street. "Judah, there is going to be a very big crowd indeed, with stragglers this far from the wharf."

"Yes, sir, a big, big crowd."

"It is going to be very interesting trying to locate Jonathan and Richard."

"Mister William, I forgot to tell you that Mister Jonathan said he would send Mister Richard to find the carriage."

"Oh, he did? That is very thoughtful of him."

It was almost six thirty when Jonathan and Richard arrived at Griffin's Wharf, along with several hundred others, most of whom came from the meeting. Over the next hour, the crowd continued to grow, swelling to nearly one thousand. Torches were everywhere, lighting the area nearly as bright as daytime.

"Richard, William and Judah should be arriving about now. It is time for you to go look for the carriage and bring William back with you."

"Yes, sir," replied Richard as he headed back into the crowd.

As the carriage continued down Hutchinson Street, the darkness rapidly faded.

"Mister William, it seems almost like it is the middle of the day down here!" exclaimed Judah, his face beaming with excitement.

"Torches, torches—they are everywhere, Judah. It does seem like the middle of day!" agreed William, with equal enthusiasm. "This is an incredible sight!"

The carriage eased into the outer edge of the crowd and came to a halt. William stood up in the carriage in an effort to see Richard and to make it easier for Richard to see him above the heads, hats, and torches.

Meanwhile Richard was quickly working his way to the edge of the crowd.

William saw some jostling in the crowd, and then Richard emerged.

"Richard! Richard, we are over here!" shouted William, as he waived his arms in Richard's direction.

"Mr. Finch, Judah," replied Richard as he ran to the carriage.

"Richard, how are you? Is everything all right with you and your father?"

"We are fine, Mr. Finch. Thank you for asking."

"I hope we did not keep you waiting long."

"Not at all; actually your timing was very good."

Just then, the stragglers from Milk Street arrived. The man who was almost hit spotted William and immediately charged over to the carriage, yelling, "There they are! There are those bastards who almost ran over me!"

Richard was startled and backed up out of the man's way as the man approached the carriage with his right fist clinched. Several other stragglers came up menacingly behind him.

"Calm down, man, and watch your language," William said in a stern, firm voice as he hopped out of the carriage in between Richard and the man. "There is no need for violence. I told you we were sorry. We thought everyone would be at the wharf by the time we got to Milk Street. Besides, no one was hurt."

"You and that servant of yours," he said, angrily pointing at Judah, "came within a whisker of killing me, and you tell me I need to calm down!"

Richard, gathering himself, moved around William and got right in the man's face. "You look here, Mister. Mr. Finch apologized to you and told you to calm down. There is not a scratch on you, so you have no complaint with him or with Judah."

"You are...Mr. Finch...Mr. William Finch?" asked the shocked man, who suddenly had an apologetic look to his demeanor, peering around Richard's glare to look at William.

"Yes, I am," said William.

"Oh, Mr. Finch, I am sorry, Mr. Finch. I did not mean to cause you trouble, but you and your servant did give me a big scare," he said, with a changed attitude, as Richard backed away.

"I am afraid the events of these recent days have had us all a bit on edge, Mr...."

"My name's Willie—Willie Boyd."

"Willie Boyd, did you say?" William asked, quickly digesting what he just heard.

"Yes, sir—is there a problem?"

"Er...no, no problem at all. Well, Mr. Boyd, I will tell you what I am going to do. You look like a man who appreciates the finer things. I am going to talk to my brother-in-law, Timothy McCaskill, a tailor who operates a store on Long's Wharf. Do you know the store that I am talking about?"

"Yes, sir, I know the store. There are some mighty fine suits in that store, mighty fine."

"I am going to tell Timothy that you can have your pick of the suits in there, a pair of breeches, coat, vest, stockings, shirt, cravat, and even a pair of shoes to go with the outfit."

"A whole outfit from McCaskill's, Mr. Finch?"

"All but a wig."

"Thank you, Mr. Finch; thank you. That is mighty nice of you, mighty nice indeed."

"You are welcome, Mr. Boyd. Go into the store at the middle of next week and tell Mr. McCaskill that William Finch sent you. He will help you pick something out and tailor it to fit you perfectly. After he is done, you are to come to my office; I want to see how the outfit looks on you. Do you understand?"

"Yes, sir, Mr. Finch—yes, sir!" exclaimed Willie, with a big grin on his face and a sparkle in his eyes.

"I trust this makes up for our little incident," said William as he extended his right hand to Willie, who heartily shook it several times.

"More than makes up for it, Mr. Finch. I am very grateful," said Willie as he continued to pump William's hand, grinning from ear to ear.

"All right then; it's time for all of us to turn our attention to the 'Indians' who are doing our country a great service tonight."

"You heard the man," said Willie, turning to the stragglers behind him. "Let us get movin' down to the wharf and watch the 'Indians' do their work."

"Thanks again, Mr. Finch," said Willie as he and his group began slipping through the crowd toward the wharf.

"You are welcome, Mr. Boyd. I will see you later. Judah, stay here with the carriage. I do not think there will be any more trouble."

"Yes, sir, Mister William."

"Richard, that was quick thinking and mighty brave of you to step in as you did. I am much obliged to you," said William as he and Richard started walking in the direction of Jonathan. "You showed considerable courage in defusing what could have been a very ugly situation. I am proud of you, and your father will be proud too."

"Thank you, sir. Truth is I was scared, but I simply could not let that ruffian threaten you and Judah like he did. Fact is, once he heard your name, everything changed."

"Fortunately my name carried weight with him."

"Sir?"

"Yes, Richard? What is it?"

"Who is Willie Boyd? He looked just like an ordinary dockworker to me, but obviously he must be more important than that."

"You are right on both counts. He may look just like an ordinary dockworker, but I assure you that he is not. He is now a major presence on the docks and the leader of the bunch that was with him. And, while I had never met him, I have heard Jean Paul speak of him. He is one of Jean Paul's lieutenants."

"So that is why you said you would give him a whole new outfit from Mr. McCaskill's when he was not hurt at all?"

"Yes. It is a good thing to have the support of someone like him, especially with what may soon be coming."

"What may be coming, Mr. Finch?"

"We will discuss it later. Now let us go to your father."

Jean Paul and Paul Revere, along with several other 'Indians,' board-ed the *Dartmouth*. Their leader immediately approached the ship's captain, James Hall, and a brief exchange followed.

"Captain, open the hatchways immediately, and give us the hoist-ing tackle and ropes. I assure you that no harm will come to you or your crew."

"And just what may I ask are your intentions, as if I do not already know?"

"Our intentions are to unload and destroy the infernal tea. None of the other cargo will be harmed. We will replace everything else and make certain that they are in their proper order. We will sweep the deck clean when we have finished. Now get me that rope and tackle, and then you and your crew must go below forthwith," he said in a commanding voice.

Captain Hall quickly ordered the tackle and rope to be delivered to him. He turned it over, and then he and the crew slipped below deck.

Both Jean Paul and Revere remained on the deck while others went below. The tea chests were brought forward in the hold, where a rope was placed around a chest, and it was then hoisted to the deck. All was conducted with smooth efficiency and in nearly total silence. Civilians came to join the work and were directed by means of point-ing or by physically taking an individual to a place on the vessel and then showing the person what to do. The tea ships' guards (guards had been assigned to protect the tea since the ships had arrived) also joined in to assist in the endeavor.

"Monsieur?" asked Jean Paul of Paul Revere in the quietest voice possible. Revere had gotten Jean Paul's attention as the two were fe-verishly working side by side.

"See that man," Revere whispered, looking and carefully pointing to a civilian who was wearing a coat.

"Oui, monsieur, what about him?"

"Looks to me as if he is stashing tea in the lining of his coat and waistcoat."

Jean Paul glanced up periodically at the man while continuing his work. After observing the man sneakily snatch tea shards and slide them into his coat, Jean Paul whispered back to Revere, "I will take care of the matter, monsieur."

With amazing alacrity, Jean Paul grabbed the man and dragged him to their leader. After the tea was emptied from the man's clothing, several "Indians" ripped his coat and waistcoat from him, hit him, and smeared muck from the harbor bottom all over him. He was then unceremoniously escorted off the ship to loud boos from the crowd, who had witnessed the whole sordid matter. The man took a pounding, running as fast as he could through the gauntlet of the crowd's jeers and hisses, finally escaping with bruises all over him and with his clothes in tatters.

After Richard left, Jonathan watched the "Indians" board the *Dartmouth* and marveled at the smooth efficiency with which they set about the task at hand, quickly hoisting the chests of tea from the ship's hold up onto the deck, smashing them open with hatchets and axes, and dumping the contents and the chests themselves over the side. This went on for a considerable time, and Jonathan, who was so focused on the activity on the ships, did not even hear Richard and William coming up behind him.

"Father," Richard said as he and William approached Jonathan.

Startled, Jonathan immediately turned around at the sound of his son's voice and, with an expression of relief on his face, hugged first his son and then William.

"Richard, William, I am so glad you are here. I was beginning to get worried about you. What took so long?"

"Jonathan, it is quite a story," replied William. "I will tell you that I am very proud of your son, and you will be too when I tell you the details of what transpired. Richard rescued me from a nasty situation that could have resulted in a very bad outcome."

"Really? Please tell me. I want to hear all about it."

"I will be happy to, but to do so, I have to start from the beginning."

"By all means, I believe we have plenty of time."

For the next several minutes, William recited the events that took place, beginning with Judah's abrupt entrance into the house.

"So you see, Jonathan, I am much obliged to Richard. His quick thinking and courage saved the day—er...the night, that is."

"Richard, I am very proud of you, and so will be your mother," said Jonathan as he heartily embraced his son.

"Oh, Father, I had to do something. That rude man was threatening Mr. Finch and Judah for no good reason."

Just as he finished saying this, word spread through the crowd around them that individual members of the governor's council had sent an urgent message to British colonel Leslie on Castle William in the harbor that he was *not* to bring his troops in to attempt to stop the "Indians." The crowd was ecstatic, and a chant went up: "The Regulars are *not* coming; the Regulars are *not* coming." This went on for several minutes, building into a crescendo. As the crowd chant slowly began to die down, Jonathan and William resumed their conversation.

"I hope and pray that what we are hearing is actually true," Jonathan said somberly.

"I do too, old friend," said William as he nodded his head in agreement. "I cannot imagine the possible bloodshed if the troops were called in and the resultant fallout that would occur from such a horrible incident."

The three men turned their attention to the harbor where the "Indians" were at work on board the three ships side by side at the wharf: *Dartmouth*, *Eleanor*, and *Beaver*.

"I marvel at how they are able to work so quietly and efficiently together," said Jonathan. "I was watching them from the time Richard left until both of you arrived."

"It is almost as if they had done this several times before," agreed William.

"It is amazing, considering the difficulties they are encountering," Jonathan said.

"Do you mean the canvas covering the tea chests?" William asked.

"Yes. The canvas coverings certainly slow the breaking up of the chests."

"True, especially when coupled with the dull axes that many of the 'Indians' appear to be using," William replied.

"And with this operation occurring hours before high tide, the stacking of the chests on the bottom of the harbor is slowing progress by the need for apprentices to get into the water to break them up," Jonathan said.

"Father, Mr. Finch," exclaimed Richard, "that hoist on the ship—it is collapsing!" He pointed toward the *Dartmouth*.

"Sir, the hoist!" screamed Jonathan and William, almost simultaneously, at the man, who looked up, but too late. The hoist came down and hit John Crane, a twenty-nine-year-old carpenter, knocking him senseless. Immediately, he was gathered up and taken off the wharf into a woodworking ship by a couple of the "Indians."

"Father, do you think he was killed?" asked a somewhat-shaken Richard.

"I do not know, son."

"I am afraid he sustained an awful blow to the head," added William. "We can only hope and pray that he survives."

The "Indians" and their civilian counterparts finished the job of dumping all the tea and chests over the sides of the three ships, completing the work at approximately the same time. The work of cleanup was now a priority. Jean Paul and Revere grabbed brooms and began, along with others, to sweep the deck clean of all debris that had accumulated on the deck of *Dartmouth* over the previous three hours, and debris there was aplenty. Bits of cloth and numerous fragments of wood from the chests mingled with dust and shards of tea to create an almost eerie scene in the dim moonlight—and a real mess.

Everything was put back in its place, including chests containing other mercantile goods. The ships and the rest of their contents were virtually undamaged.

After all tidbits of tea were removed from the "Indians," Jean Paul again grabbed a broom and cleaned up the few shards remaining on deck. Then the "Indians" and civilians quietly began to file off the ships and onto the wharf as word circulated through the crowd that John Crane, though dazed by the blow he sustained to his head, was going to be all right.

As the crowd began to disperse, William, Jonathan, and Richard started walking back to the carriage.

"It is astonishing that all the tea was destroyed and everything put back in its place, all in such a short time," said Richard.

"I agree, son; the whole thing was quite remarkable," Jonathan concurred as they wove their way through the thinning crowd. The carriage, with Judah on top, was now in front of them. "But I must say that I am very concerned about the repercussions of such a brash act in defiance of Parliament and the Crown."

Jonathan, with a furrowed brow, turned toward William, who was in the process of hoisting himself up into the carriage. "What do think, William? What do you think will come from this?"

"I do not know what the future has in store for us," William replied as he settled into the seat next to Judah. "However, I do know one thing."

"And what would that be?" asked Jonathan, with a curious look as he and Richard settled in their seats behind William and Judah.

"Now it begins..."

Jean Paul and Revere left *Dartmouth* side by side in the midst of a throng of "Indians" being led by Lendall Pitts, a young man whose father was on the governor's council and brother on the board of selectmen, back to Fort Hill from whence they had started several hours before. They passed by Coffin's house, a loyalist who had invited British admiral Montagu to spend the evening. Montagu opened a window as the triumphant "Indians" passed by and loudly proclaimed, "My, my, my, fine-feathered Indian friends, you had quite a time for your tea party tonight, did you not? But just remember, there is a price for all that fun. The piper must and will be paid!"

"Come on down here," Pitts replied, in an equally boisterous retort, "and we will take care of that bill here and now."

The "Indians," including Jean Paul and Revere, laughed uproariously, while Montagu, in a huff, slammed the window shut. The group proceeded with a quicker pace up the road to Fort Hill.

2

December 17

The day dawned cold and clear, the rising sun glistening upon the dark-brown foamy waters of Boston Harbor. Remnants of smashed tea chests had washed on shore, carrying with them shards of tea—tea that was there for the taking by anyone who was willing to risk the wrath of the Sons of Liberty.

"Richard was magnificent," William explained to a captive audience gathered for breakfast at the Finches'. "Just when I was about to be accosted by the man nearly hit by the carriage, Richard moved between us. In no uncertain terms, Richard told him to calm down, that Mr. Finch had apologized, and that since he did not have a scratch on him, he had no complaint. You should have seen the look of shock on the man's face."

William reached his right hand up to his throat, his jaw dropped and eyes bulged out. Victoria tried desperately to suppress a giggle but failed miserably.

"He said, 'You are Mr. Finch?' He peered around Richard, sneaking a peek at me. I never knew how much my name meant in this town." Richard smiled sheepishly.

Lydia—William and Annabelle Finches' eldest daughter, age seventeen, a striking, tall, black-haired, black-eyed, intelligent beauty with porcelain skin, full ruby-red lips, high, firm cheek bones, and a classic shapely figure—inquired, "Father, may I ask, who was this rude man who was threatening you?"

"His name is Willie Boyd."

"Willie Boyd," mused Lydia. "Seems as if Jean Paul has mentioned his name before."

"Jean Paul has mentioned his name before," interjected Victoria. "I think he is one of Jean Paul's lieutenants, correct, Father?"

"Very good, daughters. I realized immediately who he was. I decided to move quickly to establish rapport with him."

"Establish rapport with a man who threatened you and behaved so disagreeably?" Lydia retorted, with a look of disbelief.

"Yes. Not only is he one of Jean Paul's lieutenants, but he also operates at the docks, a very important place. That is why I told him to pick out a new outfit—breeches, coat, vest, shirt, cravat, and shoes—at McCaskill's next week."

"A new outfit at McCaskill's!" Lydia shrieked. A talented seamstress, Lydia worked there part time, at William's insistence, to help her uncle Timothy McCaskill and to keep her grounded, to make sure that her position of privilege did not spoil her as had been the case with so many other daughters of prominent Bostonians. As for Lydia, she enjoyed the work. "That is some way to establish rapport! Father, surely—"

"That is quite enough, young lady," Annabelle said sternly, interrupting her daughter. "That is no way to speak to your father. You know better. You apologize this instant."

Before Lydia could reply, William came to her defense. "It is quite all right, dearest wife. I understand Lydia's astonishment. Richard was stunned himself; were you not, Richard?"

"Yes, sir—I was and still am, sir." He nodded his head.

"I suppose on reflection that it was a bit much, but it had the desired effect. Mr. Boyd's face was beaming; he was grinning from ear to ear. He left us a very happy man and could prove useful to us on the docks, especially in light of these recent developments. I want you, my dear," William continued, now looking directly and intensely at Lydia, "to make sure that Mr. Boyd's outfit fits him perfectly. Do you understand?

"Yes, Father, I understand. I will take care of it as you wish," said Lydia, now with a resigned attitude about the matter.

"Good, that is my girl! Trust me; this outfit will produce very beneficial results."

After breakfast was finished and the table was being cleared, William, Jonathan, and Richard retired to the parlor.

"Jonathan, I am very interested in hearing the buzz around town about the events of last night. I was thinking of sending Victoria with Judah to Faneuil Hall while you and I head down to the wharf. I have some business to attend to. After that, we will talk to some dockworkers regarding their perspective on the events. Then we can go to McCaskill's and inform Timothy about the outfit for Mr. Boyd. Lastly, we will get your carriage filled up."

"It appears to be a very full day ahead of us," said Jonathan.

"Mr. Finch and Father," interjected Richard, "with your permission, I would like to go to Faneuil Hall with Victoria and Judah."

"That is fine with me, Richard, but it is your father's decision."

"Father, may I?"

"Certainly, son, I think that's an excellent idea."

"Well then, that is settled," said William. "I will have Annabelle accompany you. I will inform her, Victoria, and Judah. Jonathan and I will take his carriage to the wharf."

As Judah drove the carriage through the heart of Boston toward Faneuil Hall, Richard and Victoria huddled next to each other in the back of the carriage, providing warmth against the chill of the brisk December morning.

"I tell you, Victoria, last night was amazing—incredible—and, I guess, a bit scary."

"Scary, what do you mean by scary?"

"As my father and I were being swept down the street to the wharf, I asked my father if the 'Indians' would meet resistance from the British. I could not believe that they would allow the pending destruction of the tea without some opposition."

"What did he say?"

"He said that he was hoping that they did not meet resistance, or it could be a terrible night. He was trusting that the British would do the right thing and let the 'Indians' go about their business. Later, when your father arrived, news passed through the crowd that members of the governor's council had sent urgent messages to Colonel Leslie *not* to bring in his troops from Castle William. Needless to say, this brought a huge sense of relief, but after the event was over and we were walking back to the carriage, my father asked your father, 'What do you think will come of all of this?' Your father said he did not know what the future held, but one thing he did know."

"And what was that?"

"Now it begins…"

"What did my father mean by that?"

"I am not entirely certain, but I think that he meant that we are on the path that will eventually lead to hostilities."

"Hostilities—what do you think?"

"I think that hostilities may be inevitable. It will be interesting to hear what is being said at Faneuil Hall."

As Richard said this, Judah deftly maneuvered the carriage around the crowd milling around outside Faneuil Hall and then proceeded to bring it alongside and park it next to a rather fancy, ornate carriage not far from the entrance to the building. Richard alighted from the carriage and assisted Victoria down.

"That is Jean Paul's carriage," Richard said to Victoria.

"I would recognize it anywhere," she replied.

"Let us see if we can find him. I want to hear his thoughts on last night and what lies ahead."

"Mother, Richard and I are going to try to get closer to Faneuil Hall and see if we can locate Jean Paul."

"You two go ahead; I will stay here in the carriage with Judah," Annabelle said.

As they pushed their way through the crowd toward the entrance, Richard recognized Jean Paul Pierre DuBois and his son, Francois, from behind.

"Jean Paul—Jean Paul Pierre DuBois and Francois!"

Jean Paul, with a smile on his face, and Francois, his twenty-five-year-old son, turned around at the sound of Richard's voice.

"Monsieur Barnes and the lovely Mademoiselle Finch—bonjour! So good to see you!" Jean Paul said, firmly shaking Richard's hand and then raising Victoria's right hand and planting a kiss on it.

"Monsieur Barnes, Mademoiselle Finch," Francois added as he followed his father in shaking Richard's hand and then lifting and kissing the right hand of the now-blushing Victoria.

Francois Garcon DuBois, as he grew up, spent time with his mother at her tavern, named Maggie's and with his father, whenever Jean Paul had occasion to come to town. When Jean Paul moved to Boston, following the war, and renewed his relationship with Maggie Mae, Francois spent more time with Jean Paul, especially at JPs. Between Maggie's and JP's, Francois was exposed at an early age to almost every class and aspect of society. As an adolescent he worked periodically in the evenings in both taverns, cleaning tables and washing dishes. He also gained much business experience on weekends at his father's merchant office, learning the ropes of the merchant trade. The result was that now, at the age of twenty-five, he was an assistant manager of Jean Paul's merchant business and JP's, occasionally assisting his mother at Maggie's when she was shorthanded. Francois had the sharp nose, dark hair, full mustache, and slightly swarthy complexion of his father. He also had the same basic physical build, but he was taller, heavier, and more muscular than Jean Paul, who stood five feet nine inches tall and weighed 170 pounds. And though he was several years older than Richard Barnes and a few years older than Joshua Finch, William's oldest child, Francois became friends with both.

"Jean Paul, I could swear that I saw you on board the *Dartmouth* last night."

"Monsieur, please lower your voice," Jean Paul implored as he moved close to Richard and spoke in a muted voice. "Surely you were mistaken," Jean Paul remarked with a serious look and raised right eyebrow. "A 'French Indian'?"

"Oui," Richard now whispered the response to Jean Paul, "a 'French Indian' and a very good one at that, I might add. It was you, was it not, who nabbed that rascal civilian who boarded the ship and started stuffing his pockets with shards of tea."

Jean Paul, with a blank look on his face, feigned innocence.

"Francois?" Richard asked, getting no response from Jean Paul.

"I know nothing, Monsieur Barnes," Francois said quietly and straight faced.

Richard noticed a very slight upturn in the corner of Jean Paul's mouth.

"Jean Paul—Jean Paul, tell me the truth."

"Ah...well," Jean Paul said as he shrugged his shoulders and slightly raised his hands, a you-got-me look crossing his face.

"Yes...oui!" Richard blurted out a bit louder, which brought a stern look of rebuke from Jean Paul. "It was you!" Richard toned down his voice. "I knew it. You were magnificent! You moved with stealth and speed to nail the rat and expose him. Did he ever get a nasty reception from the assembled crowd when he was booted off the ship. That was great work!"

Jean Paul let out a muffled chuckle and then, in an almost whispered voice, replied, "Merci, monsieur, merci—the 'French Indian' was only doing his patriotic duty, along with his tribe, but that is *not* to be repeated, monsieur. Understood?"

"Oui," Richard said, nodding his head. "Understood, monsieur."

William and Jonathan opened the door to Timothy McCaskill's tailor store to a ringing bell informing the proprietor that customers had arrived. They had just finished talking to dockworkers on Long's Wharf, who echoed their sentiments about the destruction of the tea and the possible repercussions in the aftermath of it.

"May I help you?" asked the thirty-two-year-old brother-in-law of William Finch, from the back of the store.

"I certainly hope so, young man," William replied, just as Timothy came into sight.

"William, Mr. Barnes, so good to see you!" exclaimed Timothy, with a big smile on his round baby face as he came to the front of the store.

"Good to see you too," Jonathan quickly agreed.

The men exchanged handshakes, and Timothy then inquired, "What brings you gentlemen into my store this afternoon? Are you looking for a new outfit for Christmas and New Year's perchance?"

"Well, yes and no," answered William.

"Yes and no?"

"We are not looking for an outfit for ourselves," said William. "I am buying a full outfit, shoes and all, for Willie Boyd."

"You are doing what?" said an obviously shocked Timothy.

"I am buying a full outfit for Willie Boyd."

"Whatever for? Why would you ever do such a thing?"

"It is a long story—just believe me that I have good reasons."

Timothy looked incredulous.

"My reaction was just like yours," added Jonathan, "but he does have good reasons."

"Very well."

"Mr. Boyd will be in next week. He may pick out whatever outfit he wishes—coat, vest, breeches, stockings, shirt, cravat, and shoes. I have already spoken to Lydia. She has agreed to fit him perfectly. Just put everything on my tab. Any more questions?"

"I will take care of the matter for you."

"Timothy, I appreciate all your efforts. We will see you at the house bright and early Christmas morning."

"I will be there. I so look forward to spending Christmas with all of you."

Sam Adams emerged from Faneuil Hall and addressed the crowd.

"My fellow citizens, a brave renegade band of 'Indians' has done the cause of liberty a great service by taking care of a thorny problem, at least temporarily. They made us proud by the way they conducted themselves on board the three ships, quietly and ever so efficiently going about the business at hand, ridding us of the dreaded tea that had put a cloud over us for so long.

This was not something that we wanted or brought on ourselves. God knows that we tried everything in our power to avert the crisis and avoid the loss that occurred, but alas, 'twas not to be. What was done had to be done for us and for future generations; however, I can assure you that the British will not take this matter lightly. They undoubtedly will consider this to be a serious affront to their power and authority. There will be retaliation, and it will be swift and severe, though one can only speculate as to what form it will take. We must be strong and unified in the face of what lies ahead. God bless us all, and may His favor be upon us in the days ahead."

As the crowd was dispersing, Richard relayed to Jean Paul the incident the prior evening involving William and Willie Boyd.

"Willie—ah yes, he can be a bit of a hothead, but he is a very loyal and important lieutenant. Monsieur Finch did a very wise thing with him. I just hope that Willie does not become a dandy in his fancy new outfit."

"What do you think of Mr. Sam's remarks?" asked Victoria.

"I think unfortunately he is right, my dear mademoiselle, but I would say it more succinctly and harshly: there will be hell to pay."

"So, Father, Mr. Sam Adams said that the Brits would retaliate. He believes it will be swift and severe, though he is not certain what form it will take," Victoria reported to William.

"And Jean Paul—he agrees with Mr. Sam. He even went so far as to say that there will be 'hell to pay,'" said Richard.

"Jean Paul said there would be 'hell to pay'?" William's eyebrows arched at his own question.

"Yes, sir, those were his exact words."

"Those are strong words, William," Jonathan interjected, "but I am afraid that Jean Paul is right."

"Yes, so am I," a concerned William said wearily as he slowly nodded his head and furrowed his brow. He reached out to the small table next to his chair in the parlor and took a long drink from his glass of port.

"That is essentially what we heard from the dockworkers this afternoon," Jonathan added.

"You are right, my friend. It would appear that the town is in agreement that while the act of a few brave 'Indians' resolved a precarious situation, the consequences, I fear, will be severe."

The next morning, the discussion of all the recent events continued during breakfast at the Finches'. Late the previous afternoon, Judah had taken a carriage to Lexington and brought Eleanor, Margaret, and James Barnes to the Finch home.

"I do not understand why everyone seems so glum around here," Eleanor said as she cut into a golden-brown biscuit. "Did not the *Gazette* say that masters and owners were well pleased with the events that took place, that people were congratulating one another, and that even John Adams was ecstatic?" Eleanor Barnes was a wonderful, comely woman, with light-blond, shoulder-length hair, beautiful blue eyes, and a light smooth complexion. She had a warm, pleasing air about her. She was thirty-eight years old, married to Jonathan at age twenty, and was totally devoted to her husband and family. While she had complete respect for Jonathan and his position in the family and society, she was not at all afraid to make her opinions known.

"Yes," replied a solemn Jonathan.

"Well, is it not true?"

"Oh, it is true," added William, "and we too were excited and pleased with what the 'Indians' accomplished, but the consensus around town is that there will be 'hell to pay,' and that is quoting none other than Jean Paul. He is basically in agreement with John's cousin, Sam Adams, and the dockworkers that Jonathan and I spoke with yesterday."

"What kind of 'hell to pay?"

"That is just it, my dear," said Jonathan. "We do not know yet."

"I believe that it will involve the port," William said, as he was just about to put a piece of dried beef into his mouth. "The port is the hub and the heart of this town," William continued as he stabbed the air with his fork, the beef still attached. "And it is where the greatest affront to British authority occurred."

"Yes," Jonathan replied, "it is the most likely place for a blow to be struck against Boston. The port is practically everything."

"Then why not do something positive and preemptive, if you will, to lessen the impact of the anticipated retaliation?" Eleanor pleaded.

Before William could respond, Judah entered the room.

"Mister William?"

"Yes, Judah, what is it?"

"Mister Jean Paul is here to see you, sir."

"Jean Paul is here?"

"Yes, sir."

"Judah, please show him in."

"Jean Paul," said William as he rose to greet his smiling friend, "your timing is impeccable, my friend. I was just about to invoke your name."

"Not in vain I hope, monsieur," replied Jean Paul, with a mock-serious look on his face.

"Not in vain, I assure you. We were just talking about British retaliation for the destruction of the tea, 'hell to pay,' as you so aptly put it to Richard. We all agree that the port is almost certainly the place that the Brits will strike, since as goes the port, so goes this town. Eleanor astutely recommended that we do something preemptive and positive to reduce the anticipated repercussions. Just before you walked in, I was about to suggest that we call a meeting of the merchants' association and include you."

"Include me with them? Are you sure that is a good idea?"

"If any of them are opposed to your attending, they can kindly take their leave of the meeting. I thought we could hold it in the middle of next week, before Christmas and in the evening. It need not be a lengthy meeting, but it could help us get some ideas on what we need to do. My concern is where to hold the meeting. I am worried about spies."

"We could have a pre-Christmas party here at our house," Annabelle interjected. "Judah and the servants can get the house ready in short order; it will be perfect cover for a meeting. While the party is in full swing, you and your associates can retire to the parlor."

Annabelle Finch, the very beautiful bride of William, had porcelain skin, ruby-red lips, black, shining hair, and an exquisite figure. Annabelle was just as beautiful inside as she was outside and, like her best friend Eleanor, was totally devoted to her husband his work, and her family.

"That is a splendid idea, my dear," said William, now quite excited.

"Splendid indeed," said Jonathan, grinning and nodding his head in agreement.

"I could help you with shopping for the party," Eleanor said to Annabelle.

"Why not now? I will get Judah, and we will go to the market this morning to gather supplies for the party and the week ahead."

"Excellent," said William. "Now Jean Paul, what brought you here this morning?"

Jean Paul let out a huge belly laugh that caught everyone off guard.

"Jean Paul, what is so funny?" William asked.

"Monsieur, monsieur." He broke up again in uncontrollable laughter. "My apologies to all, but this is so ironic—I came here because Willie Boyd asked me to tell Mr. Finch that the British ship *Hadley* left port immediately after the destruction of the tea, bound for England."

"Willie Boyd told you that?"

"Oui, monsieur, he said that you promised to give him a full outfit from McCaskill's."

"He told you about the outfit?"

"Monsieur Richard told me about it yesterday at Faneuil Hall, but Willie was eager to tell me the whole story. Outfitting him was a fantastic idea. He will be your friend for life and a valuable asset on the docks."

"The outfit is already proving beneficial, as you said it would, William," Jonathan agreed.

"Yes, but this is even sooner than I expected."

"Jean Paul, thank you so much for the information. Give my sincere thanks to Willie. Tell him that I visited McCaskill's today and told Timothy about our arrangement. Please remind him that he is to stop by my office after he is outfitted. I told him I wanted to see him in his new wardrobe."

"You are most welcome, monsieur. I will convey the message to him this afternoon."

"Now *Hadley*'s leaving when it did means that it will arrive about the middle of next month."

"Oui, monsieur. England will be apprised of the destruction of the tea by the end of next month."

"Which means that we have even less time than we initially thought."

"We probably have until no later than the middle of next year."

"Jean Paul, I look forward to your input at the meeting."

"Just let me know the date and time, and I will be here."

"William, take a look at this," said Annabelle to her husband, following the return from their shopping.

Annabelle gave William the handbill as Jonathan and Richard looked on.

"Where did you get this?" William asked, with an inquisitive look.

"It was handed to me outside the marketplace."

"What is it?" asked Jonathan, with nearly the same look as William's.

It is a handbill that says there is going to be a tar and feathering at two o'clock today at the Liberty Tree for those caught carrying tea leaves or shards during or following the destruction of the tea."

"Who is doing this?" asked Jonathan.

"The Sons of Liberty."

"I should have known."

"It seems that the Sons are trying to send a message. Let us go to the tree, now," William said, looking at Jonathan and Richard. "Good-bye, ladies. We shall return as soon as the Sons are finished with their lesson."

The men arrived in the Finch carriage to Hanover Square and the Liberty Tree shortly before two o'clock. Hundreds had already gathered to see the Sons of Liberty flex their muscles, holding court with three poor souls caught with shards of tea. The place was abuzz with much grumbling among those who had come to see the Sons mete out punishment to the enemies of liberty. The possession of tea was now akin to committing high treason. William, Jonathan, and Richard worked their way through the crowd until they had a clear view of the culprits.

"Father, Mr. Finch," said Richard excitedly, "that is the man, the man who—" As he raised his finger toward one of the three culprits, Jonathan quickly interrupted to silence his son.

"Shh…stop it, Richard," Jonathan said in a firm voice as he brought his hand down on Richard's shoulder. "Do not say another word."

"But, Father, I am sure he is the man on board the *Dartmouth* who—"

"Richard, enough, I said," Jonathan said in a firmer tone, now looking directly at his son, who had a wide-eyed look on his face as if to say, "What have I done wrong?"

Then it hit Richard. Jean Paul had said to him at Faneuil Hall that the great work of the 'French Indian' was not to be repeated. Richard's countenance changed dramatically as he realized what he had almost done.

"Father, I…understand…I understand. I almost made a big mistake."

"Yes, but fortunately, I was here to prevent it. You must not talk to anyone about who was aboard *Dartmouth* that night, let alone blurt out the name of one of the 'Indians,' in a crowded setting such as this. Remember, we were unable to identify the 'Indians.'"

"Yes, sir."

"Nevertheless, I believe you are correct in your identification of *that* man," Jonathan said.

"Oui, Monsieur Barnes, he is correct," said Francois DuBois as he and Becky Braun quietly came alongside William, Jonathan, and Richard.

Francois, following in his father's footsteps, was a ladies' man, being seen about town with many of the fairest of the fairer sex. He had more than met his match with the flirtatious, shapely, twenty-two-year-old beauty with dark eyes, black hair, and dimples. Daughter of wealthy financier, Horace Braun, and his dark-skinned beautiful Bahamian wife, who died when Becky was five years old, Becky was an only child. She was an heiress to a fortune and spoiled by her father, who deeply loved her but had little time for her with his many business and civic duties. Hence, she looked for love in the arms of men. Francois, cautioned by the elder DuBois, was totally taken with her, though he was careful not to show his true feelings. It was a fascinating relationship with each trying hard to maintain an edge over the other.

"Francois and Miss Braun!" Jonathan said, followed by William and Richard. "You have come to see justice administered by the Sons of Liberty."

"Oui—especially to *that* man, pointed out by Monsieur Richard. He is the man whom a certain 'Indian' with whom I am acquainted caught in the act of stealing tea from *Dartmouth*."

Becky Braun, now staring intently at the man who was the focus of all the attention, said, "What do you suppose they are going to do to him, Francois?"

"I am not certain, my dear, but I am certain it will not be pleasant for him."

"He is the nasty culprit here," said William, "and I believe that the Sons will have a special punishment for him. We will find out soon enough—here they go."

"Ladies and gentlemen," exclaimed one of the Sons in a loud voice, "we proclaim a great victory over the tyrant, King George III, and his lackeys, the British Parliament and East India Tea Company. We, the citizens of this town, this province, and indeed these colonies, must be united in the cause of liberty. We cannot and must not tolerate possession of tea. Those who disobey will receive this treatment and worse at the hands of the Sons of Liberty. These two were caught with shards in their shoes and pockets, picked up from the harbor following the destruction of the tea." The Son referenced the culprits other than the one nabbed by Jean Paul. "They are about to receive just punishment for their crime."

The men were both quickly covered with the hot, sticky tar, and a canvas bag full of feathers was dumped on their heads, which covered them from head to toe. The crowd roared its approval as the poor souls were being tormented by the awful concoction.

"What these men did was bad enough," the Son almost shouted in a fever pitch, "but this one," he said, grabbing Jean Paul's man by the arm and bringing him in the front and center for all to see, "this one had the audacity to pretend to help our friends, the 'Indians,' in their peaceful and excellent work on board the *Dartmouth*. He came on board the vessel, ostensibly to destroy the tea, while his real purpose was to fill his coat pockets with as much of the hated stuff as he could. But fortunately, one of our best 'Indian' friends caught him in the act, red-handed, if you will. He was drummed off the ship and sustained some serious blows from those of you on the pier. While already punished, his crime deserves more. He will receive a double portion of the concoction as reasonable justice for his transgression and fair warning for all who would consider similar actions."

"A double portion!" Becky gasped.

With that, the first portion of tar and bag of feathers was poured on his head, and before he could move, the second dosage followed. The crowd went into a complete uproar, chanting louder and louder, calling for more punishment.

"Tar and feathering ain't enough," a loud, obnoxious man shouted from the middle of the crowd. "He needs to be flogged within an inch of his no-good, rotten life. Why, he ain't nothin' but a traitor—a traitor, I says!"

"Traitor, traitor..." the crowd yelled as they closed in on the now truly frightened tarred-and-feathered man. The raucous chant grew louder and louder as some became belligerent, threatening to wrest control of him from the Son and tear him from limb to limb.

"Francois, this crowd is scaring me," Becky said as she wrapped her left arm tightly around his right arm and looked up at Francois, who turned his head to meet her gaze. For the first time, Francois saw fear in the eyes of this charming, alluring woman who always seemed to be in complete control.

Before Francois could reply, the Son quickly grabbed his musket from a fellow Son and fired it into the air. "Silence!" he screamed at the top of his lungs. It had the desired effect. The stunned crowd went immediately and completely silent. The Son continued in a loud voice with a warning to the crowd.

"There will be no lynching here today. The lesson has been given, and I believe it has been learned. The punishment was appropriate. Now leave and go to your homes. If anyone dares to lay a hand on him, they will get this," he said, pointing to his musket, "in their belly." The frightened man stood by the Son while the crowd began to quietly disperse.

"The men got what they deserved," William said to all, before they departed, "but the crowd behavior or lack thereof is cause for great concern."

"Oui, Monsieur Finch, I agree on both points. The crowd was frightening."

"Frightening is a bit of an understatement, Francois," said a still visibly shaken Becky Braun. "They were acting wild, crazy. I have no doubt they would have killed the man had they gotten their hands on him. I thought they were going to trample us to get to him!"

"The situation was rather precarious, but fortunately, the Sons still had the matter under control," Jonathan added.

"I agree with Becky, Father. They would have killed him given the chance," said Richard, he too with a look of fear on his face.

"I do not believe that they would have killed the man, but I agree with William; it is a matter of grave concern," Jonathan said.

"Gentlemen, we must take our leave. Miss Braun, Francois," William said as he again shook their hands, followed by Jonathan and Richard doing likewise. "Francois, please, as always, give our regards to your father," William said as he, Jonathan, and Richard turned and headed back to the carriage.

"Oui, monsieur, and our regards to your family," Francois exclaimed as he and Becky departed.

"I tell you, it was a sobering experience this afternoon," exclaimed William at supper that evening.

"Why do you say that, Father, if I may ask?" asked Lydia.

"Well, my dear, if you had seen what Jonathan, Richard, and I witnessed—oh, and Francois and Miss Becky Braun joined us—you would understand what I was referring to."

"Francois and Becky Braun," Lydia said with disgust, shaking her head. "Why is he with her?"

"What do you mean by that?" William inquired. "I have not known Francois to discriminate when it comes to being with beautiful women, and besides, what is the problem with her? Her father is one of the wealthiest, most respected men in town."

"William Finch, you know perfectly well what she means about Becky Braun," Annabelle said forcefully.

"I know that she is a beautiful, charming, and intelligent young lady."

"Father, forgive me if I am being too forthright, but she is the biggest flirt in this town, and everyone knows it. She is nothing but trouble."

"Perhaps you are right, but that cold-hearted femme fatale, as you ladies seem bent on describing her, was scared out of her wits today. Her observations about what took place, were, I must say, very astute. Do you agree, Jonathan?"

"I think she was not far from the truth."

"Father, may I ask what took place today?" asked Lydia.

William proceeded to give a brief yet vivid account of the events at the Liberty Tree and then asked, "How would you describe it, Jonathan?"

"I would not call it mob rule. The Sons were in control of this situation, but when that maniac practically called for blood from the poor victim, it whipped up the crowd into a frenzy. The question is, will the Sons of Liberty and Sam Adams be able to control the masses in the future? If not, all could be lost," Jonathan replied in a somber tone.

"Father, Mr. Barnes, do you not think those men all got what they deserved? The no-good one caught by Jean Paul had the nerve to come on board the ship and pretend to help the 'Indians' when he was just trying to get some of the tea for himself? I am sorry and do not mean to be disrespectful, Mr. Barnes, but he is no 'poor victim' in my opinion."

"You are not being disrespectful to me," Jonathan quickly replied. "I do agree with you that he received the punishment he deserved, as did the others, but when I said he was a 'poor victim,' all I meant was he did not deserve to be lynched. While I do not think the man would have been torn limb from limb, I have no doubt he would have suffered a severe beating had the Son not fired his shotgun in the air. We must punish those who deserve it not just because it is the right thing to do but also to serve as a warning to others that this behavior will not be tolerated."

"What we saw was power today, raw power. The Sons had the crowd where they wanted them, but things almost got out of hand. This is the rub: There is enormous power in a crowd such as we were part of today. That power is necessary for us to have any success in redressing our grievances against the Brits, but it must be controlled and focused against them, or as Jonathan said, all could be lost. Uncontrolled power in the hands of the masses could be more dangerous than the British themselves," William said.

"May I ask why that is, Father?" Lydia inquired.

"Because it has the potential to destroy the fabric of our society. We must have order; the rule of law must prevail, or none of us is safe."

"Then the Sons must maintain control and channel the power properly," Lydia concluded, grasping the significance of her father's statement.

"Precisely, my dear." William nodded as he raised a glass of water to his lips for a sip.

"I believe that they will," interjected Jonathan. "The Sons of Liberty have an extensive network developed over considerable time, and Sam Adams is their unquestioned leader. He demands and gets their total respect and allegiance."

"What you say is true, my friend. Sam Adams controls the Sons, but can the Sons control the masses? That is the real question."

"Reverend Bacon, that was certainly a rousing patriotic message," exclaimed William as he shook John Bacon's hand following the Sunday morning service at Old South Church.

"I am glad that you enjoyed it."

"I did, but without meaning to be negative or temper enthusiasm for what the 'Indians' accomplished, I believe our citizens must realize that British retaliation will be swift and severe."

John Bacon had given a stirring message thanking the "Indians" for their great service to Boston, Massachusetts, and the colonies as a whole.

"Of course, Mr. Finch, I agree. I believe our citizens know that there may be 'hell to pay,' as Jean Paul put it, but I thought it vital that we be uplifting today, praising the Lord for his work, especially at Christmastime."

"Jean Paul—how did you know what Jean Paul said?"

"Word travels fast in this town, Mr. Finch," said Reverend Bacon, grinning.

"All right, Reverend, I trust your judgment."

"Thank you, sir, and thank all of you for attending today. It was very good to see the Finches and Barnes together in our church."

Following a noon meal at the Finches', the families said their good-byes, Eleanor and the children to return on New Year's Eve, while Jonathan would be back briefly the following week for the much-anticipated "party."

The party itself proved to be a great success. The meeting in the parlor had some tense early moments.

"Gentlemen, I have heard the grumblings about Jean Paul, and I will have none of it. You all know that he and I are very good friends and have been for a long time. I would trust Jean Paul with my life and the lives of my family. And, we all owe him our heartfelt thanks and gratitude for his contributions to his country, especially last week. I shall not say more. I have invited my best friend and loyal customer, whom you all know, Mr. Jonathan Barnes, to attend this meeting and future meetings during this time of crisis. He is a great resource, and I highly value his insights and judgment, and I believe we all benefit from his counsel."

All in the room nodded their approval for Jean Paul and Jonathan. They were very aware of Jean Paul's contributions and Jonathan's standing in the greater Boston community.

"Now I believe we are ready to get down to the business at hand. Jean Paul himself has said that as a consequence of the destruction of the tea, there will be 'hell to pay.' Will you please tell us what you meant by that?"

"Oui, merci, Monsieur Finch, I am grateful to be here. When I said that I believed that there would be 'hell to pay,' I meant that the Brits would act swiftly and ruthlessly in response to our actions. Already *Hadley* is on its way to England, so soon the king, Parliament, and all England will know of the events that have taken place here.

They will be furious, considering it an abridgement of their sovereign authority, and come down hard, punishing us not just for our 'crimes,' but to make an example, messieurs of Boston and the Bay Colony. I do not know what form it will take, but it will be very painful for us. Monsieur Finch believes that it will involve the port, since it is where the destruction of the tea took place and is the symbol of Boston."

"I believe they will do something to strangle the port in the form of imposing some sanctions to cripple our flow of goods and supplies," William said. "Jonathan's wife, Eleanor, implored Jonathan and myself to do something preemptive and positive to lessen the anticipated impact. My wife suggested this party as cover for this meeting, so that is why we are here. We are going to need all the help we can get. Our time to act is going to be short."

"Messieurs, I will begin to quietly store more clothing and nonperishables in my warehouses and to make contact with sources out of Boston, even out of Massachusetts, to funnel goods to us."

"Jean Paul, let me get in touch with Michael Beaumont," Jonathan interjected. "I have a man in mind to go to Charleston immediately and notify Michael of our needs. I know he will be happy to personally help us and will recruit Charleston merchants to come to our aide."

"Oui, Michael is a wonderful man. He will be a great asset. Please send your man."

"This is the plan that I had in mind. Make contact with sources outside of the city and even the colony to start putting supply lines together for the purpose of filling up our warehouses with goods and supplies so that when the time of Brit punishment comes, we will be ready—as ready as we can be," William said, poking the arm of his chair with his finger for emphasis.

"If we do this now, monsieur, it will be *so* much easier than waiting until the Brits retaliate," Jean Paul added, raising his hands.

"By then it would almost certainly be too late," William said. "While there are currently no sanctions being imposed, I would suggest that we attempt to, as Jean Paul put it, quietly go about the business of storing goods and supplies. Try to make it appear, as much as possible, as if it is 'business as usual' while the inflow into our warehouses increases. What is being proposed is voluntary. I am not going to impose numbers and quotas of lines and goods but simply implore you to do whatever you realistically can to put this into action. Is everyone in agreement?"

Heads nodded around the room, along with a few verbal yeses.

"Excellent."

"Just one question, William," Jonathan said. "When do we get started?"

"I would say right after Christmas."

"Oui, monsieur, as for contacting supply sources, it is imperative that we start right away. There is no time to lose."

"Gentlemen, this has been a most productive meeting. Thank you all for coming on short notice and for your cooperation. We will meet again in a few weeks at my office to see how we are progressing and to deal with other pressing issues. Merry Christmas to you and your families."

December 31

Late in the afternoon, the Barneses' carriage pulled up to the Finch residence. Judah greeted them as the carriage came to a stop.

"Mister Jonathan, Madame Eleanor, it is good to have you back here."

"Good to be back, Judah," Jonathan responded as Judah helped Eleanor and Margaret, age fourteen, down from the carriage. James, age twelve, alighted on his own.

"I will take your bags to the room, sir, but first I will open the door for you."

"Thank you, Judah."

"Mister William, Madame Annabelle," Judah said as he opened the front door, "Mister Jonathan and Madame Eleanor are here."

"Jonathan, Eleanor, children, welcome!" William greeted them with a warm smile and hugs to all.

"Please make yourselves at home, after all, this *is* your home away from home," Annabelle said as she too hugged her friends.

After the evening supper, the adults moved to the parlor.

"William, I sent a good friend and very dependable person, Thomas Gallagher, to Charleston to contact Michael and inform him of our needs. Thomas left early the day after Christmas. It will be a long time before he returns, but I am certain we will be glad we did this."

"Michael will be a tremendous help. Jean Paul has followed through with contacting some of his other sources, and I have been able to make some contacts myself. The response thus far has been very favorable. Goods should be flowing into my warehouses early next year."

"You deserve much credit, William, for putting this into action."

"We have a very long road ahead of us, my friend. I trust that all our association members are following through with making contacts of their own. This is not a one-man operation. It is and must be a concerted effort of countless individuals if we have any hope of succeeding."

"Yes, but you are our leader and the driving force behind this plan."

"That may be true, but it was your lovely wife who spurred us into action with her correct assessment of our poor attitude and the need for an adjustment of the same."

"And it was your lovely wife who came up with the idea of a pre-Christmas party here at your beautiful home," Jonathan quickly and astutely responded, "which was the perfect cover for the association meeting."

Eleanor and Annabelle smiled at each other.

"We are pleased for the acknowledgment of our contribution, but we are very proud of both of you for implementing the plan so quickly. The community may not know it now and may never know it, but your efforts could improve and even save countless lives," Eleanor said, with admiration and conviction.

"We know that we and the community can count on you to do whatever needs to be done," Annabelle agreed.

"Jonathan and I are grateful for your confidence and support," William said, glancing at Jonathan, who gently nodded his head. "We will need all of it in what promises to be a most challenging new year."

3

Year 1774

"**I** have been giving a lot of thought to pursuing a career in the law," Richard said as he turned his head to gaze into the wide-open eyes of Victoria. They were together again, this time at the Finches', as they had been more and more often in the preceding days.

"You are considering the law?" asked Victoria in eager anticipation.

"Yes—yes, I am. I think it fits my personal bent. It would provide more potential for me to contribute to and influence the lives of others than in any other business or profession."

"That is exciting, Richard. I agree that a career in the law has the potential for you to have a significant impact in society."

"That is my thinking, but the possibility of a conflict brewing between the colonies and the mother country may postpone my ambitions," he said, with waning enthusiasm.

"Richard, as you know, my father's lawyer is the famous John Adams. I would be very pleased to talk to father about introducing you to him. He is not only a great lawyer but also a leader of the patriot cause. Surely he can give you insight about the current situation and the potential effects on pursuing a career in the law at this time."

"Mr. Finch will introduce me to John Adams?" Richard said, his eyes suddenly wide open and sparkling again and his countenance reenergized.

"I am sure Father will be happy to introduce you to John Adams. Let us go to Father's office right now and broach the subject with him. I am certain that he would be delighted to hear your career aspirations and be glad to arrange a meeting."

"Victoria, Richard, what brings you to my office that could not wait until this evening?" said William as he entered the lobby of his Long Wharf office to hug and greet them.

"Father, Richard and I were talking about the future, and Richard told me that he has been considering a career in the law."

"Richard, is that true?"

"Yes, sir. I have been thinking about it for quite some time, but I am concerned about current events and their possible impact on my plans."

"Father, I told Richard that your lawyer is John Adams and that you might be willing to introduce Richard to him."

"I would be very pleased to do so. Richard, I am certain that Mr. Adams will be willing to give you his opinion about current affairs and their impact on your aspirations."

"Thank you, sir. I am most grateful to you."

"I am glad to be of help. As a matter of fact, next week I am meeting Mr. Adams for dinner, along with Mr. David Whitmore, my wharf manager, and Mr. George Manly, my assistant wharf manager, to discuss legal matters concerning the wharf. Come and join us."

"Sir, that would be wonderful! What day will it be? I must speak with my father about taking time off from school."

"The dinner meeting will be next Friday, at noon at Jean Paul's tavern, JP's. You may spend the evening at our home."

"Thank you so much, sir. I will ask Father for approval."

"I am sure he will approve, and I can tell you that Mr. Adams will be elated to know the son of Jonathan Barnes will be joining us."

On Friday of the scheduled meeting, Richard arrived at JP's at quarter till twelve and was escorted to a table in the back. As Richard approached the table, William rose from his chair to greet the young man.

"Richard, I am so glad that you could come."

Richard firmly shook the hand of his father's merchant and best friend.

"Mr. Finch, I am so grateful that you invited me."

William introduced Richard to David Whitmore, George Manly, and then to John Adams. As Adams began to rise, Richard stopped him.

"Please be seated, sir; the honor is mine."

"Mr. Barnes, I assure you that I am the one who is honored by your presence here today," Adams responded as he returned to his seat. "When William told me of your interest in the law and your desire to join us for dinner, I was naturally delighted. By the way, please say hello to your father for me. He is a true American patriot."

"I will be happy to do so."

Dinner was served, and William, David, and George discussed various legal issues regarding business at the wharf with John Adams, who deftly responded to all the matters that were brought up. Richard listened intently, especially to what Adams had to say. As business was wrapping up, Adams invited Richard to attend a criminal trial scheduled a few weeks later. Adams estimated that the trial would last no more than two days.

"Mr. Adams, I will discuss the matter with my father. I will again have to procure leave from school. I have missed several days lately."

"If I may assist with school issues, please let me know. I will speak with the headmaster, if necessary."

"I appreciate that very much, sir, but there is another matter that has been weighing heavily upon me."

"The state of affairs between the colonies and the mother country?"

"Yes. In the wake of the destruction of the tea, it is quite evident from discussions with my father, Mr. Finch, and Jean Paul and the efforts they and others are making to blunt what they foresee as coming sanctions against us, well—it just appears that a serious conflict is coming that could ruin my plans."

"I hear you," said Adams, gently nodding his head as he put his right hand on Richard's left shoulder and looked directly into his eyes.

"Your concerns are justified, son, and I would probably feel the same if I were in your position," he said. "What will happen to my plans if a major conflict develops?"

"That is the question."

"Do I think a conflict is at hand? Yes, it is already here with this whole tea business and the Brits taxing us without representation. Is the conflict going to grow? Almost certainly, especially when they impose their sanctions on us, which will be soon, I am sure. Would that stop me from doing all I could, at the present time, to pursue my ambition, my career? Absolutely not! Events will probably overwhelm and change the course of all our lives, but until that actually occurs, do all that you can do to pursue your ambitions. That is my advice. In keeping with that advice, come to the trial. You will enjoy it and learn something about our interesting legal system, and you will not be bored."

"Sir, I am grateful to you for your insights and wisdom," Richard said, his spirits again lifted.

"I am glad you asked me." Adams then filled Richard in on the details of the trial.

"In the very unlikely event that the prosecuting attorney actually comes to the realization that he has no case and does the honorable thing and drop the charges, I will let your father know immediately. Otherwise, I will see you in court!"

⚜

"John Adams is wonderful," Richard said excitedly to Victoria and her family that evening at the Finches'.

"He is amazing," William concurred. "I never cease to marvel at his intellect. He hears the facts of a situation and instantly processes them in his mind. The end results are rational, straightforward solutions to what often seemed unsolvable problems."

"I could almost hear his mind at work as he dealt with those difficult issues you presented to him."

"I am very grateful that he is on my side and the side of our liberty. There is no more ardent patriot than John Adams. He is a lion. Speaking of difficult issues, did you address with him the matter that was weighing on your mind?"

"I did, and as you said, he readily gave me his opinion. He said to do all I could do, at this point in time, and not worry about the future. He invited me to attend the criminal trial of a client of his. I cannot wait to see him in a court trial. I am sure he will prove to be a formidable opponent to the prosecution."

"He invited you to attend a criminal trial?" asked Victoria incredulously.

"Yes. He said, in the unlikely event that the prosecutor came to his senses and dropped the charges, he would inform my father; otherwise, he would see me in court."

"May I join you?" Victoria asked excitedly.

"Of course, if your father would be agreeable."

"Father, may I go with Richard to the trial?"

"Certainly, my dear. I think it would be a tremendous experience for both of you. I will accompany you."

"Richard, when is it going to occur?"

"Three weeks from Monday, eight o'clock sharp. But first are matters to be addressed," Richard said.

"Jonathan's permission?"

"His and the headmaster's."

"I know that Jonathan will embrace this opportunity for you, and I am sure the headmaster will also," said William.

"I wish I was as confident as you, sir. I have missed quite a few days of school lately."

"I will be happy to speak to your father, if it would be helpful," William added.

"I appreciate that, sir. Mr. Adams said he would talk to the headmaster for me, if necessary."

"Now what are you worried about, Richard?" Victoria added. "I am sure we are going to a jury trial!"

"Richard, you have missed several school days with all the recent events," Jonathan observed.

"I know that, Father, but Mr. John Adams has personally invited me to attend this trial, which he estimates will last no more than two days. And Mr. Finch agreed to accompany Victoria and me."

"John Adams is a great lawyer and man, and there is no more ardent and articulate spokesman for our cause," Jonathan said as he gently stroked his chin with his left hand, a contemplative look on his face as he pondered the matter, "but I am concerned that you are falling behind on your studies."

"He told me to say hello to you and that you were 'a true American patriot,'" Richard said, deciding to take the offensive in the matter.

"John Adams said that?" Jonathan said as he snapped out of his contemplative mood.

"Those were his exact words, sir. He also offered to speak with the headmaster himself, if necessary, on my behalf," Richard added, sensing that the tide had turned in his favor.

"That is very kind of him," said a pleased and flattered Jonathan, "but it will not be necessary. I will discuss the matter with the headmaster and make arrangements with him for you to catch up."

"Thank you, Father," said Richard, nearly as proud of his ability to sway his father's judgment as he was happy to receive his blessing.

"Think nothing of it," Jonathan said with a dismissive wave of his hand, the same hand that just moments ago was stroking his chin. "This is a terrific opportunity to see the legal system at work and one of Boston's greatest legal counselors in action."

William, Richard, and Victoria sat in rapt attention in the back of the Boston courtroom. They and several citizens of Boston and the surrounding towns had come to see a criminal trial featuring John Adams. It was he who had successfully defended the British Regulars who were charged following the infamous Boston massacre, when a majority of Bostonians believed that his clients were guilty of murder. Adams had just sat down after delivering his closing summation, concluding two days of trial. All in the courtroom were amazed at the clarity, logic, and persuasiveness of his argument.

The jury retired to consider the evidence and arguments of counsel. William, Richard, Victoria, and the other spectators left the courtroom to stretch and await the jury verdict.

"Mr. Adams was magnificent, was he not?" said Victoria, clearly in awe of what she had just witnessed.

"He was." Richard nodded in agreement.

"That was the John Adams I know at his finest," William added.

"I hope the jury reaches a verdict by the end of the day, because you must get back to school," Victoria said.

"I do not think that will be a concern," Richard replied. "Did you see the reaction in the courtroom after Mr. Adams finished his summation? He had the jury under his control," Richard said with admiration.

"He did, but I hope that translates into a quick verdict."

"I would be shocked if it did not."

Within an hour news spread throughout the courthouse that the jury had reached a verdict. The foreman read the verdict, which was not guilty on all counts.

After the courtroom had almost cleared, William, Richard, and Victoria spoke with John Adams as he was leaving.

"I am so glad all of you were able to come. What did you think?"

"John, this trial showcased your brilliant skills," William said.

"It did, sir. You were wonderful!" Victoria gushed.

"I agree," added Richard, nodding his head vigorously up and down. "Your summation simply destroyed the prosecution's case. Attending this trial was more beneficial to me than a month in school!"

"You are all very kind. The prosecutor had a weak case. I believe I told you Richard that this case should have been dismissed. All I did was expose the obvious weaknesses in a reasoned, rational way."

"You, sir, are too modest," said Victoria. "Everyone in that courtroom was held captive by your arguments and conclusions."

"I must admit I thoroughly enjoyed this case. The summation was like icing on the cake."

"Richard, if I have another criminal trial this summer, I will be happy to inform your father. And when you have completed your studies, you may read and study law under me."

"Sir, I am incredibly flattered, but I am not worthy to read and study law under the tutelage of the great John Adams."

"Son," replied Adams in an understanding way, "I understand, but trust me when I say that what you saw today was the culmination of years of dedication to my profession. I struggled mightily as a young lawyer but persevered. If you want to learn and are willing to work, you will be a fine lawyer."

"I am willing to do whatever it takes to succeed."

"Good," said Adams, "we will discuss this again at a later time."

4

"Judah, take this newspaper to Jonathan," said William, upon reading in the *Boston Gazette*, the full text of the Boston Port Act, passed by the British Parliament, to take effect on June 1. "He needs to read it right away."

"Yes, sir, Mister William," Judah replied. "I will fetch the carriage and leave now."

"Very good. I look forward to your return with his reaction."

❧

"Madame Barnes," Judah said as he entered the Barnes General Store in Lexington.

"Judah, how good to see you," Eleanor Barnes replied, smiling as she came to the front of the store. "You are looking for Jonathan, are you not?"

"Yes, ma'am, I am."

"This must be very important for you to come out here in the middle of the week."

"Yes, ma'am, it is."

"I will get him for you. He is out back."

"Thank you, ma'am."

"You are welcome. Wait right here."

Eleanor hurried out the back of the store, finding Jonathan at work in the garden.

"Jonathan, Judah is here, and he says it is important."

"Judah here now? It must be important for him to be here at this time of the week."

After removing his gloves and apron, Jonathan entered the back of the store and quickly walked to the front to meet Judah.

"Judah, it is good to see you, but I must confess that seeing you at this time of the week gives me cause for concern," he said, with a subdued look.

"Mister Barnes, sir, I understand. Mister William sent me to deliver this newspaper to you right away. He said it was urgent," Judah said as he handed the paper to Jonathan.

Jonathan saw the headlines and began intently reading the article on the Port Act. Aghast at what he read, he looked up mortified, his face now ashen.

"Mister Barnes, are you all right, sir?"

"No, Judah, I am not. I am feeling a bit ill right now," Jonathan said as he lowered himself into a chair along the front wall of the store. "Good Lord, this is even worse than we anticipated. This is an attempt to utterly destroy the colony! Please thank William for me and tell him that I will come to Boston this weekend to discuss what we can do in response to this reprehensible Port Act."

"I will, sir."

"Thank you all for coming," William said, at a meeting of his merchant association convened at his office and attended by Jonathan. "By now you have all seen and read the Boston Port Act. It is quite evident that we made the correct assessment when we surmised that the retaliation would be directed at our most important asset, the symbol of our town, where our so-called disobedience took place. And when you said that there would be 'hell to pay,' I believe even you will admit, Jean Paul, in light of this monstrous Port Act, that was an understatement!" William said, as he turned to look at Jean Paul seated immediately to his left.

"Oui, monsieur."

"Indeed, this is, in my humble opinion, an attempt to totally annihilate the town of Boston."

"William, with all due respect, I would have to say that it is really even worse than that. I believe this is an attempt to destroy the colony!" Jonathan interjected.

"I agree with Monsieur Barnes, and I feel certain that more sanctions will be forth coming very soon."

"You may be correct, my friends. This could very well be only the beginning. The good news, if there is such a thing, is that we saw the problem and we acted upon it. Most of our sources have been contacted, and the supplies have been flowing in for several months. How are we doing?"

"I, for one, monsieur, have contacted all my sources. The response has been very good, though I must say that some have responded much better than others. I will contact those whose response has been somewhat—how do you say—tepid and urge them to please redouble their efforts to help us."

"While I have contacted some of my sources, there are a few more whom I believe I can contact. I will set about doing this immediately and ask all those who have already sent supplies to increase their efforts," said Stephen Walker, long time Long Wharf merchant and association member.

"And I will get back in touch with Michael Beaumont. I am certain that the Charleston merchants will be willing to do even more to assist us in this time of need," said Jonathan.

"I believe that is what we all must be about doing," William said. "I too will redouble my efforts. Think about all possible sources; there may have been a few that you have missed or forgotten. Go back to the sources who have been contributing and ask if they could do more. Time is of the essence. Let us meet again next week, but somewhere else. It is time to move our meeting around to different locations."

"We can meet at my house, messieurs, if you like."

"I do. We will meet at Jean Paul's house a week from today at seven p.m."

≈

"My friends," said William to Jonathan and Jean Paul in a meeting called to discuss a response to merchants calling for payment of the tea tax following the Brit blockade of the port of Boston on June 1. "It is quite apparent that some of the other merchants do not feel the same way that we do about the appropriate response to this terrible act and its implementation. Many have begun to panic. A town meeting has been called a few days from now at Faneuil Hall to discuss the matter. We must present a united front. It is obvious that many of our cohorts want to capitulate."

"By simply paying the tea tax, they believe our problems will be solved?" Jonathan asked.

"Yes. And I surmise many of our fellow merchants will call for the disbanding of the Boston Committee of Correspondence, which is a critical cog in the organization of our anti-British protests. Let us face reality; despite all our efforts to get ready for this eventuality, the economic ramifications are still going to be devastating," William said.

"No doubt that it would be far easier to simply cower to the king and let him have his way, but can they not see that to do so means an erosion of our own basic liberties in the long run?" Jonathan asked.

"That is the point, my friend. If we give in now, where will it end?"

"It will end with the complete trampling of our liberties, messieurs, beyond erosion, as Monsieur Jonathan aptly calls it, to a complete squelching of them. It is only a matter of time with this king and his Parliament. You cannot trust them."

"So what can be done, William?" asked Jonathan.

"I will convene our merchants' association as soon as possible. We must make certain that our members will resist any efforts by merchants who would attempt to convince them to cave in to the British."

"I agree, Monsieur William."

"I too, William, as soon as possible."

"Good. Jean Paul, let us call an emergency meeting of the association tomorrow night at my office at the wharf. We will discuss this and other pressing issues. Please contact the other members in the morning. Jonathan and I will see you tomorrow night at seven o'clock at my office."

"Oui, monsieur, seven o'clock."

The association met, and nearly all members were in agreement with the need to present a united front against paying the tax. One merchant, Donald Souther, did express serious doubts about his ability to survive now that the act was actually implemented and the pain could already be felt.

"William...Mr. President," he said.

"Yes, Donald, what is it?"

"Honestly, I do not see how I will be able to survive. I have been talking with some of my other merchant friends who belong to other associations, and they are ready to pay the tax and be done with it. I am already being significantly hurt, and the Port Act just took effect a few weeks ago."

"I too am feeling the effects, even with all the advanced storage I was able to accumulate," William replied.

"That is exactly what I am saying. Even those who were able to store some goods for customers, themselves, and their families are struggling, and we are not even through June. How are we going to survive the summer?"

"Monsieur—if I may," said Jean Paul, ready to interject his thoughts about the situation.

"You may," nodded William.

"Messieurs William, Jonathan, and I discussed this matter last night, and it was decided to call this emergency meeting of the association. In that discussion, Monsieur Jonathan eloquently stated that if we cower to this king and his Parliament—and make no mistake; it is *his* Parliament—it will mean an erosion of our basic liberties. Monsieur William replied to him that that was the point; if we give in now, where will it end? I told them and submit to you that it will end in a complete trampling or squelching of our liberties. We give in now to them, and our pain is eased for a short while, but rest assured, messieurs, they will perceive us as weak, and they will soon lay an even heavier burden upon us. If you think it is bad now, just wait. The king would be a tyrant if he could, and some say he is already. What is the cost of our most precious commodity—our liberty? I assure you, messieurs, freedom is not free; the price is very high indeed, but it is worth *everything* to me. Let me say that again. It is worth *everything* to me!" Jean Paul said, pouring out his heart and clutching it as he spoke with great conviction. "That is why I chose to live in this dear country, to be free to do whatever I choose, to build a better life than I could ever have had in France, or Canada. I am determined to do everything in my power to maintain that freedom and the freedom of my fellow citizens. We must be united and say no—no, no, a *thousand* times no—to the king and his minions. We will never pay for the tea, nor your outrageous tea tax—*never!*"

The association was silent, listening with rapt attention to the words and passion of Jean Paul. All were familiar with his background and his sacrifices, and though he still did not smack of "respectability," as some defined it, all did admire where he came from and what he had accomplished.

After a several seconds of awkward silence, Jonathan said, "Jean Paul is right, gentlemen. The result of giving in today will not be just an erosion of our liberties—perhaps just an erosion initially—but ultimately, he is right; we know where it will lead."

"I could not possibly have said it better than Jean Paul. Are we now in agreement that we will fight and oppose this hated act no matter the cost? That we will do all in our power to aid and assist our fellow merchants and citizens of our fair town and our colony against this unjust law?" William firmly asked, sensing that now was the time to ask this poignant question.

All, including Souther, nodded their heads in solemn agreement.

"Very well, it is settled. I would appreciate as many of you as possible coming to the town meeting in a couple of days at Faneuil Hall, set for noon, to discuss this very issue," William exhorted. "There can be no equivocating. We must present a united front and make sure that our voices are heard, loud and clear."

"Jean Paul, you did it again," said William, grinning broadly as he slipped his arm around the shoulder of his friend as they entered Maggie's near Faneuil Hall, for a beer or two, in celebration following the town-hall meeting. The merchants who pleaded for payment of the tax and disbandment of the Committee of Correspondence saw their proposals fail by a wide margin.

"He did indeed," said a likewise jovial Jonathan, who entered right behind them.

"And just what is it that he did now?" said a curious Maggie Mae as she joined her man and his friends. Maggie had beautiful dark-brown eyes and an infectious smile.

"Maggie! My beautiful Maggie Mae!" Jean Paul greeted his long-time lover and tavern owner with a crushing hug and kiss.

"Francois and Mademoiselle Braun!" Jean Paul excitedly exclaimed as Francois, who was working in the tavern that afternoon, and Becky Braun, who had come have dinner with him, joined the group. Jean Paul bear-hugged his son and kissed the right hand of Becky. Despite his misgivings, Jean Paul was quite fond of her.

After greetings were exchanged by William and Jonathan, William answered Maggie's question.

"He simply destroyed the argument of the merchants who were ready to accede to the Brits' demands that the tea tax be paid."

"He did it by—let me guess—telling the reason why he chose to live in America following the French and Indian War," Maggie said as she looked into Jean Paul's eyes. "Liberty." A thin smile appeared on Jean Paul's face as he returned her gaze.

"How did you know that?" William asked, with a look of amazement.

"Monsieur Finch," Francois interposed, "that is practically all my mother and I have heard about for years, but especially since the tea tax was levied. My father loves liberty."

"What can I say?" Jean Paul responded, with a shrug of his shoulders and a tilt of his head. "They know me, no?"

"They know you *yes*, my friend," William said, with a slight nod of agreement.

"Francois, your father is a living embodiment of liberty. His story and the passion he brings when he relates it is a true inspiration to us all. I propose a toast to Jean Paul," said Jonathan as he turned around from the bar to the patrons in the tavern. "To the most eloquent patriot merchant in Boston."

"Hear, hear!" went up the cry, along with beer mugs from the four corners of the building.

Jean Paul was uncharacteristically at a loss for words. Finally he said, "Messieurs, mesdames, and mademoiselles, merci—*merci*—I only spoke from my heart."

"We know," said William, "and that is why your message is so effective. You speak for all of us, and most important, you speak for the cause of liberty."

"All drinks are on the house!" said a generous Maggie Mae.

"Three cheers for Maggie Mae," said a patron in the back of the tavern as he raised his beer mug.

"Huzzah! Huzzah! Huzzah!" roared through the tavern.

"Speech, Jean Paul, speech," said the same patron.

Jean Paul tried to ignore the request, but soon, "Speech, speech" was emanating throughout the tavern.

"Just speak from your heart again. They need to hear it," William said as he patted his now-emotion-laden friend on the chest.

"Oui, monsieur—from the heart."

Jean Paul raised his hands, and the sudden silence in the tavern was truly amazing and unprecedented. "We must be united, messieurs, mesdames, and mademoiselles, in that most noble of causes— the cause of liberty. Thank you for standing strong today. That is imperative for all of us, especially the merchants, since we are so vital to the economy of this town and colony.

"We will not succumb to the Brits by paying this unfair tax, a tax that was simply levied on us against our will and our sensibilities of what is fair, right, and just. We will *not* sacrifice our liberties in the face of this or any other tyrannical law or decree that they will impose, and trust me, they will impose more such decrees. This is just the beginning. We must be vigilant and oppose any and all who would infringe on our liberties, and we must be willing to pay the price, any price, even the *ultimate* price in their defense."

A spontaneous and raucous "hear, hear" went up from all over the tavern, with beer sloshing over the top of refilled mugs.

Then William got serious as he said to Jonathan and Jean Paul, "Today was a victory, no doubt, for which I am grateful, but as I have said before, I fear the days ahead will be very difficult. Some will lose the faith and passion. We must continue to remain strong for those who are weak and those who will weaken."

"Oui," said Jean Paul, "we must and will remain strong."

"Agreed," said Jonathan.

Jean Paul gave Maggie a parting kiss and Francois a hug, and then the three friends left the tavern to the cheers of all the patrons.

"Jean Paul, you are indeed a prophet," William said at a special meeting of the merchants' association, called in the wake of a barrage of acts passed by Parliament. "I believe you said that there would be more such decrees following in the footsteps of the Port Act. Were you ever right, my friend. They are known collectively as the Coercive Acts, the first of which was the Port Act."

"Coercive Acts—these are the Intolerable Acts," Jonathan added. "If there was ever any doubt about their intentions to squelch our liberties and destroy the colonies, there can be no doubt now."

"Oui, messieurs, these acts cover almost everything."

"They do, indeed, Jean Paul." William nodded. "I thought I would summarize these acts and we could discuss the possible ramifications of each and in total. The first to discuss is the Administration of Justice Act passed by Parliament on May twentieth, whereby British officials accused of crimes in the colonies may opt for trial in England or another colony."

"Administration of justice," said association member Donald Souther, with a look of disgust. "That is anything but the administration of justice. What witnesses will have the money, let alone the time, to travel out of the colonies to testify?"

"The act does say that witnesses are to be reimbursed for all their travel expenses," William said.

"But they will have to pay their own way, correct?" Souther asked.

"Yes, and there is no provision for reimbursing the witnesses for lost wages while they are doing the king's business," William added.

"Then this means the Brits can basically do whatever they want to us and not be held accountable. That *is* intolerable," intoned Souther.

"Indeed," interjected Arthur Parke, a good friend of William and Jonathan and longtime association member. "It will effectively allow the Brits to escape justice in most cases, and in capital cases, they will literally be getting away with murder!" he said as he pounded the table with his right fist.

"And along with that act, the Massachusetts Government Act also was passed on May twentieth. It modified our Massachusetts Charter of 1691 and eliminated many of our rights of self-governance, including the election of counselors and assistants who served in governing the colony. These positions, gentlemen, are now to be appointed by the king and serve 'for and during the pleasure of His Majesty.'"

"Appointed by the king—serving for and during *his* pleasure? What about elected by us—serving for and during *our* pleasure?" Parke said loudly, with his left eyebrow arched high and a scowl on his face. "We had almost no representation before—remember 'no taxation without representation'—and now we have none." The mood in the room was somber, but a look of determination was beginning to appear on several faces as William recited summaries of these abominable acts.

"The next act has already directly affected me. The Quartering Act of 1774 established on June second is similar in substance to the Quartering Act of 1765. The British, specifically 'the officer who, for the time being, has the command of His Majesty's forces in North America, may cause any officers or soldiers in His Majesty's service to be quartered and billeted in such manner as he directs by law where no barracks are provided by the colonies.' It goes on to say that if officers or soldiers remain in any of the colonies without quarters for twenty-four hours after the quarters are demanded, it is lawful for the governor of the province to order and direct the taking of uninhabited houses, barns, outhouses, or other buildings as deems necessary, to make the same fit for the quartering for such period as he should think proper."

"Your house, William, by the wharf—the Brits commandeered it, did they not?" asked Parke.

"They did." William nodded. "This has distressed me to no end. I am going to pay General Gage a visit after this meeting."

"Do you think that he will agree to meet with you, and if so, will he grant your request to have the troops removed?"

"Yes, I think so, and no, probably not, but I have to try something. We all know that this law is wrong—it is clearly unconstitutional."

"All our uninhabited buildings are subject to being taken over," mused Nathan Jeffers, another longtime Boston merchant, who came from a family with a rich history in the business. "What about our warehouses with all our smuggled supplies? Are they going to demand use of them for their precious officers and soldiers?"

"Jonathan, Jean Paul, and I discussed that possibility prior to the meeting, and while it is possible, we think it is highly unlikely, given all the abandoned houses in town and the fact that with Gage's return to Boston on the *Lively* with four regiments of troops, it is doubtful that more Brit troops will be arriving anytime soon."

"I sincerely hope you are right," Jeffers replied.

"So do we," Jonathan said.

"The last act was the Quebec Act, passed on June twenty-second," William said, "and while it is not technically a part of the Coercive Acts, it is definitely of the same substance, as them.

"It gives Catholics in the province civil equality while guaranteeing to them religious tolerance. It also vastly extends the boundaries of unrepresented Quebec, far west of the Appalachians."

"No disrespect meant to Jean Paul," Parke said as he glanced at Jean Paul before addressing the rest of the group, "but did we not help the Brits defeat the French in that seemingly never-ending French and Indian War? I mean we fought long and hard for the Brits, and if I am not mistaken, we won. We were supposed to have the spoils of victory, which included the territory west of the mountains, and now all this has been taken from us and essentially given to our enemy, the vanquished French, by the stroke of a pen!"

"Monsieur Parke, I could not agree with you more," Jean Paul said forcefully as he looked directly at Parke while addressing the group. "Your comment does not offend me in the least. On the contrary, this act offends me, along with the Intolerable Acts, as Monsieur Jonathan so aptly called them."

"So, apart from the acts themselves and the direct consequences of the implementation of them, what will be the overall ramifications to us?" asked Souther.

"I think I know what the Brits are hoping for," William replied.

"Which is?" asked Souther.

"Which is to crush us—destroy our spirit by driving a wedge between us and the other colonies, turning them against us, to the end that we and the others will be brought to heel under the Brits' authority," Jonathan chimed in.

"Monsieur Jonathan is right; that is what the Brits are hoping for," interjected Jean Paul, "but if I may make another prediction."

"By all means," said William.

"I believe the result will be just the opposite. Instead of driving a wedge between us and the other colonies, thereby destroying our spirit and bringing us all back into the royal fold, if you will, these acts will prove to be a rallying point for all the colonies, unifying us as never before, thereby lifting our spirit in the common cause."

"The common cause?" asked Jeffers.

"Why, the great cause, really the only cause," Jean Paul said, smiling.

"I know, Jean Paul," said Jeffers, now realizing the foolishness of the question, "the cause of liberty."

"I agree with what you are saying, Jean Paul, but what can we do in response to these brutish laws?" Parke queried the group.

"We must continue to carry on, even grow our smuggling operation," William responded, "because even though these acts do not directly affect our commerce, the tone is unmistakable—more and more control. Also we need to reach out to the other colonies."

"To expand on what William just said," Jonathan quickly added, "I have recently learned that the dissolved House of Burgesses has been meeting in Raleigh Tavern in Williamsburg and is proposing a gathering of representatives, a congress, selected from all colonies to address our grievances and how we should respond. Sam Adams is heading a committee in the Massachusetts House with the same objective. I believe it is imperative that we contact both of them forthwith and offer any assistance and support we can to help them to make this a reality."

"Jonathan, that is a tremendous idea!" William said excitedly, as the others nodded their heads in agreement. "The sooner the better as far as I am concerned, and gentlemen, I think we all know who would be perfect to lead the effort."

"Oui, Monsieur William, we know," Jean Paul added, looking at Jonathan.

"All right, I will be happy to, but only if you two will assist me," Jonathan said, looking back at Jean Paul and then at William. "This will be a big job."

"Oui," said Jean Paul.

"Yes, of course," added William. "I believe that is all for now. Thank you for your attention and cooperation." With that, the meeting was adjourned.

"Mr. Finch, how may I be of assistance?" General Gage asked William as he came to discuss the matter of his house near Long Wharf.

"General Gage, I came to ask you to reconsider the commandeering of a house that I own near Long's Wharf for the quartering of the king's troops."

"First of all, sir, I did not make the order, the governor did, as you are very well aware, and the house was not 'commandeered' as you say. You *are* familiar with the recent act passed by Parliament that reinstated and amended the Quartering Act."

"The governor may have made the actual order, but we both know who was behind it. And yes, General, of course I am aware of that act, but—"

"But what? Demand for quarters was made in this town twenty-four hours prior to when the order was given to take uninhabited houses, barns, or other various buildings due to lack of compliance. All that was done was within the bounds of the law, perfectly legal."

"You mean to say that it is completely within the bounds of a law that is patently illegal on its face. Taking property without due process of law. This is in derogation of the English common law, and you know it."

"Now see here, Mr. Finch—you are testing my patience and very quickly wearing out your welcome. I will not debate with you the propriety and legality of a law passed by the British Parliament, which has the power and right to put such law into effect."

"They may have the power, General, but not the right. I know that, and so do you."

"I know no such thing! I do know that if you press the matter further, *I* will take that handsome residence of yours for my headquarters, and there will be no one to stop me. As it is, I am warning you right now that your residence will be available for me, my staff, and my troops whenever the need arises and at a moment's notice, if necessary. And your house down by the wharf will quarter the troops for as long as we have need of it. Do you understand, sir?"

"My residence? That is preposterous!"

"Is it? I repeat, do you understand, sir?"

"Yes, I do."

"Very well, then we have nothing further to discuss. Good day, Mr. Finch."

"Good day, General."

As the brutal summer of '74 ground on in Boston, William continued to convene the remaining members of the association of merchants of Long Wharf, to discuss the handling of the crisis. Boston was able to endure, thanks in large part to the outside supply sources established by the merchants of the association, which kept a continuous supply of food, clothing, and other essentials flowing into the beleaguered and now-almost-ghost town. Dockworkers milled aimlessly around the wharfs with nothing to do. Lobsterbacks camped out on the commons and occupied more and more of the empty houses left by the fleeing Bostonians.

For Lydia Finch, life had changed dramatically. Gone were the golden days when she had several suitors. She had been sought after by many for her beauty, wit, and charm, though for some she was too opinionated. Lydia was furious with the king and Parliament for her predicament and that of her family and her town. Newly elected delegate, Jonathan Barnes, discussed with William the possibility of accompanying him to the First Continental Congress in Philadelphia. Jonathan thought that William, as a prominent merchant, could best enlighten Congress on the plight of Boston and Massachusetts in the wake of the Port Act and other Coercive Acts. William was very receptive to the idea, as was Annabelle, and both thought it would be good for Lydia to go as well. They thought the change of scenery would be beneficial to her.

"Lydia, Jonathan came to me and asked if I would be willing to accompany him to Philadelphia when he leaves for Congress. He thinks that, given my position as a merchant, I would be able to explain to the delegates the problems and challenges that we are facing here. Your mother and I thought that you could accompany us. We believe this could be a wonderful experience for you. We know that your mood has been depressed since the Port Act came into effect, and many eligible young bachelors in this town fled along with their parents. Additionally, Michael Beaumont is coming to Philadelphia from Charleston with his family. We thought you could spend time with Mrs. Beaumont and Lucy while Jonathan and I have discussions with Michael about our supply lines."

"Father, Mother, I would love to go to Philadelphia. I am weary of this forsaken town, and Philadelphia would be *so* exciting in so many ways. I would thoroughly enjoy being in the company of Lucy and Mrs. Beaumont. You know how fond I am of Lucy. I am certain that we can find many things to occupy our time."

"I do not anticipate a lengthy stay there, probably four to six weeks at most, depending on how much I may be needed. I do not feel that I can stay away from the rest of the family, the business, and the association for any extended period of time, given the current situation."

"I am most grateful to you for this opportunity, no matter how short the stay."

"Jonathan's plan is that we will arrive in Philadelphia about a week before Congress convenes on September 5. That should give us enough time to secure quarters and for Jonathan to get settled in. He wants to be near Carpenters' Hall, where Congress will convene."

"Then I will need to inform Uncle Timothy right away of our plans," Lydia replied.

"Actually, given the short time and your anticipated positive response, I took the liberty of telling him myself yesterday before coming home from work."

"Father, how did he respond? I know that we have been very slow, and I have only been working part time since the port has closed, but the shop is still open. I do not want my leaving even for a brief time to be a problem for him."

"He did not think that your leaving would be a problem. On the contrary, he was very supportive of the trip and thought, as do your mother and I, that the change of environment, however brief, would be a terrific experience for you. He said that upon your return, he would still have work for 'the best seamstress in the Massachusetts colony.'"

"Uncle Timothy said that?"

"He did, and he meant it."

"I am very grateful to him. I am so fortunate to have him as my uncle and employer."

During the disastrous summer, Joshua Finch, age twenty-one, who had been working for his father at the wharf for the past few years, continued to assist wharf manager, David Whitmore, and assistant wharf manager, George Manly, though there were few businesses left open, and those that remained were struggling to survive. There was very little work for Joshua to do, and he became increasingly frustrated and eager to do something to help the plight of his town and its inhabitants.

॰

"Mr. Finch," Richard Barnes said as he stood outside William's Long Wharf office.

"Richard," William said, looking up from his desk, "please come in." He gestured for Richard to enter.

"Thank you, sir," Richard said as he hesitantly entered the room.

"Richard. Something important is evidently on your mind," William said as he rose to greet his best friend's son. "Please have a seat. Is there something I can do for you or help you with?"

"Well, yes, sir, actually there is." Both men sat down simultaneously.

William studied Richard's face, which seemed to express some concern.

"Mr. Finch," Richard started, looking down toward the ground.

"Richard, does this have anything to do with Victoria?" William said in a positive tone.

"Why, yes, sir—it has everything to do with Victoria," Richard replied, now looking directly at William and noticing the slight smile creasing William's lips. "Sir," Richard said, now gaining confidence, "Victoria and I have been spending more time together of late."

William's head was nodding.

"And, actually, we have grown quite fond of each other and..." Gathering himself, Richard said, "Sir, I came to ask you if I may court your daughter. It would mean so much to me if you would approve. I apologize for not asking sooner."

"Richard," William said, now with a full smile on his face and his eyes wide open, "Victoria's mother and I were wondering when you would ask. I think you know how much we admire you." William got up and went around the desk as Richard stood up. William vigorously shook Richard's hand and said, "We are delighted at the relationship that is developing between the two of you and are very glad that you are now taking this step. And no apologies are necessary."

"Thank you. Thank you so much, sir. And please thank Mrs. Finch. Your daughter is so wonderful. I feel very blessed that she is in my life."

"I think I may speak for Victoria when I say she feels the same way toward you."

Lydia arrived at McCaskill's the following morning to report to work.

"Uncle Timothy."

"Lydia, your father informed me that you are going to accompany him and Mr. Barnes to Philadelphia when Mr. Barnes leaves for the new Congress."

"Yes, sir. It will only be for a relatively short time, perhaps four to six weeks. Father cannot stay away too long."

"So I understand."

"Father said you were agreeable to that decision. If you have changed your mind, Uncle, I would understand. While work here is slow and I am part time, I would not want to do anything that may cause you to have to close the shop."

"I greatly appreciate your concern, but I am certain that McCaskill's will survive. The closing of the port has been brutal for all of us, but folks still have need of a tailor. While obtaining needles and other materials has been difficult, as you know, we still are able to get supplies, thanks in no small part to the efforts of your father, Mr. Barnes, and Jean Paul. There will always be work here for the best seamstress in the Massachusetts colony."

"Father told me you said that," Lydia said as she smiled at her uncle. "That is so nice and flattering of you to say."

"I only say that because it is true. As regards the trip, I believe it will be very beneficial to you. I have noticed that you have been in a somewhat-depressed mood of late. The predicament of this town can do that to anyone. A trip like this to a vibrant city could be a great elixir and be invigorating to your spirits, especially with your friend Lucy Beaumont coming to Philadelphia."

"Yes, I think the trip may be just what I need, and Lucy is a joy to be with. Now I must get to work, or my employer will be most displeased."

"Your employer will not be displeased. On the contrary, he is very pleased."

Lydia smiled as she began sewing.

5

Jonathan, William, and Lydia arrived in Philadelphia more than a week before Congress was scheduled to convene. After securing quarters for Jonathan near Carpenters' Hall, William and Lydia set about locating temporary quarters for themselves, which were quickly secured nearby. While they procured two relatively small rooms on the second floor of the landlord's house, her room felt homey to Lydia, and she quickly arranged it with the few belongings she was able to bring with her. The landlords were an elderly couple who took an instant liking to the father and daughter, especially to Lydia, almost as if she was their granddaughter—the granddaughter they never had.

"Welcome to the city of brotherly love," said Mrs. Sarah Goodwin to William and Lydia.

"Thank you, ma'am; it is so good to be here and away from Boston," Lydia replied.

"You are happy to be out of Boston?"

"My daughter is especially happy to be away from Boston, if only for a short time."

"What is life like in Boston since the port has been closed?" Sarah asked.

"'Intolerable' is perhaps the best word I know to describe it. That is in fact the name of the series of acts that include the Boston Port Act, passed by the British Parliament. Parliament called them the Coercive Acts; Bostonians call them the Intolerable Acts. The Quartering Act has been a thorn in the side for our family, as the Brits took a small house of ours on the wharf, but more than anything, the acts have been especially grievous on the general population. Many had no choice but to flee the city. Dockworkers, who seem completely lost without any work to do, mill around the docks at all hours of the day and night. These acts are bent on destroying our fair town, excessively penalizing many for the actions of a few. As George Washington said, 'The cause of Boston is now the cause of America,' and that is my hope," William said.

"That is terrible. It certainly does sound as if the Brits are bent on destruction."

"They are indeed, Mrs. Goodwin. It has been a real struggle to survive," William said.

"Fortunately, Mr. Michael Beaumont from Charleston rallied merchants there to smuggle supplies into Boston. And my father's and Mr. Barnes's good friend, Boston merchant Jean Paul Pierre DuBois, has done a tremendous job of working with merchants in other towns and ports to smuggle supplies overland to our town. Of course, many others have helped in supplying Boston," Lydia added.

"That is so wonderful to hear."

"It is, and I dare say that the net result of these terrible acts will not be to destroy Boston but to unite the colonies," said William, his head nodding.

"And that is why our friend Mr. Barnes is here, as a delegate to Congress," Lydia added.

"I am very impressed, sir, with your daughter's political astuteness."

"My parents have always been involved in the local political process, and so have our good friends, the Barneses. I am not shy about expressing my opinions, which is not very ladylike."

"It may not be very ladylike, but I find it refreshing. These are times when all folks need to be engaged in what is happening in our country; too much is at stake for us and for future generations."

"You are absolutely right, ma'am. That is exactly how I feel."

Jonathan and William arrived early at Carpenters' Hall on the morning of September 5. Delegates from twelve out of the thirteen colonies, all but Georgia, gathered for this first sign of unity and solidification of the colonies: the First Continental Congress. The delegates in attendance included John Adams and Samuel Adams from Massachusetts and George Washington, Richard Henry Lee, Patrick Henry, and John Jay among the others. *What an* amazing *group*, thought William.

Jonathan and John Adams helped pave the way for William to present the case to the delegates regarding the economic struggles in Boston, having talked to several of them prior to the official start of Congress. As Congress got underway, the choice of president came to the fore, and Peyton Randolph from Virginia was nominated by Thomas Lynch, also from Virginia. After brief discussion, Randolph was unanimously elected. The next position to be addressed was secretary. Charles Thomson was also nominated by Lynch. James Duane and then John Jay of New York were at first inclined to seek other nominations, but when it became evident there were none, Thomson was also selected by unanimous vote. He was put to work immediately when a motion was made to seek God's guidance.

"Mr. President, I move that we open our sessions with a word of prayer."

"A motion to open our sessions with a word of prayer has been made by Mr. Thomas Cushing, honorable delegate from Massachusetts. Do I hear a second?"

"Mr. President, I object to this motion," John Jay, delegate from New York said as he rose. "We all come from diverse religious backgrounds. Unity at this time is of the utmost importance. I fear prayer may cause divisiveness among our body."

"I echo Mr. Jay's sentiments and concerns, Mr. President," said Edward Rutledge, delegate from South Carolina.

"Mr. President, if I may," Sam Adams said, rising from his seat. Adams who was of limited financial means, was resplendent in a new outfit from McCaskill's, furnished to him by Bostonian friends, who also paid his way to Philadelphia.

"You may, Mr. Adams. Proceed."

"I am no bigot and would be most pleased to pray with anyone who has sincere religious sentiment, so long as he is a true patriot. I have heard very good things regarding Reverend Jacob Duché from Christ's Church and proffer him to this body. I move that we invite him to lead us in prayer tomorrow morning."

"Is there a second to this motion?"

"I second the motion of my esteemed colleague from Massachusetts," Jonathan Barnes said. The motion passed handily, and Reverend Duché arrived the next morning and prayed Psalm 35 from the Book of Common Prayer. Much to the surprise of the delegates, he followed this with a sublime extemporaneous prayer, which was delivered with passion and zeal.

"O Lord, our God, creator and master of the universe, you reign with power over all governments and kingdoms of the earth; look with mercy, we pray, on our beloved country who hath fled to you for your protection from the hand of what should be a benevolent mother country but instead is proving to be a brutish regime bent on bringing its subjects to heel. We appeal to thee for justice for the support that you alone mayst provide. Take our dear country under your nurturing care, we beseech thee; provide sound judgment in council and bravery in the field of battle and convince our adversaries of the unrighteousness of their actions, and if they persist, force them to drop their weapons when the battle comes! Bless these delegates brought here to Philadelphia; enable them to resolve matters in accordance with your divine will that harmony and peace may be restored and that justice and piety resound among the people of this great land. Give these esteemed representatives of their people physical strength and strong minds, a touch of your wisdom and such earthly blessings as you see fit, and crown them with glory in the hereafter. All this we ask in the name and through the work of your Son and our Savior, Jesus Christ, whom we pray. Amen."

All the delegates forcefully and in unison said amen! The body was buzzing in the aftermath of Duché's powerful prayer—the atmosphere was incredible.

"Reverend Duché, we have been blessed by your wonderful prayer," Randolph said as he stood and shook Duché's hand. "I cannot think of a better way to begin the initial session of the First Continental Congress."

"I want to thank you, kind sir, and this body for allowing me the privilege of opening this great and historical session with a plea to the Almighty. Remember, with Him success is assured, but without Him, you are doomed to fail. So as you embark on your solemn duty, may His presence always guide and direct you," Duché said, and then he left to thunderous applause.

"Mr. President," said Jonathan, rising from his chair.

"The Honorable Jonathan Barnes, delegate from Massachusetts has the floor."

"Thank you, Mr. President. My fellow delegates, prior to our convening this honorable Congress, I spoke to nearly all of you about the dire economic situation facing Boston and the colony of Massachusetts. I mentioned to you that I brought with me my best friend and a leading merchant from our fair city, Mr. William Finch, with the hope that he may, perhaps better than anyone, be able to convey to this esteemed body the extent of the suffering there and what we are attempting to do to alleviate the problems. I believe that it is imperative for all of you to hear firsthand what we have been going through these past several months."

As Jonathan sat down, John Adams quickly rose to his feet.

"Mr. President, if I may say a few words."

"You may. The Honorable John Adams, delegate from Massachusetts, now has the floor."

"Mr. President, honored delegates, I am in complete agreement with my friend and fellow delegate from Massachusetts, the Honorable Jonathan Barnes, in requesting that his best friend and my longtime friend and client, Mr. William Finch, address this esteemed body as to what Boston, Massachusetts, and indeed New England have been facing since the imposition of the Boston Port Act and the other Coercive Acts. I wholeheartedly agree with my colleague that it is imperative for you to understand what has taken place. This is why we are gathered here for this Congress, in large part due to the efforts of delegate Barnes, I might add. He was instrumental in calling for this body to meet for the purpose of dealing with the monumental crisis we are facing. Thank you, Mr. President," Adams said, and he then sat down.

"Thank you, Delegate John Adams. Mr. Finch, you have the floor," said President Randolph.

"Mr. President, distinguished delegates of the First Continental Congress," William said, after rising from his seat next to Jonathan Barnes. "I consider it to be a great honor and privilege to appear before this esteemed body and to briefly apprise you of the crisis that has gripped Boston and the colony of Massachusetts. I would tell you that, following the destruction of the tea by dumping it into Boston Harbor in December of last year, thanks in large part to an inspiration from my best friend's wife, Eleanor Barnes, my merchant association, spearheaded by the Honorable Jonathan Barnes and good friend and fellow merchant Jean Paul Pierre DuBois, began a concerted effort to store goods and supplies in our warehouses in anticipation of what might be forthcoming from the British. Jean Paul himself let it be known that he believed that there would be 'hell to pay,' for the adventures of a few noble 'Indians' who participated in the momentous event."

William went on to recite the imposition of the Port Act, the vote of the merchants at the town-hall meeting, the imposition of the other Coercive Acts and their impact on the colony, and William's meeting with General Gage.

"It is one thing to punish for a perceived violation of authority—à la the destruction of the tea—it is altogether another thing to attempt to annihilate a town and colony that a benevolent mother country is duty bound to nurture and protect. Gentlemen, the British wish to crush our spirit and drive a wedge among the colonies with these brutish acts. I trust and agree with my good friend, Jean Paul, when he said to our merchants group and others that he believed the result would be just the opposite; it will be a rallying point, unifying the colonies as never before, lifting our spirit in the great common cause, the cause of liberty. We can and we must do everything for our liberty, for without it, nothing else matters. Thank you all for your kind attention," William said and then sat down.

There was total silence, and then one by one, the delegates rose, applauding, until the room was filled with standing delegates applauding. Deeply moved, William stood, nodded his head, and then began to applaud the delegates. Finally, President Randolph called the body to order and thanked William for his remarks.

"Mr. Finch, I believe that I speak for all present, when I say thank you very much for coming here today and briefly relaying to this Congress the terrible predicament that you and your family, your town, and your colony have been subjected to these past several months. If a committee is created, as I believe it will be, to address the grievances that you have enumerated, I feel certain that they would welcome your attendance and input in formulating the response to the king and his Parliament," Randolph said.

William nodded his head in response and then rose to say, "I will be pleased to assist you in any way that you deem appropriate."

"Thank you, sir," Randolph replied. "Now one final very important point before we adjourn," the newly elected president said, in a manner that conveyed all the authority of the position they had just bestowed upon him. "There must be absolute secrecy, for obvious reasons. There are British spies all over town. Our sessions will be closed to the public. When we are ready to make official announcements, we will, but there must be no leaking of information to the press, and be careful in your discussions in the taverns and public places. You certainly can and will discuss business in public settings, but I urge caution in how, what, where, and with whom you discuss business."

With that, Congress was adjourned. Later that evening, Jonathan wrote to Eleanor about the events that had occurred since their arrival in Philadelphia, with special emphasis on William's presentation to the Congress. Jonathan described in detail for his bride the important men who graced the opening session of the First Continental Congress and how humbled he felt to be counted among them. But the event that garnered the majority of the attention in the letter was the extemporaneous prayer of Reverend Duché and the moving and uplifting effect it had on all those in attendance. What an incredible way to start the institution of Congress!

Eleanor received Jonathan's letter with eager anticipation. Since he had left, she and the children kept quite busy running the store and tending the garden. On a couple of the weekends, she took the children to Boston to visit the Finches. Eleanor shared the letter from Jonathan, which Annabelle was very pleased to read.

Back at Congress, Jonathan solidified his relationship with John Adams, John's cousin, Samuel Adams, and the rest of the Massachusetts delegation, and with the Virginia delegation of Richard Henry Lee, Patrick Henry, and Peyton Randolph, president of the Congress. Much of the friendship building by Jonathan and other members of

Congress was accomplished at taverns after congressional sessions and during frequent dinners, suppers and gatherings attended by nearly all, though not Sam Adams.

As Congress got underway, the Pennsylvania, New York, and New Jersey delegations were, as Jonathan and John Adams anticipated, touting reconciliation with the mother country as the top priority of the new body. This proposal brought sharp division in the body, which had begun the Congress so unified. Debate was passionate and strong as to the best approach to deal with the restoration of rights lost through the implementation of the Intolerable Acts. Into this environment Paul Revere rode into town and had Sam and John Adams removed from a session of Congress to read the Suffolk Resolves.

"Sam, John, I present to you the Suffolk Resolves, the result of meetings of delegates of the county to protest the Brit Coercive Acts," Revere said intently as he pulled a document from a satchel slung over his shoulder and handed it to Sam. Sam intently studied the document.

"John, these resolves call for a complete boycott of all trade that we have with Britain. Think about the potential ramifications of that..."

"They are enormous," John replied. "Practically all our trade is with or involves the Brits."

"Additionally, these resolves actually call for enforcement of the boycott, though it is bereft of specifics as to what this entails."

"The mere fact that enforcement is called for at all means that this is serious."

"Now this is really amazing," Sam said, glancing up from the document.

"What is amazing?" John asked.

"The resolves suggest that Massachusetts become an independent state—well, at least until the Coercive Acts are repealed."

"An independent state—now that is truly amazing!" John replied, with eyebrows arched and eyes opened wide.

"I think we all agree that the Coercive Acts are a clear usurpation of English law and therefore unconstitutional," Sam said as John and

Paul nodded their heads in agreement, "but to say that anyone who even attempts to enforce these dreadful acts is to resign their position of authority—"

"That is a rebuke of the king and his Parliament," John said, completing Sam's statement.

"Indeed."

"The resolves go on to say that taxes collected from now on are to remain with the colony, and they urge the arming of citizens and appointment of officers to head the militia in the various locales."

"Those sound quite logical and appropriate," John said.

"Agreed, but listen to this, John. The resolves issue a warning to Gage that if he arrests citizens for political reasons, he can expect the detention of the officer or officers involved in those arrests."

"This is powerful!" John remarked excitedly. "A very strong statement by our colony."

"It certainly is," said his cousin Sam. "It is in my opinion a fair statement of the sentiments of our brethren in the colony. Paul, your timing is impeccable."

"What do you mean?" queried Revere, with a slightly quizzical look on his face.

"I will explain later, but right now I want the rest of our delegation to see this."

"I will get them," John said, and with that, he left. In a few minutes, he returned with Jonathan Barnes, Thomas Cushing, and Robert Treat Paine.

"Fellow delegates," said Sam, addressing them, "Paul Revere rode all the way from Boston and came straight here to Congress. He brought with him this document." He handed it to Jonathan.

After reading through it, Jonathan handed it to Thomas Cushing, who then passed it on to Robert Trent Paine. When all were done reading it, Jonathan remarked, "I believe this accurately and succinctly sums up what our people are feeling and dealing with."

"Tom and Robert, what do you think?" Sam asked.

"These resolves send a message that is unmistakable," said Cushing.

"Agreed," Paine replied as he handed the resolves back to Revere.

"This should put a stop to Galloway and his weak, compromising plan," Sam said.

"Is that what you meant when you said my timing was impeccable?"

"Yes, Paul. You see, the conservatives in Congress, primarily from Pennsylvania, New York, and New Jersey, are pushing for reconciliation with the mother country. Joseph Galloway, a delegate from here in Pennsylvania, while he has not yet formally introduced it, will be proposing his Galloway Plan. The cornerstone of the plan is an American Parliament, a grand council that would act together with Parliament, each having veto power over the other on issues affecting the colonies. He believes that the king and Parliament will go along with it, but they will not cede any power or authority over us. And besides, we cannot be seen as weak. If the British want to improve relations with us, they need to immediately repeal the detestable tea tax and all the infernal Intolerable Acts. When the delegates see these resolves, I think they will embrace them, and hopefully this will stop or at least weaken Galloway's plan before he has an opportunity to introduce it."

"I am very glad I arrived when I did."

"So are we, Paul," Jonathan added, "so are we."

"Mr. President, my esteemed fellow delegates," Jonathan said, as he began reading a draft of the Declaration and Resolves of the First Continental Congress, or Declaration of Rights, which were a result of a committee formulated just two days after Congress convened. Jonathan had been appointed to the committee, and William was invited to offer his thoughts. Jonathan, as a member of the aggrieved colony of Massachusetts, was chosen to read the draft, which was addressed to the king.

"Whereupon the deputies so appointed being now assembled, in a full and free representation of these colonies, taking into their most serious consideration the best means of attaining the ends aforesaid, do in the first place, as Englishmen, their ancestors in like cases have usually done, for asserting and vindicating their rights and liberties, declare…" Jonathan's powerful voice carried across the room, resonating with all those who supported the radical agenda. "That the inhabitants of the English colonies in North America, by the immutable laws of nature, the principals of the English constitution, and the several charters or compacts have the following rights:

"One, that they are entitled to life, liberty, and property, and they have never ceded to any sovereign power whatever, a right to dispose of either without their consent."

"That our ancestors, who first settled these colonies, were at the time of their emigration from the mother country, entitled to all the rights, liberties, and immunities of free and natural-born subjects within the realm of England.

"That by such emigration they by no means forfeited, surrendered, or lost any of those rights, but that they were, and their descendants now are, entitled to the exercise and enjoyment of all such of them, as their local and other circumstances enable them to exercise and enjoy."

Jonathan's strength and passion seemed to grow with every word. He was speaking from the bottom of his heart, and all in attendance could feel it. John Adams, the great orator himself, was hard pressed to contain himself, so thoroughly was he enjoying the oratory of his friend and fellow Massachusetts delegate.

"That the foundation of English liberty, and of all free government, is a right in the people to participate in their legislative council: and as the English colonists are not represented, and from their local and other circumstances cannot be properly represented in the British parliament, they are entitled to a free and exclusive power of legislation in their several provincial legislatures, where their right of representation can alone be preserved, in all cases of taxation and internal polity, subject only to the negative of their sovereign, in such manner as has been heretofore used and accustomed…"

Jonathan continued on for five to ten minutes more, listing the rights of the colonists, and when he finished, Congress adjourned until September 24. At that time Jonathan again had the floor, to proclaim the grievances, including a recitation of certain acts of Parliament that were considered infringements and violations of the rights of the colonists, stating that the repeal of them was necessary in order to restore harmony between Great Britain and the American colonies. As he did when reciting the rights, Jonathan seemed to get stronger the longer he spoke. When he finished, the radicals in Congress rose to their feet with wild, boisterous shouting and clapping, with William joining them. That drew the ire of the conservatives, especially Joseph Galloway, who stood and was prepared to demand a restoration of order, when Jonathan bowed and then raised his hands, requesting silence.

"My esteemed fellow delegates, I am deeply humbled by your response to this work by our committee. I was simply attempting to do my best to convey to you not just what is in my heart but also what is in the hearts of the members of the committee and what I hope is, or will be, in the hearts of each delegate to this Congress. Thank you one and all."

Following the session, many radical delegates, including Jonathan and William, retired to City Tavern, a favorite gathering place for members of Congress, located on the west side of Second Street between Walnut and Chestnut. Jonathan was greeted by cheers upon joining the already burgeoning group. John Adams was the first to personally offer his congratulations. With a firm handshake and a broad smile, he offered to buy Jonathan a beer, which he readily accepted.

"Jonathan, you were magnificent. You expressed our sentiments so poignantly in your reading of the declaration—outrage, frustration, and righteous indignation. I am very proud of you."

"Thank you so much, John. I am truly honored to have praise from such a great orator as yourself. But I did not create those lofty words, as you so often do when giving one of your speeches or when you present your closing arguments, your summation to a jury. No, rather those words emanated from the hearts and minds of the committee members of whom I had the privilege of being a part."

"My dear fellow, you are far too modest. I happen to know, on good authority, that much of what is set forth in that declaration is your doing. And besides, it is the *way* that the words are conveyed almost as much as the words themselves that can make or break an oration, and believe me, your delivery made the oration. You conveyed the real essence of the declaration, and all assembled in that room felt it—in *their* hearts. That, my friend, is what true oration is all about."

"Mr. Adams is quite right, you know."

"Colonel Washington!" Jonathan excitedly exclaimed on hearing the voice and now seeing the great man himself. George Washington simply had commanding presence. His height alone, some six feet two inches and slightly more, set him apart from his peers. He towered over most of them, whose average height was approximately five feet six inches. His face was slightly pocked, thanks to a brush with smallpox (which providentially was a most fortuitous event in his life). He carried himself with a grace and dignity unlike mere mortal men. Here was clearly a leader among leaders.

"Allow me to introduce myself."

"No, Colonel, please allow me the privilege," John Adams interceded, "Mr. Jonathan Barnes and Mr. William Finch, I am very pleased to introduce to you the most distinguished delegate in the delegation, the gentleman planter from Virginia, Colonel George Washington."

"Colonel, this is my good friend, client, and merchant, William Finch, who as you know came with me to inform the Congress of the plight of Boston and the colony."

"Mr. Finch, I am very pleased to make your acquaintance and am grateful to you for leaving your family and business under trying circumstances to tell us about the effects of these brutish acts," Washington said, as he shook William's hand.

"Thank you so much, Colonel. You do not know how much that means to me."

"And you, sir," Washington said to Jonathan, "your reading touched the delegates, and as John said, that is the key. Your great colony has been brought to heel by what has been purported to be the most civilized and benevolent nation in the world. We must present a united front against this unacceptable and despicable behavior. The cause of Boston, indeed of Massachusetts, is and must be the cause of America. United we shall stand; divided we shall fall."

"I could not agree with you more," replied Jonathan, "and I am truly humbled that you approve of my reading."

"You are very welcome. Debate will occur, but I believe the essence of the declaration will remain intact, thanks in no small measure to you," said Washington.

"I certainly hope that you are right, sir."

"Oh, I am certain he is," said Adams.

"And gentlemen, you have done commendable things, such as heading up the effort, supported by you," Washington said, looking at Jonathan and then William, "and your colleagues, which led to the formation of Congress and organizing the merchants and others to smuggle food and supplies to you."

"The smuggling effort has been a lifeline, some generated by our merchants, such as Jean Paul Pierre DuBois, others generated by patriots from other colonies, such as Michael Beaumont from Charleston, which has literally saved us from total ruin," said Adams.

"Michael has been an inspiration to me and my family," Jonathan interjected. "He has taught me what being a true patriot is all about."

"With patriotic families such as yours, Mr. Barnes, and yours, Mr. Finch, the cause of liberty is in good hands," Washington observed, nodding his head approvingly, "but I do believe that this declaration, which so magnificently sets forth the rights and grievances of our colonies, will unfortunately fall on deaf ears in Britain. If that is the case, the fate of the future of our country and this great experiment in liberty will largely be in your hands and your families'."

"That is a very sobering thought," Jonathan said contemplatively.

"It is indeed," added William, nodding his head.

"Colonel Washington is, among other things, a very astute judge of character, my friends," said Adams, "and I agree wholeheartedly with his assessment."

"Gentlemen, I am very grateful for your kind words about me and my family, but it is great men such as yourselves, in my opinion, who will be the critical factor in determining whether or not the American liberty experiment will survive and flourish and captivate the imagination of mankind or whether it, like so many others, will end up on the ash heap of history," Jonathan remarked with great conviction as he looked firmly and squarely into the eyes of first Adams and then Washington.

"You may be right," said Adams. "Leadership will, without a doubt, be critical, but I agree with Colonel Washington that we must rally the support of patriotic families in this country, from north to south, or all the leadership in the world will not suffice."

"Come, come, esteemed colleagues, I believe you are getting way ahead of yourselves."

All eyes of the quadrumvirate turned to see Joseph Galloway of Pennsylvania approaching.

"I tell you, my plan to create an American Parliament to act in concert with Britain's Parliament, I feel certain, will be embraced by the king and his Parliament and bring about the reconciliation we should be striving to attain. We must move toward reconciliation, not a break from Britain."

"Who said anything about a break from Britain?" asked Adams.

"I overheard your discussion, and it certainly sounded to me as if you were contemplating a break. And, those Suffolk Resolves that you pushed on the delegates, do you mean to say that they do not contemplate a break? Suggesting Massachusetts be a free and independent state, calling on a boycott of goods and trade, urging future collected taxes remain in the colony, advising citizens to arm and elect militia officers, and, warning the British that arresting citizens on political charges would result in detaining the arresting officials! The Resolves are contemptible and, I dare say treasonous!"

"See here, Mr. Galloway, we do *not* wish for a break; we do seek reconciliation," Washington interjected.

"And your notion that we pushed the resolves on the delegates," said a passionate and irritated John Adams as he raised his voice, furrowed his brow, and pointed and wagged his index finger at Galloway, "is simply ludicrous, and you know it. Paul Revere, unbeknownst to us, arrived as the debate for how to deal with the restoration of our rights was raging. The timing was impeccable for us, but we had nothing to do with it. We hardly pushed the resolves on the delegates. We presented them as a fair statement of what the embattled people of our dear colony are thinking and feeling, which obviously you do not understand, nor seem to care about. Besides, what you have consistently failed to mention to us, or anyone for that matter, is that all the Suffolk Resolves are tied to repeal of the Intolerable or Coercive Acts. Get rid of them, and then we can move toward reconciliation. For all your talk about your grand plan, you have yet to introduce it to Congress."

"How dare you point or wag your finger at me, John Adams! You say all this about the resolves, and yet we have this declaration being proposed to the Congress, and you expect me to believe that it is a document that expresses a desire to reconcile with the mother country?" said an equally passionate Galloway. "And do not tell me when I should submit my Galloway Plan. It will be in my good time and not yours."

"We believe that the declaration succinctly and clearly recites our history and rights as British citizens and the legitimate grievances that we have for serious and unjust infringement upon those rights. We certainly trust that the declaration, whose essence was so eloquently expressed by the reading of Mr. Jonathan Barnes, will be overwhelmingly adopted by Congress, and then it is our fervent desire that it be embraced by the king and Parliament. Unfortunately, we believe it will fall upon deaf ears."

"And if that does happen, Colonel Washington, then what?"

"We must, at the very least, meet again early next year to address how to respond to what most certainly will be considered as a snub to Congress and its delegates."

"But you believe that separation is inevitable?"

"We believe in the cause of liberty, Mr. Galloway," Adams again interjected. "We must not and will not compromise the cause of liberty for anyone or anything, no matter what the cost. If this declaration is cast aside by the powers that be in Britain, then the fate of this country and of our liberty is in the hands of people and families such as the Barneses and Finches, as Colonel Washington so aptly stated before you joined our gathering."

"Do you agree with these gentlemen, Mr. Barnes and Mr. Finch?"

"I do," said Jonathan. I stand with these gentlemen, though I believe the leadership of great men such as these two will be the key for our cause."

"I agree wholeheartedly with Jonathan," William said, looking directly at Galloway.

"You are going too far. Rest assured that I will fight you every step of the way. Good day, gentlemen."

"Good day," all four replied, practically in unison, as Galloway abruptly turned and headed for the door of the tavern.

Leaving Philadelphia was bittersweet for both William and Lydia. Friendships had begun, and others had grown for William, while Lydia had a wonderful time with the Beaumont family, seeing the sites of the flourishing city of Philadelphia.

Lydia, while looking forward to seeing the rest of her family after a month-and-a-half absence, knew she would be returning to a desperate city on the verge of a New England winter.

They gathered their belongings and loaded up the Finch carriage. William assisted Lydia in getting up and into her seat, and then after lifting himself into the driver's seat, he took the reins in his hands and started the buggy out of town.

"I am very grateful to you, Father, for bringing me with you. It was so good to be out of Boston even if only for a short time. I had a fabulous time with Lucy and her mother. I learned so much about Philadelphia."

"It has been my pleasure having you along. Your face has a glow, and there is a sparkle in your eyes! And so you know, Jonathan already told me that the delegates would welcome me back next spring, so you may have a return trip to Philadelphia, if you wish."

"You know I would, but is not the next session of Congress dependent upon the British rejecting the declaration that Mr. Barnes so convincingly read to the body?"

"You are right; the British must reject the declaration for there to be another session, but I agree with George Washington and John Adams that rejection is almost a foregone conclusion."

"Well, Sam and John, here we are on October twenty-second, and the Galloway Plan of Union has finally been laid to rest with the rejection of a motion to reconsider the plan," Jonathan Barnes said as he and Sam and John Adams left Carpenters' Hall together following another session of Congress.

"Yes. Good thing that Paul Revere arrived with the Suffolk Resolves. I would hate to have seen the Galloway Plan reconsidered, especially in light of the passage of the final draft of the Declaration of Rights," said Sam.

"I was very pleased that the final draft was approved," Jonathan replied. "I believe that it sends a very strong message to the king and Parliament."

"It does," said Sam, "and coupled with the Continental Association establishing a complete boycott of all British goods beginning in December, if the Intolerable Acts are not rescinded, well, I think this Congress made great strides in a short time."

"It may all come for naught and probably will, but I agree with you," said John.

"If nothing else, in a few days I will leave this Congress believing that there is a greater understanding of what we are facing in Massachusetts," Jonathan said, "and while we are far from united, we are closer than when this Congress began less than two short months ago."

John and Sam nodded their heads in agreement.

"And if it is all for naught, we will gather together again next spring," John said.

6

"**B**ecky, I do not understand your attraction to Mark Wilson," Francois said to Becky Braun as he drove his two-seater carriage down the narrow streets of Boston on a chilly late-October evening. He was taking Becky back to her home, the stately mansion of Horace Braun, after a quiet supper together at JP's.

"I can and will now ask you the same about Lilly Turner," Becky replied as she turned her head, which was underneath a covering shawl, to look directly at Francois, who met her stern gaze.

"Becky, you cannot compare the two. You cannot believe that I really care for her; she is just a fling. But what am I supposed to do nowadays with your constant companionship with the loyalist-leaning doctor?"

"First of all, I cannot believe that you do not care for her. I have seen you two look at each other, and what I have seen tells me she is not a fling. Secondly, Dr. Mark Wilson is a wonderful man and a true patriot. He introduced me to Dr. Warren and Dr. Church, two of the greatest patriots in Boston."

"Oui, they are great patriots, but word around town is that Dr. Wilson has been seen with some of the high-ranking Brits, even General Gage himself!"

"I have heard that, but he told me that was with Dr. Church, and the meeting dealt with efforts to ease the pain inflicted by the awful Intolerable Acts."

"So were they able to accomplish anything?"

"Not yet, but they are still trying."

"How do we know that your doctor friend is not relaying some information about our cause in some secret way to the general or his underlings?"

"Stop it, Francois—he is not doing that, especially not in the presence of Dr. Church."

"Perhaps you are right, but he bears watching. There is something about him. I just do not trust the man. Besides, he is old enough to be your father!"

"You are just jealous, Francois DuBois, insanely jealous. The man is not old enough to be my father; he is only thirty-eight-years-old."

"Well, Mademoiselle Braun, he is *almost* old enough to be your father, and he certainly looks old enough!"

As the carriage pulled up in front of the Braun house, Becky turned to Francois.

"Can we stop this now, Monsieur DuBois? I do not care about him anymore than you care for Lilly Turner, but he is charming and witty, and he gives me tokens of affection."

Francois was about to respond, but before he could say a word, Becky embraced him and gave him a long, hard, passionate kiss.

"Think about that," she said, after the kiss was over and as she stepped down from the carriage.

"Bonne nuit, my darling," said Francois.

"Good night, dearest," she said as she blew him a kiss.

William and Lydia arrived back in Massachusetts to an ever-darkening landscape. It had now been several months since the port of Boston had been shut down. The town was literally being strangled

into submission. Jean Paul and the association were working fever-
ishly with the wharf merchants and Sons of Liberty to smuggle in as
many goods and supplies as possible. Jean Paul's lieutenant, Willie
Boyd, had been instrumental in rallying dockworkers to aid in the
endeavor to stave off starvation and total economic collapse.

For Lydia, the return home, the return to reality, was difficult. Life
in Boston was now very hard and seemed to be a world apart from the
excitement that she had experienced in the vibrant and growing metropolis that was colonial Philadelphia. Then there were the young
men of Philadelphia, the handsome young men of Philadelphia, she
saw when out and about with the Beaumonts. They whetted her ap-
petite for companionship with males of her age and similar upbring-
ing. Philadelphia was energizing, intellectually stimulating, so alive.
She was thrilled to be there, and then in a short time, it was over. Mr.
Barnes and her father said it was highly unlikely that the king and
Parliament would accede to the wishes of Congress as set forth in the
declaration. Thus, it was very possible that she would be returning to
Philadelphia in the spring, but even if this was the case, springtime
seemed an eternity away. There was still the brutal and long New
England winter to endure again, under the harshest conditions ever
experienced in her life, and all without any prospective suitors or
grand balls! Within days of their return, the glow on her face and the
sparkle in her eyes had all but vanished—it was *so* depressing!

It was the end of November 1774, and the Barneses gathered with the
Finches for a day of thanksgiving. While not an official holiday, it had
been celebrated by the colonists ever since the pilgrims first celebrated it in the early sixteen hundreds. Though the remnants in Boston
were in great despair and distress, time was taken by individuals and
families throughout the city to give thanks to God for His provision.

The Barneses arrived in Boston early in the morning, the carriage rolling along through the practically deserted streets of the

city. Everywhere there were signs that the Intolerable Acts had accomplished their dastardly task—bringing the city to heel. Redcoats, "lobsterbacks," as the locals irreverently referred to them, were seemingly everywhere, roaming the streets, living in tents on the common, living in houses under the quartering act—red, everywhere there was red!

"I have seen this scene too many times over the past several months," lamented Richard.

"Son, I totally understand your frustration. Believe me, no one shares your sentiments more than I do, but unfortunately, it may take some time before our great city is finally rid of these dreaded lobsterbacks."

"I thought that the First Continental Congress was convened for that reason. Pardon my saying so, Father, no disrespect intended, but just what did the Congress actually accomplish? I mean, it has been a month since Congress finished business, and there does not appear to be anything different about life in Boston or in Massachusetts, other than what was taking place outside of Boston while Congress was in session with the shutting down of the courts and the lieutenant governor being forced to resign. And truth is Congress had nothing to do with those events. From my perspective, Congress accomplished little if anything. Am I wrong?"

"There is nothing different about life here due to what Congress accomplished—at least not yet. But mind you, I believe that it was a tremendous accomplishment just for the colonies to send representatives to such a body as the First Continental Congress. Then for that body to unite with the adoption of the Suffolk Resolves from here in Massachusetts and pass the Declaration of Rights —that was very special, even if it falls on deaf British ears. Uniting the colonies in a common cause, the cause of liberty, is our objective—and I believe it has begun."

"Uniting the colonies in the cause of liberty—that would be fantastic, but Father, do you really think it will happen? These colonies are so independent minded, correct?"

"Correct. Understand that the reason for gathering in Philadelphia was to seek redress for the wrongs inflicted on the colonies, especially our colony. We really do seek reconciliation with the mother country, though it appears unlikely to me. But despite disagreements, we came to understand the difficulties, struggles, and aspirations of others in different colonies. Thus, in my opinion, the process of unifying us all in the great cause has now begun. So do I think it will happen? It will take time. We have some very conservative members in Congress who want reconciliation at all cost, but yes, I think it will happen."

Early that evening, William and Jonathan relaxed in the parlor prior to supper. William had numerous comments and questions for his friend, whom he was seeing for the first time since leaving Philadelphia at the beginning of October.

"Jonathan, Annabelle and I again want to express our sincere gratitude to you for asking me and Lydia to join you. It was a tremendous experience for me and her—even more than we anticipated."

"The gratitude is mine. The delegates were very impressed with you and what you contributed. As I told you, they have conveyed to me that Congress would welcome you back should we reconvene, and I believe we will in the spring."

"If that occurs, I will be very pleased to return with you, and I am sure Lydia will be as well. Jonathan, I must again commend you on your reading of the Declaration of Rights."

"It was a very emotional and humbling experience for me. The committee worked hard to create the document, and they did a wonderful job. All I did was read it."

"Remember that I sat in on the committee meetings. You did much more than read it."

"I must confess that working on the document really impacted me. I read it from my heart—I guess that was what made an impression."

"It obviously did. It certainly made an impression on Colonel Washington."

"Father, Mr. Barnes," Lydia said as she knocked on the open door to get their attention, "supper is served."

"Thank you, my dear," William said as he and Jonathan got up from their chairs and joined Lydia on the walk down the hallway toward the dining room.

As the family all began to be seated at the table, Lydia said, "Mother, I overheard some of the conversation between Father and Mr. Barnes as I came to get them for supper. They were discussing meeting Colonel Washington and his response to Mr. Barnes's reading of the Declaration of Rights to Congress. Colonel Washington also added that if the declaration fell on deaf ears, the fate of the country and the liberty experiment would largely be in the hands of families such as the Barneses and Finches."

"Where did you hear that?" Jonathan asked, amazed that she was privy to this statement from Washington.

"Mr. John Adams told me before the next session of Congress convened, following your reading, when the Beaumonts and I dined with him," Lydia replied. "Colonel Washington also said that, with such patriotic families, the cause of liberty was in good hands."

"How wonderful of Colonel Washington to say such kind things about us," Annabelle said as Eleanor smiled.

"Yes," said Jonathan. "Thank you, Lydia, for sharing this. Let us hope the Brits will take notice of what our Congress has placed before them—for all our sakes."

"Agreed," William said, "now let us give thanks for the evening meal and for God's provision for us and for our nation during this time of need."

The conversation continued as plates were passed for second helpings of one Grace's classic dinners. She was a longtime Finch head cook and servant.

"Now, may I ask you, Timothy," Jonathan said, "how are things down on the wharf with this terrible Port Act?"

"Life is a tremendous struggle. As you know my store is still open, but many—definitely the majority of establishments—have closed, with many of the proprietors fleeing the city. While many dockworkers are milling about with nothing to do, Jean Paul has Willie Boyd and his group storing smuggled goods and distributing other goods to needy families around the wharf and throughout the city."

"Willie Boyd, my friend Willie Boyd," William said, with a slight smile on his face.

"He has turned out to be Jean Paul's most trustworthy lieutenant," Timothy added, "and his men have become very adept at evading the Brits and getting the goods to those who need them the most."

"That is great news," Jonathan said.

"Jean Paul has raved about the work Willie has been doing." William nodded. "His men have worked closely with the men of the association in disseminating goods throughout the city as Timothy said. It certainly would be helpful if we could have another Willie Boyd to assist the effort."

"Well, why not approach Jean Paul about the matter? If there is another Willie out there, he would certainly know who it could be or where to find him," Timothy suggested.

"Good idea."

"Father, Uncle Timothy, if I may," said Joshua.

"Yes, Joshua?" William asked, with a curious look on his face. "What is it, son?"

"I may not be the next Willie Boyd, but I would be happy to assist him in the efforts to store smuggled goods and get them distributed to the needy. There is not much work Mr. Whitmore and Mr. Manly can assign to me. They have enough help to take care of storing goods and distributing them to your customers still in Boston. If you would give me the chance, I know I could help with any goods you and Jean Paul may have available for the needy."

"Joshua," William said, "that is very admirable, but you must realize that distributing smuggled goods to the needy is a very dangerous undertaking."

"I am twenty-one years old; I am sure Jean Paul and Willie can teach me whatever I may need to know. I want to contribute, in some way, to our cause."

"I will contact Jean Paul next week for all of us to discuss it and the overall operation with him."

"Gentlemen," Eleanor interjected, "I am in complete agreement with all you are saying and planning, but there must be something more we can do, as Christmas approaches, to help this suffering city."

"Mother," Margaret said, "I for one do not need any gifts. My gifts could go to the needy people of Boston, especially to help the children who seem to have been hurt the most by this cruel Port Act."

"I do not need any gifts either. I too want to help the poor children," said young James Barnes.

"That is a splendid idea and a wonderful gesture, Margaret and James. I totally agree. I too do not need any gifts," Annabelle said, her face lighting up.

"I have an idea," Lydia said. "I would be happy to make clothing for the needy during my spare time."

"This is fantastic! This could truly be one of the most blessed Christmases ever," William said enthusiastically. "I will check with the wharf store owners who are still in town regarding needy children of employees, and while we are meeting with Jean Paul, I will ask him about people he knows who have children in need. I am certain there will be several families we can help to make their Christmas a little brighter."

Richard spent most of the day and the ensuing weekend with Victoria as their relationship grew ever stronger. They talked about the current hardships that were evident in Boston but had also engulfed the surrounding towns, including Lexington. There was a very strong chill in the air, and it was not just the coming winter. To Richard, his world was forever changed. He believed the writing was on the wall and America would soon be plunged into war and he would be part of it. All this weighed heavily upon him as he discussed events with Victoria.

"I am afraid it is coming, and it may be sooner rather than later," Richard said rather forlornly as he and Victoria sat in the backyard of the Finch house.

"What is coming, Richard?" asked Victoria expectantly.

"War with the Brits—a split with the mother country."

"Do you really think so? I mean your father made an impassioned reading of the declaration to Congress, who passed it and sent it to the king and Parliament."

"Yes, but you heard Father. Colonel Washington, John Adams, my father, and your father all agree that the declaration will almost certainly fall on deaf ears. If that happens, there will be another Continental Congress in the spring of next year. How long are we going to be able to endure these terrible sanctions without taking action? Something has to change. I sense a yearning for freedom from the Brit yoke in this town and in Lexington. I have a feeling that my plans to become a lawyer are going to be delayed for some time."

"Richard, are you sure?" Victoria said, concern etched upon her face.

"As sure as I am about anything," he responded. "Our militia in Lexington is now training in earnest. There is a heightened awareness in the men, a real tension since this terrible Port Act and the rest of the Intolerable Acts have been implemented. Something is going to happen—soon."

"Richard, you are scaring me," Victoria said, looking anxiously into his eyes. "I do not know what I will do if you go off to war."

Richard gently put his arm around her head and pulled it into his chest. "I am very sorry, my dearest; I did not mean to frighten you. Please calm down. It is going to be all right," he said as he lowered his head upon hers. "Everything will be all right…"

"Jean Paul, good to see you, my friend," William said, smiling as Jean Paul came into William's office at the wharf.

"And you, Messieurs William and Joshua, bonjour!" he said as he shook hands with the father and son.

"Thank you for coming, Jean Paul. This meeting should not take long. We have a couple of matters to address with you.

"Oui, monsieur."

"At our dinner of thanksgiving, Timothy brought up the subject of Willie Boyd and how he has done a superb job of getting his men to work closely with the men of the association to distribute goods and supplies throughout Boston."

"Oui, Willie is proving to be a most capable leader."

"I said I thought it would be helpful if we could have another Willie to assist in the effort. Timothy agreed and suggested I approach you about the matter since you would be the best person to know if there was another Willie in town, when—"

"When I spoke up," said Joshua, interrupting his father.

"Yes, when Joshua spoke up, and what did you say, son?"

"I said that, with the shutting down of the port and with the other terrible decrees, Mr. Whitmore and Mr. Manly just did not have much work for me. They have men distributing most of goods to Father's remaining customers in Boston. While I am not Willie Boyd, I know I could help."

"This is most interesting, messieurs," Jean Paul mused.

"What is?" William and Joshua asked, almost simultaneously.

"I was just thinking the same thing a few days ago, when my new blacksmith, Robert Malone, asked me if I had work for his son, Amos, who wants to be a merchant someday. I told him that I did not have much for him to do around the office, but if he was willing to work, he could be a real help to Willie in distributing smuggled goods."

"That *is* interesting, Jean Paul," said William.

"How old is he?" asked Joshua.

"About your age, Monsieur Joshua."

"Do you think I could assist Willie?"

"Absolutely. I am sure he will be very happy to have not one but two strong, able-bodied young men. But you do understand, Monsieur Joshua, that this can be extremely dangerous. The Brits are everywhere, and they will severely punish anyone caught delivering or attempting to deliver smuggled goods."

"Father warned me that it could be dangerous, but I was hopeful that you and Willie might be willing to teach me what I need to know."

"If you are willing to work and learn—I am sure I can speak for Willie—we will be more than happy to teach you what you will need to know."

"I am willing."

"Then report to my office first thing tomorrow morning. Amos will be there. You two can get to know each other and spend the day with Willie. You will learn from him firsthand."

"Thank you, Jean Paul; thank you so much! I am most grateful."

"Merci, Monsieur Joshua, we are grateful to you for your willingness to help. Now Monsieur William, what is the other matter?"

"Also at the dinner, Margaret Barnes said she did not need gifts this Christmas and that her gifts could go to the needy people in town, especially the children. We all agreed that it was a wonderful idea, but we do not know the needy as you do. If you will provide us with names and addresses of families all over town, we will try to brighten their Christmas."

"Sacre bleu! That is such a magnanimous gesture on all your parts. I would be honored to assist you in this effort. I shall have a list for you next week!"

᳕

"Monsieur Joshua Finch, meet Monsieur Amos Malone," Jean Paul said as Joshua entered the door of Jean Paul's wharf office.

"Pleased to make your acquaintance," said a somewhat startled Joshua as he shook the hand of Amos Malone.

"Likewise, Mr. Finch," said Amos, his ebony face smiling, revealing beautiful pearl-white teeth. He had a strong nose and jaw and a friendly manner about him. He had rather large biceps and a full, muscular chest, tapering down to a smallish waist, all supported by strong thighs and powerful legs.

"My name is Joshua," Joshua said, with a smile on his face, quickly recovering.

"Joshua then." Amos nodded.

"As I said yesterday, Monsieur Joshua, Monsieur Amos's father is my new blacksmith. He does very good work, and so does his son."

"I hope I am not being too forward, Joshua, but have you never met a free negro before?"

"Yes, but I must admit that I am surprised to find out that you were one. I trust I did not offend you."

"Not at all. I would have been surprised if you had not reacted as you did when you saw me," Amos said matter-of-factly.

"Jean Paul told us it was your dream to become a merchant?"

"Yes, it is—someday." Amos nodded.

"Mine, as well" said Joshua. "If I am half the merchant that my father and Jean Paul are..."

"That would be the ultimate," Amos finished the thought, as he concurred.

"You flatter me, messieurs, mentioning me together with Monsieur William."

"You deserve to be, and my father would agree."

As he said this, Willie Boyd entered the office.

"Jean Paul, Joshua, and Amos. Good morning to all of you. I see that you and Amos have met," Willie said to Joshua.

"Yes, sir, we were just getting to know each other."

"Good. I am happy to have both of you assisting our very important effort. By the way, Joshua, please let your father know that I still wear the outfit he got for me, just not quite as often as I once did. With more hands-on work since the port has been closed, it is too nice to be wearing."

"I understand, sir, and I will pass the information on to Father. I know he will be pleased to hear it."

"Messieurs, I must leave. I have much business to attend to. Have a good day!"

"You as well, Jean Paul. Thank you again for the recruits. I am sure they will prove most valuable," Willie said as Jean Paul started out the door.

"You may use the office for as long as you have need. Please lock the door when you leave."

"Yes, sir," Willie said.

ॐ

During the next several weeks leading up to Christmas, Joshua and Amos proved to be fast learners and invaluable to Willie Boyd. Willie remarked frequently to Jean Paul, who passed on the plaudits to William and Robert, that these two had quickly become his best workers. They worked together as a team and became good friends. William was especially pleased to see the change in attitude of his son as Joshua frequently mentioned their "adventures" in giving the slip to the Brits while helping needy families.

❧

"Christmas is approaching, and every effort must be made to assist families in need, families that have been nearly starved into submission by the Intolerable Acts," said Dr. Mark Wilson. A recent widower with no children—he was of medium height and build with above-average looks; though with a touch of gray on the temples and a few lines in his face, he appeared somewhat older than his thirty-eight years. He had done well financially, being widely regarded as one of the area's leading physicians.

"Yes, I agree," said Becky Braun as she was finishing the sumptuous meal provided by Wilson's chef, Jacques LaFete. "Francois informed me that Mr. Finch obtained the names of several needy families from Jean Paul. The Finches and Barneses are going to be giving those families gifts on Christmas morning."

"A worthy endeavor, but more must be done."

"What do you propose?"

"I will speak to Warren and Church about donating free medical service to all who cannot afford it. My plan is to do this on Wednesday and Thursday of the week before Christmas. This is something that has been on my mind and heart for some time," Wilson said as he took a sip of port following his meal.

"Mark, that is such a wonderful idea and so gracious of you and the others," said Becky, who was visibly moved by what she had just heard.

"Thank you, but I am not so sure the others will feel quite the way I do," Wilson replied.

"Oh, I am certain they will. They are good men and true patriots. They will welcome the opportunity."

"I hope so, but if they do not, I will proceed on my own. I am set to meet with Church tomorrow, and I will discuss the matter with him at that time. I will then speak to Warren."

"Please let me know their response."

"I will, my dear, and then I will need your help."

"My help?"

"I would like handbills to be distributed to the needy, the ones that truly cannot afford medical care. The handbills will provide all the information they will need to know, such as our office locations and dates and hours of availability. If you would give them to Francois, who can pass them on to Jean Paul, I know that he will be able to deliver them to those we need to help."

"Yes, I will be glad to do it, and I am sure that Francois and Jean Paul will be delighted."

⚘

"Dr. Wilson, do come in," said Benjamin Church as he invited his colleague into his office and closed the door. Church, a renowned Boston physician, was one of the most colorful characters in all Boston. He, along with Dr. James Warren, who was on General Ward's staff, were widely regarded as two of the leading patriots in Massachusetts.

"Doctor, I am going to offer free medical services to all who cannot afford them, on Wednesday and Thursday of the week leading up to Christmas, and I would like to recruit you and Dr. Warren to join in the effort. I mentioned the idea to Becky Braun. I will provide her with handbills that will contain all necessary information. She is going to give them to Francois DuBois, who will give them to Jean Paul for distribution."

"Free medical services for the poor. That is indeed a wonderful gesture on your part. I like it, especially at this time of the year and the circumstances in this town. I agree to offer my services, and I have no doubt that Warren will be of the same mind about the matter."

"I will speak with Warren immediately and then will have Becky give handbills to Francois."

"Mark, I truly appreciate your thinking of me," Church said, smiling broadly as he arose from behind his desk and gave Wilson a firm handshake.

"And I appreciate your willingness to participate," said Wilson as he turned and left the office.

"This is for you, my dear," said a smiling Mark Wilson as he slipped a beautiful silver necklace with silver pendant inlayed with jewels around Becky Braun's neck. It was Christmas Eve at Wilson's house, and Becky came to have supper and exchange gifts. On Christmas morning she would be with her father at his elegant residence, and then she would spend the afternoon and evening with Francois at Jean Paul's. "Paul Revere fashioned that piece."

"Oh, Mark, it is so beautiful," Becky said as she smiled and gave him a peck on the cheek. "I love it."

"Glad you approve," said Wilson.

"I approve even more of what you did for all those poor people."

"To think that I treated over one hundred patients in a couple of days and Warren and Church approximately the same number. I believe the endeavor benefited us more than it did the patients."

"It was well received, and the accolades for you and Drs. Warren and Church were much deserved," said Becky as she was becoming more and more enamored with this man. Gone were the days of flirting with the men of Boston. Now it was two men, very different, yet much to admire in both. The young, debonair, handsome Francois and the older, seemingly steadier, respectable Mark. She could not believe that she was beginning to feel strongly about this man Wilson, who not long ago was just someone who could make Francois jealous.

"It was worth everything to see the lovely look on your face just now," Wilson said as he raised Becky's right hand and planted a soft kiss on it.

Becky blushed.

᠙

Lydia set right to work knitting sweaters and mittens of various shapes and sizes, along with caps, hats, and blankets, working many evenings into the late hours. William and Annabelle were impressed with her fervor, passion, and determination to help the many who were hurting in the community around her. To them, it was obvious that Lydia had grown significantly from her experiences in Philadelphia. To Lydia, this gesture was just a part of her patriotic duty.

Christmas Eve finally arrived, and appropriately snow was falling with big, wet flakes.

The Barneses arrived at the Finches in the early afternoon for a gift exchange. Each person was to receive a single gift, with names drawn in advance.

Christmas dawned a beautiful, brisk, sunshiny morning with a few inches of freshly fallen snow on the ground. The Finches and Barneses set out at around eight o'clock for the distribution. The Barneses headed for the north side of town, while the Finches headed for the south. They all arrived back at the Finches' in time for the large noon meal prepared by Grace and the other cooks.

"What a wonderful idea that was, Margaret," said Annabelle as the families sat down over the delicious Christmas meal.

"It was indeed," agreed William. "The best moment of all was when Judah lifted a big package off the carriage and took it into what can be best described as a dilapidated house. He placed it in front of two children dressed in rags—correct, Judah?"

"Yes, sir, Mister William," said Judah as he circled the table, attending to the families.

"You should have seen the look on those children's faces when Judah opened the package and pulled out a dress for the girl and an outfit for the boy, with shoes for both. Those children were beaming and grabbed Judah in a tight hold. The parents were overwhelmed and heartily thanked us all. Joshua and Lydia were especially touched, were you not?"

"Yes, Father," said contemplative Lydia. "I would have to say this perhaps has been the most gratifying experience for me," she said as she passed a bowl of brown gravy to her mother.

"I actually felt that I was contributing, directly touching those who have borne the brunt of the wrath of the Brits," she said, almost moved to tears. "Those poor souls—" She lowered her head.

"They do not deserve this fate," Joshua interjected, completing Lydia's thought.

"That is right, Joshua," Lydia said, her head suddenly straightening and eyes wide open. "How did you know what I was thinking?"

"It was very apparent from your expression, dear sister. Besides, it was what I was thinking. I also feel as if I am now making a contribution, however small."

"Both of you are making contributions. You certainly did today," William said. "Jonathan, how was your morning?"

"We too had similar experiences," Jonathan agreed. "It was amazing the response that a sweater or knit cap could bring to a child and a family. As Lydia and Joshua said, these families are truly hurting—their spirits have been virtually crushed—but today we could see a glimmer of hope."

"Yes, a glimmer of hope in their eyes!" Eleanor interjected.

"Is that not what Christmas is all about—hope?" Margaret exclaimed as she surveyed the faces of the two families.

"Absolutely." William nodded in agreement. "And hope, that most precious feeling, is exactly what we gave to some of the citizens, thanks to all of you."

"Becky, I am telling you again that I do not trust him. I believe this necklace is evidence that he is just using you. Do you honestly believe that he really cares about you?" Francois said as he and Becky went onto the balcony over the entrance to the stately DuBois mansion, following a gift exchange and delicious Christmas meal. The air was crisp and cold as the two stood together, arms around each other, Becky staring up into Francois's face.

"Francois Garcon DuBois, Dr. Wilson is one of the most generous, caring people I have ever known. What he did for those poor souls was fantastic—it touched my heart," she said as a little tear formed in the corner of her right eye.

"Oui, it was a great gesture by him and Drs. Warren and Church, but I still think—and you may hate me for this—that there was and is another motive."

"How can you say that, Francois? You are beginning to aggravate me. As I said before, you are jealous of him."

"Oui, I am jealous, but it does not change my thoughts and feelings about the good doctor. And you still have not answered my question."

"Yes, I do think he cares about me."

"And do you feel the same way?"

"I am not certain that I care for him the same as he cares for me, but I admit to you, and I never thought I would say this, that I do care about him," Becky said as her eyes moistened further and her lower lip began to quiver. "Probably more than I should," she added softly.

"And me—what about me?" said Francois, with a furrowed brow. "Do you still care about me—or perhaps I should rephrase that. Did you ever care about me?"

"Oh, Francois, you know I care about you—deeply," she said as she pulled his head down next to hers. They held each other tightly for several seconds. "It is just that I am a bit confused at this moment," she whispered in his right ear. As they pulled back from each other, she looked up at him. "I just need some time."

"So you no longer want to be with me?"

"Yes—I mean no, I do, Francois, of course, but please try to understand."

"Mademoiselle Braun, you are a most perplexing young woman," Francois said, slightly shaking his head back and forth. "I will try to understand, but I am telling you to watch yourself with *that* man. In my heart," Francois said, putting his right hand over the left side of his chest as emotion began to build, his voice cracking, "I know that he does not care for you, like I do. Be careful."

Before he could finish, they were back in each other's arms, and her full, moist, red lips parted and engulfed his lips in a passionate kiss unlike any either had ever experienced.

Who is this woman? Francois thought, his mind spinning, *and what is she doing to me?*

7

"Amos, I am going to Gage's house on my way home," Joshua said. They were distributing perishables to a family across town, and the hour was late. "He split off his elite troops for training a couple of days ago, and with everything that has been happening lately, I have a feeling that something big will soon occur."

"I do as well, Joshua. So what is your plan? What are you attempting to learn?"

"I plan to hide across the street from his house for a while, just to see if there is any activity—any comings or goings. There may be members of Paul Revere's network already staking the place out, but I doubt it at this hour."

"How long do you plan on spying on the place?"

"I do not know, but probably two or three hours."

"That will be late. Your parents will be worried."

"Yes, but they will understand, especially if I am able to learn anything of significance. Amos, I must be off."

"Good luck, Joshua, and please be careful."

Joshua arrived at Gage's house and was able to find a good place to observe the front door. It was across the street, in the shadow of a tree, cast from the light of the nearly full moon. He stood quietly as he waited, searching the area. While it was possible that Revere's spies were in the area, he saw no signs of them. Joshua waited and waited. Though quite tired, he was determined to stay awake, pay attention, and not miss anything. One hour became two; two hours became three. He was beginning to fall asleep. He knew he would have to leave soon when it happened—a carriage arrived, a special carriage that he had seen before with Willie and Amos. Willie had pointed it out and said it was the carriage of Brigadier General Lord Hugh Percy of the elite Fifth Foot regiment. Joshua had an unobstructed view of Percy as he stepped out of the carriage and went to the door of Gage's house. He was greeted by Gage's servant, who welcomed him in. An elated Joshua started for home, being careful to stay in the shadows. To be out at this hour and be intercepted by Brits asking questions—he could not think about it.

"Joshua, where have you been?" said an upset William as Joshua came through the back door into the kitchen. "I have been very concerned about you."

"Father, please give me an opportunity to explain."

"Joshua, do you know what the hour is?"

"No, but I know that it is late."

"It is nearly two o'clock," William said sternly.

"Father, I saw him tonight!" Joshua said excitedly, ignoring his father's disapproval.

"Saw whom? Who are you talking about, son?"

"General Lord Hugh Percy."

"Lord Percy?"

"Yes!"

"Where did you see him?"

"Getting out of his carriage and entering General Gage's house."

"Are you sure it was him?"

"Absolutely. I had an unobstructed view, and with the bright, nearly full moon, I recognized his carriage and got a clear look at him."

"When was this?"

"About thirty minutes ago. I decided to come home past Gage's house after a late delivery with Amos. Father, with all that has been taking place lately—well, I have had this feeling that something big is brewing."

"I have had the same feeling," William acknowledged.

"So I decided to hide in the shadow of a tree across from his house and wait to see if there would be any comings or goings. I was very tired and just about to leave when Lord Percy arrived."

"Percy arriving at Gage's house after midnight. That tells me that whatever Gage is planning is imminent, probably as soon as tomorrow...er, later today."

"That is what I have been thinking."

"Joshua, that was excellent work. But, if you had been intercepted by the Brits—"

"I know, but this idea came to me as Amos and I were making our rounds tonight, and I thought I had to act upon it right away. Besides, I took precautions."

"We must get this information to Jean Paul first thing after daybreak."

"I will do it, Father."

"No, you have done enough. I will wake Victoria just before daybreak and have Judah take her to Jean Paul's. Now please get some rest."

William had barely slept, between his anxiety over what Gage was planning and the late hour when he finally went to bed. He arose early, dressed, and quietly entered Victoria's bedroom. He began gently shaking her from a deep sleep.

"Victoria—Victoria," William whispered into her ear as he shook her in what seemed to be a futile attempt to wake her from her slumber. "Victoria, it is almost dawn," William said as he continued gently shaking her. "You must get up and get dressed right away."

Slowly Victoria opened her eyes and mumbled, "Father...is that you, or am I dreaming?"

"You may still be dreaming, dearest, but it is your father. You have got to wake up now."

Victoria stirred and then slowly sat up, stretched her arms skyward, yawned, and rubbed her eyes.

"Why do I need to wake up now?"

"Joshua saw Lord Percy entering General Gage's house after midnight. He had an unobstructed view, and though dark, there was a nearly full moon. He recognized the carriage and got a clear look at Percy. I need you to go with Judah to Jean Paul's and deliver the message that I have suspicions that Gage's excursion could be today or tomorrow."

"And Judah and I need to do that now?"

"Yes. No more questions. You must get dressed."

"I will, Father; I will," she said as she pulled herself out of the bed. She slowly moved across the room to the chest, where she removed her favorite everyday dress, which while attractive, was comfortable.

"While you are getting ready, I will have Judah bring the carriage around to the back door of the house. When you return from Jean Paul's, Grace will have a good breakfast waiting."

Victoria nodded her head slowly, half-asleep as she slipped on the dress and then proceeded to reach for her shoes.

William quickly walked to the stairwell and practically ran down the stairs. He entered the kitchen, where the woman servants were just coming in to fix breakfast.

"Mornin' Mastuh William," said the large black woman who was in charge of the kitchen and the other female cooks.

"Good morning, Grace. Have you seen Judah?"

"I'se believes he's out back in dah shed wit dah carriages."

"Thank you," said William as he headed out the door and rapidly walked toward the shed. As he approached, he could see the shed door was pulled back, but there was no sign of Judah.

"Judah—Judah, are you in there?"

"Yes, sir, Mister William."

"Where are you?"

"Behind the big carriage, sir. Several wheels on the carriages have been squeaking, so I decided to start greasing them, sir."

"Judah, I appreciate your initiative in taking care of these carriages, but now I need you to bring one of the two-seaters to the back door. Joshua saw Lord Hugh Percy arrive at Gage's house after midnight. I have suspicions."

"Mister William, Colonel Smith of the Tenth Foot has been in serious training the last couple of days with a detachment of Regulars, and everybody knows that Lord Percy is in charge of the Fifth Foot, the best regiment the Brits have."

"That is why when Joshua said he saw Lord Percy, I knew that Gage must be planning a major operation soon, perhaps today or tomorrow. We have to get the word out to Jean Paul immediately. Bring one of the two-seaters to the back door. Victoria will be waiting. You are to take her a back way to Jean Paul's. Be very careful that no redcoat spies see you, but if they do, make sure that you lose them and go in a different, roundabout direction to get to his house. Understood?"

"Yes, sir, I understand. I will get Miss Victoria to Mister Jean Paul's, and no one is going to know about it."

"Good, Judah, I know I can depend on you."

William left and headed back to the house. He opened the back door and entered the kitchen, where Victoria was waiting for Judah.

"Victoria, Judah will be along in just a few minutes. I see Grace has already started you on your big breakfast."

"I told her that I was starving, and she gave me this delicious big biscuit."

"And dey's be moh waitin fer you'se when you'se git back wit Judah."

"Thank you, Grace, I know I will be ready for more when I return."

"There is Judah now. Remember what I told you."

"I will, Father."

"And be very careful."

"Please do not worry."

"Oh, and Victoria?"

"Yes, Father?" she said as she was going out the back door.

"Please give my kind regards to Jean Paul."

"I will. Good-bye."

※

Judah quickly but quietly maneuvered the carriage through the back alleys of the city, keeping a sharp eye out for anything suspicious along the route.

The morning was eerily still for what Victoria felt was about to happen. On the basis of what she had seen and witnessed and what her father and Richard had told her, she had a feeling deep inside that soon nothing would ever be the same. As the carriage quietly rolled along, she felt chills all over her body and a tightness developing in the pit of her stomach. She was glad she had not had the time to eat a full breakfast, or the journey undoubtedly would have been much more unpleasant. While she had been on virtually all the streets in town, she was not yet familiar with all the backstreets and alleyways frequented by Judah as he made runs to various locales at all hours of the day and night.

"Judah, are we almost there?" Victoria asked expectantly as she wrapped her soft woolen shawl around her shoulders to fend off her nervous chills and the dampness of the morning air.

"Almost, Miss Victoria. We have a couple more turns to make, and we will be at Jean Paul's house."

No sooner did he say this than Judah yanked old Betsy, the Finches' speckled gray mare, to the right into a side street, almost throwing Victoria from the carriage.

"Judah—why did you do that?"

"Ssh, missy, be quiet," he practically whispered to her as he brought the mare to a halt in an alley off the side street located in the back of a shoe-repair store. Judah jumped out of the carriage and peered around the corner, looking up and down the side street. After a few minutes, Victoria carefully stepped down from the carriage and crept up behind Judah. She gently tapped him on the right shoulder. Judah reared back with a start.

"Miss Victoria," he somehow managed to say in a low, muted voice, with a look of fright on his face, "you scared me."

"I am sorry, Judah," she whispered, "but what or whom did you see?"

"A redcoat whom I thought I recognized as one of General Gage's spies."

"How do you know him?"

"Mister Jean Paul—he has pointed out several of them to me when I have been with him on various occasions."

"Do you think this redcoat spy knows who you are?"

"I do not know for certain, but I know he has seen me with Mister Jean Paul. And Mister William gave me strict orders to make sure no redcoat spies see us."

"Judah, do you really think that he saw us?"

"Probably, though I did my best to turn quickly so he could not get much of a bead on us."

"You did turn quickly."

"I am sorry, Miss Victoria; I just reacted."

"I know, but now what do we do?"

"Well…Mister William said if we see a redcoat spy, we should go in a different, roundabout direction to get to Mister Jean Paul's house— so we will start down this side street and double back around."

"How far out of our way will that take us, and how much time?"

"It is a hard to say, but I guess it will be about an extra quarter mile or so and take us about ten or fifteen minutes more."

"All right, then let us get going right away."

Victoria and Judah headed back to the carriage, and Victoria climbed aboard. Judah grabbed the halter and gently backed old Betsy and the carriage from the alleyway behind the shoe repair shop and into the side street into which they had darted. After completing the maneuver, Judah climbed back into the driver's seat, picked up the reins, and lightly snapped them. The carriage started moving slowly down the street. The sun was rising higher in the eastern sky, taking the chill out of the air as a beautiful spring morning was unfolding. Victoria removed her shawl and placed it in a holding storage space behind the seats.

Judah carefully took the carriage through a couple more side streets, looping back to the original street from whence they came, taking approximately ten to fifteen minutes as he had estimated.

"Judah, it appears that we are back on the correct street in just about the time you said."

"Yes, Miss Victoria—and it appears that the coast is clear."

In another five minutes and a couple of additional turns, they arrived at the back of Jean Paul's beautiful mansion.

Judah pulled old Betsy to a stop right behind the back door and quickly alighted, moving around the carriage and helping Victoria down. They then went to the back door, where Judah knocked on the door with three fast, hard knocks, followed by two soft knocks followed again by three more rapid, hard knocks.

"It is a signal code that Mister Jean Paul and I devised a long time ago."

Within a few seconds, the door cracked open, and Cheebs, Jean Paul's chief servant, inquired.

"Is that you, Judah?"

"You know it is, Cheebs. I have with me Miss Victoria. We need to see Mister Jean Paul right away."

"Come in; come in—I will get him. Please sit down."

Within a couple of minutes, Jean Paul came bounding into the kitchen and heartily shook Judah's hand and placed a delicate kiss on Victoria's outstretched right hand.

"Mademoiselle Victoria, Monsieur Judah, it is so good to see you, but so early?"

"Jean Paul, if this were not of the utmost importance, I assure you, we would not be here at this hour," Victoria replied assertively.

"Then please proceed," he said as he pulled up a chair and sat down across from them at the kitchen table. "Oh, before you do, please accept my humble apologies. Do either of you want something to eat or drink? Naomi makes the best breakfast in Boston."

"No, thank you," Victoria said. "I had a biscuit before we left, and Grace has more waiting for me when we return. I know that Naomi is a fantastic cook, but Grace's biscuits are delicious."

"Oui, mademoiselle, Grace's cooking is superb. I did not mean any offense to you or to her."

"Oh, Jean Paul, I did not take offense. It was good of you to say that your cook makes the best breakfast in town."

"How about you, Monsieur Judah?"

"Yes, sir. I would be much obliged. I could sure use a piece of ham and one of Miss Naomi's golden biscuits. Oh, and some cider, if I may."

Jean Paul smiled. "Wonderful—coming right up!" To his cook, Jean Paul said, "Naomi, a piece of your delicious ham and one of your very best golden biscuits, with a mug of cider for my friend Monsieur Judah."

"Yessuh, Mastuh Jean Paul, I'lse git it for Judah."

As Naomi put a huge piece of tender ham, a flaky, golden-brown, hot, buttery biscuit and mug of cider in front of Judah, Jean Paul turned to Victoria.

"Now, Mademoiselle Victoria, what may I do for you?"

Victoria proceeded to relate the events witnessed by Joshua to Jean Paul, who, listening intently, nodded at the mention of this.

"Father thinks that some major operation may be coming, possibly as early as tonight. That is why he had Judah bring me first thing this morning."

"Mademoiselle Victoria, this is consistent with what I have been hearing from my other sources. In fact Francois reported to me a couple of nights ago that one of Madam Jayne Kitt's ladies overheard two Brit Regulars at Maggie's saying they believe something big is going to be happening soon."

"They were foolish enough to talk about it in public?"

"Oui, it happens all the time, mademoiselle."

"Especially in the taverns, Miss Victoria," Judah chimed in. "The alcohol loosens the tongue."

"Oui, Monsieur Judah is right, and that is why I have Francois and tavern workers paying close attention to what is said and done when the Brits visit. It is like being given a gift."

"Apparently so," marveled Victoria.

"Getting back to what we were discussing, I agree with Monsieur William. A British excursion of some sort is soon to be forthcoming, and my guess is that it will begin tonight."

"If that is true, what will you do, Jean Paul?"

"I will contact Monsieur Revere immediately with this information. He has been in readiness for quite some time for Gage to make a move. He is probably gathering reports from other sources as we speak, confirming this intelligence. He will know exactly what to do."

"I am really worried about the Barneses in Lexington," said Victoria. "How will they receive an advance warning in the event the Brits head in their direction?"

"Not to worry. Revere's network is prepared to warn all the towns and countryside around Boston."

"That is comforting."

"Anything else?"

"No, sir, I believe that is all that Father wanted me to convey to you."

"I have a question for you two. Were you seen by any Brit spies?"

"Yes, sir, well, most probably by one of General Gage's redcoat spies you pointed out to me when we were together," Judah said.

"That is good to know. Monsieur Revere and I thought this would happen. It was more important to get this report than to be fearful about being spotted. It will not affect our plans, though we must assume that ole Gage will know that we know he is planning something. Now I must get this message out to Revere. I am most appreciative of the information, but be very careful to avoid those Brit spies on your way home. Please be sure to give my personal regards to your father and mother. They are the best people I know."

"And that reminds me that Father did want me to convey his kind regards to you, as always."

William was at the carriage-house door waiting to greet Victoria and Judah upon their return when Judah pulled old Betsy to a halt right in front of William.

"Mister William, are you all right, sir? I did not see you until I almost hit you."

"I am just fine," William replied, with a grin. "I saw you all the way; I was never in any danger."

"Father, Father, are you sure you are all right?" Victoria practically shouted as she stepped down from the carriage, with a hand from Judah.

"Victoria," William said as he gave his daughter a strong hug, "I said I was just fine, especially since you and Judah are back home safely."

"Father, how long have you been waiting for us?"

"Probably about half an hour. I must admit I was beginning to be concerned. Did you have any issues on the trip? Did you encounter any spies?"

"As a matter of fact, we did, on the way to Jean Paul's, correct, Judah?"

"Yes, Miss Victoria."

"Where? Did you recognize them?"

"Close to Mister Jean Paul's. Miss Victoria had just asked if we were almost there, and I told her that a couple more turns, and we would be there, when I saw him. I yanked old Betsy hard to the right into a side street."

"Who was it?"

"I do not know his name, sir, but I thought I recognized him as one of General Gage's spies. Mister Jean Paul—he has pointed out several of them to me."

"Did he see you?"

"I do not know, sir, but probably. I pulled the carriage into an alleyway off the side street and stayed there for several minutes. I know he has seen me out and about with Mister Jean Paul. I looked up and down the side street for any signs of him. Then we got back in the carriage and headed down the side street in a different direction, as you instructed me to do, Mister William."

"Excellent, Judah."

"It took us about fifteen minutes more to get to Mister Jean Paul's."

"Any more sightings?"

"No, sir, no more sightings."

"You did the right thing. Nevertheless, since you were probably spotted early in the morning with Victoria, it is reasonable to assume that the word is getting passed on to General Gage. But it was worth it to get the message to Jean Paul."

"That is what Jean Paul told us, Father. He and Paul Revere figured that, with their spy network, the Brits would probably encounter us and other patriots on their way to report Brit activities. It will put everyone on heightened alert but will not affect the plans."

"How did Jean Paul react to the message of my suspicions?"

"He said it was consistent with what he was hearing from his other sources. He agreed with you that some sort of British excursion would be happening soon, and his guess was that it would begin tonight."

"So he thinks it is tonight?"

"Yes, he said he would contact Revere immediately with the information. Revere has been in readiness for some time for Gage to make a move. Revere will know exactly what to do. He said that Revere's network was ready to warn the towns and countryside surrounding Boston of any Brit excursion, so we need not worry about the Barneses; they will be forewarned should there be any move toward Lexington."

"Thank God! Victoria and Judah, I am grateful for your courage and quick thinking. Your actions may have saved the lives of many of our citizens."

"Father?"

"Yes?"

"I forgot to tell you that Jean Paul sent his personal regards to you and mother. He says that you are the best people he knows."

"That is one of the nicest compliments I have ever received. I will tell your mother; she will be touched by it."

"And, Father?"

"Yes?"

"May I please get some breakfast? I am starving!"

William laughed. "Let us go in—Grace is ready for you. You have earned it."

8

When Revere received word on the morning of the eighteenth from Willie Boyd about William Finch's suspicions, it only confirmed what Revere had suspected and gleaned from some other, though less reliable, sources.

"I have no doubt now that Gage is planning some sort of excursion that will be getting underway very soon. The questions are, where is he heading, what is his goal, and how will he move his troops? Tell Jean Paul that I am grateful to receive this intelligence, and I am happy to finally meet you. I have heard many good things about you."

"It is my privilege to meet you. All of us in Jean Paul's network feel honored to serve under your leadership."

"The feeling is mutual. Now I must get this information to my superior."

"Dr. Warren, I have reliable, credible intelligence that General Gage is planning an excursion, which in all probability will begin tonight," Revere said, after arriving at the office of Dr. Joseph Warren.

"I have been accumulating more and more information that seems to support what you say, Paul, but nothing definitive. I must say that I have been confused by HMS *Somerset* and HMS *Boyne* having dropped boats into the harbor near the stern of the ships."

"Doctor, I have a signal system prepared in the event the Brits make a move by land or by water. Your observation suggests water."

"That is logical, but if so, where are they headed?"

"Across the Charles perhaps to Concord. Rumor has it that Gage has learned of Hancock and Sam Adams hiding in Lexington and that he is determined to seize the gunpowder and ammunition stored in Concord."

"Are the powder and ammunition still there?"

"I do not know for sure, but I am certain that if and when the lobsterbacks make it that far, they will surely be disappointed."

"I do hope you are right, or our cause could be dealt a severe blow. I want to attempt to verify that the Brits are planning an excursion before we make a move."

"And how do you propose to do that, Doctor?"

"I have a certain 'unimpeachable source' in the British high command. I believe it is high time I paid that source a little visit."

"An 'unimpeachable source'? That sounds intriguing."

"After my visit, if my source confirms that the Brits are going tonight, I will visit with Jean Paul and inform him. He will contact you and Dawes to join me back here. If you do not hear from Jean Paul, you will know that the excursion is not tonight."

"Trusting that it is likely the Brits are going forward tonight, I will proceed to the Old North Church this afternoon, where I have a signal system in place. Then I will be heading home."

Late in the afternoon, Revere arrived at the Old North Church. He had come to see Robert Newman, an unemployed leather worker who was serving as sexton at the church.

"Robert, I need to talk with John Pulling right away—is he here?" Revere said as he firmly shook Newman's hand.

"Yes, I will get him for you."

"Very good, thank you."

Within a few minutes, Newman had returned with John Pulling Jr., a church vestry, and a friend and neighbor of his by the name of Thomas Bernard.

"Paul, this is my friend and neighbor, Thomas Bernard."

"Pleased to meet you, Mr. Bernard."

"Please, call me Thomas."

"And please call me Paul. John, all signs indicate that tonight is the night."

"I have noticed increased activity among the elite troops, but it seems a bit early for them to make a move."

"Reliable sources that I have point to it, so I want you to be ready. It appears to me that Gage will be moving his troops across the Charles toward Charlestown, but this is still speculation. Remember the signal that I have alerted Charlestown to be ready to receive: one lantern if the Brits move by land, and two if they move by water."

"I remember."

"Any questions?"

"No questions."

"All right. If it is indeed tonight, I will be back here later; otherwise, it is a false alarm."

Revere next met with Whigs Joshua Bentley, who was a boat builder, and Thomas Richardson, a shipwright, and conveyed the same message to them of the need to be ready that night with the boat on the Charles.

At the same time, Dr. Benjamin Church bid adieu to his mistress and was seen by Willie Boyd leaving General Gage's house, parting "like old friends." Later in the evening, Church held a clandestine meeting with a Brit Army major.

Meanwhile, in Menotomy, five miles east of Lexington, prosperous merchant and active Whig Elbridge Gerry was surprised by two members of the local Provincial Committee of Safety who had hastily entered and then left a meeting of the committee.

"Sir, after leaving the committee meeting, while heading home in our chaise, we spotted two mounted Brit officers who had dined in Cambridge. They were moving in this direction, away from the city."

"Away from Boston," said Gerry, briefly musing. "Gentlemen, thank you for informing me of your observation."

"What do you make of it, sir?"

"I strongly suspect that the Brits are planning an excursion to Lexington tonight, especially with all the recent Brit troop activity and rumors that have been flying about town. I must send a messenger there immediately to warn them."

In Lexington, shortly before eight o'clock that evening, Reverend James Clark received a message in his parsonage and immediately informed houseguests John Hancock and Samuel Adams, who were staying there while conducting a Provincial Council meeting in Concord.

"John, Sam, I just received a message that mounted Brit officers who dined in Cambridge were spotted moving away from the city, no doubt they will very soon be in our vicinity."

"My carriage is close to the road, only a few hundred yards away. I am certain that it is visible from the road. We have to move it as soon as possible," Hancock stated.

"Yes, John," Sam Adams said. "We had better move it now."

"Let us go," Hancock said as headed for the front door.

Hancock and Adams quickly moved the gilded carriage back toward the house and into a grove of trees, effectively sheltering the view of it from the road.

While they were hiding the carriage, Sergeant William Munroe, a militia sergeant who owned a tavern, was informed by Solomon Brown about a band of Brit officers and sergeants who were in the area. They were passing through Lexington, headed toward Concord, led by Major Mitchell of the Tenth Regiment of Foot. Munroe walked to the nearby Clarke parsonage to tell Hancock and Adams that the Brits might be out to capture or kill them.

"Sergeant Munroe," said Sam Adams as Munroe entered the parsonage, "your being here tells me there must be Brits about."

"How did you know?"

"Reverend Clarke recently informed us that mounted Brit officers, who were dining in Cambridge, were moving away from the city."

"That is interesting. I just received word from Solomon Brown of a band of Brit officers and sergeants in the area. He saw them passing through Lexington heading toward Concord, led by none other than Major Mitchell."

"Mitchell," chimed in Hancock. "Whatever the Brits are doing, if Mitchell is involved, it must be important."

"I would agree," replied Munroe. "I must say with these many redcoats in the area, I am worried that they are looking for you two to capture you."

"That may be the case," added Adams, "but it appears as if there is something much more important to them than us."

"I am not sure what could be more important to them than to capture two of the leading proponents and symbols of our cause. I am not going to take any chances. I am assigning a squad of eight militia to maintain guard all night around the parsonage."

"We certainly appreciate your concern sergeant, but will not a squad of militia draw more attention to our location than if we do not have the guard?" said Hancock.

"Perhaps, John. I will make certain they stay out of sight."

"Very good," Adams concurred. "There is plenty of cover around this house."

"They will be here within the hour."

"Sergeant Munroe, thank you for your kind concern and provision for us. We are greatly appreciative," Hancock intoned.

"Not at all, gentlemen. If you have any other needs, please inform one of the guards, and he will see to it that I receive the message."

"We will," said Adams as he showed Sergeant Munroe to the door.

Within the hour, there was a knock on the door.

"Mr. Adams, Mr. Hancock, my name is Billie Jacobs. I am the militia squad leader, and I am here with my squad. I have deployed them around the house."

"Are they sufficiently hidden from view?" Hancock asked.

"Yes, sir. I made certain that they would not be detectable by any Brits who may come into the area."

"Excellent. Mr. Adams and I will be retiring for the evening. If you need us for any reason, do not hesitate to wake us."

"Understood, and good night to both of you."

Adams and Hancock headed up the stairs to their room, a single room where they would sleep. Adams, a light sleeper, slept in his clothes.

"Good night, Sam. I see you will be ready for anything," remarked Hancock as he slipped into his nightshirt.

"You know I wake up at the drop of a feather, and besides, with all the commotion going on, who knows what may yet happen tonight."

The crew of the HMS *Somerset* set about the job of seizing all ferries and anything else they could find that could be rowed in anticipation of the excursion to take place beginning later that night. Meanwhile, Dr. Warren went to pay his visit to the "unimpeachable source" he had inside the British high command.

"Mademoiselle Braun," said a smiling Jean Paul, greeting Becky Braun as she entered JP's. She arrived in the early evening to meet Francois for supper, but he was nowhere to be found.

"Is Francois here, Mr. DuBois? I was supposed to meet him here for supper."

"No, mademoiselle, Maggie needed him to help her at the tavern. He told me to send his regrets, but nothing could be done about it. Duty called."

"I understand. Thank you."

"Mademoiselle, Francois suggested that you join me instead, for a sumptuous JP's meal, on ole Jean Paul. What do you say?" Though Jean Paul had concerns about his son's involvement with Becky Braun, which he made known to Francois, he remained fond of her even after she also became involved with Dr. Mark Wilson.

"Are you sure you want me to join you? I mean, I know that Francois's mother does not approve of my involvement with Francois and—"

"I am not Maggie Mae, Mademoiselle Braun. Maggie is very protective of Francois," Jean Paul said firmly. "While I am always concerned about him and his choices, he is a man, and he makes his own decisions. Now, will you please join me?" Jean Paul said invitingly, as he reached for Becky's hand. "We will dine at the finest table in all Boston."

"All right, I will be happy to join you. Thank you for the lovely invitation."

Jean Paul led her toward the back of the tavern, near his office, to a beautiful solid-oak table and matching chairs, exquisite in quality, shape, and design.

"It is a beautiful table," Becky remarked as Jean Paul pulled a chair back and sat her at the table.

"So glad you like it."

Instantly they were waited upon and soon were eating their fill of JP's famous ham, golden biscuits, and yams. Dr. Warren, who had left his source and hurried through the dark streets after the visit, carefully entered the back door of JP's and knocked on Jean Paul's office door. Jean Paul, who was engrossed in his conversation with Becky Braun, heard the knocking on his office door, looked up, and saw Warren standing in front of it.

"Dr. Warren, good evening, my friend. Please come to our table and join us for supper," Jean Paul said as he gestured for Warren to sit in an empty chair. Warren turned around at the sound of Jean Paul's distinctive voice.

"Jean Paul—Miss Braun, so good to see you. Thank you, Jean Paul, but I will not be long. If you please, I really must meet with you privately," Warren said as he approached the table. Warren was visibly anxious, and Becky Braun noted that he seemed uneasy.

"Why, certainly, doctor," Jean Paul replied. "Mademoiselle Braun, please excuse me for a few minutes. I shall return momentarily."

"Take as long as you need. I have plenty left to eat."

Jean Paul and Warren retired to the office, whereupon Warren relayed his message.

"I just came from an 'unimpeachable source' in the British high command who informed me that the target is definitely Concord, and they will move by water later tonight. The Brits know that Hancock and Sam Adams are in Lexington, and they intend to capture them."

"An unimpeachable, unmentionable source, Doctor?"

"Unmentionable, yes, but trust me, definitely unimpeachable."

"I trust you; besides, the information that I have been receiving from my very reliable sources is basically the same as yours."

"I met with Revere this morning after he received your information from Willie Boyd. I told Revere that I would visit my source, and if the information that we had received was confirmed, I would have you contact him and Dawes and have them report to my office immediately for further instructions."

"I think Monsieur Revere has anticipated this, but I will make certain that he and Monsieur Dawes are informed immediately. I will have them report for instructions, as you wish, Doctor."

"I appreciate your help."

"You are welcome. Be very careful; there are many Brits prowling about tonight."

"Indeed," said Warren as he opened the office door.

"Is everything all right, Mr. DuBois? I could not help but notice that Dr. Warren seemed anxious," Becky said as Jean Paul returned to the table.

"Everything is just fine, mademoiselle. Dr. Warren frequently meets with me."

"But he did seem to be uneasy."

"Do not be concerned. As I told you, everything is fine. Well now, I hope you enjoyed the meal. Thank you for the pleasure of your company. I must now depart, as I have business to tend to," Jean Paul said as he took Becky's right hand and kissed it.

"Thank you again for the delicious meal. I am grateful, and I thank you for the pleasure of your company. Please tell Francois I missed him but that his father was a wonderful substitute."

"You are welcome, any time, mademoiselle, and I will tell Francois. He is quite fond of you, as I am sure you know. Bonne nuit."

"Good night to you, Mr. DuBois."

"Mark, Maggie needed Francois at her tavern, so Jean Paul invited me to dine with him at JP's tonight. We were eating when Dr. Warren arrived to see him," said Becky Braun as she sipped a glass of wine in the parlor of the Wilson home. Wilson had invited her to have wine with him in the late evening since she was not available for supper.

"Oh?" said Wilson curiously.

"Yes, and when Jean Paul invited him to dine with us, he said that he would not be long but that he must meet with Jean Paul privately.

Warren appeared anxious, uneasy, and in a hurry. The two of them met in Jean Paul's office. I continued eating my meal, and Jean Paul returned a few minutes later. Warren left the office and went out the back door into the alleyway."

Wilson sipped his wine and gently nodded his head, paying attention to her every word.

"Then what happened?" he asked.

"I asked Jean Paul if everything was all right, that Dr. Warren seemed anxious."

"And Jean Paul said?"

"He said everything was fine and that Dr. Warren frequently meets with him. He then graciously dismissed me, saying he had business to tend to. He said good-night and left."

"That is interesting," said Wilson, he himself now getting anxious.

"I have never known Jean Paul to act that way before. He has always been the consummate gentleman to me, though I know that he has misgivings about my involvement with Francois. While he was not rude, he was abrupt."

"I am sure Jean Paul did have business to attend to, after all he is one of the leading businessmen of this town."

"But coming after this meeting with Dr. Warren—"

"I would not make too much of it, my dear," Wilson cut her off, now fidgeting in his chair. "However, please forgive me. The hour is getting late, and I must be up and to the office bright and early tomorrow morning," Wilson said, rising from his seat, as he took the hand of Becky as she rose from her chair.

"This is indeed an unusual evening," Becky said. "Business matters do seem to be pressing the men in my life."

Wilson led her to the door, kissed her gently on the cheek, and then on the lips.

"Thank you again, my dear—it has been wonderful."

As Becky left the Wilson house, she maneuvered her carriage around the corner and into dark shadows where she could not be easily seen but where she had a clear view of the back of the house. She did not want to believe what she feared and told herself she should go straight home, but she could not. Wilson's reactions to her story were so out of character for him but also too obvious. She had to know the truth. She waited, her heart racing, perspiration forming on her brow, her breath heavy in the cold air—and then her heart sank. Wilson emerged from the back of the house and quickly went to the stable. With the nearly full moon, she could make out the distinctive walk; it was him! Soon a carriage left the stable and rapidly headed down the dark, deserted street. The carriage not only took Wilson to wherever was his destination but also took with it a piece of Becky's heart.

"Doctor, what are you doing here at this hour?" asked General Gage as he greeted Dr. Benjamin Church at the back door of his home. "You are taking a risk coming here."

"That may be, General, but I had to come."

"Come in then, and state your business."

"I will not be long. I got here as quickly as possible," Church said as he entered the house.

"It does appear that you have been in a hurry."

Church then informed Gage that Wilson came to him after having wine with Becky Braun and shared with him the events of her evening.

"And what do you make of all this?" asked Gage.

"What I make of it is that the rebels are on to us; they know that the excursion is tonight."

"Interesting. One of my spies told me that he thought he saw William Finch's daughter and servant traveling not far from Jean

Paul's early this morning. However, he only got a glimpse, and then the carriage disappeared down a side street. When I queried him further about it, he confessed that he was not sure it was them and he could not be certain where they were headed, so I did not give it much thought."

"I would speculate that he did see them, and they did meet with Jean Paul."

"I agree. But even if what you say is true, what am I supposed to do about it?"

"Call off the excursion—now! If the rebels spread the news, the troops will be vastly outnumbered. They will never be able to get to Concord and back without serious repercussions."

"I will not call off the excursion, as you call it. It is too late. And even if I could do something about it, I would not. They are the king's finest men. The rebels will flee from their presence, and if they do not, that rabble is no match for our men."

"General, I beg to differ with you, with all due respect. I have lived among these people, and I know them. While they are not professional soldiers, they are on their home soil. And with Warren and Jean Paul involved, it means that Revere is well apprised of the scheme. He has a sophisticated network, not just in Boston but also in the surrounding towns and countryside. Trust me; he will get the word out to those people, and the militia will turn out in force to greet the Regulars. They will fight, and I fear that the king's troops will be decimated."

"I believe that our men are more than up to the task, but I have conveyed the plan to General Percy and told him to have his regiment ready in the event they might be needed as reinforcements. I will send word to him first thing in the morning to move out."

"Good. Percy and his regiment are the finest, but why not contact him tonight?"

"Dr. Church, I appreciate the information and your concern, but I think you are overblowing this situation. I will have the general contacted in the morning, and he will be able to have his men on the scene in plenty of time to assist the contingent of Regulars, should they need it."

"But General Gage—"

"No more, Doctor; I have had quite enough for one evening," Gage said rather curtly, stopping Church in midsentence. "Now go home, and get a good night's sleep. Everything will be fine," Gage said as he adroitly led Church out the back door. "Good night."

"Good night, General," Church said as he turned to shake Gage's hand, only to realize that the door had already been closed behind him.

No sooner did Church depart than Percy arrived at Gage's house to tell the general that their plan had been uncovered. Gage discussed his meeting with Church and then told Percy to ready his troops to move out in support of the Regulars first thing in the morning.

"Billie, tonight is the night," said Dr. Warren to William Dawes, a twenty-nine-year-old tanner by trade and an excellent horseman, as he entered Warren's office.

"So I have heard from Jean Paul."

"Since you are friendly with all the guards there and you are such an excellent rider, I am sending you through the neck to Lexington to warn Hancock and Adams of the threat of their arrest and then on to Concord. Revere will go across the Charles. Hopefully the two of you will meet up, but in any event, warn as many as you can on the way."

"I will, sir. You can count on me to get the word out."

"Very good. Godspeed."

With that, Dawes quickly got aboard his mount and headed off into the night toward the narrow Boston Neck.

Shortly after Dawes had departed, Revere arrived at Warren's office. After briefly conferring with Warren, Revere left to find Newman, Pulling, and Bernard at ten o'clock, waiting behind Revere's house.

"I just came from Dr. Warren. It is confirmed by his 'unimpeachable source' inside the Brit high command tonight is indeed the night; the target is Concord, and the Brits will move—by water."

"Water—that means two lanterns in the steeple," said Pulling.

"That is correct. Make sure you hold the lanterns clearly before the window of the steeple, but do not hold them there for too long. The Brits might see them and get suspicious."

"Understood," said Newman, nodding his head.

"Joshua, Thomas, the hour has arrived," said Revere as he approached Joshua Bentley and Thomas Richardson, the two rowers who were waiting for him on the bank of the north end of the Charles River with the small boat that Revere had hidden under a wharf.

"Paul," said Bentley, "we are ready."

"It is imperative that we be as quiet as possible. We are going to pass very close to those Brit ships. Do we have something to muffle the oars?"

"Actually we do. We have a petticoat from a fair patriotic lass, who gave it for the cause," Richardson volunteered.

"A petticoat?" Revere replied, with a raised eyebrow.

"Yes, a petticoat."

"That may be one of the most interesting and unique contributions to the cause that I have heard thus far, gentlemen," Revere said, a grin on his face.

"Joshua and I were just commenting on the uniqueness of this contribution before your arrival," Richardson added, with an amused look, "but if it works—and we are sure that it will work just fine—then why not?"

"Why not indeed," Revere agreed.

"I need help tearing the fabric and wrapping the oars," Richardson added as he handed the precious fabric to Revere.

"I will be happy to assist you," Revere said as he took the petticoat and tore it into two approximately equal parts. "Any rope to tie the fabric as it is wrapped around the oars?"

"I brought plenty of twine and a small pocketknife," Bentley said as he handed them to Revere.

"Good, now let us get this done," Revere said.

They quickly placed the fabric pieces over the oars and secured them with the twine, which was wrapped around the fabric several times and tied tightly, and then they shoved off into the dark waters of the Charles. Bentley and Richardson dipped and pulled the oars as the boat, using the shadow of the skyline as camouflage, silently glided past and into the shadow of the *Somerset* cast by the nearly full moon.

As they were crossing, the Brits were forming at the edge of Boston Common, moving toward the beach to board longboards, which would take them across the Charles in the wake of Revere's boat. As Revere arrived on the other side of the river, Whigs were waiting with Deacon Larkin's strong, outstanding mare, Brown Beauty.

"Gentlemen," he said as he disembarked from the small flatboat and walked briskly toward the Whigs, "with your being here, I gather that you received the signal on time?"

"We did, Paul. It was not only on time but also quite clear."

"Not too long, I hope, so as to tip off the Brits?"

"I do not think so, but I assure you the Brits are out there, as thick thieves, and they will be looking for you."

"I am sure they will be," Revere said. "What is this horse's name?" Revere asked as he petted her nose.

"Brown Beauty. Deacon Larkin gave his father's best mare for your ride."

"She is indeed a beauty, a magnificent animal, and I am most grateful to be able to ride her on this most important of missions. Please give Deacon Larkin my sincere thanks."

"I will be happy to do so. Have a safe ride, and be very careful."

"I will. I must be off; there is not a moment to lose."

Revere mounted the big mare around eleven o'clock and headed off down the road to Lexington about twelve miles away. Several roadblocks of Brit horsemen commanded by Major Mitchell were out in front of him. While racing along, two Brit riders suddenly appeared out of the shadows into his path. With the adept precision of an expert horseman, Revere deftly turned Brown Beauty, without missing a beat, outmaneuvering them and outracing one pursuer. As he came to houses along the way, he banged on shutters and pounded on doors while Brown Beauty was prancing back and forth. Revere shouted in his powerful voice, "Turn out! Turn out! the Regulars are out!"

In house after house, the residents were stirred from their slumber. Other designated riders from each town rode to a predetermined series of other towns in a network, radiating outward from Charlestown, waking militia while leaving behind ringing bells, signal muskets, and beating drums. The countryside quickly came alive with activity as militia riders jumped on their mounts and poured into the road to Concord, which also had some twenty Brit officers and sergeants.

Revere galloped into Lexington, heading straight for Buckman Tavern. He pulled up the fast-racing Brown Beauty right in front of the tavern's famous bright-red door, shouting at the top of his lungs to the thirty or so militiamen or minutemen (so known because they could be ready at a minute's notice) inside, "The Regulars are out!" Immediately the minutemen poured out of the tavern and onto the green. Sergeant Munroe and other minutemen, including Jonathan Barnes and son, Richard, went about arousing the rest of the militia of Lexington, who came running for muster on the green.

At the same time, Revere and Brown Beauty started down the right fork in the Bedford Road, soon arriving at the Clarke parsonage. Revere pounded on the front door, yelling for Hancock and Adams over the protests of Sergeant Munroe.

"Mr. Revere, Mr. Paul Revere—what are you doing? Stop your pounding immediately, sir!"

"I shall not, Sergeant, not until Adams and Hancock appear before me." He immediately let out a loud shout, "The Regulars are out! The Regulars are out!"

"We hear you, Paul," said Adams as he and Hancock appeared in the door. Lydia and Dorothy Quincy appeared at a second-floor bedroom window. Parson Clarke, his wife, and some of their eight children looked out other windows.

"About how much time do we have?" asked Hancock.

"Not much. Brits are everywhere around here, and Major Mitchell and his regiment are on their way."

Billy Dawes finally arrived to join Revere after a three-hour ride.

"Let us head over to Buckman Tavern to talk with the minutemen," Adams remarked.

"Fine, Sam, let us go," Hancock replied.

Off they went, Hancock, Adams, and Reverend Clarke walking the few hundred yards to Buckman Tavern and engaging several minutemen in conversation, including Jonathan Barnes, who was in charge of them until Captain John Parker arrived. Jonathan, like Parker, was a French and Indian War veteran. He had assisted Parker in training the militia, drilling them extensively over the last few weeks.

"Jonathan, what is your assessment of the militia in the face of the approaching Regulars?" Adams inquired.

"I believe we have done all that we could to get them ready, Sam, but how they will actually handle the situation when the moment arrives—"

"I feel certain they will acquit themselves with honor," Hancock said.

"We will all know soon enough."

Revere and Dawes, after leaving Buckman Tavern, hit the road to Concord and continued to warn residents all along the way. They met up with Dr. Samuel Prescott, a Son of Liberty and brother to one of

Revere's express riders, who was riding home after a visit with Miss Mullinex of Lexington, to whom he had just proposed marriage.

"Dr. Prescott," Revere said as Prescott pulled his horse alongside Revere and Dawes.

"Paul, Billy, what are you doing here at this hour? I have never seen the countryside so full of activity, so I am assuming your presence is linked to that?"

"Yes, Doctor. Brits are everywhere. Gage is sending his elites on an excursion."

"To where?"

"The information we have says that they are first attempting to capture Hancock and Sam Adams in Lexington, whom I have warned, and then on to Concord to seize ammo and gunpowder. Billy and I set out to warn as many as possible along the route and especially to get the militia out."

"Good Lord! The Brits are trying to capture Hancock and Adams?" asked an incredulous Prescott. "That would be a disaster!"

"It would indeed. They would be a feather in the hat of General Gage," Revere replied, "but as I said, I have warned them of the impending danger. Our job right now is to alert as many as possible along the route to Concord."

"May I be of assistance?"

"We would welcome your assistance, Doctor; please join us," said Dawes.

Revere, Dawes, and Prescott continued down the road, when Major Mitchell and three Brit officers stepped out into the roadway in front of them, the officers waving pistols and swords while shouting threats.

"You rebels, what are you doing out here in the middle of the night? Get into that pasture right now!" said Major Mitchell, screaming at the trio and pointing to a nearby open area.

Immediately Revere, Dawes, and Prescott scattered, with Prescott's horse jumping a stone wall. He escaped and headed back down the road to Concord. Dawes was thrown from his horse but was able to crawl into the bushes and escape on foot. Revere, however, was not so fortunate. He was surrounded, and then Major Mitchell pointed a gun at Revere's head.

"Mr. Revere, I am going to ask you one time what you and those others were about at this hour of the night. I would suggest, for your sake, that you be truthful."

"We have been notifying the citizens and militia all over the area that you were coming soon."

"From all the activity and noises that I have been seeing and hearing, it would appear that you were successful in your endeavor," Mitchell said, with a tinge of sarcasm, withdrawing the gun from Revere's head.

"You are free to go, but I have need of this excellent horse of yours."

"It is not my horse. I must return her to the rightful owner."

"I am now the rightful owner, Mr. Revere. You were riding in defiance of the Crown."

"No, Major, I was riding in defense of my country," Revere forcefully uttered as he turned and headed down the road to Lexington.

"Francois! Francois DuBois!" Becky shouted out as she rushed into Maggie's, spotting the distinctive features of Francis DuBois at the far end of the tavern. The din of many conversations was deafening, but as Becky hurried to meet Francois, who was heading toward her, several patrons stopped talking and looked at Becky. Realizing that she was an unwanted center of attention, Becky, who had nearly knocked a patron into a waiter carrying meals and drinks, slowed down. Francois was now upon her as Becky, nearly out of breath after running from her carriage, attempted to compose herself.

"Becky...Becky," said Francois as he quickly embraced her and then pulled her back. All eyes were upon them as Francois led her through the crowd to the office in the back. As he opened the office door, the patrons returned to their conversations, and the din was as loud as ever. Francois helped the shaking Becky Braun into a chair as he pulled up another chair in front of her.

"Becky, are you all right?" Francois said as he slipped into his chair.

"Oh, Francois…Francois," said Becky, now sobbing uncontrollably.

"What is it, Becky? What is this all about?" he asked as he reached over with a handkerchief to wipe the tears off her cheeks. Suddenly there was a bang at the door.

"Who is it?" Francois asked.

"Your mother," Maggie Mae said, in a loud voice.

"Come in."

Maggie Mae opened the door, stepped inside, and stood right above her son and the visibly shaking Becky Braun. Maggie had not been happy when Francois initially became involved with Becky. Though Maggie was well aware of Francois and his love for the ladies, Becky's reputation for being the biggest flirt in town was well deserved and a serious concern to Maggie. Like Jean Paul, she had made her concerns known to Francois. She was slower than Jean Paul to accept the situation. However, she finally began to do so, grudgingly, and had to admit to herself that she might have misjudged this young lady; that is until Dr. Mark Wilson came on the scene. Any semblance of acceptance of Becky turned to disdain. Maggie was equally upset with Francois because he refused to end his involvement with Becky, though her affection for the good doctor was becoming well known all over town. Perhaps more important than anything to Maggie, Francois was increasingly becoming the butt of jokes.

"Francois Garcon DuBois," Maggie said, in a stern voice, glaring down at him as he sat beside the whimpering Becky, "I told you I needed you tonight, all night. Now get back out there and tend to your job."

"Mother, Becky is in distress. I will be out in a few minutes."

"Distress? She is in distress? I am the one who is in distress," said Maggie as Francois looked up. "She is making a mockery of you, Francois, by getting involved with a man who is old enough to be her father!"

"He is not old enough to be my father," Becky managed to squeak out between the sniffles.

"Be quiet! If I want to hear from you, I will ask!"

"Mother, that is enough. I will be out in five minutes. Now leave!"

Maggie gave Francois another glare. "Five minutes and not one minute more!" Then she turned around, opened the door, left, and slammed it shut.

"Please excuse my mother. She is protective of me and is well meaning, but—"

"She is right, Francois," Becky said between sniffles, "as much as I hate to admit it, she is right, though not in the way she imagines."

"Whatever do you mean, dearest?"

"I have been a fool, my darling."

"Dr. Wilson?"

Becky nodded. She proceeded to tell Francois about her planned evening engagement with Mark Wilson and relaying to Wilson the events of her supper with Jean Paul.

"No, Becky—you did not tell all that to Wilson. How many times have I told you about my suspicions of him?"

"I know, Francois, I know. It is just that I could not believe that Mark was anything other than what he purported to be—a fine doctor, upstanding citizen, and true patriot."

She then related how she waited in her carriage in the dark close to Wilson's house and saw him take his carriage and head down the street, undoubtedly to relay the information she just conveyed.

"Where do you suppose he was going?" Becky asked.

"My guess is to a go-between," Francois replied.

"A go-between?"

"Oui, someone whom he has contact with, who would relay the information up to the British high command, eventually to Gage himself."

"General Gage?"

"Oui."

"What have I done? What have I done?" Becky began to sob again.

"Becky, do not worry. You did not impart any direct piece of information about what might be happening on our side. I feel certain that what was communicated to Gage or the Brit high command was not unexpected."

"I hope you are right—I could not forgive myself if I betrayed my country."

"You did not betray your country, but you were used. Do you understand that now? What have I been trying to tell you for months? Wilson is not to be trusted."

"You were right—I have been such a fool. Please forgive me, my darling," she said as they stood up and embraced each other.

"You must stop your involvement with him immediately."

"No. If I did that, he would be suspicious."

"But you could be in danger if he finds you out."

"I could be in more danger if I suddenly stop seeing him for no good reason."

"So what are you going to do?"

"Pretend as if nothing happened—at least for now—until I have a legitimate excuse for ending my involvement with him."

"Becky—I am scared. Be careful—be very careful."

"I will be; do not worry, my darling."

"All right, but please do not see him again until I can pass this information on to my father. I need to let him know our suspicions about Wilson."

"When will that be?"

"I will try to see him tomorrow. Come back here tomorrow night about the same time. I should have seen him by then, and we can discuss his thoughts."

"I will be back tomorrow night."

"I love you," Francois said as they embraced. He again sought Becky's full, receptive lips.

"John, may I ask what you are doing?" asked Sam Adams, incredulously.

"I am sharpening my sword," said Hancock.

"Yes, but why?"

Just as he was finishing the question, up walked Revere, joining Hancock and Adams at the parsonage.

"Why, to fight those despicable lobsterbacks!"

"John, you cannot do that!" said Adams as he approached and put his hand on Hancock's back. Adams leaned over, attempting to look Hancock in the eyes, as the sharpening continued.

"Why not?" Hancock asked, oblivious to Adams's efforts to dissuade him.

"John, it is Paul Revere," Revere interjected.

"Paul," said Hancock, looking up with a startled look on his face, "I thought you were gone to Concord."

"I was headed there, but Major Mitchell and his officers intercepted me, Billy Dawes, and Dr. Prescott, who joined us. Dr. Prescott got away on his horse, Billy escaped on foot, and I was held at gunpoint and then released—horseless."

"What did you tell Mitchell?" Adams asked.

"That the citizens and militia have been alerted all over the area."

"And he let you go?"

"He was convinced with all the activity and noise in the area. He took Brown Beauty and let me go. I decided to head back here to the parsonage."

"I understand," said Adams.

"But getting back to the matter at hand," Revere said, "John, I completely agree with Sam. Stop the sword sharpening; you cannot fight the Brits. You are far too valuable to the cause. In fact, we all must leave immediately."

Hancock shrugged his shoulders, sheathed his sword, and said, "All right then, let us get going."

"My wardrobe," said Adams.

"Forget it, Sam," Revere replied. "Let us get into the carriage—now!"

Adams, Hancock, and Revere, plus Sergeant Munroe and John Lowell, who was with Munroe, quickly climbed into Hancock's gilded carriage.

"Where are we headed?" asked Adams.

"To a clergyman's widow's house in Woburn," said Revere. "We should be safe there."

"Wait a minute," said Lowell. "John, your trunk is not strapped to the back of the carriage. It is in my room at the tavern."

"The trunk—with all that has been happening, I completely forgot it! We have got to fetch it!" exclaimed Hancock excitedly. "The papers in it could be very damaging if the Brits get their hands on it."

"Lowell and I will get it," Revere said. "The rest of you head to Woburn."

Revere and Lowell jumped out of the carriage and headed toward Buckman Tavern.

Upon arrival in Woburn, Hancock sent the coach back for the salmon he left at the Clarke parsonage. The salmon was cooked immediately upon the coach's return.

At about the same time, Revere and Lowell entered the tavern, and a mounted scout came riding up the road, shouting, "The Regulars are coming on the quick march! They are only a mile away."

Revere and Lowell headed up the stairs to get the trunk while Captain Parker, who had arrived some minutes earlier, ordered the drummer to beat the call to arms. Seventy-seven minutemen lined up in the two ranks along the green as Parker walked up and down the lines, encouraging the men and boys who made up the ranks and exhorting them, "Do not fire unless fired upon, but if they want a war, let it begin here." Jonathan Barnes walked alongside Parker, also encouraging all to remain calm and focused, to not do anything rash. Richard Barnes, in the first line of the ranks, was attempting to remain calm and in readiness, but it was very difficult to control the emotions that he was feeling. He knew the Brits would soon be arriving, and the cool, damp morning air was filled with the threat of war with the mother country—the greatest power on earth. The thought of seeing those bright-red coats coming out of the morning mist was enough to panic the most seasoned veteran, let alone one who had never before been tested in the heat of battle.

"Mr. Hancock, Mr. Adams!" said the messenger excitedly.

"Son, sit down and catch your breath," Hancock said, pointing to another chair at the table where he was eating. Hancock had just begun eating the salmon that had been brought to him and cooked.

"Thank you, sir, but there is not time. The Brits are coming; they are very near. You must leave right now!"

"Here we go again. Sam, we need to conceal the carriage first and then ourselves."

"I am with you," said Adams as he started out the door.

Hancock followed close behind, along with the messenger, quickly reaching the gilded carriage. They moved it well back into the trees near the house, and then they went back into the woods to conceal themselves. Several Brits passed very close by, but fortunately, neither the carriage nor the men were spotted. Adams had to stifle a sneeze just when a Brit sergeant came within a dozen feet or so of where he stood. The sergeant halted at the muffled sound, looked around, and then finally left after several minutes. When the Brits were gone, Adams suggested they head for the house of Amos Wyman, which they did a few minutes later.

"I am certainly glad that this trunk contains important papers," said Revere, as he pulled the trunk down the stairs, with Lowell hanging on from behind.

"Why is that?" Lowell asked as they both strained under the weight of the big, full trunk.

"Because if it did not, I would have abandoned it and left it for the Brits. This is extraordinarily heavy—and very awkward to move."

"Agreed," Lowell grunted as he strained on the steps to hold the trunk back to keep it from sliding down into Revere.

"Let us just hope we can get this trunk out of here before the Regulars arrive," Revere offered as he lowered the front of the trunk and then raised it back up as he reached the bottom of the stairs.

With surprising alacrity, they carried the trunk out the front door of the tavern and none too soon. As they struggled to move it out of harm's way, Major John Pitcairn appeared, leading his Regulars toward Lexington Green.

"Father agrees that in all likelihood Dr. Wilson was going to see a go-between, but he emphasized that we have no solid proof. In light of Wilson's sterling reputation as a patriot, we need to tread very carefully. Father is going to attempt to pass this information on to Dr. Warren, but only Father, Dr. Warren, you, and me are to be privy to this, for if it leaks to the public, you could be in danger," Francois said as he met with Becky in Maggie's office.

"Then he agrees that I should continue to see Mark?"

"At least for the time being. He agrees that to stop right now would be too obvious.

However, he said that if you begin to feel uncomfortable or if you have any legitimate reason to terminate your involvement with him, you should do so."

"All right. Mark has asked me to supper tomorrow night, so I will accept the invitation."

"Again, be careful, my darling, and let me know how he acts while with you."

"I will, though I may be more concerned about how I act while with him."

9

"Throw down your arms! Ye villains! Ye rebels!" yelled Major John Pitcairn, from the top of his lungs, sending shivers up the spines of the assembled militia, including young Richard Barnes. Pitcairn, alongside Major Edward Mitchell, were mounted, accompanied by Lieutenants Barker and Gould, who were on foot.

The Brits, in their brilliant red coats, white tights, and black boots, moved closer and closer. Captain Parker swiftly surveyed the situation, realized he was completely outnumbered, and ordered his troops to disperse.

"Militia disperse; militia disperse!" Parker yelled.

Jonathan and Richard Barnes followed orders and began to fall back, walking away, but like most of their comrades, holding onto their weapons.

Then it happened. A shot rang out and echoed across the green. It was immediately followed by a volley from the Regulars, which sent a huge cloud of acrid white smoke wafting over the retreating rebels.

Parker exhorted the men to pull back, "Retreat, men; retreat! The regulars are out of control."

Jonathan, Richard, and the militia began to run to the other side of the green with all due haste as the Regulars followed the volley with a bayonet charge. Chaos ensued. During the retreat, some of the militia turned and got off shots, including James Parker, Lieutenant Benjamin Todd, and Richard, but they had no effect on the onslaught; indeed nothing seemed to until Colonel Smith arrived on the scene with the main contingent of Regulars. Smith was appalled to see that the initial contingent of Regulars was preparing to assault private homes.

"Play 'Down Arms,'" Smith crisply barked to the drummers. The startled drummers hesitated, and Smith more forcefully said, "Play 'Down Arms!' Do it now!"

"Yes, sir," said the young drummers, almost in unison as they loudly banged out the tune, not once but several times.

Before the Regulars heeded orders, carnage struck the green. Jonas Parker, kinsman to Captain Parker, was wounded in the volley. While lying on the ground, reloading his gun, he was fatally bayoneted. Jonathan Harrington was shot in the chest. He crawled across the road, his wife peering out the front window. Seeing her husband coming toward her, she opened the door as Harrington pulled himself on the doorsteps.

"I die, my dear, in service to my country," he uttered as he died before her eyes.

Two other militiamen were shot in the back while running away from the enemy. When the smoke had finally cleared and the din had died down, eight militiamen lay dead on the formerly pristine Lexington Green. Nine others were wounded. Only one Brit was a casualty, Private Johnson of the Tenth Foot, who was shot in the thigh. As the Regulars drifted back into line, Colonel Smith gathered them together.

"That behavior is totally unacceptable. I was appalled to see Regulars ready to plunder private residences. That cannot and will not be tolerated. And when the drummers play 'Down Arms,' you obey, and you do it the first time it is played; no more second, third, and fourth renditions. Understood?" said Smith, in an unmistakable tone and equally unmistakable look on his face.

"Yes, sir," the troops said.

"I cannot hear you."

"*Yes, sir!*" the troops shouted.

"Troops, dismissed; officers, gather around me."

The officers quickly closed in around Smith.

"Our destination is Concord," Smith said to the visibly shocked body. "A munitions stash that must be taken from the rebels' hands."

"Sir, with all due respect," said Major Mitchell, still on his mount, "the troops are wet and nearly exhausted. There is much rebel activity all around us. I intercepted that rebel leader and rabble-rouser, Paul Revere, who was out here tonight with a couple of others, warning militia and civilians of our approach. I am fearful for the safety of the men should we march all the way to Concord and then have to pass back through Lexington to Boston."

"I, sir, agree with the major," echoed Lieutenant Barker.

"I also, sir," said Lieutenant Gould. "The whole countryside has been alerted to our presence. Other militia and the civilians will be out in force."

"Balderdash! We are the king's finest, the greatest fighting force on the face of the earth! Are we to be afraid of rabble? Will we tremble before mere peasants? I think not! We will do our sworn duty and move on to Concord and seize the ammunition from this rebellious lot!"

"I am in total agreement with you, sir," Pitcairn said. "We will do our duty, and these rebels will flee before us."

"Drummers, beat your drums; gentlemen, fire a volley, and give three cheers for our victory here!" Smith said.

With that, a volley was fired, three cheers went up, and with the drums beating loudly, the Brits marched out of Lexington on the road to Concord.

"Ah, what a glorious day," Adams remarked, turning toward Hancock on the road to Amos Wyman's house, as guns reverberated in the distance.

"Yes, yes," replied Hancock, "a glorious day indeed."

"For America, I mean."

"Yes, of course—for America."

"I am here to inform you that the Brits will soon be here, coming up the road from Lexington. My information is that they are headed for a stash of ammunition on the other side of town," said Dr. Samuel Prescott to the leaders of Concord who had assembled. He arrived in Concord at about two o'clock in the morning after arousing the countryside.

Reverend William Emerson said loud and clear for all to hear, "I say let us stand our ground. If we die, let us die here."

Sixty-four-year-old Charles Barnes, father of Jonathan Barnes, who had been in the Concord militia since its inception, said, "The Brits will be sorely disappointed. I have it on good authority that the weapons stash has been moved and that James Barrett and his sons buried the few remaining weapons, but I echo the reverend's sentiments. We must stand our ground regardless of the consequences."

"Hear, hear, we will stand our ground. Let them come. If we die, we will do so with dignity, defending our country," was a statement that could be heard emanating from the midst of the men.

As the Brits came into the edge of town, Colonel Smith called a halt to them, conferring with his officers, Mitchell, Pitcairn, and Lieutenants Gould and Barker.

"We have now reached the town of Concord. I am going to send seven companies in two groups into the town to cross the North Bridge. One group will go to the Buttrick farm and another to the Barrett farm, which is several miles away. Major Pitcairn, I am sending you into town. I want all rebel ammunition confiscated and brought back to me or destroyed; it must not stay in rebel hands. Do your job, and do it well."

"Sir, I must again ask you to reconsider this course of action," said a visibly agitated Barker. "The men are wet and exhausted; they are in no condition to engage a large contingent of the enemy. To carry on with this excursion with the entire countryside alerted to our presence is tantamount to consigning the men to the grave. Even if we succeed in locating this ammunition, which is doubtful, since I believe it has long ago been moved or hidden, how are we going to destroy it and then get out of here and back to Boston safely?"

"Lieutenant, what you are saying, sir, is very nearly insubordination. I will not hear any more of this nonsense. Our men will do the job; they will acquit themselves with honor and dignity. Now, you have your orders. Do your duty."

"Yes, sir," said Lieutenant Barker as he snapped to attention and saluted Colonel Smith.

"Grenadiers, break this door down," Major Pitcairn said as he and his troops arrived at the Jones Inn, owned by Ephraim Jones, the town jailer. The hour was seven o'clock in the morning. Pitcairn believed that Jones had hidden the town's three cannons. Pitcairn had dispatched troops to search for them while he and some grenadiers headed for the inn. Within a few minutes, the door came crashing in, and Pitcairn stormed in with his troops. Pitcairn knocked Jones down to the ground, put a pistol to his head, and cocked the gun.

"Mr. Jones, now would be the time to tell me the whereabouts of those three cannons," Pitcairn demanded.

"If you would be so kind as to remove the pistol you have so rudely placed on the side of my skull, I will lead you to them immediately," Jones replied.

"Get up, Mr. Jones, now!" Pitcairn ordered as he pulled the pistol back and uncocked it.

"Follow me," said Jones as he got up from the floor.

Out the door they went with Jones leading the way. Pitcairn had the pistol pointed at Jones's back as they went to the prison yard next door, where the cannons and accessories were located.

"Troops, commandeer these cannons and make certain they are spiked. They must be of no use to the rebels," Pitcairn ordered as he went inside the prison, where a Tory was being held. "And Mr. Jones, release my Tory friend over here," Pitcairn said, pointing at Floyd Clements, behind bars, all the while keeping his pistol trained directly at Jones's back. "He has been held in this hellhole for far too long. After he is released, we are all going to take a little walk back to the inn." Jones dutifully obeyed, releasing a grateful Clements, who eagerly shook Pitcairn's hand, thanking him profusely.

"Thank you, thank you, Major," said a beaming Clements. "I was beginning to wonder if I was ever going to be released."

"Mr. Clements, please come join me for breakfast at Mr. Jones's inn," Pitcairn said as he directed Jones back to the inn, with Clements alongside.

"Breakfast at Jones Inn?"

"Do you have an objection to my inn and my food, Mr. Clements?" Jones asked as he turned to look at Clements as they approached the inn. "As I recall, you have eaten there several times in the past."

"No, sir, not at all. The food is excellent, and I would be most grateful to partake of breakfast with the Major. It is just that, given the circumstances, I did not think I would be eating at your inn at this time."

"You will be, and you may order whatever you like; I will pay," Pitcairn said, patting Clements gently on the back as he pulled open the door and ushered Clements and Jones inside, with the gun still pointed at Jones's back.

"Thank you, Major, that is most generous."

"Not at all," Pitcairn replied, "I applaud your support of His Majesty, King George III," he said as they sat down at a table. Pitcairn carefully placed his gun on the table in front of him and proceeded to order breakfast. As they were doing so, several Brit Regulars drifted in.

"Mr. Jones, if you would be so kind," Pitcairn said, looking up at Jones.

"Yes, Major," Jones said as he picked up a bottle and began going around the room, pouring rum for several of the Regulars.

Meanwhile, at the North Bridge heading out of town, Captain Laurie no sooner crossed the bridge with one hundred troops than he sent an urgent message to Colonel Smith for reinforcements.

"Take this message immediately to Colonel Smith," Laurie said to Private James Blair. "We must have reinforcements, as many as can be spared and as soon as possible. We are in a dire predicament. If we do not get additional troops immediately, all may be lost. Make sure that the colonel understands the urgency of our situation. Do you understand?"

"Yes, sir," Blair said, and he turned and headed back over the bridge and into town. Upon locating Colonel Smith, he relayed the important message.

"Sir," said Blair as he approached Smith.

"What is it, Private?"

"I came from Captain Laurie with an urgent request for reinforcements, as many as can be spared, sir, and as soon as possible. We are greatly outnumbered, sir," Laurie said with conviction, reflecting the gravity of the predicament of Laurie's troops.

Colonel Smith, anticipating the request, turned the other way.

"Sir," said Blair again, more forcefully, "did you hear me?"

"I do not have time for such nonsense, Private," Smith replied equally as forcefully, as he briefly turned to face Blair. "Tell Captain Laurie that he has more than enough of the king's men to do the job. I will *not* hear any more of this matter," Smith said as he turned and walked away, leaving a stunned Blair in silence.

Smith then located several lead muskets, which he proceeded to dump in a pond. He also found wooden gun carriages and barrels of wooden spoons. These he had piled high and then set ablaze, but unfortunately too close to the courthouse, which was also set on fire.

"Colonel—Colonel," Mrs. Moulton, an elderly resident, said in a stern voice and almost as stern a demeanor as she approached Smith.

"What is it—ma'am?" Smith said as he turned around to see the diminutive white-haired lady staring up at him with a menacing look.

"You started this fire, which is burning our courthouse and will undoubtedly threaten our homes next. I demand that this fire be put out immediately."

Pitcairn, who was nearby and overheard the conversation, interjected, "Colonel, I will have my troops take care of the matter."

"Very well, Major."

Pitcairn ordered several of his troops to put out the fire, and they were soon joined by Concord residents who together were able to smother the blaze in a relatively short time.

However, the smoke rising from the fire alerted the American troops on the hill that trouble had struck the town.

"Colonel Barrett," Captain Davis said, "I fear that the Brits may be torching our town!"

"I fear you may be correct, Captain," replied Barrett. "We must take immediate action. I will give the order."

"Men, form a line, face the bridge, and load your weapons. Forward, across the bridge!" Barrett said exhorting the troops.

"Retreat, men; retreat across the bridge now!" Lieutenant Gould shouted to his Brit company and various other troops who were guarding the bridge. Captain Davis and minutemen from Acton led the way. The Brits scrambled back in the face of the coming onslaught from Barrett's advancing columns adopting a street-fighting style, partly forced upon them by the circumstances and partly adopted due to sheer panic. A Regular fired a shot, which set off a fusillade from the Brits. Captain Davis was shot through the heart and dropped to the ground. Barrett gathered his men into position, and

Major Buttrick, a militia leader, yelled, "Fire, fellow soldiers; for God's sake, fire!" The retort from the Americans was swift with a powerful volley that exacted a terrible toll on the redcoats.

"Hold your positions, men; hold your positions!" Lieutenant Gould screamed as he attempted to rally his troops to protect the North Bridge, but all for naught. Barrett sent half of his troops, including Charles Barnes and his neighbor and close friend, Andrew Gibson, over the bridge, pushing onward toward a stone wall up the hill where he could take up a defensive position. Gould waited for Smith to arrive, and when he finally did, Gould stopped out of musket range and then withdrew.

"Andrew, do you see what I see?" Charles asked.

"I do," Andrew responded. "Those four Brit units that were beyond the bridge came running onto it right past the militia."

"And none of our militia fired a single shot!" Charles replied, looking back on the scene.

"They look as if they were too stunned by what was taking place, to react."

"Amazing!" said Charles, shaking his head.

For all the plans and exertion that were involved in this operation to wrest ammunition from the rebels, Colonel Smith had to concede to himself that he had very little to show.

I simply cannot believe what is transpiring before my eyes. Can it be we came all this way for nothing? And the king's men, my men, could they possibly be in jeopardy—is that really possible? Yes, unbelievably, yes—as much as I do not want to admit it, the sheer number of the rabble—they are pressing on us from all sides. It is noon, and we must get moving. This would be difficult enough under normal circumstances; there will be a fight—a very nasty fight, I fear. "Men," Smith barked, pointing toward several troops, "to the flanks, immediately, on both sides of the road—do it now! The rest of you men, move out!"

Soon thereafter Barrett yelled his own directive to the militia, "Those flankers are keeping us at bay, so let us give them a taste of our style of warfare. Head for cover, men. Keep moving from tree to tree and stone to stone." Charles and Andrew, avid hunters and marksmen, as were many of the other militia, followed Barrett's directive, seeking cover, which enabled them to load and fire their muskets at close range. "Keep pressuring them; we have them on the run," Barrett added, as acrid smoke hung menacingly in the clear air, drastically reducing visibility and irritating eyes and noses. The wailing cries of the wounded added to the assault on the senses.

"Charles," said Andrew Gibson, "the Regulars are approaching Merriam's corner."

"I was thinking about that myself. That narrow bridge poses a big problem for them. Those flankers will be forced to pull in and walk along the stream, which means that they will be even more vulnerable to our fire," Charles replied as he, Andrew, and the militia closed in.

"Look at them trying to quench their thirst; they are making a fatal mistake," Andrew said to Charles.

"Yes. We are going to make that stream turn red," Charles replied as he squeezed the trigger on his weapon and dropped a redcoat into the stream just as he was about to scoop the crystal-clear water into his mouth. Sure enough, blood from the wound oozed forth into the stream, and red appeared. Before long the entire stream had become bright red from the blood and coats of the dead and wounded Regulars. The Brits scrambled and stumbled back over the bridge as they pushed on toward Lexington.

Back in Lexington, Captain Parker saw his opportunity for revenge. After the Brits had passed through, he gathered the remainder of his men, positioning them for the inevitable return of the Regulars.

Jonathan and Richard Barnes crouched behind a stone wall, along with several of their fellow militiamen.

"Men, I know that you desperately want to avenge the murders of our fellows, and you shall soon enough," said Parker as he slowly walked behind the line of his men, "but we must be patient. We will have the element of surprise. Do not—I repeat—do not fire until I give the order. Understood?"

"Yes, sir" was the reply from the men.

Within a few minutes, the harassed Brits came into view.

Jonathan nudged Richard and whispered, "There is Colonel Smith on the white horse."

"He is mine, Father, as soon as Captain Parker gives the order."

Closer and closer came the Regulars, appearing far different than they did just a few short hours ago. Instead of the proud, triumphant troops who marched victoriously out of Lexington, a now-ragged, defeated-looking group staggered back into town, not realizing the fate that awaited them. The hidden militia were getting very itchy to fire upon the hated Regulars, but they followed orders and exercised restraint. Just when it seemed that the Regulars could not get any closer, Captain Parker barked the order that the militia had been waiting for: "Fire, men; fire now!"

The men rose from behind the wall and unleashed a stinging volley of musket fire. Richard aimed, fired, and hit Colonel Smith in the thigh, knocking him from his saddle. The stunned Brits came to a standstill, leaving them in a precarious situation. Jonathan, Richard, and rest of the militia reloaded and fired again, mowing down several other Regulars in what can only be described as an amazing turn of events.

Then upon Lexington Commons, none too soon for Smith, arrived the fresh brigade of Brit troops, led by none other than Brigadier General (Lord) Hugh Earl Percy. The Regulars, spotting their rescuers, shouted for joy and ran, with strength they did not think they had, to their comrades in arms.

"Get those cannons on those hills; our flanks have to be protected right now!" Percy, after quickly assessing the difficulties, yelled out his order, pointing to the cannons in front of him and then to hills overlooking Lexington on each side of the road. This swift action had immediate results, at least temporarily stopping the militia's relentless pursuit.

Percy set up headquarters in the tavern belonging to Sergeant Munroe, using it as a hospital for the wounded and to give the bedraggled Regulars a much-needed respite.

"General," Colonel Smith said as he limped toward Percy, Smith's leg bandaged at the wound inflicted by Richard Barnes, "the rebels may use houses as cover for snipers. Request permission to fire the houses."

"Permission granted, Colonel. We will teach them that if they use these uncivilized, guerrilla-type tactics with houses as cover, they will pay a dear price."

"Excellent, sir," replied Smith, "I will order the firing of three suspicious houses immediately."

The order was given, and within a few minutes, the three houses were all ablaze.

"Dr. Warren, I have a plan," said a confident Brigadier General William Heath as he met Warren in Watertown, having left his farm in Roxburg when he was informed of fighting in Lexington and Concord.

"General Heath, you have a plan?" Warren said as the two men saluted each other and then firmly shook hands. "A plan to harass the Brits?"

"I do indeed. Let me show you what I have in mind," said Heath enthusiastically as he unrolled a scroll he was carrying. It outlined a skirmishing plan whereby there would be a moving ring of fire around the Brits. Units would continuously be replaced with new units, replenishing ammunition while watering and feeding the troops.

"That looks impressive on paper, General, but do you really think it will work?"

"I do, Dr. Warren. While the Brits are unprotected and exhausted, our men will be refreshed, replenished, and protected. I am quite certain that the Brits will regret that they ever left Boston."

"All right, General. Time to put your plan into action. I will join you."

After receiving the blessing of Warren, Heath arrived in Lexington, took charge of the militia, and immediately began implementing his plan.

"Keep it up, men; keep up the pressure on them. You have them on the run," said Warren, as he walked behind the lines with Heath, exhorting the militia to keep on the offense with the retreating Brits, who Percy had led out of Lexington on the road to Boston.

Jonathan and Richard and the Lexington militia joined in with the circle of troops, firing, reloading, and firing, all while moving in a seamless flow around the harassed Regulars, finally to be replaced by another unit. As Heath had confided to Warren, the militia were able to replenish their ammunition, rest, and quench their thirst. The same could not be said for Percy's men, who were being fired upon from all sides, killing several of them, to the horror of Percy and Smith.

"Father, I can see it," said Richard as he wiped his brow on his sleeve and took a long gulp of cold water from his canteen.

"What can you see?" asked Jonathan, happy to have the much-needed break that Heath's ring afforded.

"Fear and panic. I can see fear and panic in their eyes."

"You are quite right, son. But we must keep the pressure on them as Dr. Warren said. Remember, they are professional soldiers."

"Father, look at those Brits coming out of those houses. They are murdering and plundering our innocent citizens!" Richard exclaimed, as the Brits moved into Menotomy.

"This despicable behavior is from what is supposed to be the most civilized fighting force in the world. We must make them pay for this most unseemly behavior," Jonathan replied.

※

"General, the rebels have thrown the boards of the Cambridge Bridge into the river," a distraught Colonel Smith said to Percy.

"Good Lord! Then we must reach Charlestown."

"That means crossing the narrow and treacherous Charlestown Neck, General."

"I am aware of that, Colonel, but do you see any other choice?"

"No, sir."

"Send the troops down the Charlestown Road, immediately, while continuing to fire the cannons at the militia. We must reach safety soon, or we will all perish. That is an order!"

"Yes, sir!"

※

"This is it, Father; now we have them!" Richard exclaimed excitedly, upon seeing Colonel Thomas Pickering arrive on the scene with troops gathered from Salem and Marblehead, Massachusetts.

"Yes, but Pickering must prevent their passing."

"Father, surely he will stop them—oh, no! What is Pickering doing! I cannot believe what I am seeing!"

"The man does not have the intestinal fortitude to stand his ground," Jonathan said, with complete disgust.

"Colonel, how could this possibly have happened?" said an outraged Jonathan, confronting Pickering after Pickering had let

Percy pass without firing a single shot. Within minutes of passing Pickering, Percy and his men had reached Charlestown and later collapsed on Bunker Hill, where the guns of the HMS *Somerset* assured their safety. "We had the Brits caught between our forces. All you needed to do was stand your ground, yet you let them get through to safety and without even firing a shot. Almost certainly we would have forced their surrender. What a prize that would have been for our cause, yet they now live to fight another day. How can this be? It almost appears to be treasonous, sir!" Jonathan's face was red, the veins bulging in his neck as he practically screamed the words at Pickering. Richard, standing next to Jonathan, while also very upset with Pickering, was mortified at his father, never having seen him act like this before.

"Father, please—calm down," Richard said as he placed his hand on Jonathan's shoulder.

"You better listen to your son," Pickering said. "How dare you insult a superior officer or question my loyalty. General Heath ordered me to stand by."

"I did no such thing," said a visibly agitated Heath as he approached them, "and you know it. I must say Lieutenant Barnes got it quite right. This is nearly treason, Colonel. I could have you court-martialed. I would suggest you retract that claim."

"Sir," Pickering said, saluting, turning, and walking away, without a retraction.

"Thank you, sir, for supporting me," said a now-much-calmer and in-control Jonathan. "I apologize for my behavior. I simply could not believe what was happening, especially after all we went through and suffered today."

"No apology is necessary," said Heath. It is that man's behavior that was inappropriate and cannot be tolerated. And then to say I ordered him to stand by."

"We all know the truth, sir."

"Father," said Richard.

"What, son?"

"I am proud of you."

The damage was severe to both sides, especially to the Brits. Gage, who was across the Charles River, was inconsolable as he observed his beloved Regulars struggle up Bunker Hill, disheveled, exhausted, dispirited, and defeated. Downcast, he wondered, *How am I ever going to be able to explain this to His Majesty King George?*

10

"Father, I am deeply concerned about the safety of Victoria and the Finches. To tell you the truth, they have been on my mind for some time. But now I fear that Gage will take out his frustrations upon our people in Boston. While we suffered losses today, there can be no doubt that we put a whipping on the Brits," said a worried Richard to Jonathan.

"I share your concerns, son. I too have been worried about the Finches, particularly as it became increasingly obvious that Gage's men were taking a beating. Tell me, what do you have in mind?" said Jonathan, with a furrowed brow, anticipating his son's response.

"Sneaking into the city to talk to them about getting out and bringing them back to live with our family in Lexington."

"That is what I thought you would say," Jonathan replied, shaking his head. "I completely support the idea of them coming to live with our family, but do you realize the difficulty getting into and out of Boston at this time and what the Brits will do if you are captured?"

"I know how to get in and out, and besides, if I go right away, they will not be ready for me. I have to do something. I cannot stay here, knowing the danger the Finches may be facing."

"There is no sense arguing with you," said a resigned Jonathan. "Truth is, I would do the same if I were you. Let us seek Captain Parker's permission."

"Captain Parker," Richard said as he and Jonathan approached their superior officer.

"Private Barnes, how may I help you?"

"Sir, request permission to go to Boston to warn the Finches of their need to leave as soon as possible."

"Private, I appreciate your concern for that family. I know how close your families are to one another, but I do not have the authority to grant you permission. You will have to take this directly to General Heath. If it is any benefit to you, you may tell him that you have my blessing."

"Request permission to see General Heath," said Richard as he approached Heath's attaché.

"He is busy right now, Private; come back later."

Before Richard could say anything, Heath, who had seen Richard and Jonathan approaching, came to greet them. Richard and Jonathan quickly stood at attention.

"Gentlemen, at ease, what may I do for you now?"

"General, I just spoke with Captain Parker to ask him permission to enter Boston to speak with the Finches about leaving the town as soon as possible. I fear for them in light of the licking we gave the Brits today. Captain Parker gave his blessing but said it was your decision."

"Private, I know them and believe that they are capable of fending for themselves; however, I understand your concern for their safety. They certainly are a family that could be targeted by Gage for retribution, and if anything would happen to them, it could be a blow to our cause. I am going to grant you permission. Gather whatever information you can about the enemy. Report back to me personally at Watertown as soon as you complete your mission."

"Thank you, sir."

With that, Jonathan and Richard took their leave from Heath.

"All right, son, you best get going. Please convey my heartfelt thoughts to the Finches and let them know that I fully support your position. Be careful."

"Annabelle, please pass the ham and potatoes," William said to his wife as the family gathered for a late supper. The Finches knew that Gage's troops had set out for Lexington and Concord, but they had not yet heard what had transpired on this fateful day.

As Annabelle passed the plate, she said, "William, I am very worried about Jonathan, Richard, Eleanor, and the children."

"Me too, Father," Victoria agreed. "I must confess that I have been anxious about Richard all day. With Richard and Mr. Barnes in the Lexington militia, no doubt they were directly in the path of Gage's troops."

"Ladies, I share your concern. I will send Judah out first thing in the morning to Jean Paul's to gather any information he may have about what transpired today."

Eleanor Barnes was assisting in caring for the wounded in the Barneses' family general store back in Lexington, which she volunteered for use as a temporary hospital. Eleanor spent most of the grueling day assisting the town's lone doctor in cleaning and dressing the wounds of the militia, who were brought to the store from up and down the road traveled by the troops. The store had been promptly converted to a hospital shortly after the Brits left town, leaving behind carnage on the Green earlier that morning. While she was tending to the wounded, she left her children Margaret and James with her parents, Frederick and Deborah Williams, who also resided in Lexington. When the Brits came back through town shortly after noon while being harassed by the militia, Eleanor saw the number of wounded continuing to climb as the battle raged all around them.

As is frequently the case in these situations, the doctor had to make difficult decisions as to whom to treat, how extensively to treat them, and in what order to treat them; there were simply too many wounded and far too little help.

"Eleanor," Dr. Walmsley said as he pointed to her right, "you have done what you could for the soldier you are treating. The one I am pointing at needs your immediate attention."

"But, Doctor, if I leave this soldier, he will almost certainly die," Eleanor replied, with a pleading look on her face. "I cannot abandon him now."

"You can, and you must. As I said before, you have done everything you could for him. He will die whether you continue to tend to him or not. This man"—again the doctor pointed to the patient to her right—"has a chance to live if you will take care of him now. Do you understand?"

"Yes, Doctor, I understand—I understand," a weary and somber Eleanor said, nodding her head slowly, sweat dropping from her brow.

"I am very sorry, my dear. We cannot save them all. We must do what we can to save some. That means hard choices, choices that simply have to be made. Now please get to work on that soldier. Time is wasting, and the one thing he does not have is time."

"I will take care of him."

"Good. Now I can take care of this poor soldier over here," the doctor said as he wandered off to the other side of the store.

Richard managed to sneak into Boston around eight o'clock in the evening. After quietly taking back alleys and staying close to houses and buildings, avoiding guards, he arrived at the Finch residence about thirty minutes later. He knocked on the back door, which was next to the kitchen.

"Judah, who dat at dah door?" a startled Grace asked. Grace had finished cleaning up from the evening meal and was getting ready for the morning.

"I do not know, Grace," Judah said, peering out the window next to the door at the figure, shrouded in darkness. "I will tell Mr. William," he said as he swiftly went to the parlor, where he knew his master would be at this hour.

"Mister William," Judah said, when he reached the open parlor door. William was seated in his chair by the fireplace with a glass of rum in his hand.

"Yes, Judah, what is it?"

"Mister William, there's a-knockin' on the back door by the kitchen."

"Knocking on the back door at this hour? Are you certain?"

"Yes, sir, Mister William, I am certain."

"Then go out the front door and go quietly around back. Take this pistol," William said as he reached inside his coat pocket. "It is loaded but only has one shot. Be careful."

"Yes, sir," said Judah as he took the pistol, turned, and headed for the front door. Judah stealthily slid along the side of the house with the pistol in his right hand. As he got close to the end of the house, he heard the continuing knocking.

"Mr. Finch, Judah, it is me, Richard Barnes," Richard said as he continued pounding.

Judah heard this just as he reached the back of the house. He quickly put the pistol away and rounded the corner.

"Mister Richard!" Judah said excitedly as he approached Richard, with a big grin on his face.

Richard startled and jumped back.

"Mister Richard, are you all right?"

"Judah! You scared me!"

"I am sorry, Mister Richard."

"It is all right, Judah—it is just that I have been knocking on the door for quite some time. I expected someone to answer the door, not come around the corner of the house."

"I told Mister William that there was somebody a-knockin' on the back door. He said, 'at this hour?' I said yes, and he sent me to see who it was back here. He gave me this pistol," Judah said, pulling it out and showing Richard.

"Whoa, Judah! Be careful!" Richard said as he pushed the small barrel away.

"I am sorry, Mister Richard. I did not mean to scare you again," Judah said as he put the pistol in his coat pocket.

"Judah. May we go in the house now?"

"Oh, yes, sir—come with me."

Judah led Richard around to the front of the house and through the front door.

"Mister William, it was Mister Richard who was doing the knockin'," Judah said as Richard emerged from behind Judah.

William nearly jumped out of his seat in the parlor and quickly walked across the room to Richard, who was standing in the entrance. William grabbed Richard's right hand in both of his hands, shaking it heartily.

"Richard, Richard—it is so wonderful you are here! Please come to the kitchen. You must be absolutely starving."

"I am, sir, but if I could make a request—"

"Victoria?"

"Yes, sir."

"I will have Judah get her right away. Meanwhile come with me. Grace will make something for you to eat in no time."

"Judah, please have Victoria come to the kitchen right away, but do not tell her why."

"Yes, sir, Mister William."

William and Richard headed for the kitchen as William inquired as to the day's events.

"I must tell you that Victoria, well everyone, expressed concern for you and your entire family while we were eating supper. We were quite worried about you and your father, especially figuring that you two were probably directly in the path of the redcoats on their mission. Were you?"

"Yes, sir, as a matter of fact, we were. The Brits arrived at Lexington Green early in the morning."

"Hold that thought, son," William said as they arrived in the kitchen. "Grace, please rustle up some of your best stew and biscuits for Richard and also bring him a big glass of cider."

"Mistuh Richard? Yes, sir, Mastuh William, I'se be glad to—we was all worried 'bout you'se today."

"Thank you, Grace. I truly appreciate your concern."

"Richard! Richard!" shouted Victoria as she ran to him and threw her arms around him, hugging him and kissing his neck. "Oh, Richard, I was so worried about you!"

"And I too am worried about you and your family," Richard said as he looked into her big, beautiful, moist eyes.

"What do you mean by that, son? That you are worried about our family?" asked William, with a quizzical look.

"Well, it is probably best if I first relate the events of this incredible day."

"Yes," said William, "you said the Brits arrived early this morning at Lexington Green."

By now William, Richard, and Victoria had moved into the dining room and were joined by Annabelle, Joshua, and Lydia. As they gathered at the dining-room table after greetings to the rest of the Finch family, Richard continued with his recitation of the day's events.

Just then Grace emerged from the kitchen with a steaming bowl of stew, a plate of her big flaky biscuits, and a large glass of hard cider. She sat them down right in front of Richard.

"Thank you, Grace, it looks and smells wonderful."

"You'se most welcome. Please try it. If it needs a pinch of salt or pepper, I'se will git it for you."

Richard grabbed a spoon and eagerly delved into the thick, rich stew as everyone watched in anticipation. He put the spoon next to his nostrils and smelled the enticing aroma of a hearty, well-cooked dish.

"Mm, mm, that smells so good," he said, and then he practically gulped down the contents.

A big smile creased his face. "Delicious—absolutely delicious; does not need a thing—you cannot possibly improve on perfection!"

Grace had a wide smile, bigger than Richard had just flashed.

"Grace, I dare say your smile is even better than the stew!"

"Oh, stop it, Mistuh Richard, you'se 'barassin' me's now. If'n you'se still hungry afta you'se done wiff dat, dey's moh where dat comes from."

Richard continued eating the stew and biscuits in between gulps of cider.

"Before I restart my story, I promised Father that I would extend his warmest greetings. As I was saying, as the Brits approached the green, Major Pitcairn screamed at us to throw down our arms. I was petrified after hearing him say those words in such a commanding way. Before I could do anything, the Brits were moving closer and closer. Suddenly, our Captain Parker made a quick decision, realizing that our situation was hopeless. He ordered, 'Militia disperse! Militia disperse!' Understand he did not say, 'Lay down your arms.'

"Immediately my father and I, as well as other militiamen, heeded the order and began falling back, taking our arms with us. Then it happened. A shot rang out. I swear that it came from behind their lines. It seemed as if, pardon my expression, all hell broke loose. A volley by the Regulars as they continued to push across the green had all of us running for our lives. It was followed by a bayonet charge. The Regulars were out of control. Jonas Parker, kinsman to our captain, was wounded and on the ground, reloading his gun, when he was fatally bayoneted by the so-called civilized redcoats. I shall never forget it as long as I live," said Richard, his lower lip quivering and eyes beginning to well up.

"Oh, Richard," said Victoria as she wrapped her arm in his and put her head on his shoulder, "it must have been absolutely awful."

"Yes, dear, it was—it truly was."

After a few moments, Victoria raised her head and released his arm.

Richard gathered himself and continued, "Two other militiamen were shot in the back. I thought all of us would be cut down, but thank God, Colonel Smith arrived on the scene and immediately had his drummers play 'Down Arms.' He had to give the order again and again before the Regulars finally heeded the call. When they left with a volley and three cheers, it set my blood to boiling. Eight of our comrades had been killed—no, murdered—I believe it was nothing less than murder."

"I must agree," William said as he gently nodded his head, a grim look on his face.

Richard related how Captain Parker rallied the militia after the massacre, lifted their spirits, and got them in position to inflict severe damage to the Brits on their way back through to Boston. He went on to tell them about the militia being quietly crouched behind the stone wall eagerly awaiting the Brits return and how he rose up when Colonel Smith came within range and shot him in the thigh, knocking him off his horse.

A grin creased William's face as he heard this story. "Well done—well done."

Richard continued on, explaining that Brigadier General Heath arrived on the scene, took control, and related his "ring of fire" plan, which resonated with all the troops.

"General Heath's arrival was vital, especially since the Regulars were saved with the arrival of Brigadier General Hugh Earl Percy and his reinforcements."

"Father, there is that name again," said a suddenly engaged Joshua. "It seemed clear with his late arrival at Gage's house that something big was up, and for him and his troops to come to the rescue..."

"Is only fitting," said William, finishing Joshua's thought.

"Sir?" Richard said, with a questioning look.

Before William could respond, Joshua related his story about seeing Percy at Gage's house.

"I rushed home to tell father. Father said he thought a big event was imminent, with everything else that was going on around town," Joshua said.

"What was going on?" Richard queried.

"Gage detached about seven hundred of his elite troops for special training, under the command of Colonel Francis Smith of the Tenth Foot," Joshua answered.

"That training, along with the heightened alert that Jean Paul and his lieutenants have been under this spring, well it seemed obvious that Gage was planning something," Victoria added.

"Then when Percy arrived at Gage's house, it was evident that the time had arrived," Joshua said.

"I woke Victoria at daybreak and told her to dress quickly and go with Judah and pay a visit to Jean Paul to relay to him my suspicions," William said.

"Pardon my saying so, sir, but that sounds dangerous," Richard said, with concern etched on his face.

"I agree; it was," said William, "which is why I made sure that Judah took all the back streets and alleys and kept an eye out for redcoat spies."

"Did you see any spies, Judah?" Richard asked, turning toward him.

"Yes, sir, Mister Richard, I saw one," Judah, who had been sitting in a separate chair in the dining room with Grace, ready to assist with the needs of the family, replied.

"The more important question is, did he see you?"

"I think so, though I do not know for certain. I tried to turn the carriage quickly when I saw him."

"Judah turned very quickly," Victoria jumped in. "This might have been a dangerous mission, but we had to get the information to Jean Paul."

"What did Jean Paul say?" Richard asked.

"He said it was consistent with information he received from his other sources, including from Francois, who said that one of Jayne Kitt's ladies at Maggie's told him she overheard two Brit Regulars say there was soon going to be a big event occurring."

"Very interesting," Richard pondered.

"Richard," we have gotten a bit off track with your story as you have been filled in about what was happening with us. You were saying about Percy and his arrival."

"Oh yes, Percy," Richard said, collecting his thoughts. He went on to relay Percy's arrival on the scene, telling them his assessment of Percy, which prompted William to nod his head in agreement.

Richard finished his stew and looked over at Grace, who had been listening with rapt attention. Without a word being spoken, Grace smiled and said, "Comin' right up," as she reached for Richard's bowl.

Richard went on relating the success of the ring of fire and, if not for Pickering's strange behavior, who knows how much of a blow would have been inflicted on the king's finest. Grace set another steaming bowl of her best stew in front of him. Richard attacked this bowl with nearly the same vigor as the first.

"Father and I went to see Pickering following this incident, and Father confronted him."

William's right eyebrow arched upon hearing his old friend confronted a superior officer. "Interesting," he said, more as a statement about his thoughts than a question.

"Father was angry—I do not recall ever seen him that mad before. His face was red; the veins on his neck were bulging—he nearly accused Pickering of treason. I was concerned about what could happen to father from making accusations against a superior officer, so I told him to calm down."

"Then what happened?" William asked.

"Pickering claimed that Heath had ordered him to stand by. It was fortuitous that General Heath approached us just after Pickering told us that story, and Heath denied it."

"What did Pickering say?"

"Nothing. He stood there for a second and then said, 'Sir,' saluted, turned, and walked away."

"Without a retraction?"

"Without a retraction. General Heath said he could have him court-martialed."

"And Jonathan?"

"He calmed down and apologized to me, but Heath backed him up and said that he got the whole thing quite right."

"I am sure he did," said William. "He always does."

"Yes, he does. I told him I was proud of him."

"As well you should be."

Richard continued eating and sipping on his cider. "That sums up the day's events, the best I can remember them."

"Richard, I commend you, your father, and the militia on a job well done," Joshua remarked.

"Thank you very much, Joshua. You do not know how much I appreciate that."

"Oh, Richard, I thank God that you are here and that you are unhurt," Victoria added as she turned his head toward her and looked into his eyes.

"I thank God also, my dear, that I am here with you and your family. Many of the militiamen whom I knew were not so fortunate."

"Richard, do you know anything about your mother, brother, and sister?" Annabelle inquired.

"No, Mrs. Finch, I have not heard anything since all these events transpired today. However, Mother told me last night that she planned on assisting Dr. Walmsley if there was need. She said the general store would be used as a temporary hospital if there were casualties. I am sure she was there shortly after the initial fighting and probably spent the rest of the day there, tending to the wounded."

"And James and Margaret?"

"Mother said that they would go to my grandparents in Lexington."

Richard finished up the last of his second bowl of stew and second big biscuit.

"Grace, I am completely stuffed and could not be happier."

"I'se so glad, Mistuh Richard. With a day's like's you'se been through, you'se needed all the nourishment you'se could git."

"Well, I got it. Thank you."

"Richard, when you came here, you said you were worried about us. I assume, in light of your story, your concern is due to the casualties sustained to Gage's troops by the lowly Americans."

"Yes, sir, you are right. I am very worried that Gage and his men may try to retaliate at Bostonians for the humiliation suffered by the Brit troops. You, being a prominent patriotic family, would be high on the list, in my opinion. And now that you have told me that Victoria and Judah may have been spotted by a redcoat spy, I am that much more concerned for your safety. I have come to implore you to leave the city and come to temporarily live in Lexington. Father supports my position. The rooms above the store will accommodate Grace and other female servants. Judah can stay in the outbuilding behind the garden, used for storage. Father has his office there. It is quite roomy and has a stove, which keeps it comfortable during the winter. Father even has a bed there for those few occasions when my parents have a disagreement."

"I am familiar with the rooms above the store and the outbuilding. The accommodations are more than adequate, and the offer is very generous, but we cannot accept. General Gage is well known to us. I am grateful to you for your brave service to our country and for the courage you displayed coming here tonight, but Boston is our home, and we are not about to be forced out—at least not yet."

"With all due respect, sir, if a Brit or Brit sympathizer or loyalist spotted Victoria and Judah heading toward Jean Paul's house, it is all the more reason to flee and flee now."

"I appreciate your thoughts and concern for us, but the answer, at least for now, is no."

"Yes, sir. Before I leave Boston, I must gather information about the enemy and report back to General Heath upon my return."

"It is much too late to be going out and about on an intelligence-gathering mission, so I insist that you spend the night here, with us," Annabelle said authoritatively.

"Yes, ma'am, thank you; I could use the rest, but I must get off early tomorrow morning."

"I would suggest that you pay an early visit to Jean Paul. With his network, he will almost certainly have the information that you need. Just be very careful. I have a feeling that the Brit spies will be thick," William said.

"I will, Mr. Finch. Yes, Jean Paul will almost certainly have the information I need to deliver to the general."

"I'se have some warm biscuits, brown bread, bacon, and hot coffee ready for you'se first thing in the mornin'," said Grace.

"That would be wonderful, Grace. I am most appreciative to all of you for your hospitality," Richard said as he looked directly into the adoring eyes of Victoria.

"Richard, one more thing before you leave. Our house will assuredly be closely watched by the Brits. In the future, you must be exceedingly careful. When you come to the back door, rap on it with three quick, hard raps, followed by a brief silence, and three more quick, hard raps, then we will know that it is you. If no one answers, wait several seconds, and repeat the sequence again and again, if necessary, until someone comes. Do you understand?" William asked.

"I understand, sir, three quick, hard raps, then silence, and then three more quick, hard raps."

"That is correct. Do you have it, Judah?"

"Yes, sir, Mister William."

"Now off to bed for you, Richard. You need your rest," said Annabelle.

Early in the morning, Richard met with Jean Paul, who informed him that the preliminary indications were that the Brits were truly devastated by the "successful operation." It was in reality a humiliating defeat, one that would undoubtedly have serious repercussions for the leadership at the top.

"Do you think that you, the Finches, and the people of Boston will be facing the wrath of Gage and his minions?"

"That is a good question, Monsieur Richard. Only time will tell, but I do not believe that we are in any immediate danger."

"I certainly hope you are right. With Victoria and Judah coming to you about Mr. Finch's suspicions, well if ole Gage suspects that they tipped you off about the operation, I am just worried about possible retribution to them and to you."

"I understand, monsieur, and your fears may be well founded, but I believe that General Gage was stunned by the day's events. It appears, from the information that I have received from reliable sources, he realizes the magnitude of what took place and the rather severe consequences that will almost certainly follow. He has a lot of explaining to do to King George. I do not think that he is concerned about us right now. That, of course, is always subject to change."

"I will trust your judgment on this. I appreciate the information and your insights, and I will pass them on to General Heath."

Richard quietly slipped out of town and headed straight for Watertown. He met briefly with General Heath to inform him of what he had learned from Jean Paul.

"So General Gage realizes that the so-called successful operation was in fact anything but that. Thank you, Richard, for the information. It is good to know that the Brit command agrees with our assessment. I am sorry that you were disappointed regarding the Finches, though I cannot say that I am surprised. Things may change in time. I believe this was the beginning."

"Of war, sir?"

"Yes, of war."

"Gentlemen, I must go," said Dr. Church to Revere and Dr. Warren, in Watertown. Dr. Warren was on General Ward's staff and enlisted justices of the peace to take affidavits from eyewitnesses to document Brit cruelty during the battle. Church, who was helping Dr. Warren with the enlistment process, had blood on his stocking, which he proceeded to show Paul Revere, informing him that it was from the blood of a dying militiaman whom he led in battle. Revere was dubious. Church decided to head for Boston.

"And where is it that you are heading, Dr. Church?" asked Revere. "If I may ask."

"You may, Mr. Revere. I am leaving for our fair city immediately. I have business that I must attend to."

"And what business might that be, Dr. Church?" asked Revere again, this time with a tinge of sarcasm in his tone. "If I may ask again."

"You may again. Why, the business of our glorious cause, of course. Boston needs me."

"Do not be a fool, Church," Warren pleaded. "You must know that if the Brits catch you, they will surely hang you."

"I assure you that I will be careful, very careful."

As Church left, Warren turned to Revere and said, "Paul, I have known Church for a long time and have never had cause to question his loyalty, but this makes absolutely no sense, not for someone as prominent as he is. Given the situation, only a complete fool would dare to venture back into town at this time—unless—I wonder what he is really doing. Somehow I am struggling with it being our glorious cause."

"I agree with you, Doctor," Revere nodded, a skeptical look on his face.

"And I just received word from Jean Paul that casts doubt upon the loyalty of Dr. Wilson," Warren added.

"The loyalty of Wilson is in question?"

"Jean Paul thinks that Wilson may have met with a go-between, relaying information about our awareness of the pending Brit operation. While there is no direct proof, Wilson was observed, by Becky Braun, leaving his house late at night right after she relayed some details to him about a meeting between me and Jean Paul earlier that evening."

"Do you think Church was the go-between?" asked Revere.

"Though there is no solid proof that there even was a meeting, I think the evidence points to it. And, given the close relationship between Wilson and Church—"

"Let us just say that our other good doctor friends will bear some close watching."

"Abigail, it certainly appears to me that the Brits gave no quarter," John Adams said to his wife upon his return from a ride along the battle route, surveying the scene of destruction. Adams was deeply distressed by what he observed. "They burned houses to weed out snipers and undoubtedly entered houses to do as they pleased. If I am not here and you sense any danger, I want you to grab up the children and immediately fly to the woods. I do not trust the 'civility' of the king's men. I have no doubt of their desire to capture you and inflict serious harm. Understand?"

"Yes. I will gather the children, and we will flee immediately."

"Our troops were magnificent!" said an excited, beaming Dr. Mark Wilson as he and Becky Braun sat down to dinner at his stately mansion. Becky was taken aback by his false enthusiasm. *It is false, is it not?* She tried not to act surprised.

"Oh, why, yes, they were…they were indeed," said Becky as she bit into a delicious yam.

"You do not sound very convincing, my dear," said Wilson skeptically as he looked at her, chewing a piece of succulent sugar ham, followed by a sip of water.

"Oh, but I am, Mark," Becky said, now concerned that despite her efforts, her true thoughts might have shown through. She decided to go on the offensive. "From what I have gleaned from my father and Francois, the Brits had a very bad time of it as they left Concord to return to Boston, and if not for General Percy and perhaps our Colonel Pickering, the Regulars might have been forced to surrender."

The effect on Wilson was exactly as hoped. His skepticism seemed to vanish in the wave of her zeal and sanguine delivery.

"Yes, Percy saved the Brits' day, but Pickering's actions were appalling. He should be court-martialed," Wilson said, with apparent conviction.

"I agree completely," Becky said as she continued to partake of the exquisite meal prepared by Wilson's French chef.

"They can claim victory, but the truth is it was a resounding and humiliating defeat."

"It was, and I am sure that there will be consequences for General Gage."

"Oh, indeed," Wilson said slowly, lips slightly pursed and with a slight nod of the head. "The king will not take this so-called victory lightly."

Who is this man? I know what I saw that night, but he sounds so convincing. Could I be mistaken? Is he really a great patriot—or perhaps just a great actor?

11

While the army and officers were gathering at Watertown, the delegates to the Second Continental Congress began the trek back to Philadelphia.

Hancock and Samuel Adams left together and arrived in New York to a tumultuous welcome. Thousands of people, including militia members and grenadiers, lined the road to greet them and show appreciation for who they were and what they meant to the cause.

Jonathan sent Richard, who had become adept at sneaking into Boston, to fetch William and Lydia to accompany him back to Philadelphia. Jonathan and William had discussed the travel schedule and itinerary well in advance, and an added bonus was that John Adams would be joining them.

"Richard, I am so grateful your father is willing to take William and Lydia again on his long journey back to Congress," Annabelle said, upon Richard's arrival at the Finch home. Please make sure to convey to him and your mother my deepest gratitude for all that they have done and are doing for my family."

"Yes, ma'am, I surely will." Richard nodded.

"Oh, and Richard…"

"Ma'am?"

"The same goes for you."

"I am happy to be of service."

"Lydia, are you ready to go? Do you have all your things in order?" William asked.

"Yes, Father, I have been anticipating this day for weeks!"

"Very well. I will get Judah, and he will load your bags and mine on Richard's carriage, and we can leave right away. We should reach Lexington before dark."

Within a few minutes, Judah had the carriage fully loaded, and it was again time for good-byes.

"Please travel safely," Annabelle said as she hugged first her husband and then her daughter. "And please write often."

"Do not worry about our journey. Our travels will be safe and enjoyable. Jonathan and John Adams will be wonderful company. I am looking forward to the actual trip, almost as much as returning to Congress and Philadelphia."

Victoria, who had joined them for the farewells, added, "I will greatly miss you both but look forward to hearing, on your return, about all the things you experienced. This is so exciting, especially for you, Lydia!" She hugged her sister tightly. Both sisters shed tears. "Perhaps you will even meet a man who is handsome and interesting."

"Now that would be exciting!" Lydia said, pulling back from Victoria's embrace.

"Time to go, ladies," said William. And with that, they climbed aboard the carriage and waved good-bye.

"This is a place that I almost do not know anymore," said Benjamin Franklin to John Adams. Franklin had arrived back in Philadelphia in early May after a voyage of nearly one and a half months. It had been an exhausting trip for the now sixty-nine-year-old who had been living in London for nearly eighteen years. Franklin and Adams walked around the area near the State House, between Fifth and Sixth Streets, the Congress having moved there from Carpenters' Hall. Franklin continued, "John, this town has become a thriving metropolis with new buildings that have sprung up everywhere. My, my, there are so many people here now."

"Ben, it has been eighteen years since you left Philadelphia, eighteen long years. All this did not happen overnight. When you left, I was a young man of twenty-one years."

"You are right, John; it has been a very long time. It just seems somewhat foreign to me. I hope that I am not too out of touch."

"You will adjust soon enough. Just having you here is a wonderful boost to our cause—a real blessing. You know the Brits better than anyone. That could prove to be invaluable."

"I suppose you are right. I do know the Brits quite well after having lived among them for so long. While I trust the basic goodness of the people, the king and his Parliament—now that is another matter."

"It does appear that King George has become a despot."

"In my opinion that is an accurate assessment. The former benevolent monarchs of our mother country appear to be just a fond memory. This monarch and his minions have made their intentions perfectly clear—not just to punish Boston, the Bay Colony, and indeed all America for the destruction of the tea but to bring us to heel and squelch out the last vestiges of our dear, sweet liberty. I do not see any turning back now."

"Nor do I. We cannot and will not let them succeed, Ben. There is too much at stake."

"You betrayed me to that rebel, Dr. Warren. How could you do this to me?" An angry General Thomas Gage said to his American wife, Margaret.

"Whatever are you talking about, Thomas?"

"Do not lie to me, Margaret. You know very well what I am talking about. I know that you and Warren are friendly. I strongly suspect that he came to you for information about our plans for the excursion."

"I repeat, Thomas, I do not know what you are talking about."

"I could not understand who warned the rebels of what was about to take place. I was writing a report to secretary of war, Lord Burlington about what had transpired, when a terrible thought occurred to me. I remembered you said to me that you hoped I would never be an instrument of sacrificing the lives of your countrymen. I could not, did not want to believe it, but I knew it must be you."

"Thomas—"

"Enough! I have heard enough of your denials—your lies! I will book passage for you on the next available ship bound for London. Good-bye, Margaret!"

"Dr. Church, will you please take this note to Paul? I know he needs it right away," said Rachel Revere, Paul's wife, as she placed £125 together with a tender note in the hand of Dr. Benjamin Church.

"I am very flattered, madam. Rest assured that they will be delivered to your beloved forthwith," Church replied.

"Doctor, you have been gone for two days. Where have you been?" asked Revere.

"Upon returning to Boston, I was arrested and taken to Gage's headquarters for questioning. I never expected this to happen."

"How could you possibly have gotten out so soon?"

"I have friends in high places. It did not take long to secure my release."

Revere, stared at Church with a look on his face that betrayed his thoughts.

"You do not believe me, sir," Church replied rather tersely.

"That you have friends in high places, yes, of that I am certain. As to being arrested and taken in for questioning—."

Before Revere finished his reply, Church, showing obvious disgust, turned and walked away without delivering Rachel's £125 and tender note.

❧

"The Congress will come to order," Peyton Randolph of Virginia, president of the First Continental Congress loudly proclaimed as he pounded the gavel over and over.

"Gentlemen—please."

Finally order was restored, and then Randolph continued.

"Let the record reflect that the Second Continental Congress is now officially in session."

"The first matter of business is the election of a president to preside over this Congress."

"Mr. President," said Jonathan as he rose to address the Congress.

"The chair recognizes the Honorable Jonathan Barnes, delegate from Massachusetts."

"I move for the election of the Honorable Peyton Randolph of Virginia as president of the Second Continental Congress."

"Is there a second to the motion?"

"I second the motion of the Honorable Jonathan Barnes," said John Adams, rising from his seat.

"There is a motion from the Honorable Jonathan Barnes and a second on the floor from the Honorable John Adams, delegate from Massachusetts, to elect Peyton Randolph of Virginia as president of the Second Continental Congress. Is there any discussion?"

Randolph patiently waited several seconds, hearing nothing.

Jonathan continued, "Mr. President, I move that the nominations be closed and call the question."

"There is a motion on the floor to close the nominations. Is there a second?"

"I also second this motion of the Honorable Jonathan Barnes," John Adams said.

"Any discussion on the motion and second to close the nominations and call the question? Hearing none, the nominations are closed, and the question is called. All in favor of the motion say aye."

The entire Congress said aye.

"All opposed, nay. Hearing no opposition, the motion has passed. Peyton Randolph is unanimously elected president of the Second Continental Congress."

Shortly thereafter, Randolph was asked by the Virginia House of Burgesses to preside there. He accepted the position, leaving the presidential post empty. The delegates considered Henry Middleton of South Carolina, but he decided not to accept owing to ill health. Hancock was next to be considered. Interestingly, his credibility and stature among the delegates increased significantly when it was learned that General Gage issued pardons to all but Sam Adams and John Hancock. Hancock was elected and installed as president of the Second Continental Congress.

Jonathan Barnes did not believe a word of rumors that were swirling about Congress that Dr. Benjamin Franklin was a spy and made it known to every delegate he spoke with. Calling the rumors "utter nonsense," he lambasted all who disseminated them, declaring the perpetrators to be petty and jealous of the "great man who had done more to advance the cause of mankind and the standing of this country in the eyes of the world than all the other delegates combined." Jonathan was eager to formally meet Franklin, whom he revered as a living legend.

"John, I cannot believe that such an august body as this would stoop so low as to attempt to destroy our most famous and loyal citizen, all, in my opinion, over petty jealousy. Just because he rarely contributes during the sessions, though some believe he should be passionately engaged at this time, has no bearing on his loyalty to his country and our cause," Jonathan remarked to John Adams on the way to City Tavern following a session.

"I agree with you, Jonathan, that much of this foolishness stems from petty jealousy, but that, my friend, is part of the political arena, as difficult as that is to accept. I believe Franklin's seeming indifference stems from his respect for Congress. Rather than proclaiming his stance on all matter of issues, I think he has gone to great lengths to avoid claiming any special wisdom. Perhaps he has gone too far by remaining silent. But to say that he may be a spy—why, that is ridiculous—outrageous."

"I intend to introduce myself to him and let him know that I, for one, am a strong supporter."

"That is most admirable," Adams replied, "but I am certain that he is already aware of your support. Word travels quickly around here."

"That it does."

"Dr. Franklin, my name is Jonathan Barnes, and this is, as I am sure you know, my best friend and prominent Boston merchant, William Finch, and his daughter, Lydia."

"Mr. Barnes, yes, Delegate Barnes. Oh, I know who you are, sir. And you, Mr. Finch, I have heard wonderful things from other delegates about your contributions to the First Continental Congress. We are very happy to have you back with us, and I look forward to your input to this Congress. And this lovely young lady—you are most fortunate to have such a prominent man as your father. I am very pleased to make your acquaintances," said Franklin as they all exchanged handshakes.

"Dr. Franklin, I want you to know that these rumors about you are utter nonsense, inconceivable for one who has done more for his country than all the other delegates combined," Jonathan said.

"Kind sir, I am most grateful. I know that you have been supportive of me in this body."

"I personally believe these rumors stem from petty jealousy among certain factions of the delegates. Very sad to me, considering the stature of the men assembled here."

"It is an esteemed body, but it is a political body, and politics—is well—politics. Backbiting is just a part of it. Do not worry; it will all blow over in time."

"I certainly hope you are right, but I cannot help but say that all this is beneath the dignity of this institution."

"I am right, rest assured, and yes, it is beneath the dignity of this institution, but I will be just fine. Now, on to a brighter subject, I would be very grateful if all of you would join me for supper with my Sally and Richard and Mr. James McDonnell, a junior partner with my former partner's sons and William Sellers."

"We would love to. Where and what time?"

"At my house, right after the next session of Congress. We can all leave together."

"We are already looking forward to it, are we not?" asked Jonathan.

"Yes, we are," William responded. "It will be so nice to meet your family and Mr. McDonnell."

"Wonderful," Franklin said. "And with that, I bid you a good day."

Lydia surveyed the sumptuous meal set before her at Benjamin Franklin's house and the very handsome, debonair young man seated across the table from her. There he was, a junior partner in Hall and Seller's printing business. Twenty-three years old with dark, wavy hair, a solid jaw line, sparkling brown eyes, small dimples in his cheeks, and a dazzling smile. Lydia was instantly smitten; her heart pounding in her chest, she fought to control herself. And the wit! Oh, what wit he displayed! She flirted; he flirted—it was heavenly!

All the while Jonathan and William were telling Franklin about the struggles of Massachusetts since the implementation of the Port

Act. Boston was squeezed to the maximum. The Finches and other merchants were desperate, and the dockworkers were beyond desperate. Then they discussed Lexington and Concord, and Jonathan was able to give a firsthand account of the events of Lexington and the "massacre at Lexington Green." Jonathan went on to explain the horrific treatment of the civilians at the hands of the "world's most civilized fighting force."

"Jonathan, this is appalling, yet I am all too familiar with our 'civilized friends.'"

"What do you mean by that?" William asked.

"At the beginning of last year, I was called before the Privy Council in London for a meeting that ostensibly had been called for a hearing on a petition by the Massachusetts House to remove both Hutchinson and Oliver from office. But it was obvious when the opposition brought the Solicitor General, Alexander Wedderburn, that much more was at stake," Franklin said.

"And that was?" Jonathan asked.

"Not just a hearing on the petition, but a personal and a legal assault on me."

"A personal attack on you? Did that stem from those letters written between Hutchinson and Oliver?" William asked.

"You mean those outrageous letters that made it plain where our governor and lieutenant governor's sentiments resided?" Jonathan added.

"Yes, the assault on me stemmed from those letters." Franklin nodded.

"Those so-called Massachusetts men showed that they were anything but—it is obvious they betrayed us. Their loyalties lie with the Crown," Jonathan continued passionately, his voice rising. "Those letters confirmed that the Brits see us as contemptible and ungrateful."

"Agreed," Franklin responded, "but the crux of the furious fusillade launched on me by the solicitor pertained to whether the letters were private or in the public realm."

"No doubt they were public exchanges between men in public office," William said.

"That is how I saw it," Franklin said, his head slightly nodding, "but not according to Wedderburn. He equated the privacy of the letters to a gentleman's family heirlooms."

"Ridiculous," Jonathan said.

"He claimed that I was the leader in a conspiracy to remove Hutchinson and Oliver from office."

"He did not!" William exclaimed.

"Yes, he did," Franklin added, "he was screaming vindictively at me. He said I was corrupt and that the object of the conspiracy was that I wanted to be governor. The council then rejected the petition and dismissed me as deputy postmaster."

"You defended yourself before the Privy Council, did you not?" Jonathan queried.

"Actually, I did not," Franklin stated solemnly.

"You did not respond to those ludicrous accusations?" William asked, his eyebrows raised and head slightly cocked.

"I did not respond during the Privy Council session. I stood silent and showed no emotion. I did not want to give them the pleasure of thinking that the attacks had an effect on me."

"That is absolutely amazing," Jonathan said, slightly shaking his head. "I am afraid I would have attempted to strangle that bombastic Wedderburn."

"Well, in a sense, I did later."

"How so?" William asked.

"I wrote a lengthy article in the London newspapers with the name 'Homo Trium Littercurrim,' which basically means 'a man of letters.' That was a moniker given to me by Wedderburn himself."

"That is poetic justice." Jonathan chuckled.

"I thought so."

"So in the article, you defended your position and let your thoughts about the council and solicitor be known, correct?" Jonathan asked expectantly.

"Oh yes—not only did I defend my position but all in England now also know exactly what I thought about their precious Privy Council and solicitor general," Franklin deadpanned.

Both Jonathan and William laughed simultaneously.

"But it is not really the people. They are by and large gracious and well-meaning folks, but the king, Parliament, and evidently the Brit Army, their venom toward us has obviously bent the rules of civility."

"Yes—it has indeed," said William, as he and Jonathan nodded their heads.

A few days later, Jonathan, William, and Lydia again supped with James McDonnell, but this time at City Tavern. John Adams, who was there, referred to it as "the most genteel tavern in America." Lydia was thoroughly taken with James, though she had told herself that while she was still an adolescent, she could no longer behave like one. She was determined to control her emotions. While she wanted him to know she was very attracted to him, she could not afford to be too obvious. While she was chatting with James, John Adams brought a very famous delegate from Virginia to their table.

"Miss Finch, I consider it my distinct honor and privilege to formally introduce to you one of the truly great men of our country, Colonel George Washington of Virginia."

"And Colonel Washington," said William, looking at James, "this is Mr. James McDonnell, a junior partner with Benjamin Franklin's former partner's sons and William Sellers."

Washington, ever the gentleman, bowed to all and took Lydia's right hand in his and raised it to his lips, gently placing a kiss on it. The effect upon Lydia was electric, especially when he said, "Miss Finch, I am so pleased to make your acquaintance," while looking directly into her eyes.

Lydia blushed, feeling warm all over. "Colonel Washington, I am flattered beyond words."

"Miss Finch, I had the honor and privilege of meeting your distinguished father at the time of the First Congress; now I have the honor and privilege of meeting his lovely daughter at the time of this, the Second Continental Congress."

"Colonel—thank you so much for your kindness."

"Miss Finch, I previously remarked to these esteemed gentlemen that I believe that the fate of our liberty experiment is in the hands of patriotic families such as yours."

"Yes, Mr. Adams informed me of your flattering assessment."

"Then, I am certain that he told you that I believe the cause of liberty is in good hands," Washington said, looking at Lydia and then John Adams.

"Yes—" Lydia responded.

"I did indeed," John Adams, finished the reply with a smile.

Washington nodded. "I stand by that assessment, Miss Finch," he said, looking at Lydia, then William and Jonathan.

"Thank you so much, Colonel; that means so much us," Lydia said, glancing over at William and then at Jonathan.

"I can think of no greater compliment," William said.

"Nor can I," Jonathan concurred.

"As I said when Colonel Washington made that previous assessment, the colonel is among other things a very astute judge of character," John Adams interjected.

"And you, Mr. McDonnell," Washington said, turning his attention to the young printer, "to be a junior partner with such a distinguished partnership, which not only prints the Pennsylvania Gazette, but the official government documents and currency for Pennsylvania—well, you are most fortunate."

"Thank you, Colonel Washington. I am incredibly fortunate to be a junior partner in this firm. It has been an amazing learning experience. I am very excited about what the future holds. Dr. Franklin has told me that he thinks that if I work hard, I will have great success, because he believes that opportunities in this business are limitless."

"I wholeheartedly agree with Dr. Franklin," Washington nodded. "And speaking of him, I have it on good authority that your family ties to him go back many years."

"That is true. My grandfather, who was a merchant, joined his Junto group shortly after Dr. Franklin came back to Philadelphia from London the first time, and became great friends with him. My grandfather, and my father, who also became a merchant, spent considerable time with Dr. Franklin and his now deceased, former partner, David Hall. And, when Dr. Franklin went to London for nearly eighteen years, my father and I went to visit him on several occasions. Dr. Franklin encouraged me to get into the printing business."

"Excellent. I feel certain you will do your family and Dr. Franklin proud."

"Thank you, sir. That is my fondest wish."

"Of that I have no doubt. On that note, please excuse me, but I must leave. It has been a pleasure to meet you all," Washington said, as he gently bowed and left.

"Colonel Washington is a very impressive man," William remarked to Lydia as they started back to their quarters from their wonderful evening at City Tavern. "I cannot help but think that he will be a very prominent figure in the future of our country."

"I agree, Father. He is one of the most impressive gentlemen I have ever met."

"He possesses wonderful qualities: charm, an imposing physical presence, intelligence, wit—there is an aura about him."

"He does have an aura about him."

"Then there is James," William said, with a hint of a smile at the corner of his lips and a glint in his eyes. "Now *there* is an impressive young man—and handsome, I might add."

"He is impressive—and very handsome," said Lydia with a smile, showing her dimples as she began to blush again.

"He is completely smitten with you."

"Do you think so? James smitten with *me*?"

"Lydia, I assure you that he is taken with you."

"And I have been so worried that I was being too obvious."

"Dr. Franklin told me that James asked him when we could all have supper again. I told him in a couple of days—if it is all right with you."

"All right with me? Yes, it is all right with me! Thank you, Father!"

"Esteemed delegates," said Samuel Adams's emissary, John Brown, as he entered the hall to address the delegates on May 17, 1775, "I am pleased to inform you that Fort Ticonderoga is in our hands!"

"Hear, hear!" the cry went up throughout the room. When the cheering subsided, Sam Adams rose.

"I will propose a resolution," said Sam Adams, "that Ethan Allen and Benedict Arnold be put in charge of Fort Ticonderoga artillery and for them to make inventory of everything to be returned to the Brits when peace and order is restored."

The resolution was seconded and passed.

Then John Adams proposed a military plan to Congress to protect those patriots still in Boston. His proposal was that each colony seize Brit officials as hostages for the Boston patriots, with each colony initiating its own new government.

"Then Congress shall declare independence and at that point offer to negotiate peace with Britain. The army in Massachusetts would become a continental army, pulling in additional volunteers from all other colonies. A general would be appointed to command the army, with Congress to underwrite their pay and all their expenses."

The reaction in Congress was one of shock, especially among the peace-loving delegates, many of whom were in the Pennsylvania delegation. John Dickinson of Pennsylvania, a leader of the peace coalition, rose to propose a resolution.

"My fellow delegates, I am proposing a resolution for this esteemed body to ask His Highness, King George III, to open negotiations to heal this serious breach that has occurred between the mother country and her colonies. Let us take the lead in this matter, a matter of great import to pull us all back from the brink of war."

John Adams immediately rose to attack Dickinson and his position.

"Distinguished delegates, the Honorable Mr. Dickinson is proposing a resolution asking the king to open negotiations to heal the breach. Why should we be the ones to take this first step, 'the lead,' as Mr. Dickinson phrased it? It is abundantly obvious who caused this breach, which is growing bigger day by day, who has been the oppressor, choking Boston and the Bay Colony, who proceeded to murder several Massachusetts militiamen and who ignored our Declaration of Rights. And we are the ones who are supposed to 'take the lead' and ask, better *beg*, that tyrant, George III to open negotiations to heal the breach? I say no, no, never, Mr. Dickinson."

"Mr. Adams," Dickinson said as he hastily approached John in the courtyard after the speech. The State House yard, to the rear of the State House, was about the size of a city block. It was enclosed by a brick wall some seven feet in height with a high, arched gate on the far wall, where ammo and gunpowder were stored, and opened into Walnut Street. It was the perfect place for delegates to talk in private, which they did frequently.

"What is it, Mr. Dickinson?"

"What are you attempting to do? If you persist in your radical policies and approach, many colonies will abandon New England and proceed as they see fit. I have the votes; you do not. Heed my warning, and vote for my resolution. If you persist in opposing me, you do so at your peril."

Dickinson stomped away, leaving Adams quietly seething when Sam Adams put his hand on John's shoulder.

"John, he is right; he has the votes, we do not—not yet. Be patient; our time is soon coming, but for now, you must vote for Dickinson's resolution."

"I agree with Sam, John," Jonathan Barnes said as he approached the cousins, "as much as I do not want to—"

"Yes, Sam, Jonathan, I suppose you are right. I will." He hesitated, taking a long, deep breath.

"John, John," Sam said, grabbing John by the shoulders.

"Sam, I was about to say that I will vote for that detestable resolution even though that man would like to take us back thirty years."

Sam and Jonathan winced at the same time at this "affirmation of support" from John.

"Do not worry, gentlemen—I will vote for it."

"Well, my dear, how would you like to stay in Philadelphia for a while?" William said as he and Lydia were taking a carriage ride back to their quarters, following supper with Franklin and his family and James McDonnell.

"Father, that would be wonderful, but how will I support myself?"

"I have spoken with Jonathan about the matter. He is familiar with some seamstresses and upholsterers in this town. He is willing to go with us tomorrow to meet some seamstresses. Until you are able to procure a position, I will support you. It is imperative that I leave for Boston very soon. I have also spoken with the landlords, and they would be most happy to have you stay on."

"They are dear people. That is very kind of them."

"It would only be until Jonathan makes a trip back to Boston, which will likely be sometime in the fall."

"I will be very happy if it is only for a couple of months."

"That is what I thought, my dear. Very well, it is set. We will go with Jonathan in the morning to attempt to secure you employment."

"Father, I am *so* excited!" Lydia said as she leaned into William's arm, snuggling up to her father.

He wrapped his arm around her and said, with a smile on his face, "So am I!"

"William, Lydia, I thought that we would go visit a young couple who recently started their own upholstery business. I thought it would be a good way to end our day," said Jonathan.

"What are their names?" William asked.

"John and Betsy Ross," Jonathan said. "Colonel Washington has had very positive things to say about them."

"Colonel Washington has? How does he know them?"

"Apparently through Christ Church, which the colonel occasionally attends while in town for Congress."

"If Colonel Washington vouches for them, that is good enough for me," William said, nodding his head slightly in affirmation of his statement.

"My dearest Eleanor," Jonathan Barnes wrote to his wife, "much is taking place here in Philadelphia, both on the political front and on the personal." He went on to describe the activities, assuring her that he was doing his part, urging John Adams to be patient and support Dickinson's resolution to have the king open negotiations with the colonies, knowing that the time would soon come when independence must be embraced. He informed her of his meeting and getting to know the legendary Franklin, explaining the terrible unfounded rumors circulating in Congress about him. He related the introduction by Franklin of James McDonnell, describing James'

junior partner position in Hall and Sellers and how James and Lydia were quite enamored with each other, spending as much time together as possible. This, of course, with the blessing of William, who was quite impressed with the young man. "William is leaving in a few days; he will probably be home by the time you receive this letter. He gave Lydia the opportunity to stay in Philadelphia for a while, at least until I come home. William asked me, and I readily agreed to chaperone Lydia on her visits with James. I also went with William and Lydia to procure a position for her as a seamstress while she is here. We visited with a young couple who just started their own upholstery business, John and Betsy Ross—very delightful. They immediately took to Lydia, and though they did not have much work at this time to provide for her, they agreed to hire her on part time. While not much income, it should be sufficient to meet her needs, at least temporarily. William was pleased with the couple and satisfied with the arrangement." He also discussed his growing friendship with another great man, Colonel George Washington of Virginia, who, Jonathan wrote, might be the best hope to unite the colonies.

Eleanor wrote back to applaud Jonathan's participation and expressed excitement at the developing relationship between Lydia and James. But for the most part, she related, much as Abigail Adams did to John, the extreme hardships in Massachusetts, her struggles with the store, and issues with the children, who, though very proud of their father, missed him terribly.

"James especially misses you. He simply cannot wait until you come walking through the front door. Richard is doing his part to provide manly leadership, but with his position in the militia, he is not here as often as we would like. And there is simply no replacing you. I am so happy for your contribution to our country at this critical time, but I sincerely hope that you will be able to return soon for the sake of our family. As for the store, we are pressed on all sides— shortages with regard to nearly every item that we sell, and prices are very high, largely due to the embargo. Abigail told John that they had shortages of many staples, such as coffee, pepper, sugar, shoes, and pins, and that the cost of pins had nearly tripled in price. We face the same issues here as in Boston. All the while Richard continues to make periodic forays into Boston to see Victoria and the Finches and gather information from Jean Paul and other sources to report back to Heath and the militia command. It is quite a life we are living here; I do not know if you can fathom it. I pray constantly for you, my darling, and I covet your prayers."

"Sam, Jonathan, I tell you that I am determined to get these reluctant delegates to declare for or against something," John said as they walked in the shade of the large trees encompassing the State House yard, during a break in the sessions. He had invited them to walk to discuss an important proposal.

"What are you proposing, John?" Sam asked.

"I am going to make a motion this morning that Congress should adopt the army before Boston and appoint Colonel Washington as commander of it."

Sam Adams looked seriously at his cousin but said nothing.

Jonathan thought a moment and then said, "John, I am in agreement that Washington is the right choice to unite the country, and I believe it is necessary to bring leadership and direction to the army."

"I appreciate your support and would greatly appreciate any support you can give me in there," said John as he pointed toward the State House.

"I will be very happy to support your motion," Jonathan said.

"John, you know I have had deep reservations about having a standing army, but I now realize that it is essential to our cause. I too will support you," Sam now proffered, with a slight nod of his head, "just get ready for a raging controversy."

"Yes—a raging controversy. Well, if that is what comes of it, then so be it. It is time we move forward, gentlemen."

John Adams quickly rose to speak as Congress came back into session. All the delegates sat in rapt attention, for he was already acclaimed as the preeminent orator among distinguished orators in the still very young institution known as the Congress.

"Mr. President, my fellow delegates, this is a crucial moment in the history of our new nation. There are many issues facing us in the wake of recent military engagements. While the militia performed admirably in these encounters, there are serious uncertainties that exist in the minds of our people. The many distresses of the army, including the clear and present danger that the army may soon dissolve and if that terrible possibility becomes a reality, there will be numerous difficulties in attempting to raise another. You can rest assured that the enemy will take advantage of any delays or mistakes on our part. The time for action is now; we cannot afford to wait any longer. We must be united in both direction and leadership. Therefore, I am now moving for the adoption of the army by this Congress and the appointment of a general to lead it as commander in chief. I have one man in mind. He is a gentlemen who has experience as an officer, an independent fortune, the character and talent to fulfill the nearly impossible duties of the job and who will, better than anyone, be able to unite the various different factions of all the colonies."

Washington, who was seated next to the door, got up and went into the library.

"I refer to the distinguished gentleman planter and delegate from Virginia, Colonel George Washington."

"There is a motion for the adoption of the army by Congress and for the appointment of Colonel Washington as the army's commander in chief," said a visibly shaken John Hancock, who secretly coveted the position for himself and was mortified that his own Massachusetts delegate would propose a Virginian. "Is there a second to the motion?"

"Mr. President," said Sam Adams, rising from his chair.

"The chair recognizes the Honorable Samuel Adams, delegate from Massachusetts."

"I second the motion as proposed by the Honorable John Adams."

"There is a second to the motion. Is there any discussion?"

Then to add insult to the injury inflicted upon Hancock, Jonathan Barnes rose to speak.

"Mr. President," Jonathan said.

"The chair now recognizes the Honorable Jonathan Barnes, delegate from Massachusetts."

"Mr. President, my fellow delegates, I must add my support to the motion and second put forth by my esteemed colleagues from the Bay Colony. It is essential that we adopt the army at this time, and I firmly believe that Colonel Washington is the one man to lead it."

No sooner did the words come out of Jonathan's mouth than opposition was voiced.

Several delegates declared themselves against the appointment, with the entire army being located in Massachusetts, with a general already leading the army, and with the Brit Army pinned in Boston. The motion was postponed, and then after much lobbying by John Adams, the motion was again brought to the body with Thomas Johnson of Maryland making the formal nomination. Washington was unanimously elected to serve as general and commander in chief of the army, and the army was adopted by Congress.

"But lest some unlucky event should happen unfavorable to my reputation, I beg it be remembered by every gentleman in the room that I this day declare with the utmost sincerity, I do not think myself equal to the command I am honored with," declared the new commander in chief to the Congress. "I will not accept a salary, but I will pledge everything that I have to our glorious cause."

"Let me be first to call you commander in chief, General Washington. Congratulations," John Adams said to Washington, following the address.

"I am indebted to you, sir. Without your enthusiastic support of me and the adoption of the army, none of this would have happened."

"I appreciate that, General, but I want you to know that there is absolutely no question in my mind that you are by far the most qualified man for the job."

"I am very humbled by your faith in me, but in my opinion, no one is qualified for this position. This may be close to an impossible task. I am afraid, sir, and I do not say this lightly, that the odds against our victory are very great indeed. We are opposed by perhaps the greatest fighting force in the world."

"It may be close to an impossible task, but I know you will rise to the challenge. Please understand that I will support you in any and every way possible and do everything within my power to make certain that Congress supports you to the fullest."

"And I give you my word that I will give this command my full and complete attention and effort."

Later Washington wrote to his wife, Martha, and his brother, saying that his appointment "is a trust too great for my capacity," and said that he had done everything in his power to avoid it. "A unanimous vote left me no choice but to accept."

12

"General, I urge and implore you to land two divisions on those hills at daybreak and not a moment later. The rebels are up to something; I feel certain they are constructing earthen works to thwart a thrust by us into the interior, and if they place cannons on the hills, Boston is in danger," Clinton said, at headquarters, to Gage, who was listening intently and considering his options. Clinton had been reconnoitering on the prior evening, when he heard faint sounds coming from the vicinity of Bunker Hill and Breed's Hill. He had arrived in Boston, along with Generals Howe and Burgoyne.

In fact, Jean Paul learned that Clinton, Howe, and Burgoyne were planning on attacking Cambridge in the near future. He passed on the information to Richard, who conveyed it to General Artemus Ward. A council of officers was convened, and they were in unanimous agreement to construct earthen works on Bunker Hill with all due haste, which was also authorized by the Committee of Safety. General Putnam then ordered the building of a fort on the hill, and General Ward ordered Colonel Prescott to carry out the orders.

"I am afraid I must concur with General Clinton." Howe nodded in agreement. "We cannot afford to allow the rebels to get a foothold on the heights. It would be a disaster for us."

Gage replied, "I hear you, gentlemen, but I do not agree with landing two divisions at daybreak. However, I will call a council of war to discuss the matter with all the officers."

Prescott arrived on Bunker Hill with eight hundred fifty men, which included Richard Barnes and forty artillery gunners and weapons.

Prescott gathered his officers around him for council and then said, "After listening to you and reviewing the situation myself, I am in total agreement with that we need to move from Bunker Hill to Breed's Hill. That move will put us right on top of the British fleet. Let us begin as soon as possible."

The men quickly and silently began the move from the top of the taller, larger Bunker Hill to the smaller but more strategically placed Breed's Hill. They trudged through almost waist-high grass near the top of the hill. It was midnight, and Colonel Richard Gridley began stacking a redoubt, and Prescott directed men, including Richard Barnes, to begin digging.

"We must build a fort tonight and do it in almost total silence. All right, men, you have your orders."

Richard grabbed a shovel and started digging in a line of several men, all working in total darkness and remarkably quiet. Richard's arms, legs, and back ached as never before. Water breaks were few but a blessing. Sweat poured from his forehead and soaked through his shirt, but he and his fellow militiamen kept up a blistering pace.

By three thirty in the morning, amazingly, the fort was nearly done, surprising even Prescott. The ramparts were five and a half feet high, with a rather narrow entrance on the north side, but it was lacking openings for guns.

Richard and the other militiamen were starving, having not eaten since noon the previous day. Additionally the water supply was getting low, a major concern for Prescott since the heat of the June day was looming before him and his men.

As day broke the Brits awoke to a startling sight. On Breed's Hill loomed a four-sided, square redoubt with the east side being more than one hundred thirty feet long with a redan with the pointed angled protrusion on the southwest side and a six-foot wall on the east side extending for fifty yards. This was an amazing accomplishment by the rebels, and it forced Gage to call a council of war. Clinton urged an attack to be mounted on the rear of the fort.

"I am telling you, gentlemen, that the rear of this fort is very poorly defended. Why be foolish and send our men right into the strength of the enemy?"

"General, I respect your judgment, but these are peasants, rabble going up against the finest force in the world. We must make a statement and make it now," Howe responded.

"With all due respect, General," Clinton replied, "I believe that rabble put quite a thrashing on the king's men at Lexington and Concord."

"You are correct, General," replied Howe. "However, in that situation there were far more 'peasants' than now. They came from everywhere. Here the numbers are much more favorable."

"I hear you, General, but—"

"Enough—I have thought about the matter, and I am in agreement with General Howe. We will launch a frontal attack, and General Howe will lead it. However, you must wait until late afternoon when the tide will be high," Gage said as he walked to the window, staring out intently at Breed's Hill. "This time we must make them pay."

Prescott meanwhile used all the time awaiting Howe's attack to prepare his men for what was to come. A cannonball screamed through
the air and tore the head off a farm boy not more than a few paces
from where Richard Barnes was standing. Richard, visibly shaken,
collapsed to the ground and vomited. Prescott immediately came to
Richard's aid, putting his hand on Richard's shoulder.

"Son, are you all right?"

"Yes, sir," Richard replied as he looked up, wiping the vomit on
his sleeve.

"I know what you are feeling right now. I experienced a very similar situation."

"I was just talking with him, sir, and then—"

"So was I, Private. I was in the trench, talking with my best friend
one moment, and his head literally flew over my shoulder the next.
I almost went into shock, but my superior officer grabbed me, shook
me, and brought me to my senses. We quickly buried my friend without ceremony."

"Without ceremony, sir?"

"Yes, Private." Prescott addressed the troops, "Men, we must bury
this man immediately without ceremony."

The men, including Richard, protested, and Prescott finally relented. A clergyman was brought in, prayers were made on behalf of
the deceased, and he was buried. Some of the men deserted, but the
ceremony helped to calm Richard and strengthen his resolve to fight
the redcoats.

Prescott then turned his attention to the troops. His assessment
was that he needed more, so he issued a request to the Committee
of Safety for additional troops. The committee gave the order to
General Stark to move from his location four miles from Breed's Hill.

"Men, the fate of Boston, perhaps the fate of British control of the
colonies, is in your hands today. We must prevail; we must drive

the rebels from the top of the hill. Failure is not an option. To fail would almost certainly mean that Boston will be lost, and we will all board ships and leave, which is quite disagreeable. Do your duty to the king and your country, and our victory is assured," said Howe to the troops at Hancock's Wharf, ready to go to Moulton's Point.

❧

"Sirs," Major Andrew McClary said, addressing officers camped on Charlestown Neck, "General Stark is coming up and requests that you and your troops move aside so that our troops may pass."

"Yes, sir, Major, tell the general to come up. We will clear the way," an officer relayed to McClary.

McClary saluted, turned his horse, and galloped back toward Stark and his troops. Within a few minutes, Stark and his men were coming up the neck, heading toward Breed's Hill with cannonballs falling all around them.

"Colonel." Stark arrived at the top, addressing Prescott with a salute. "Reporting for duty."

Prescott saluted Stark and then shook his hand. "We are grateful that you are here, General, and none too soon."

"Glad to be here. Let me have a look at the situation, Colonel."

"Please, General," said Prescott, "follow me."

Prescott then led Stark to the front of the fort and then down to the far east end, closest to the Mystic River. From the height of the hill, Stark saw a problem.

"Colonel, I fear that we are vulnerable to a flanking maneuver by the Brits, right there," said Stark as he pointed toward the Mystic.

"I agree, General."

"Let me send men to that rail fence," he said, again pointing to the fence some forty yards from the fort. "That should help shore up our position."

"Send as many as you deem necessary, General. If you need anything additional, please let me know, and I will provide it for you."

Stark dispersed troops immediately to the rail fence. The troops fortified their position with hay and grass, piled stones to the edge of the river, and then hid, three deep, behind the fence and the wall.

Richard was positioned just to the east of center in the fort. Standing on a wooden platform constructed inside the fort, he had a view of Stark's troops and could see that they were hidden and ready to repulse an attack by the enemy; the flank was secure.

Through the haze rode Dr. Warren, a major general, to join Prescott on the hill. Warren, who dined with Mrs. Betsy Palmer the night before, had a premonition that he would die in battle, and he intimated as much to her that evening, to her horror.

"Betsy, I must tell you, I have had a premonition about tomorrow," Warren said matter-of-factly.

"What do you mean? What sort of premonition?" said Betsy, shaken by the sudden dark turn in their conversation.

"Betsy, I hesitated to tell you this, but I feel that I must since this premonition is so strong. I will die tomorrow in battle."

"Joseph…oh, Joseph, no! It cannot be!" Betsy cried.

"My dear friend, I am very sorry to put you through this, but I simply felt compelled to tell you. Do not worry for me. I am very grateful to God that I will die for our glorious cause. Death is a small price to pay for the liberties of our people."

"No, Joseph, you must not go! The premonition was given to you to warn you not to go!" Betsy desperately pleaded.

"I must go, and I will go. If I am to die, so be it. I consider it to be the greatest honor that could be bestowed upon me—to give my life for my country."

"I cannot possibly change your mind?"

"No, I know this is my fate."

"Then it is good-bye, my friend—my wonderful friend. I have cherished our friendship," a resigned Betsy said, tears welling up in her eyes as she dabbed them with a kerchief.

"As have I...as have I," Warren said, nodding his head slowly and sadly. "Good-bye."

"Colonel Prescott," said Warren as he approached Prescott, whose back was to Warren. Prescott quickly turned around at the mention of his name.

"Dr. Warren...General Warren," Prescott said as he saluted, "I accede command to you, sir."

"Thank you, Colonel, but I defer to you with your military mind and experience. You know far better than me how best to handle this operation."

"All right, sir. Quite frankly, I am not sure that there is much more to do at this time. Our troops are set. I believe we are in a good defensive position, as good as possible. Now we wait."

"To their left flank," Howe ordered the troops, upon landing in the southeast corner of the peninsula, to what he believed was the rebel weakness. Richard Barnes, from his perch high on Breed's Hill, peered over the redoubt and down upon the American left flank. Though smoke wafted through the air from the burning of Charlestown by the Brits to weed out snipers and the bombardment leveled upon the rebels prior to the Brit offense, Richard could clearly see what Howe and his men could not; a trap awaited them.

"Do not fire, men," General Stark said, speaking to the men behind the stones, "until the redcoats are here." Stark pointed to the line. Stark had five hundred men and two artillery pieces, while to their right, between them and the breastworks, some fifty to seventy five waited in entrenchments ready to deliver an enfilading fire on the Brits. "For you, men," he said, speaking to those huddled behind the fence, "do not fire until you see half gaiters or, as Old Put says, 'until you see the whites of their eyes.'"

At about the same time as Stark was addressing his men, Prescott gave the final instructions to his. Prescott, Putnam, and Dr. Warren had roughly fifteen hundred men in the center, three hundred in the redoubt, and twelve hundred behind the breastworks with artillery pieces. "Men," Prescott said, "the moment is now at hand. If you follow my orders, the redcoats will not reach us. We must use our ammunition wisely. Do not fire until they are within forty yards of the fort, until you can see the whites of their eyes. Then fire and fire quickly. Remember to shoot low; these muskets tend to fire high. Stay calm; we have prepared and are in the best defensive position possible."

As Prescott concluded, Richard could feel his throat tighten and his stomach tie in knots. Though he had recently been in the battle of Lexington and along the ring of fire back to Boston, he still was very new to combat. This time he sensed he would be directly engaged, without the protection involved in guerrilla warfare as had been the case with the ring. He began to break out in a cold sweat. The waiting was excruciating. He actually longed for action. It would help relieve the stress.

General Howe, a bit impatient, decided to proceed without artillery, since he had the wrong-sized cannonballs for his cannons. The troops quickly closed on the rebel left flank, two hundred yards, one hundred yards—closer and closer. The infantry moved briskly along the river. At approximately two hundred yards, they were exposed to crossfire from riflemen and snipers on their left and others on their right. They continued to close in on the last fence. A few Americans fired but ceased immediately upon the loud exhortations of their officers.

The Brits kept coming—fifty yards, forty yards, thirty yards. Finally at approximately twenty-five yards, the order was barked out, "Fire!" The Americans rose as one, leveled their muskets, and poured a frightening, withering volley into the heart of the astonished British line. The volley, which erupted like an exploding volcano, had the desired effect, as the Brit line staggered back, regrouped, attacked again, and were met with another equally devastating volley. The black, acrid smoke from the rebel guns temporarily hid a horrific scene. The Americans targeted officers, including Pitcairn, who was carried away, dying, from the field of battle by his young officer son.

Howe exhorted his troops in a direct assault, slowly moving up the hill toward the top, but men were falling all around him.

"Forward, men—press forward! We must take that fort at all costs!"

Richard was itching to unload on the redcoats again, with the memory of Lexington Green burned brightly into his mind. Nevertheless, he controlled himself as Prescott again addressed the troops.

"Remember, men, we have to conserve our powder and ammunition. Do not fire until you see the whites of their eyes."

Onward and upward, relentlessly came the Regulars. A magnificent though seemingly suicidal sight.

Richard could hardly stand it. When would he be able to fire? It seemed as if the redcoats would soon be in the fort. Then it happened—he saw the whites of their eyes! Almost simultaneously he heard Prescott scream, "Now, men, for God's sake, fire now!"

Richard and the men all around him immediately pulled the trigger, and a tremendous roar thundered down the hillside. The Brits absorbed a terrible blow and then retreated to regroup near the base of the hill.

Somehow Howe managed to escape unfazed, which was truly remarkable, leading the assault and being directly in the line of fire. Two members of his own staff were cut down, stunning Howe and briefly rendering him immobile. He gathered himself and pulled his men back several hundred yards, well below the redoubt.

Howe led his men up a second time, slowly moving in the famous British precise lines. Again, men were falling all around Howe, who was in disbelief that his men had been unable to take the hill.

"This cannot be happening to us; I simply cannot believe it. This is preposterous! We must retreat once again! Retreat, men, retreat!" he yelled to Regulars who were already on the move.

Down the hill they fled, and then they regrouped and moved forward one last time, now quite late in the afternoon. Howe now had an additional four infantry regiments and battalion of marines. At about three hundred yards from the fort, the Brits were hammered by crossfire and artillery fire from above, but they kept on coming, higher and higher.

"That is it, men—now we have them, at last. Forward—the fort is ours!" Howe exhorted as the troops, finally sensing victory was at hand, quickened their pace.

The third attempt was a major problem for the Americans. The Brits were on the upward move again, and this time nothing could stop them. It was a frightful yet awesome wave of red and white with gleaming but menacing bayonets. Gunpowder was almost gone, reinforcements were needed, and while Prescott had sent messengers to Putnam for that purpose, much to his disgust and chagrin, no troops were forthcoming.

"What is Putnam doing, or should I say, not doing?" Prescott said to Dr. Warren, with a look that conveyed his extreme consternation and annoyance. "If those reinforcements that I asked for are not forthcoming immediately, our doom is sealed. There is no possible way that we can hold this fort, General."

"Colonel, I cannot say what Putnam may be up to, but I am afraid it is too late. Here they come!"

Just then the redcoats stormed into the west wall of the redoubt, loaded with ammunition and bayonets bearing down on the over-matched American soldiers, who had neither. Several American troops had already dropped their weapons and started running, anticipating the onslaught. Others grabbed anything they could get their hands on to jam into their muskets for ammunition. Before Richard could reload his musket again with what little powder he had left, the Brits were on top of them. The Americans did the only thing they could: swing their muskets like clubs. Richard quickly flipped his musket upside down and began swinging it wildly at anyone in his sight, while he was sweating from head to toe. Somehow he was able to continue to maintain his grip, though his hands were getting slipperier by the moment. All around him his colleagues were being slaughtered. Everything seemed to be in slow motion for Richard as he literally fought for dear life.

Dr. Warren was also in desperate straits, swinging his musket at the charging Brits, while rallying the Americans around him to stand and fight.

"I see the villain, the treacherous, Dr. Warren! Out of my way; he is all mine!" a Brit officer who recognized the famous patriot blurted out as he quickly pushed aside others struggling around him to get a shot at the doctor. At the mention of his name, Warren turned to face his accuser. Before he could raise and swing his gun, a lone shot was fired from no more than five feet away. The musket ball smashed into Warren on the left side of his face, between the nostril and eye, exiting his skull at the base, just to the right of center. Without being able to utter a word, he fell to the ground, dying instantly, thus fulfilling his premonition.

Meanwhile, Richard, musket still swinging, headed for the back of the fort. It was total chaos all around him, and the rear exit was too small and narrow, with too many bodies trying to push through at the same time. Somehow he managed to squeeze out, only to be nicked by a musket ball in his upper left arm as he turned to run to Charlestown Neck. Richard grabbed his left arm with his right arm as he ran, managing to hang on to the musket with his left. He bounded down the back of the hill with bullets whizzing all around him, sounding almost as if he were in a swarm of angry bees. He quickly moved out of musket range and sought to address the matter of his left arm, which, though a rather small flesh wound, stung terribly.

All about him fellow Americans soldiers ran by at full speed from the fort, though they were now far from danger. The vast majority of the Americans survived owing to the fact that the Brits entered from three sides, forcing them to hold fire lest they shot their own men.

The body of Dr. Warren, a man hated by the Brits due to all the trouble he had caused them, was stripped of his clothes. He was later buried in his father's coat.

Bunker Hill had lasted about three hours yet seemed to be much longer for the Brits. The hill was strewn with redcoats, both wounded and dead. The cries of the wounded were pitiful and continued long after the battle was over, while medics dressed wounds in the field and carried off those who were unable to walk.

"Generals," said Gage, addressing Howe, Clinton, and Burgoyne, "this is victory? Nearly fifty percent of our Regulars were killed or wounded and forty percent of our officers—this is victory?" His shallow voice trailed off. "How am I to explain this to my lord the king? The loss we have sustained is greater than we can bear," he said as he slowly lowered himself into his chair at headquarters, his face ashen and his knees weak.

"General Gage, it was a victory," Clinton replied.

"A dear-bought victory, another such would have ruined us," Howe said as he paced about headquarters. "I will concede, General Clinton, that it was a victory, but my God, my God, my men, my officers were dropping all around me," Howe said as he continued pacing and began wringing his hands. "It is miraculous that I was spared."

"It is incomprehensible to me that these people fight like this. They show a spirit and conduct against us that they never showed against the French," Gage said, shaking his head.

"Stop this talk. All is not lost, despite the terrible price we paid. We will defeat this rabble; they simply must not prevail against the most powerful and glorious fighting force on the face of the earth," Burgoyne interjected, with a stern look of determination on his face, "or my name is not Gentleman Johnny Burgoyne."

"General Putnam," Prescott said as he wagged his finger in Old Put's face, "I should have you court-martialed." Troops were milling around the slopes of Bunker Hill as Prescott confronted the popular leader.

"Go ahead, Colonel, if you must, but the men here," he said, gesturing to those around them, "might have something to say about it."

Prescott realized that Putnam was simply too popular among the troops for a court-martial to occur, lest mutiny became the order of the day. Nevertheless, Prescott continued his scathing criticism.

"Why did you not support me, General, with your men?"

"I could not drive the dogs up," Old Put said defiantly.

"If you could not drive them up, you might have led them up," Prescott retorted.

"Why are you berating me, Colonel? Should not your wrath be directed at General Ward? The men all around us are saying, 'Where was General Ward our commander in chief? What was he doing?' Those are the real questions here."

"I have told you why I am 'berating' you, as you have called it, and for that I have good cause. As for General Ward's leadership, I will personally address the matter with the general, but as for you, the next time that I am in charge and I ask for support, you will deliver."

Richard emerged from the battle only slightly wounded physically, but he grew and matured from his second taste of battle, knowing that he was indeed blessed to escape without a more serious wound and most importantly, with his life. Many who were all around him in the fort were not nearly as fortunate.

13

A few days later, word reached Boston of the appointment of George Washington and the adoption of the army by Congress. William had just recently returned to Boston, and when he heard the news, he and Annabelle had serious discussions about the implications for him and the family. William decided to meet with Jean Paul at JP's.

"Come in, my friend," Jean Paul said as he heard the knock on his office door at the appointed hour. "It is good to see you, as always."

"Likewise, Jean Paul," said William as the two close friends exchanged a hearty handshake and brief hug.

"Please be seated, Monsieur William."

"I will not be long, Jean Paul," William said as he slid down into the comfortable chair across from Jean Paul's desk, "but it is very important."

"General Washington, perhaps, monsieur?"

"General Washington and the army."

"You have come to tell me that you are going to volunteer your services, no?"

"No—I mean, yes," said William with a surprised look. "How did you know?"

"Because I know who you are—besides, I was going to come to you to tell you the same thing, monsieur."

"You were going to tell me that I should volunteer my services?"

"No, monsieur, I was going to come to you to tell you that I plan to volunteer my services. Now that General Washington is commander in chief, it is obvious that Congress and the country are finally getting serious about our liberty."

"But you cannot volunteer your services, Jean Paul—not now anyway," said William, with conviction.

"I cannot, monsieur? Why not? No one believes more in liberty than me. I must give everything for my country to support this noble cause."

"Yes, yes, Jean Paul. You are a symbol of liberty, of freedom, and what it means. No one appreciates it more, nor lives it more than you, but right now our country—and me and my family—we need you right here doing what you are doing."

"Monsieur?"

"Look, with the vast spy network that you have in this town, working with Paul Revere, you are the eyes and ears of the army. General Washington needs you to continue running this network. And that is to say nothing of the supplies. Without your distribution of supplies to your own customers and the needy families of Boston, this town would be at the brink of destitution and starvation."

"Monsieur, begging your pardon, but that tyrant the king has us all at the brink of destitution and starvation, even with all our distribution efforts. Paul Revere can certainly handle the spy network. He knows all my people, and they would have no problem working directly with him."

"All right, I know we are close to destitution and starvation now, and I know Revere is quite capable of handling the network on his own, but it would not be the same without you. Besides, and this may seem selfish, I need your help."

"How can I help?"

"In addition to volunteering my services, Annabelle and I decided to take up the Barneses' offer to temporarily relocate our family to Lexington, now that Gage announced that those who want to leave town may do so. To be frank, my business has taken substantial hits since the embargo. I am fortunate to have half the volume and customers I had at about this time last year. And though I feel confident that David Whitmore and George Manly can take care of what business is left, it would be so comforting to me if Willie and Amos could assist them in distribution efforts to those loyal customers that remain. Additionally, and I have already spoken to David and George about this, and they are in full agreement, they would relish any advice you may provide them in getting more smuggling sources and distributors. Also, I need you to take over leadership of what's left of the merchants' association in my absence."

"Monsieur William, I will be happy to help with smuggling sources and distributors. And, Willie and Amos may be able to assist in distribution to your customers. I will confer with them about it. But you want me to assume leadership of an association that did not want anything to do with me?"

"Yes, because you are the only one capable of leading it. Besides, they know you are my friend. They also know if they do not follow your orders, there will be 'hell to pay,' to borrow your phrase, upon my return."

"But how do I know they will believe me when I tell them Monsieur William left me in charge?"

"Do not worry. I have already taken care of it. I convened a special meeting of the board and told them that you would be acting in my place and stead."

"You did? And how did they receive this news?"

"Actually quite well. You see, you have earned their respect and admiration. They know you are the right man for the job."

"All right, monsieur, if you say so, I will do it for you."

"I knew you would, my friend. You have put my mind at ease. The association is in good hands. Now I have another matter."

"Oui?"

"I want you and Timothy not to worry about our house. Gage helped himself to quartering his troops in our house by the wharf, and he made a bold statement to me, when I protested to him, that he could commandeer our house anytime he wanted to at a moment's notice."

"Are you saying that we should just let the Brits take over your beautiful house, monsieur?" Jean Paul said, with a look of mild surprise written all over his face.

"I am. Honestly, I do not know how you could prevent it anyway. If Gage, or Howe or whoever is in charge, decides he wants it, then he is going to get it, and I do not want either one of you to risk his wrath just to protect my property. I have given this matter a lot of thought, and Annabelle and I thoroughly discussed it prior to my making the decision to volunteer my services. I must now serve my country; the safety of our property is secondary. I could never forgive myself if any harm came to you or Timothy from protecting our property. Do you understand?"

"But, monsieur—"

"No buts—do you understand?"

"Oui, Monsieur William," he said reluctantly, nodding his head slowly.

"Now, having said that, I will ask you to 'keep an eye out,' on the house to see if the Brits do occupy it, who actually occupies it, and for what purpose. I know this may be a lot to ask, but I believe Gage wants my house as his headquarters, though his stay here may be short lived. If any of this happens, valuable intelligence may be gained by paying attention to the comings and goings from the house."

"I will put my network on alert, monsieur, as soon as you leave, to keep a nonobvious watch on it."

"What would I do without my friend, Jean Paul?" said an obviously relieved William as he stood to leave. "You are making this difficult transition much easier for me."

Following his personal meeting with Jean Paul, William convened a meeting of the family, including Timothy and Jean Paul, to discuss this new and very important development.

"I called you all together to tell you about a very important development. Colonel George Washington from Virginia was recently appointed as general and commander in chief of the army by Congress."

"Father," asked Victoria, with a concerned look, "do you believe his appointment is a good thing for our country? The army primarily consists of northeastern, New England men, correct?"

"Correct."

"Then why is a man from Virginia being called to lead the army?"

"That is an excellent question. Colonel, now General, Washington is a great man of character and integrity, with military experience. He is a large, physical man, with the look of a leader. Not only that, but Virginia is our most populous colony and centrally located. We need to unite against the Brits, and George Washington can be the man to help unite us."

"If he is all that," said Victoria, "then we are most fortunate."

"My understanding is that General Washington will soon be coming here to assume command. I wanted to inform all of you that with General Gage's recent announcement that all who want to leave Boston may do so and with General Washington's appointment and the adoption of the army by Congress, I believe that the time has come for me to volunteer my services. Annabelle and I have had some serious discussions about this, and we also agree that it is time to take Richard up on the Barneses' offer to move, temporarily, to Lexington. Richard should be arriving soon. Jean Paul is aware of this since I had an individual meeting with him to discuss several matters."

"Father, I am proud of you for making this decision," said Victoria as she hugged William, with tears welling up in her eyes. "There is no doubt in my mind that your country is in need of your service and leadership."

"That is special coming from you, my dear," William replied as he pulled her back and planted a soft kiss on her now moist right cheek. "I want you all to know that your mother and I did not come to this decision lightly. It is going to take considerable sacrifice on all our parts."

"Father, I too am proud of you, but I want to stay here in Boston. I feel that I am contributing to the cause with my work with Willie and Amos. Perhaps I could stay with Jean Paul temporarily until the family is able to return home, that is, if it would be agreeable with him," Joshua said.

"Oui, Monsieur Joshua, you may stay with me, but the decision is not for me to make—it is your parents' decision."

"Thank you, Jean Paul, for your generous offer, but Joshua will be leaving with the family in the morning."

"But, Father, I am an adult now and—"

"Son, you may be an adult, but you have been living in this home and have been subject to the rules of the household. Your family needs you now; that is the important thing. Besides, I could not have you imposing on a dear friend."

"It is no imposition, Monsieur William."

"You may not consider it as such, Jean Paul, and I am very appreciative of your very generous offer, but I consider it to be such. This matter is settled."

"But if I cannot stay in Boston, may I enlist in the army?"

"Not now, son. Your mother and sister need the presence of a man as they make this difficult transition, and you must be that man, with my departure. While the Barneses have been our closest friends for several years, it is an altogether different thing to move the family in with them in tight quarters under trying circumstances. Once all are fully adjusted to their new life, if you are still interested in enlisting in the army, we will evaluate it and discuss it then. In the meantime I would suggest we speak to Richard when he arrives. I am sure that he would be happy to introduce you to Captain Parker of the Lexington militia. From what Jonathan and Richard have said to me about Captain Parker, he is a very fine man, and I am certain he would welcome you. You could receive valuable training so that if you ever do enlist, you will have an advantage on many others."

"Yes, Father, I would like that very much," Joshua said. "At least I would feel as if I am doing something worthwhile."

"I am certain that what Eleanor and I have planned for you will be more than worthwhile, young man," added Annabelle, with a scolding look. "Just because household chores and work in the general store and garden are not glamorous or directly connected to our glorious cause does not mean that they are not worthwhile."

"I know that, Mother, but—," Joshua said, rather sheepishly, deciding the better of getting in any deeper with his mother, who was obviously having none of it.

"But?" Annabelle said with a slight smile as she nodded. "You see Richard and now your father going off to war and Mr. Barnes in Congress, so helping a bunch of womenfolk and their families around the home, that is not the same, is it?"

"Well, maybe not quite," said Joshua, not sure if he was off the hook yet. He knew he had to choose his words carefully. "But do not misunderstand me; I know that helping all of you is important."

"It is important, son," interjected William, in a somber tone. "It is important to me, especially with me being gone. I am counting on you."

"Do not worry, sir; I will do everything that is asked of me."

"I know you will, and trust me, that is a great contribution."

"Now the wharf," William said, changing the subject.

"You do not have to worry about the wharf, William," Timothy interjected. "It has been an enormous struggle since the embargo, but I will be fine, and the few remaining shop owners—well, they have managed to hang on thus far, so I am sure they will survive."

"That is good to know, Timothy, and I do not want you to worry about our house." William proceeded to recite to Timothy what he had discussed with Jean Paul regarding the house and indicated to him that he need not be concerned with watching it since Jean Paul already agreed to conduct a nonobvious surveillance.

"While Jean Paul's men are watching this house, I will continue to surveil your house at the wharf for any Brit changes."

"Good, any thoughts or comments, Jean Paul?"

"Oui. I have already alerted my men regarding the surveillance, Monsieur William."

"Excellent."

"Oh, and Monsieur William."

"Yes, Jean Paul?"

"I spoke with Willie and Amos, and they both indicated that they would be happy to assist your manager and assistant manager in the distribution efforts to your customers."

"That is great news, Jean Paul, I am very grateful to you, Willie, and Amos. Please give them my heartfelt thanks and appreciation. Anticipating their approval, I have already spoken with David and George about appropriate compensation to your men."

"Merci, monsieur, but I have a question of you."

"And that is?"

"How are you going to receive any funds from the business if you and your family are not here to collect?"

"I intend on discussing this matter with Richard. While a primary reason for his sneaking into town has been to see our family, specifically Victoria," William said as he glanced at his daughter, "he has proved invaluable at gathering intelligence on the Brits from you and other sources and conveying that information to our command. I am certain that General Washington will be pleased to allow Richard to continue to assist in this important endeavor. Thus, he will periodically be coming to town to visit with you for intelligence. I will ask him if he would be willing to collect money from David and George and then take it to Lexington and give it to Annabelle."

"Very good," Jean Paul said, nodding.

As if on cue, Richard arrived, to the delight of everyone, especially Victoria.

"Richard—oh, Richard," Victoria said as she ran into his arms. "I am so happy you are here."

"Victoria, my darling, I am very happy to be here," Richard replied as he wrapped his young love tightly in his arms.

"Richard, I have been so worried about you, especially after that awful Battle of Bunker Hill." As she pulled back from his arms, she looked into his eyes and saw his pain. "Are you all right, my love? I see pain in your eyes; are you hurt?"

"I am fine," said Richard, trying to cover the pain.

"What happened to you, son? You can tell us," William said.

"Well, sir, before the battle really began, I was talking with a fellow soldier, a farm boy in the fort, and a cannonball flew over the wall and tore his head off. I mean, he was standing not more than a few paces away from me. That shook me; it shook me real bad. Colonel Prescott said a similar thing happened to him when he was a young soldier. His commander said there would not be a memorial service, and Colonel said we would not have one either. I could not accept that, nor could the others, so he relented, and we had a brief service. It seemed to quiet me down. Then, the battle got underway. The Brits came charging up the hill. After two unsuccessful charges up the hill, the Brits tried a third time, and this time they made it. They scaled the wall of the fort and charged in on us with bayonets. We were all out of powder and ammo, so we grabbed the barrels of our muskets and swung our guns like clubs. I was able to hit several redcoats, but to tell you the truth, sir, all I could think about was getting out of there. We were severely outnumbered, and our men were doing their best to fend off the Brits and escape. I worked my way toward the back of the fort, swinging my musket with all my strength. It was so difficult to get out the back. It was such a narrow exit, and everyone seemed to be trying to escape at the same time. Sir, I must admit, though I am not proud of it, I was scared, really scared, and I was sweating profusely, head to toe. My hands were so sweaty I do not know how I was able to keep a grip on the musket. Men were screaming and dropping all around me. All I could think about was getting out fast. I squeezed into the exit, and then suddenly, I was hit. It was my upper left arm. I popped out the back and started running for my life. Bullets were whizzing all around me." Richard's face reflected the tension that he experienced during that perilous time, his brow now wet with perspiration. His lower lip quivering, his eyes bulging, he continued. "I ran, sir; I ran for my life, I am ashamed to say. The wound was just a nick, but it really stung. I must say that it still hurts, but I am one of the fortunate ones. I am alive." Richard wiped the sweat from his brow.

"Richard, you have nothing to be ashamed of. You had no choice. The fort was overrun, and you had no powder or ammo. You clubbed as many of the enemy as you could before getting out of there. What else could you have done?"

"I do not know, Mr. Finch—I just feel ashamed."

"Son, there is no shame in fear, and there is no shame in running when there is no other option. Clearly you were not alone. Others did the same, and others were attempting to do the same but did not make it. We are so glad that you did."

"Thank you, sir, I certainly appreciate your words and thoughts. Sir…"

"Yes, Richard, is there something else?"

"Dr. Warren came to the fort. I later heard that he did not make it. He was shot in the face and fell over and died instantly."

"We heard the terrible news immediately following the battle," said Annabelle, her voice cracking.

"He was a great patriot," William said sadly. "He will be sorely missed—our cause has suffered a substantial blow by the loss of this man of liberty."

"Yes, sir, you and Jean Paul always spoke highly of him," said Richard.

"Oui, messieurs, he was a great man—a tremendous asset to us—a champion of liberty and—" Jean Paul said, fighting back tears, "a true friend."

"Richard," Victoria anxiously interjected, changing the subject, "your arm—is it all right?"

"Let me take a look at that dressing, if I may," said Annabelle.

"Yes, ma'am," Richard said as he removed his shirt.

After seeing the somewhat worn bandage, Annabelle offered to clean and bandage the wound, which Richard readily accepted. Within a matter of minutes, the job was done, and Richard was buttoning up his shirt.

"Richard, before you arrived, I gathered the family together to discuss a very important development."

"The appointment of General Washington, sir?"

"Yes. Mrs. Finch and I discussed this matter at length and concluded that now is the time for me to volunteer my services in the Continental Army. We have decided to accept your offer and move our family temporarily to Lexington. I already discussed the matter with your mother."

"That is wonderful, sir. General Washington and the army will be very fortunate to have your services. I am sure you will receive an excellent commission from him. I am very happy and thankful that your family is getting out of Boston and going to live with my family in Lexington. I have been concerned for your safety ever since the events of April."

"It is we who are thankful and very grateful to your family for this tremendous sacrifice. As close as our families are and have been, to actually live together is another matter. It is quite an imposition."

"Sir, I assure you that it is no imposition. All of us have wanted it for some time."

"You are most gracious; however, I have a couple more favors to ask of you. If you would be so kind as to introduce Joshua to Captain Parker, we would be most appreciative. Joshua has decided to join the Lexington militia."

"I will be glad to do so, but I must tell you that Captain Parker is gravely ill with tuberculosis."

"That is terrible news. Another hero soon to be gone."

"Yes, sir, but I believe he would be willing to meet Joshua and discuss the militia. They can use all the help they can possibly get."

"Good, I would like to thank him personally for his service. Also, I have talked with Jean Paul and Timothy about several things. They are going to be monitoring Brit activity as it pertains to our house and our house at the wharf. My belief is Gage or his successor will take over our house as soon as he realizes it is vacant. Willie and Amos have generously agreed to help David and George with distribution of goods to my customers. I mentioned to them that I would expect General Washington will continue using you as an intelligence-gathering resource."

"Yes, sir. I would anticipate that."

"No one is more adept at getting through enemy lines than you, and you have plenty of intelligence sources already established; the most prominent of which is right here now. Jean Paul and I had a heart-to-heart discussion when I went to tell him about my decision to volunteer my services. He told me that he was about to come to me and tell me that he had decided to volunteer his services. I said, not now; he is far too valuable to our cause in the position that he is in at this time. He has the best goods-smuggling and distribution network in town, and his intelligence-gathering network is superb. We need him here so long as the enemy remains in Boston."

Richard nodded in affirmation, glancing first at William and then Jean Paul.

"Thus when you come to town to gather information, if you are willing and are not too pressed for time, if you could, please proceed to the office and collect money from David and George and take it to Mrs. Finch. If you have time to pick up the funds but not enough time to go to Lexington, just bring the monies to me in Cambridge, and I will make arrangements for their delivery to Lexington. I will compensate you for your efforts."

"I will be very happy to assist you in this way, sir," Richard said as he looked at Annabelle and then Victoria, "but I do not want any compensation."

"I insist that you be paid appropriately. This is too important to me and my family and too much to ask of you without remuneration, understood?" William said firmly.

"Yes, sir," Richard said, conceding the matter. "Now may I ask you a question, sir?"

"Certainly."

"When do you plan on leaving?"

"My plan is that we leave right away, early tomorrow morning."

"Tomorrow morning?"

"Yes, we will load up early and go to Lexington. Then I thought you and I would leave the following day for Cambridge."

"One other matter. If I could speak with Jean Paul about the status of the Brit operations, I will not have to take a trip around town to gather information."

"Certainly, Monsieur Richard, let's talk alone, now—that is, if we are done," Jean Paul said as he looked at William.

"We are done, Jean Paul. Thank you and everyone for your support and attention. These are very difficult days with very difficult decisions, but with God's strength and blessing and with us working together, we will make it through. I believe we will be the better for it." After talking at some length with Richard, Jean Paul and Timothy said their good-byes to everyone.

"I need to see Mark right away," Becky said in a loud voice as she approached Dr. Mark Wilson's assistant, early on the morning following the battle.

"Miss Braun, he is with a patient. Please take a seat, and he will be with you when he is done."

"It is all right, Miss Jones," Mark Wilson said as he emerged from his patient rooms into the office lobby, "the patient can wait a few minutes. Now, Becky, what is so urgent?"

"Mark, terrible news—Dr. Warren was killed during the battle!"

"Joseph? Oh, dear God—not Joseph!" said Wilson, visibly shaken. His legs getting weak, he collapsed in a chair. "How...how did it happen?"

"The information that I received is that he was in the fort when it was breeched by the Brits. He was involved in hand-to-hand combat when a Brit recognized him. Dr. Warren turned toward the man and was shot in the face. He fell, struck dead immediately."

"That is awful—a terrible tragedy—an immeasurable loss to the medical community and our glorious cause. I will miss him; he was a wonderful man—a pillar of the town and a dear friend. It is just like him to risk his life in the field of battle—he is irreplaceable."

"Yes," said Becky as she pulled up a chair next to Wilson and tried to console him, "he was all those things."

"Thank you for sharing this with me."

"You are welcome, though if I had known it would affect you this much, I would have waited."

"No, no, you did the right thing. I am glad I received the news from you; however, I am in no condition to proceed with my patient. Miss Jones, please tell the patient to come back tomorrow morning around eight o'clock. Please offer my apologies."

"Yes, Doctor, I will take care of it for you."

"And I will take you home," Becky said.

"If you take me, how will I get my carriage home?"

"I will bring Mr. Archibald back here in my carriage, and he can then take yours back home."

"Thank you, my dear. That is so very kind of you."

"Miss Jones, will you please help me hoist Dr. Wilson into my carriage?"

"Certainly."

Becky drove Wilson home, brought Mr. Archibald back to Wilson's office for the carriage, and then proceeded to Maggie's, hoping to find Francois on duty.

"Francois...oh, Francois."

"Becky, mon chéri—are you all right?"

"I am fine."

"Are you sure? You look like you are stressed."

"Well, I am somewhat..." Becky said, her voice trailing off. "Francois, I need to speak with you for a minute."

"I am very busy right now; can this wait?"

"I promise that I will only take a minute of your time."

"All right, let us go to a table in the back where you can sit and settle down, and we can talk in private. Maggie is in the office right now."

After proceeding to a table, Becky sat down, and Francois brought her a glass of water.

"Here, this should help."

"Thank you, darling," Becky said as she took the glass and took a long gulp.

"Now what is the matter?"

"I went to Mark's office to tell him the terrible news of Dr. Warren's death in the battle."

"Oui, that is terrible, terrible news," Francois said, with a somber look on his face. "He was a great patriot whom we all admired."

"That is true, but Mark was utterly devastated. He collapsed in a chair and put his head in his hands. He had to release a patient. His assistant, Miss Jones, and I had to hoist him into my carriage. I drove him home and then brought Mr. Archibald back to Mark's office to fetch Mark's carriage."

"Is Wilson all right?"

"I think so. He seemed to gain color and strength as we reached his home. He was able to get down from the carriage with only minimal assistance from me."

"So what is the problem?"

"If Mark is a traitor, then why did he react as he did? Why would he be so completely weakened physically by this news?"

"Fair question," Francois said, shaking his head, "but even though he is a traitor, it does not mean that he could not be very fond of Dr. Warren. They did spend much time together. It is possible that Wilson became quite attached to Warren even while Wilson was betraying Warren's confidence. Does that seem reasonable?"

"I think so," Becky said, slowly nodding her head, "but I am not entirely certain—I do not understand how a real traitor can react like that; that was not faked, Francois."

"Are you still doubting that he is a traitor who is collaborating and conveying vital information to the enemy?"

"Well…"

"Becky, you saw the man commit treachery with your own eyes."

"But all I saw was him leaving his house in his carriage."

"Right after you in essence told him that Dr. Warren and my father were on to the Brit excursion to Lexington and Concord. Given his suspicious reaction to your news, then cutting the evening short for no good reason, and immediately leaving the house in the dead of night, it is clear cut—he is a traitor. But I must admit he is a darn good actor."

"But I told you he was not faking."

"Perhaps. You would be surprised at what some men can do to cover their true feelings. But again, it is also possible that it was a genuine reaction borne out of a close, though deceptive, relationship."

"I suppose you are right, but my heart still does not want to believe it."

"Believe it, Becky; I am right. This man has been using you. I am not saying that he does not have any feelings for you, but I am certain his motive from the beginning was to gain your confidence and gather as much information as possible to pass on to his go-between. I know that this is difficult for you to acknowledge, but it is the truth."

"Yes—I have known that in my mind for a long time."

"It is time for you to believe it in your heart. Be careful."

14

"Congratulations, Mr. Jefferson, on your selection by the leadership in Congress to the committee to draft the document that will succinctly state our rationale for taking up arms against the mother country. Since penmanship is your strong suit, it was thought that you would be the right choice for this important endeavor," John Adams remarked to Jefferson during a brief recess, regarding the latter's appointment to the committee to draft what would be known as the Declaration of the Causes and Necessity for Taking Up Arms or Causes and Necessities. Jefferson, the distinguished Virginia planter and youngest member of Congress, had just arrived in an ostentatious carriage with three slaves.

"Thank you, kind sir. I am flattered that the leadership in Congress would choose me, a delegate who has only arrived a few days ago."

"While that is true, your earlier work, *A Summary View of the Rights of British America*, which was brilliantly stated, has preceded you. In *Summary View*, you got to the point when you said that 'the British Parliament has no right to exercise authority over us.' And the charges you leveled at the king and his handling of the monarchy and treatment of the colonies were bold, perhaps harsh, but they made a positive impression on me and many in the leadership. The recitation of English history, woven into your citing of monarchial transgressions, was masterful and enlightening. Thus, on the basis of what we have read of your work, we are all confident that you will deliver the right message. But I must warn you that on the committee are some of the moderates in Congress, most significant of whom is John Dickinson of Pennsylvania."

"I am familiar with Mr. Dickinson."

"Then you are aware that he still seeks reconciliation with England, even at this late date and after all that has transpired. He will be drafting a petition to that effect to the king."

"So I understand."

"He was put on the committee so that we will have bipartisan support for the final product. I can assure you that Mr. Dickinson will not hesitate to make his opinions known, speaking from personal experience."

"I have heard of his outspoken approach and of the issues between the two of you, but if called upon to draft the document, I will do so as I deem appropriate, on the basis of the facts and circumstances as I know and understand them."

"Very good. I wish you the best in your assignment."

"Thank you, sir."

The morning dawned bright and clear, perfect for travel. After a special farewell-to-Boston breakfast, prepared by Grace and the cooks, William, Richard, Joshua, and Judah began loading the carriages with the family essentials, which included much of the women's clothing.

"Mister William, if I may say so, there sure are a lot of ladies' clothes."

"You are right, Judah; there are a lot of ladies' clothes, but far be it from me to make an issue of it. I am certain if I said anything to them, they would let me know they were making a sacrifice in taking only a small fraction of their wardrobes."

"I know they have a lot of clothes, but this is a small fraction? Wow, Mister William, that is amazing!"

"Yes, Judah, it is amazing. There is nothing I can do about their clothes, so let us get everything loaded into the wagons and carriages as quickly as possible and head down the road and out of town."

"Yes, sir, Mister William," Judah said as he hoisted another chest full of clothes into a wagon. Richard assisted in the endeavor, and shortly they were ready to go. William locked the house up tightly, and the whole family bid adieu to their spacious but warm house for a life in much more crowded quarters in Lexington.

The carriages pulled away from the stately home as the sun rose rapidly in the sky. Judah, with Grace next to him, was sitting at the front of a loaded-down wagon, while the other female servants walked quietly alongside.

After arriving in Lexington, the men unloaded the wagons and carriages, first moving Annabelle, Joshua, and Victoria into the Barneses' home and then Grace and the other servants above the store. James and Margaret Barnes went to their grandparents, Frederick and Deborah Williams, who lived across Lexington Green. Finally Judah moved into Jonathan's office in the outbuilding.

"Annabelle, Eleanor, I realize that we just arrived and there has not been much time to adjust, but does everything seem satisfactory, at least thus far?" William asked the ladies, prior to going to a meeting with Captain Parker.

"Everything is quite satisfactory," said Annabelle. "You do not have to worry about us; we will be just fine."

"It may take a little while before everyone is completely settled and comfortable with their roles and environs, but everyone will be soon. Your family will be safe and loved while they are here with us," Eleanor added.

"I know they will be," William said, "especially loved."

"We consider it to be a privilege to have your family stay with us during this difficult time. We are all very proud of you for your decision to serve your country, which is in great need of your leadership."

"You do not know how much your family means to me and my family. Our relationship spills over the bounds of friendship. I will give everything that I have on behalf of my country, and certainly my mind can focus on the job before me knowing that my family is here with you. Now before Richard and I leave, Joshua, come with us to Captain Parker's, and Richard will introduce you to him. Are you ready to go?"

"Yes, Father."

"All right. Ladies, we will return shortly," said William as he, Richard, and Joshua boarded the carriage.

"Richard, if you will direct us to Captain Parker's house."

"It will be my pleasure."

"Captain," Richard said, saluting John Parker.

"Come in, gentlemen, come in," said Parker, gesturing. "Please have a seat."

William, Richard, and Joshua pulled up chairs around the kitchen table. Parker was gaunt, the dreaded consumption that he had contracted before that fateful day of April 19, had ravaged his body. He coughed repeatedly as William began to speak.

"Captain, I promise that we will not be long. I am honored to meet you, and I wanted to personally thank you for your service to our cause. Your contribution, I am sure, will never be forgotten in the annals of our nation."

"I appreciate your kind assessment," Parker managed between coughs.

"The reason for our visit is that since Congress adopted the army and George Washington was appointed as commander and given the rank of general, I decided to volunteer my services. Additionally, General Gage gave his blessing to all who would leave Boston to do so at this time with no repercussions, so my wife and I decided to take the Barneses up on their offer to move our family in with them. My son Joshua, who was working with my assistants in my merchant business, has over the past several months been aiding the cause by delivering smuggled goods to needy families in Boston. He will now be the man of the combined households. While the women will have plenty of worthwhile tasks for him, I believe it best for him to join the militia to receive training and be available if called upon."

Captain Parker gathered himself and after a hard cough replied, "I was not able to be at Bunker Hill for obvious reasons, and for those reasons, I am stepping down as head of the militia," he wheezed. He took a drink of water and continued, "I will write out a note of recommendation that you may take with you," he said, looking at Joshua, "though I doubt that you will need it. I am sure they will be quite pleased to have an able-bodied young man join them." Parker pulled himself up, walked slowly to the only desk in the house, opened the top drawer, and got out a piece of parchment, quill pen, and ink well. He wrote out a brief note, signed and dated it, and handed it to Joshua. Joshua read it over and gave it to William.

"Thank you very much, sir. I truly appreciate this," Joshua said.

"You are most—" a loud, long hacking cough emanated from deep within the man—"welcome," Parker finished.

"Captain, we are most grateful to you for your recommendation. Again, it was an honor to meet you. We will not take any more of your time and do not trouble yourself; we will show ourselves out," William said as he gently shook Parker's frail hand. Parker nodded, and the three guests departed.

Upon their return to the Barneses' residence, Judah assisted William and Richard in loading the carriage. After brief, tearful good-byes were exchanged, Richard and Victoria firmly embraced for several seconds, followed by a kiss.

"Good-bye again, my darling," Victoria said, looking with moist eyes into the face of her beloved.

"Good-bye, my love," Richard replied, as he again tightened his embrace and whispered his words into her ear. "Do not worry; I will be just fine. I will be back as soon as possible."

"I will be praying for God's hand of protection upon you and Father," Victoria said as they released their embrace and he held her hands in his.

Richard raised her right hand and placed a gentle kiss upon it. "I feel a certain comfort knowing you are petitioning the Almighty on our behalf," he said as he gazed into her eyes.

"Richard, we must be off," William said, gently tapping Richard on the shoulder.

Richard released Victoria's hand but continued to gaze at her.

"Now, Richard."

"Yes, sir."

And with that, Richard turned and climbed up into the carriage while William boarded on the driver's side. As Richard waved to Victoria, they started down the road to Cambridge.

"General Gage," said his attaché as he approached.

"What is it, James?"

"I have it on good authority that the treacherous William Finch and his family have left Boston for Lexington."

"And his house is left empty and unattended?"

"That is what I have been told, General."

"I fear, James, that I will not be in charge here for much longer. The audacity of Finch to protest the quartering of troops in his house down by the wharf, when it was perfectly legal under the Quartering Act. He actually was so brazen as to tell me the law was unconstitutional! I have suspected that William Finch sent his daughter and chief servant to warn that scoundrel, Jean Paul Pierre DuBois, of what he believed was an imminent excursion by our troops. One of our spies thought he saw them in the vicinity of DuBois's house. James, it would give me great pleasure to make that house my headquarters, if only for a day. So go, James—go to the house right now and personally verify the status of the dwelling and report back to me at once."

"I will be back momentarily."

William and Richard arrived in Cambridge on the evening of June 30. Richard introduced William to all his acquaintances in the army the following day, and they together met the officers, who were especially pleased to have a man of William's stature now on board. The buzz throughout the camp was the imminent arrival of the new general and commander in chief, George Washington.

"Welcome, Mr. Finch," said Colonel Prescott, "we are very glad to have you here with the army."

"And I, sir, am very happy to be here."

"Your timing is impeccable. We await the arrival of General Washington."

"What is the feeling in the army about the general, sir? Are there issues or concerns since he is a Virginian and this is primarily a northeastern army?"

"There were rumblings initially, especially among the officers. Several wanted Ward to continue on, but I noticed a change of heart as we learned more about General Washington. It appears that he is a man of significant reputation and standing."

"I am glad to hear that because I can tell you from personal experience and observation, having met the man myself in Philadelphia, that he is indeed a man of significant reputation and standing. I know of no one better to lead this army and unite the country."

"It should be a momentous occasion for the army and our young country, when he and his bride arrive."

"She is coming with him?"

"Yes, Martha Washington is her name. I understand that she is quite wealthy and a perfect hostess, the epitome of a southern plantation woman."

"It sounds as if…if I may say this in our current political climate, that they may be our royalty."

"You may be correct. If so, let us hope that they will be royalty with a heart for the people."

15

General George Washington and his bride, Martha, arrived on the morning of July 2, amid much flourish and fanfare. A ceremony was held in Washington's honor, attended by many dignitaries, including Abigail Adams.

William introduced Richard to Washington, and they immediately struck up a conversation.

"Private Richard Barnes, are you, perchance, the son of delegate to Congress Jonathan Barnes?"

"I am, sir."

"Your father is indeed a man of distinction. I had the great pleasure of meeting him along with Mr. Finch, here, his best friend," said Washington, gesturing toward William, "at City Tavern in Philadelphia during the First Continental Congress."

"Yes, sir," Richard said.

"That was following his stirring reading of the Declaration of Rights."

"My father was thrilled to meet you, sir. It was following a second meeting with you at City Tavern during the Second Continental Congress that he wrote to my mother and told her that he believed you might be the best hope to unite our country."

"He did, did he?"

"He was right, as he usually is," William interjected.

"I am certain that he was right in this instance," said Eleanor Barnes as she and Annabelle Finch approached.

William and Richard were stunned as they turned to see the ladies, but before they could utter a word, Annabelle said to them, "We decided to surprise you, and we simply had to welcome General Washington to the Bay Colony."

"I understand. And Joshua?" said William, with a look of mild concern on his face.

"Joshua is doing very well. Do not be concerned," Eleanor said.

"Then he has become the man of the house in my absence and quite quickly,"

William said, with a slight nod of the head in appreciation of his son.

"General Washington," William said, as he turned his attention back to him, "it is my pleasure to introduce you to my wife and Lydia's mother, Annabelle Finch."

"And, General Washington, sir," Richard added, "I am pleased to introduce you to my mother—"

"Eleanor Barnes, General," Eleanor interjected. "I am so very pleased to make your acquaintance. Welcome to Massachusetts."

Washington, with the utmost grace and ease, quickly took the outstretched hand of Annabelle and then of Eleanor and lightly planted kisses on them.

"Mrs. Finch and Mrs. Barnes," Washington said as he looked first at Annabelle and then at Eleanor, "it is my great pleasure to meet you, the matriarchs of such distinguished families."

"Thank you, sir. I must say that we are very proud of our families," Eleanor said, smiling as she squeezed Richard in a side hug.

"As well you should be. You have a son who is risking his life in defense of his country and a husband who is making a major contribution in creating and legislating policy for his country. And Mrs. Finch, you have a renowned merchant husband who has volunteered his services to serve in the Continental Army and a very lovely daughter. Much indeed to be proud about."

"Sir, my decision to volunteer my services now was due to your having been given the command of this army. With your arrival to unite us in the common cause and the stature that you bring to the command, I knew that I must now come and offer my services, such as they may be, to you. I am at your disposal, sir," William said.

"I am flattered that you placed such faith in me. I will confer with the other officers and soon offer you a commission. I am grateful for your willingness to serve your country and the cause of liberty at great personal cost to you and your family."

"I am the one who is grateful, and I know that *your* service is at great personal cost to you, sir, and to your family. I believe I speak for everyone here when I say we are indebted to you for the example that you have set for us all."

Washington nodded, shook hands again, and the Finches and Barneses took their leave.

Abigail Adams wrote to John to tell him that Washington was much more than John had said. Eleanor Barnes also wrote to Jonathan regarding the day's developments:

> My dearest Jonathan,
>
> What a glorious day for our country! Everyone was here to see the arrival of General Washington and his wife and hostess, Martha Washington. There was much pomp and circumstance, not unlike what would be befitting royalty. As I understand it, William even made such a remark to Colonel Prescott before the Washingtons' arrival, and Prescott replied something like if they be royalty, then "let us hope that they will be royalty with a heart for the people." I do not think that will be a problem; they seem to be very gracious. General Washington has great physical presence. You

can immediately tell that he is a leader. He exudes strength and confidence. As Abigail Adams has observed, he is "dignity with ease." My impression is that he is everything we could hope for in someone to take charge of this army. He commands respect. You and the Congress chose wisely when you picked him to be commander in chief. I am very proud of you and of William, who has decided to join in the fight for our glorious cause. I am certain that General Washington will give him a commission worthy of his ability. I miss you more than words can say, and the children long for your return. I am so grateful for your service to our country, especially at this critical juncture.

All my love,
Eleanor

"Now this is the headquarters that I should have had from the beginning," Gage said to James, his attaché, as he surveyed the spacious house, now filled with his furniture from his prior headquarters, along with all the Finches' furniture, which he decided to keep.

"General, it really is quite becoming, a place worthy of being your headquarters."

"Gentlemen of the committee," John Dickinson said, addressing the committee of five selected for drafting the Declaration of the Causes and Necessities of Taking Up Arms, "I have reviewed Mr. Jefferson's draft and would urge you to consider the following revisions."

Jefferson, seated across from Dickinson, flinched inside at the mention of modifications to his draft, but showed nothing outwardly. To Jefferson, his writing was as natural as breathing, such that any changes, however small, would alter the poetic feeling of his work.

"Our cause, the cause of establishing a nation whose cornerstone is liberty, is just and noble. In this we citizens of the colonies are as one."

Jefferson was puzzled. Were these the words of a man who was even now preparing a peace petition for the king? Was it reconciliation or justification?

"Our internal resources, many yet untapped, are substantial, and if needed, we shall seek and obtain help from foreign nations."

The committee adopted many of Dickinson's revisions, and so did Congress on July 6, 1775, just a day after it adopted his so-called Olive Branch Petition, a last-ditch effort by the Congress, particularly the moderates, to end the conflict and heal the wounds between the mother country and the colonies. Both reached Britain about the same time, along with a letter that had been intercepted from John Adams to a friend, whereby Adams referred to the petition and its author in a rather disparaging, derogatory way.

"Captain William Finch reporting, sir," William said, saluting Colonel Henry Knox. Knox, the portly proprietor of the London Bookstore in Boston, who learned military tactics from his own books, had become the chief artillery officer of the army.

"Captain, though you have only been in camp a short while, I have heard many fine things about the leadership and organizational skills that you have shown from your civilian life. I need a man of your talents to assist in an important ongoing undertaking."

"How may I be of service, sir?"

"Captain, I am putting you in charge of the fortifications. Though you do not have an engineering background, I am confident in your ability to do the job, which of course I will oversee. Our breast works and trench works are thick and deep in some places, but, as I am sure you are aware, our defenses are stretched thin over several miles."

"Yes, sir," William said, gently nodding his head.

"And, what with the scattered firing that occurs and the bombardments from the Brits, this can be dangerous, though tedious work for the troops."

"I understand."

"The intelligence we have been able to gather, thus far, largely through Private Barnes, points to no attack forthcoming from the Brits, which is confounding to His Excellency and to me."

"And to me as well, sir."

"Despite these reports, His Excellency is intent on remaining vigilant, which is why I have chosen you. Your job will entail not only directing the physical work but also boosting and maintaining troop morale, which is vital."

"I appreciate your confidence in me, sir. I assure you I will devote my full efforts to the task set before me."

"I am confident you will, sir," Knox said with a slight smile. "And I am certain His Excellency will concur. You are dismissed."

"Sir," William said, as he saluted and left.

"Excellency," said Joseph Reed, Washington's personal secretary, who accompanied him from Philadelphia, as he approached Washington in his headquarters study, located in a large drawing room on the first floor and which was tastefully decorated by Martha Washington. Headquarters was a spacious three-story Georgian mansion abandoned by loyalist John Vassall. The house was chosen over Samuel Langdon's home, which was too small for Washington's needs.

"Yes, Mr. Reed, come in. What is it?"

"Excellency, the Massachusetts legislature and Congress have learned of the letter to Virginia, where you said the New England troops are an 'exceedingly dirty and nasty people.' Excellency, they are outraged. You must apologize immediately."

"Apologize?" Washington peered over the top of this glasses, which were slid down on his nose. "Whatever for? What I wrote is true. You have seen these people yourself. Am I not correct in my assessment?" Washington said with conviction.

"Well...yes, Excellency, but..." Reed said with some hesitancy.

"But what, Mr. Reed? These people are filthy, and that shows a lack of discipline. They must clean up their physical appearance and condition, learn manners that comport with being a good soldier, and learn discipline. Only then will we have any hope at all of defeating the Regulars. And it is not just the individual soldiers. You saw the condition of this camp when we arrived and for that matter the current condition. The place has a foul odor and that is understandable when men urinate and defecate anywhere that seems convenient to them."

Washington shook his head while relating these details as Reed cringed.

"Trash strewn everywhere—let us be truthful, the place is only slightly better than a dump, and I am probably being generous in saying that."

"I do agree that they are a dirty people. Most of them being outdoorsmen or at least spending much time in the outdoors in hard labor, though I do not think that I would call them nasty. With your leadership I feel certain they will in time become good soldiers."

"Perhaps I have been a bit harsh," Washington said, upon reflection.

"But all this is irrelevant. It really does not matter whether what you wrote is true or not. You must have the full support of the Massachusetts legislature and especially the Congress if you expect to lead this army. If you do not retract that statement in a full apology that shows true contrition, you will have to proceed alone."

"Yes, yes—I suppose you are right." Washington slowly and gently nodded his head, his eyes fixed with a far-off hollow look.

"Do you wish for me to draft the letter of apology?"

Washington snapped out of it and replied, "Yes. Draft the letter of apology, and express my sincere and heartfelt regrets to the legislature and Congress. I will sign it, and you make certain that it gets delivered. Let them know that it will not occur again."

"I will take care of it at once, Excellency," Reed said as he turned to leave.

These are exceedingly dirty and nasty people, Washington thought, as he seethed inside. *Troop cleanliness and discipline must characterize this army, but I must be careful in expressing my opinions, lest I lose the support of my superiors. Now is the time to address these issues, while it is still early in my command.*

"Mr. Reed, before you go," Washington said, as Reed was about to open the door.

"Yes, Excellency?"

"Let us take this opportunity to alleviate some of the problems we have been discussing."

"Sir?" Reed said as he slid back down into one of the beautiful royal-blue chairs situated in front of Washington's desk.

"I am issuing a series of orders; take these down," Washington said, again peering over his glasses while pointing his right index finger, not at Reed but as a gesture of emphasis.

Reed quickly pulled out parchment and was in readiness to write.

"The troops must bathe regularly—that is an order—and while I will not order where they do their bathing, I will make it clear that they are not to bathe near the bridge, where the local citizens, especially the women, can gaze upon them. They are ordered to have their clothes washed regularly, and this is important." Washington took his right index finger and gently pounded it on the table, causing Reed to momentarily look up from the parchment. "All latrines are to be at least one hundred yards from the dining tent. Also, while this is not an order, I do want all to realize that I will not countenance or tolerate public drunkenness or profanity; they shall no longer characterize this army but rather proper discipline and respect. Now regarding the officers, while I have admonished them regarding their proper conduct with the troops, I think it would be expedient to remind them in writing. Do you recall my admonishment?"

"Yes, Excellency, 'be easy—but not too familiar, lest you subject yourself to want of respect.' I think these are excellent orders and rules of comportment." After finishing his writing on the parchment, Reid handed them to Washington for signature.

"Circulate the orders and rules, as you called them, to the officers," Washington said as he signed and handed them back to Reed.

"I will take care of the matter, forthwith," Reed said as he once again turned to leave and this time went out the door.

"How can this possibly be?" Washington asked Henry Knox, shortly after Washington took command.

"You are informing me only have thirty-eight barrels of gunpowder for this entire army?"

"Yes, Excellency, that is our entire supply," replied a rather embarrassed Knox.

"And the word that I received was that there were four hundred thirty barrels."

"Sir, I am not sure who provided you with that number, but we have never had even close to that figure."

"How is this army supposed to fight with only thirty-eight barrels of gunpowder?" said Washington, an incredulous look on his face. The stark realization was that while cleanliness and discipline were major problem, this was the biggest challenge he faced.

"Obviously, we cannot," replied Knox glumly.

"Yes, obviously we cannot. And I was concerned about four hundred thirty barrels being enough!" Washington said, shaking his head. Please summons Mr. Reed. I must write to Congress immediately about this woeful situation."

"Yes, Excellency."

"Your Excellency," said William as he was ushered into Washington's office, saluting the general and commander in chief, who returned the salute.

"Captain Finch, how are you? I am hearing good things from Henry about your work on the entrenchments and fortifications," Washington said as he rose from behind his desk, gently placing his spectacles on the papers before him.

"I am quite well, sir; thank you for asking, and thank you so much for the compliment."

"Captain, please take a seat," Washington said as he gestured to William to sit in one of the chairs stationed in front of his desk.

Washington sat back down, and William then sat down and continued.

"The work is not so much challenging as it is tedious. Keeping the men motivated to build defenses—that may be the biggest challenge of all. Truthfully, sir, if I may be at liberty to speak freely."

"You may."

"The men are itching for a fight, Excellency," William said as he fingered his hat in his hands, gazing intently at Washington.

"I completely understand. I too am 'itching for a fight,' as you say, but all the intelligence I am receiving is that the British are not ready to make a move. Nevertheless, we must be vigilant in building our defenses and be ready for anything."

"I assure you that we are vigilant and ready."

"I am certain you are, and for that I am very pleased. Now, what may I do for you? I know that you had something on your mind to discuss with me."

"Yes, Excellency. I wanted to compliment you on the orders and rules of comportment that you circulated to the officers. Camp cleanliness, personal hygiene, and discipline are critical. I especially appreciate your admonishment to all of us officers to 'be easy—but not too familiar, lest you subject yourself to want of respect.' I believe that was the perfect statement as to how we are to conduct ourselves. It is very relevant to us here in New England, who tend to be a bit too friendly to enlisted men. I am trying very hard to incorporate your approach in my daily dealings in the men."

"I am very glad you feel this way. I do believe this approach is critical to our cause. It is not just a Virginian or southern gentleman attitude, but a 'rule of comportment' among successful armies and military operations. Separation, distinction between officers and the men, is a key foundation, vitally important, especially in the heat of battle."

"There must be a defined chain of command. All must know and respect the officer in charge, especially when bullets are whizzing about and cannonballs are flying overhead." William paused. "When lives are at stake—matters of life and death—and a battle may hang in the balance."

"Indeed," said Washington, nodding his head, with a slight smile on his face, a look of admiration in his eyes. "I could not have said it better myself. I need your help in spreading this message to your fellow officers."

"I will do all that I can, although I may not be the best to convey the message."

"Why is that?" asked Washington, with a puzzled look.

"Because you gave me a commission. I am not subject to reelection by the enlisted men as are most of the other officers."

"Yes, I understand."

"Nevertheless, I will do everything in my power to lead by example, sir, keeping a discreet distance from the men."

"I am sure that you will be a splendid example, Captain," said Washington, maintaining a slight smile and gently nodding his head. "Anything else that I may do for you?"

"No, Excellency. However, I just want you to know that your presence here has had a profound effect upon the troops."

"How so?"

"You have brought joy and confidence to the army. We are so glad that you are here to lead us."

Hearing this ringing endorsement, Washington was very happy that his comment about New Englanders in his letter to Virginia had not leaked out to the troops.

"Captain, it does my heart good to hear that I have the troops' favor."

"Oh, you do, sir; you do."

"Thank you so much for your visit," Washington said as he stood up from behind the desk and moved around to William as William got up from his chair. "This visit has lifted my spirits immensely." Washington smiled warmly and took William's hand firmly in his large right hand, squeezed, and shook it firmly.

"Mine too, Excellency," William said, saluting and then taking his leave.

As William left, Washington thought, *This is the kind of officer I so desperately need. Oh, but for more men like him!*

"Messieurs Willie and Amos," said Jean Paul as he greeted his chief lieutenant and his lieutenant's worthy assistant, in his office at JP's, "General Gage moved very quickly to commandeer the Finches' house as his new headquarters. While Monsieur Finch made it clear that I was not to attempt to interfere if this occurred, he did ask me to keep an eye out to find out who occupied the premises and to what purpose and to watch for comings and goings. Willie, you are familiar with Gage's officers and staff, but are you, Amos?"

"Yes, sir, I believe I know them all."

"He does, sir. During our distributions around town over the course of the past several months, I have had opportunity to point them out to him," Willie said.

"Very good, then I want you, Willie, to pick two of your best men for this assignment, which is to do what I promised Monsieur Finch I would do. I want you to each take one of the men with you when you go for this surveillance, so they can learn what you do and you can point out the officers and staff. If your men already know them, so much the better. I do not care how you two split up the assignment. Obviously, messieurs, you will need to be very discreet. Make certain that you are not detected. You should probably move around to different locations somewhat removed from the house so that you do not fall into a pattern. Same goes for time of the surveillance. I would vary it, messieurs, again to avoid falling into a pattern that could lead to detection. I want daily surveillance, and while it will not be the entire day, it needs to primarily be early morning, around noon, late afternoon, and early evening, times when there is most likely to be activity and people coming to and going from the house. I want you to report back to me weekly unless you see or sense any suspicious activity, and then you need to report back to me immediately. After you have done this for two or three weeks, if you feel comfortable with the progress of the men, I will have you pick two other men to be trained by your trainees so that no one will be overburdened."

"Will we then be relieved of our duties, sir?" Amos asked.

"Good question, Amos. Oui, but not entirely. I want you two to periodically join whoever is doing the surveillance to make certain that it is getting done properly. As Monsieur Finch said, some very valuable intelligence may be gathered from this endeavor. I know that both of you have a great deal to do, but you are my best, most trustworthy men. However, our primary focus is still distributing the smuggled goods throughout town to the needy. These people are dependent upon whatever we can provide for them, so if this process is simply too burdensome for us, I need to hear that from you and your thoughts about what, if anything, can be done to solve the problems. Questions?"

"Where and when do you want us to report to you, sir?" Willie asked.

"Come right here to my office at JP's. I would say it would be best to come in the middle of the night and enter the back door in the alleyway. Be on the alert to make sure no one sees you. If you notice one or more Brit spies or Gage's officers or staff in the tavern, just order a drink, act very casual, and leave. I will understand if you do not appear at my office. If this persists for several nights or seems to be occurring regularly, then come very discreetly to my house, knock with three quick, hard knocks, followed by two soft knocks, followed by three more hard, fast knocks. This is a code that I worked out with Monsieur Judah a long time ago, and I will let Cheebs know that it will be you. We will then discuss either changing our meeting place or time or both. I will see you a week from tonight. All right, messieurs?"

"Yes, sir," Willie said, while Amos nodded.

Summer had been a time of adjustment for Annabelle, Joshua, Victoria, and Judah and the rest of the Finch servants, as well as a time of adjustment for Eleanor, Margaret, James, and Eleanor's parents, Frederick and Deborah Williams.

Annabelle was grateful to be out of Boston what with the constant surveillance by the hated Brits and the scourge of smallpox, not to mention the struggle for food and supplies that even they had to deal with on a regular basis. Even though she, the children, and the servants had been inoculated, she knew that the disease was taking a devastating toll in the city, affecting every aspect of life. Yes, it was good to be out of there at this time, especially with William joining the army. Nevertheless, life in Lexington with the Barneses was not easy for the Finch clan. It was a major change for everyone concerned, and all did their best to cope with the difficult, albeit temporary situation that the circumstances of life had dealt them. And while there was food available in Lexington, primarily due to the large garden the Barneses maintained behind their general store, which produced an abundance of delicious vegetables, there was a definite shortage of other supplies. This shortage left far too many empty spaces on the shelves of the store, shelves that in the past were overflowing from goods supplied from none other than Annabelle's wonderful merchant husband and Jonathan's best friend, William. Now their chief supply line was Michael Beaumont, who saw to it that supplies smuggled up from South Carolina would first stop in Lexington before heading to Boston.

William was close by and did manage to come to Lexington with Richard a few times over the summer months, but the stays were brief, and it was clear that William's mind was elsewhere. Worries about Timothy, Jean Paul, members of the merchants' association, the status of the Finch house, and the progress of the defenses and entrenchments that Henry Knox had put him in charge of all made his visits less than fulfilling for Annabelle, who had worries of her own about William's safety.

Additionally, while Eleanor was a most gracious hostess and the home was homey and adequate for the Barnes family, it was a far cry from the lovely, spacious Finch abode in the heart of Boston. It was even tougher for Victoria, who actually saw less of Richard than when she was in Boston. She missed the political intrigue in the city and the spying that she occasionally engaged in for Jean Paul and his network. But it was most difficult for Joshua, now twenty-two years old, who had been, along with his friend Amos, assisting Willie Boyd in delivering smuggled food and other goods throughout embattled Boston. Service in the militia had proved to be a godsend for him, as he learned a great deal about preparedness, but he felt rather useless.

He no longer had the distribution work, and his father and friend were off in a noble cause serving in the army, and his friend's father was serving his country in Congress. Joshua did work very hard, tending the garden, stacking shelves in the store with what supplies were available, and making wagon runs with Judah to and from the store, including trips to take supplies to the troops. But with each visit of William and Richard and each touch with them and other soldiers in the camp, he grew more and more restless to see action of any kind.

"Benjamin," Jonathan Barnes said as he quickly approached Franklin, following the vote to name him postmaster general, "congratulations on your appointment to the new and vitally important position of postmaster general. You are the right man for this position."

"Jonathan, thank you; thank you so much. I certainly have appreciated all your support," Franklin replied as the two friends shared a firm handshake.

"Not at all, you have always deserved not just my support but also the support of all in this room, and now you finally have it. The brilliantly conceived Articles of Confederation, while premature for many of the members of Congress, clearly had a soothing effect regarding your loyalties."

"Though the rumors were already dying out, as I knew they would, I believe that you are correct; the articles may have squelched the matter for good. I certainly hope, however, that they will serve a far greater purpose than just relieving concerns about my loyalties."

"I have no doubt that they will, sir. I have discussed the terms with several delegates. Some were admittedly horrified, but others were equally impressed by the detail and breadth of your proposal. Providing for the common defense of the colonies, securing our liberty and safety, providing for our general welfare—all are important foundational and overreaching concepts, which are critical for our survival as a nation."

"We must no longer think provincially, if we hope to endure and flourish."

"I wholeheartedly agree, sir. And giving Congress the power to determine war and peace, to enter into alliances and treaties, and to make ordinances regarding commerce and currency enables it to effectuate the broad concepts."

"Congress must have authority to implement the broad concepts, or all is for naught."

"Absolutely. And by further giving Congress the power to create and oversee a post office for the entire country, this may be the most vital detail of all."

"Without a regular and reliable means of communication, we cannot hope to be a unified people."

"I am grateful that my fellow delegates at least saw the wisdom in creating the postal system at this juncture."

"I am very pleased. I was well aware that the Articles as a whole would be too radical for many at this time; that is why I did not ask for a formal record or vote. Even with the provision in the Articles terminating them, if the Brits make full restoration of our rights and privileges and compensation for all the economic damage they have done to us, it was obvious that my assessment was correct. However, I believe we must be forward thinking, which is why I brought them to Congress when I did."

"The day will come when that plan will play a big role in the establishment of a new government for these colonies; of that you may rest assured."

"Excellency, you sent for me?" Joseph Reed said as he quietly entered Washington's office.

"Mr. Reed, please come in," Washington said, looking up over the top of his spectacles as he sat at his desk, reviewing several papers. "Please take a seat." Washington gestured to one of the chairs in front of his desk as Reed came in and sat down.

"Well, Mr. Reed, we have attempted to clean up the men and the camp, and I believe the orders that were issued have, by and large, improved things considerably."

"That they have, Excellency. The men have made great strides in personal hygiene, and the camp is notably improved from the squalid place that you inherited upon your arrival."

"Yes, but nevertheless we are still facing a crisis of tremendous proportions. I am referring to the scourge of smallpox."

"The dreaded disease is taking a toll, Excellency."

"And that is why I am making a general order that applies to all troops in the army that they shall receive smallpox inoculations."

"Inoculations? Excellency, that would be a very controversial order. Do we really know if inoculations help prevent the spread of the disease or cause it?"

"That is the question. However, I must say that my brief encounter with the pox while in the Caribbean, and Jean Paul Pierre DuBois's encounter while he was in the Caribbean, have apparently immunized us from coming down with a debilitating or life-threatening case of the disease."

"That is interesting—Jean Paul, huh?"

"Private Barnes told me about Jean Paul's incident, which sounds not unlike my own. He said that Jean Paul is able to work in hospitals set up in Boston to deal with the smallpox epidemic that is occurring there. He has shown no ill effects whatsoever from his many encounters with the disease's victims. And perhaps even more importantly, Private Barnes said that Timothy McCaskill, Captain Finch's brother-in-law, decided to get inoculated. Although he was ill for about a week, he is now doing fine. Jean Paul recruited him to volunteer in the Boston hospitals, and thus far he has had no signs of contracting the pox."

"So you and Jean Paul were in essence inoculated by actual brushes with the disease itself?" asked Reed, with a more receptive look on his countenance.

"Apparently, Mr. Reed, for which I am most grateful."

"But in addition to your natural inoculation, Mr. McCaskill at least provides some evidence that taking an inoculation *may* ward off the disease."

"'May' is the word. Timothy's situation is just one case, and more could be involved in his seeming immunity than just the inoculation. Regardless, I am convinced that it would be far worse to do nothing than to aggressively attempt to alleviate the problem. So you have my order, Mr. Reed," Washington said, after reviewing the written document that Reed had quickly scribbled and then dating, signing, and returning it to his secretary. "Make sure that it is circulated to my officers immediately. Let them know that I plan to implement the program forthwith, because with an army of this size, it will take many months."

"I will take care of the matter, Excellency," Reed said as he left.

"Gentlemen, I have called this council of war on instructions from Congress. I am deeply concerned about the future. I do not think that I need to tell you that this army is crumbling, what with disease and desertion, and I will soon be facing a massive problem with six-month enlistments ending. I simply cannot afford to have to recruit a new army, especially with winter approaching. Now is the time to act and act decisively," Washington said to the gathered council on September 11, consisting of three major generals and several brigadier generals. "I am proposing an amphibious assault across Back Bay. I believe it can be successful and be that bold strike that can reignite the fervor that we desperately need for reenlistments and new recruits."

"Excellency," Major General Putnam said, "I understand your predicament, your desire to make a bold strike and all that a successful attack could mean for our cause, but it is far too risky."

"General Putnam is right, Excellency," said Nathanael Greene. "If we do not perfectly time the tidal movements, the result may be a major disaster."

"And the Brit defenses in Boston are too strong. In my opinion, it would be a huge mistake to make such a strike," added John Sullivan. "I understand the predicament, but I do not believe that this plan is the answer, with all due respect."

"Excellency, I must agree with my esteemed colleagues," William Heath said somberly.

"And I also. The odds of failure far outweigh the odds of success," Major General Charles Lee interjected, "at least at this time. We cannot afford to have the army destroyed at a single stroke, especially because of our own initiative."

"I hear your objections, gentlemen, and while I agree that there is an element of risk involved, I firmly believe the obstacles that you noted can be overcome. Let us take a vote on the proposal."

"Now that my plan has been unanimously rejected, does anyone have any suggestions on what can be done to seize the initiative in this interminable stalemate?" Washington asked, imploring, almost begging, for positive input.

"Excellency, I agree that something needs to be done," Major General Ward said, "and I again urge all of you to approve the taking of Dorchester Heights. This would be an ambitious initiative that I believe has little risk. All that is necessary is to put cannons there, with some supporting troops. If we control the heights, we control Boston. The Brits will have no choice but to withdraw or be pulverized. I reiterate it would be a huge mistake if we do not act now. If the Brits take it, a great opportunity will be missed."

"Thank you, General Ward, for your thoughts," Washington said while gently nodding his head, while pondering Ward's advice. "Does anyone have any comments about this proposal or any other proposals?"

"Excellency, I do not believe the Brits would take this threat seriously. Would they really believe that we would destroy the town to rid them of it?" Sullivan queried.

"If they do take it seriously, we may be facing another Bunker Hill–type assault," Putnam interjected.

"Perhaps a more elementary question is where do we get the cannons?" Heath asked.

"Excellent question. Any more comments or proposals?" Washington asked, glancing around the room. "Hearing none, let us vote on General Ward's proposal."

"Gentlemen, thank you for your input. With the rejection of General Ward's proposal and my proposed initiative, there is nothing further to discuss. This council of war is now adjourned," Washington said, graciously accepting the decision of the council. However, his big problem was not going away. *How may I keep this army together?* Washington wondered as the council members took their leave.

"The rejection of that so-called Olive Branch Petition should finally end the ludicrous debate once and for all," John Adams said to Jonathan Barnes as Jonathan approached the two cousins, John and Sam Adams, in the State House yard during a brief recess.

"And to think of all the time and effort to prepare that petition, and the king would not even look at it," Jonathan replied.

"In fact, he had already written the Declaration for Suppressing Rebellion and Sedition prior to Lord Dartmouth receiving the petition, thereby declaring us to be in rebellion against the mother country," Sam interjected.

"John, your letter intercepted by the Brits, which criticized Dickinson and the petition, may have had a great deal to do with the king's attitude toward the petition," Jonathan said.

"If that is in fact the case, then I am indeed happy," John responded. "Now we can reap the rewards, the harvest, if you will,"

John replied with a smile. "The issue is now very evident: either a total break and independence or complete subjugation at the hands of the Brits. There can be no middle ground."

"As you said, this should end this ludicrous debate, once and for all," Jonathan said.

"It should, and indeed it must," said John. "The time is ripe for us to make the big push for independence, not just for ourselves but also for generations to come."

16

"This plan must succeed," Washington said, examining Bendict Arnold's map. "The capture of Quebec will restore the only link wanting in the great chain of Continental Union." Arnold had led his militia company up from Watertown after Lexington and Concord. Rejected for the main western attack on Quebec through the Champlain Valley, he proposed an eastern push through the Maine wilderness, up the Kennebec River, for support. Unfortunately, his map was faulty, showing the distance to be traversed to be half the actual distance.

"You shall have it, Excellency," said Arnold forthrightly, "if I get the men and supplies I need."

"How many men do you need?"

"For this undertaking, I must have one thousand men."

"You shall have the men and all the supplies you need," replied Washington, "on the condition that General Schuyler gives his blessing. I will get word to him immediately."

"I have now received word from General Schuyler, and he lends his total support to the plan that you have proposed, Colonel Arnold," said Washington, a few days later.

"Colonel?" replied a somewhat surprised Arnold.

"Yes, you are a colonel in the Continental Army. I have given you the rank that you need and deserve to lead such a daring and important expedition."

"Excellency, I am most grateful to you for the rank, but my men and supplies? I am primarily looking for woodsmen and men skilled in handling bateau."

"You may choose your men from among all the troops in the army. I am certain that you will be able to find men who can fill your criteria. I do have someone whom I am asking you to consider but who does not quite fit your profile for this expedition."

"Who might that be, Excellency?"

"His name is Joshua Finch. His father is—"

"Captain William Finch."

"You know Captain Finch?"

"Know of him, sir. He is one of the best-known merchants and patriots in New England. He is best friend of delegate to the Congress Jonathan Barnes and good friend of merchant and patriot Jean Paul Pierre DuBois."

"My, that is impressive—impressive that you know so much about Captain Finch."

"There is much more that I know. He is a good man, Your Excellency."

"I totally concur, Colonel. Since he joined the army, when I assumed command, Henry Knox put him in charge of fortifications. Henry has raved about the job Captain Finch has done. And the man came to me and told me that he was in total agreement with my assessment of an officer and an officer's position with regards to enlisted. I need more like him."

"And his son, sir?"

"Captain Finch came to me and asked me if his son Joshua could join your expedition."

"What did you say?"

"I said that it would be your decision, Colonel. It will be your regiment, but I told him that I would put in a good word for the young man."

"Do you know Joshua, Excellency?"

"I do not, but I do know that he worked for his father in his father's merchant business. He also eagerly volunteered to help Jean Paul's men in delivering smuggled goods to needy families in Boston, because he wanted to 'do something for the cause.' Then when Captain Finch joined the army, he moved his family to the Barneses' in Lexington. Joshua readily agreed to join the militia and has been training with them on a regular basis. Though it has been a relatively short time, he has gained valuable experience. He does not quite fit your prototype, Colonel, but I am hoping you will consider him."

"I will be happy to consider him, sir. He comes from good stock, and that means a great deal. He has shown personal initiative, and that is vital. However, this could be a very difficult undertaking, the likes of which he, who has spent most of his life in the city, has never experienced. I will personally speak with him and give you my assessment."

"Private Joshua Finch reporting, sir," Joshua said, saluting Benedict Arnold. Joshua had begun to think that he was never going to see any action, but fate smiled on him in the form of the small yet stout fireball that was Arnold. After hearing about Arnold's expedition to Canada, Joshua rode out to camp in Cambridge to discuss the matter with his father. William approached Washington regarding Joshua's interest to join up with Arnold and was assured by Washington that Arnold was a great leader who would do everything possible for his men. Washington told William that he would put in a good word for Joshua but that the decision had to be Arnold's. With that, William took a brief leave from his duties to confer with Annabelle and Eleanor. They conveyed to him that although the going was exceedingly difficult in Lexington, it was primarily due to supplies, or lack thereof, and that they believed it best for all if Joshua pursued his dream of seeing action and joining the army. William told Joshua, and with that, Joshua immediately made himself available to Arnold.

"At ease, Private. Thank you for coming," Arnold replied, after returning the salute. "I understand that you are with the Lexington militia."

"Yes, sir, I am. I recently joined after my father, William Finch, joined the army upon General Washington assuming command. My father moved our family out of Boston to live with our friends, the Barneses."

"So I understand. Your father is a fine man and a great patriot, and so is Mr. Jonathan Barnes. And I have heard good things about his son Richard. You have a very impressive pedigree and friends with impressive pedigrees; however, I must tell you that our mission will test every part of that pedigree of yours. We will be traveling through beautiful country, but it is wilderness. Are you certain you are ready for the challenge?"

"Yes, sir, I know I am. I have got to do something to contribute to our cause. My father and best friend are with the army, my best friend's father with the Congress, and while I have helped to deliver smuggled goods to people in need in Boston and have trained with the militia in Lexington, I feel as if I have done nothing."

"If I take you, you will get your opportunity to contribute, but let me just say that distributing smuggled goods to those poor souls in Boston and training with the militia are not 'doing nothing.' I feel certain that they have contributed to your overall physical conditioning, but I am specifically looking for woodsmen and those who know something about boats. You are from the city; do you have any experience in the outdoors?"

"Yes, sir. When I was younger, my father took our family into the mountains of western Massachusetts for a couple of weeks for several summers. We went camping along with the Barneses. I learned to fish, hunt, use a canoe, repair a canoe on occasion, and help carry canoes to and from the lakes and streams we fished in. We dealt with all different weather conditions, from heat to cold to light rain to violent thunderstorms. Our families, women included, had to endure almost everything. Father and Mr. Barnes wanted us all to experience the outdoors, both to see nature and to be prepared in case we ever had to survive in the wilderness. While I am not a woodsman, I am not just a soft-handed city dweller either, if I may say so, sir."

"Apparently you are not a 'soft-handed city dweller,' as you put it. Your father and Mr. Barnes are truly wise men who did you and your families a very great service. And while this is not going to be a picnic or a summer vacation, it appears as if you possess the skills and qualities I want. You certainly possess the fire and determination so important to achievement. All right, Private, I will inform General Washington that you will be joining us. I for one am happy to have you. When we capture Quebec, it will be a glorious victory that will cement Canada in our corner and prevent the Brits from maintaining a stronghold to our north. Go ahead and finish your preparations. We head out within the week."

The expedition got underway, heading up the Kennebec River with high hopes. The men's spirits were soaring as they began what many, including Joshua and his new friend, Private Jeremiah Greenman from Rhode Island, believed would be a great adventure, the adventure of their lives. Little did they know the incredible hardships that awaited them.

"This is completely unacceptable!" Arnold said to Lieutenant Colonel Christopher Greene, commander of one of the divisions, not long into the journey. His face had a look of utter disgust, when it became quite obvious that his expedition had a very big problem: leaky boats.

"We are just underway, and nearly one-quarter of our food supply has already been ruined because of water leaking into the boats. What inferior workmanship!"

"Yes, Colonel Arnold, I agree, though due to the brevity of preparations for this expedition, there was scarcely time to build the requisite number, let alone the quality of watercraft this undertaking required."

"I suppose you are correct, but even with the time constraints, this situation is nearly intolerable, especially given the money that was paid for them! We *will* make do, Colonel, nothing must stop us from reaching Quebec!" Arnold replied emphatically.

"Read it, young lady," Washington said sternly to a woman who attempted to deliver a coded message to a British major, late in September. The message was received by a man named Wainwright, who delivered it to Washington. Washington held the letter out for her to take from him. "I shall not wait any longer for a response from you."

The woman sat, head down, not saying a thing.

"Very well, you leave me no choice but to order you to jail."

The tactic worked. The poor young woman quickly took the message in her trembling hands and barely looked at it before she broke down crying. Head still down, she began sobbing profusely.

"Sir...sir..." She could barely speak.

"What is it, child?"

"Dr. Church...Dr. Church."

"What about him?"

"He kept me...would not let me go...and now...I am pregnant by him. He had me deliver coded messages to the British officers," she said, gaining some semblance of composure.

"For how long has this been going on?" Washington asked firmly.

"Several years, sir."

"Several...several years?" Washington asked incredulously, his voice trailing off, his eyes reflecting stunned disbelief.

"Yes, sir, several years."

Washington, visibly shaken, sat down, taking a deep breath as he digested the magnitude of the treachery perpetrated by one of the so-called leading patriots of the colonies and "leading proponents" of the glorious cause.

"And Dr. Church—he wrote this message?"

"Yes, sir, he wrote it, handed it to me, and told me it was urgent and needed to be delivered immediately."

"I see..." Washington's voice again trailed off as he tried to absorb what his mind did not want to believe, though he knew in his heart that he had suspicions about Dr. Church for quite some time.

"Young lady," Washington said as he got a grip on his emotions and rose from his chair, "while I cannot excuse your actions in delivering these messages to the enemy for such a long time, I do understand the control that was wielded over you by one such as Dr. Church, a powerful man. I am grateful for this information, which despite all the ill that has taken place over these last years, has proved to be invaluable to me. You are dismissed for now; however, I expect full cooperation if I am in need of your testimony about these matters. Do you understand?"

"Yes, sir, you shall have my full cooperation, I assure you."

"Excellency, how could you possibly believe that I, Dr. Benjamin Church, a patriot's patriot, could do such a thing? You would believe the word of a harlot over my word?"

"Stop the pretense, Church. You are no more a patriot than King George III. And, yes, I would and do believe her word over yours. She is telling the truth, whereas you, your whole life is one big lie, you worthless...the code has been deciphered. How long has this been going on, Doctor?" Washington demanded.

Church suddenly sat silently in his chair across from Washington's desk. Washington got up and walked around the table and leaned over Church's chair, his large physical presence hovering over Church, who had beads of sweat breaking out on his forehead.

"Doctor, I am going to ask you one more time," said Washington as he pressed his face almost into Church's, "how long?"

"I am innocent—innocent, I tell you," Church whispered, wiping his brow with his handkerchief.

Washington pulled back in disgust and moved back around the table to his chair.

"Innocent. You are no more innocent than Judas Iscariot! Anyone who would betray his country for, in my estimation, the equivalent of thirty pieces of silver—death is too good for him. Get out of my sight!" Washington nearly screamed as he gestured powerfully with his right hand.

With that, Church quickly and quietly took his leave.

"Becky, I just received word that Dr. Church has been arrested for spying for the British. That is treason," Francois said as he helped Becky into his carriage, picking her up for a supper engagement.

"Dr. Church...Francois, no!" Becky said, her eyes wide open, a stunned look on her face.

"Oui, Becky—Dr. Church."

"How did you learn of this?"

"My father just received word from Paul Revere. You see, my father, Paul Revere, and Dr. Warren all have suspected Church for a long time."

"Honestly?" Becky said in disbelief.

"Oui. I believe it now makes sense," Francois said as he gently flicked a whip to his beautiful burgundy horse, which he named Red Knight, or Red, for short.

"What do you mean, Francois? What now makes sense?"

"I am now quite certain that Church was Wilson's go-between. He was the one whom Wilson relayed the message to after you told Wilson about your encounter with Dr. Warren and my father at JP's."

"Are you sure?"

"I am sure. You know how close Church and Wilson are and how both of them did free public medical work, donating their time and talents to the poor," said Francois as he took his eyes off the street and glanced at Becky, who had slumped in her seat and now had a forlorn look on her face.

"Becky..."

Becky glanced over and slowly nodded. "Yes, I suppose you are right." Then a thought struck Becky, and she quickly sat up. "Francois," she exclaimed, "do you think they will arrest Mark for treason?"

"I doubt they have the direct evidence to prove it; that is, unless—"

"Unless what?" Becky asked.

"Unless Church squeals on Wilson, which he might if he thinks it will save his neck."

Joshua and Jeremiah gathered around the evening fire, discussing the difficulties already encountered just a few brief weeks into the Maine interior.

"I am worried, Joshua, that this mission is going to be much more difficult than anyone, especially Colonel Arnold, ever imagined. We have already lost a good portion of our food supply in those lousy, leaky boats. Each day more and more of the men are forced to walk, many with bare feet. The grumbling is getting louder."

"It does seem apparent that the perils of this excursion were woefully underestimated. Doubtful that many of us were prepared for this, and that includes Colonel Arnold. However, he is strong, a real leader of men. I know that he will see us through."

"I wish I had your confidence in Colonel Arnold," said Jeremiah as he shivered, rubbed his hands together, and stared blankly into the dying fire.

"You will in time," Joshua said firmly.

"I do not know, maybe—maybe in time," Jeremiah said softly.

"Becky, I just cannot believe that—Church, the great Dr. Church, a spy for the British—for years? How can that be?" Mark Wilson said, during supper, to Becky Braun, who carefully observed the doctor's mannerisms and expressions.

"Yes, how indeed can that be, especially for as long as he was involved in the treachery? It seems almost impossible to believe that someone did not suspect something. You, Mark, were close to the man. Did you notice anything that seemed even remotely suspicious?" Becky said as she nibbled on a potato.

"What are you saying, my dear?" said Wilson, rather abruptly and defensively.

"I am not saying anything—I am asking. Think—did you or did you not notice anything about the man, including those who he associated with, that seemed even remotely suspicious?"

"What difference does it make now? Church has been caught."

"Yes, he has been caught, but how many others may be in complicity with him, either working with him in his endeavors or knowing about what he was doing and not reporting it to our authorities?"

"And I can somehow shed light on others who may be or may have been involved with him?"

"Perhaps."

"Well, the only other person I remember spending much time with him is dead."

"Dr. Warren?"

"Yes. You do not believe that Warren was a spy, do you? He died a patriot, shot directly in the face by a Brit on Breed's Hill. Then his coat was stripped bare by the Brits—at least that is what I have been told."

"Warren was no spy. That man was one of the greatest patriots this country has ever known and will ever know, for that matter, and I think you know that," Becky said emphatically.

"I would say that is correct. I just do not know anyone else Church associated with, and I cannot say that I noticed anything suspicious about his behavior."

"Think about it, Mark—it could be important. I will talk to you about it later."

"I will, Becky—I will think about it," Wilson said somberly, with a slow nod of his head.

"Mr. Boyd," said Amos as he practically ran up to greet Willie, late in the afternoon of an early-October day.

"Yes, Amos—calm down. Are you all right?"

"I am fine, sir," said Amos, catching his breath.

"What is it?"

"I think this is one of those moments when we need to go see Mr. DuBois."

"Oh?"

"I saw General Gage leave the Finch house, with his belongings and servants, and staff, at noon, and shortly thereafter General Howe arrived with his. Michael noticed activity this morning and informed me, so I was able to be there with him and witness the transition."

"Wow! So ole Gage's time has finally arrived! Jean Paul thought as much after the Brit catastrophes at Lexington and Concord and Bunker Hill. I agree with you; this is one of 'those moments.' Let us go to Jean Paul immediately."

"Becky! What a pleasant surprise," Mark Wilson said as he greeted Becky Braun in the front of his office in the patient waiting area, where he had been speaking with Miss Jones while awaiting the arrival of his last patient.

"Mark, we need to talk. Do you have a few minutes?"

"Yes, I think my last patient is scheduled to arrive in fifteen minutes or so; is that right, Miss Jones?"

"Yes, Doctor, that is correct," Miss Jones said, nodding.

"Then let us go back to my patient room," Wilson said as he escorted Becky to the back of the office.

Upon closing the door to the patient room, Wilson asked, with a look of concern, "Now what is so important that it could not wait until the weekend?"

"Have you been thinking about what we discussed the last time we met?" Becky said somewhat pointedly.

"And that was?"

"Mark, do not be disrespectful to me. You know what we discussed."

"You mean if I noticed anything suspicious about Dr. Church's behavior or of the behavior of anyone he associated with?"

"Yes."

"And why is this so important to you, if I might ask?" Wilson replied, now getting perturbed by where all this seemed to be leading.

"Because I care about this country. Dr. Church was found guilty at his court-martial, so any question of his innocence has been settled. If there are any spies who were associated with that despicable man, I must learn who they are," Becky said forcefully.

"What are you implying, my dear?" Wilson replied with equal force as he stared directly into her eyes.

"Mark..." Becky hesitated, momentarily glanced away, and then pushed forward, looking directly at Wilson, "where did you go that night?"

"What night?"

"The night before Lexington and Concord when I was at your house. The night I told you that Jean Paul and Dr. Warren met at JP's while I was having dinner with Jean Paul. I told you about the meeting and the result, and you then started to act very strange and mumbled something about an early morning, and you quickly showed me to the door."

"So…"

"So I waited outside in my carriage. I had a feeling deep inside of me about what was going to transpire. Then you quickly came out of the back of your house and drove down the street in your carriage—late at night—in a great hurry, just after you told me you had an early morning and abruptly showed me to the door. Where did you go that night?"

Wilson was caught off guard, though he maintained a stoic facade that conveyed nothing.

"You went to Dr. Church's, did you not? You went to tell him that the Americans were aware of Gage's excursion to Lexington and Concord for later that night."

Wilson stared at her, saying nothing.

"I did not want to believe it—could not believe it," Becky said, "but the truth of the whole matter was unavoidable."

Finally Wilson said, "I went to see a patient whose husband came to the house before you arrived. I told him that I would be along later that evening."

"Do not lie to me, Mark Wilson. You told me that night you had to bid me adieu because you had an early morning, and now you tell me that you went to see a patient after having wine with me? What doctor would do such a thing?"

"There was nothing life threatening or requiring extraordinary attention. I do not have to answer to you, young lady, about the care of my patients."

"What is the patient's name?"

"You know very well that there is a matter of doctor-patient confidentiality."

"Yes, I know and understand the whole situation very well."

"What does that mean?"

"It means good-bye, Dr. Wilson. While you do not have to worry about me, I would keep a low profile if I were you. I have many friends who will be watching you. If they sense any spy activity on your part, they will not hesitate to involve the appropriate authorities."

Becky whirled about and stomped out of the room, through the waiting area, and then out the front door, just as the last patient was arriving.

"Is everything all right, Miss Jones?" the patient asked as she entered the waiting area, with a startled look at the receptionist.

Before Miss Jones could respond, and mercifully for her, Wilson entered and said, "Everything is perfectly fine, Mrs. Gray. Please follow me." Miss Jones smiled her relief as Mrs. Gray followed Wilson back to the patient room.

"So you see, sir," said Amos, "Michael deserves the credit. He smelled it out, knew something was up, and got my attention."

"Excellent work, messieurs, this is exactly why I wanted you in charge and for you to get good men involved," said Jean Paul approvingly as he sat behind his office desk at JP's. "Amos, I know you have worked with Michael for some time. Do you think he could make it through the lines, get to Cambridge, and tell Monsieur Finch of what has transpired?"

"Absolutely, sir. Michael is one of the best men I have ever seen at avoiding the Brits. I have no doubt that he can give them the slip and make it to the army camp at Cambridge."

"Splendid. But it is not just the Brits whom I am concerned about; he best be careful, or he could be shot entering American lines."

"I will speak to him. He can handle it."

"Then tell him to leave this evening. When he arrives at the camp, he is to ask for Captain William Finch and to tell him that Jean Paul sent him. He is to tell Monsieur Finch that Gage is out as of this afternoon, and Howe is now the Brits' commander in chief and is now using the Finch house for his headquarters. Also, tell him to let Monsieur Finch know that we will continue with our vigilance in watching his house. Questions?"

"No, sir."

"Merci, gentlemen," Jean Paul said as he stood up and shook their hands, "and again, that was outstanding work."

"All in the line of duty, sir," Willie said as they turned and walked out the door.

"Sir," Michael said as he approached Private Richard Barnes, who was on the defensive lines of the army and on the evening watch.

Richard had his gun raised to his shoulder, pointing it at the youngster from Boston.

"Put your hands in the air, soldier, state your business, and do not take another step."

"Sir, I am not a soldier. My name is Michael, and I have been sent by Mr. Jean Paul—Jean Paul Pierre DuBois—to speak to a captain William Finch."

"Jean Paul?"

"Yes, sir."

"You are not a Brit, are you?" Richard said.

"No, sir, I am an American."

"Come closer—slowly, with your hands in the air, so I can get a better look at you," Richard said, not yet lowering his weapon.

"I work for Mr. Jean Paul, Mr. Willie Boyd, and Mr. Amos Malone," Michael said as he slowly approached Richard, with his hands held high.

"Willie Boyd and Amos Malone? What do you do for them?"

"I help distribute smuggled goods and supplies around Boston, and lately I have also been doing some surveillance of Captain Finch's house in Boston. That is why I was sent here to see him."

"Well, why did you not tell me that before?" Richard said, lowering his gun and shaking hands with Michael.

"Do you know Captain Finch?"

"Know him? Why he is my father's merchant and best friend."

"Then you must be Mr. Richard Barnes, sir."

"I am he. And stop that 'sir' stuff. I am not that much older than you, and besides, I am just a private in this man's army. Look, I will take you to Captain Finch right away; follow me."

"Captain Finch, this is Michael," Richard said as he introduced the young man to William. "He has some important news to tell you."

"Mr. Jean Paul Pierre DuBois sent me on this mission, sir."

"Jean Paul?" William said, with a surprised look. "Then I am sure it is important. How is Jean Paul?"

"He is quite well, sir. He wanted me to tell you that General Gage has been relieved of his command, and General Howe has taken over. I witnessed it today with Amos Malone, who recruited me to do surveillance of your house."

"My house."

"General Gage took over your house as his headquarters shortly after you left."

"I knew Gage would do that; I told Jean Paul as much."

"Yes, sir, Mr. Jean Paul had Mr. Willie Boyd and Mr. Amos Malone conduct surveillance. Mr. Jean Paul had them recruit two men for training in surveillance, and another gentleman and I also recruited a man each for the job. We have all been sharing time watching the house. And Mr. Jean Paul wanted me to let you know that the surveillance will continue."

"I knew Jean Paul would follow through," said William, with admiration. "That is exactly what he said he would do. I certainly hope your surveillance efforts are not adversely affecting the distribution of goods and supplies, which is vital to the town."

"No, sir, we all assured Mr. Jean Paul that with split shifts and the additional manpower, the distribution would not be affected."

"That is good to know. So Gage is out, and Howe is now in as commander in chief, and he is using our lovely home as his head-quarters. Hopefully the Brits will treat it with respect, but somehow I doubt it."

"I am sure they will, sir, at least as long as they occupy it."

"You are right, son, but when they finally leave—and God willing they will be leaving and hopefully soon—who knows what they may do to the place."

"Yes, sir."

"I cannot be concerned about my house. But as for the matter at hand, you will stay in my quarters tonight, and tomorrow morning the three of us will visit His Excellency."

"General Washington—sir?"

"The one and the same."

"I am going to meet General Washington?"

"You are, son."

"This is a true honor, sir. Thank you."

"No thanks are necessary. You should be the one to deliver the message about the change in the Brit leadership since you were the one who witnessed the events."

"Your Excellency," William said as he and Richard saluted General Washington in his headquarters.

"Captain Finch, Private Barnes," said Washington, returning the salute, "it is good to see both of you again. And this is…" he said, looking at Michael.

"This is Michael, Your Excellency. He is why we are here this morning."

"Michael, what can I do for you?"

"Well, sir, I came to tell you what I observed in Boston. I work for Mr. Jean Paul Pierre DuBois, distributing smuggled goods throughout Boston and doing some spying too, sir…"

"Go on, son," said Washington.

"Mr. Jean Paul's best lieutenant, Mr. Willie Boyd, recruited Mr. Amos Malone to help with surveillance of Mr. Finch's house after the Finches left Boston. Shortly thereafter, General Gage took over the Finch house as his headquarters. Then Mr. Malone recruited me to help him, and yesterday in the morning, I sensed that something was about to occur. I contacted Mr. Malone, and he joined me. We witnessed, at noon, General Gage and his staff leaving the Finches' and General Howe and his staff coming in shortly thereafter."

"You are certain that it was Howe?" Washington asked.

"Yes, sir, I am certain. Mr. Malone had pointed him out to me before as we were on delivery and spying missions around town. Both of us saw him come out of the carriage, climb the steps, and enter the house. It was Howe."

"Very interesting," Washington said, listening intently to the young man.

"Mr. Malone and I contacted Mr. Boyd, who, with Mr. Malone, went to see Jean Paul immediately. He directed them to send me to camp to tell this to Captain Finch."

"You have done well, son, very well. I am very proud of you for your bravery and service."

"I was just doing what I was supposed to do, sir."

"That may be true, but the information is invaluable to me. I will call a council of war to discuss this matter, and I want you to be in attendance, Captain Finch."

"Yes, Excellency."

"If there is nothing further, you are dismissed."

"Your Excellency, General Howe did exhibit uncommon bravery at leading his troops up Breed's Hill, not once, not twice, but three times in the face of disastrous fire from our troops in the fort at the top," said General Artemus Ward at the hastily called council of war. "He kept on going even when his aides were killed right next to him."

"So I have heard," said Washington, pondering this new development of Howe taking command. "Do we think that Howe will take the initiative where Gage has failed to strike?"

"If I may, Your Excellency," interjected William.

"Please, Captain Finch, I am interested in your thoughts on the matter."

"Our fortifications are strong, probably as strong as they will ever be, though a direct assault by all the Brit troops could be problematic. We need more men on the lines. I understand that the Tories in Boston feel positively about Howe because of the battle, but I have also heard some rumors, prior to when I left, that he has lost some of his nerve, his will to fight, since his 'victory' at the battle of Bunker Hill. I hear that he was truly stunned by the ferocity and tenacity exhibited by our brave men that day."

"So what do you propose?" asked Washington.

"Prepare the men for an assault. Send Private Barnes through the lines to meet with Jean Paul Pierre DuBois, with instructions that we need all the information we can muster about Howe and his predisposition toward making an attack before winter comes."

"I like your proposal." Washington nodded. "Does anyone else have any other thoughts?" There was silence for several seconds. "All right, hearing none, let us get our troops ready for a Brit initiative, and Captain Finch, I am giving you the responsibility of instructing Private Barnes as to the information we are seeking about Howe."

"Yes, Your Excellency, I will speak to him immediately."

"Thank you all, gentlemen. This council stands adjourned."

"Captain Finch, Private Barnes," said Washington, smiling and motioning William and Richard into his headquarters, "please be seated." Washington took a seat behind his desk.

"Thank you, Your Excellency," said William as he and Richard sat down in the beautiful royal-blue chairs across from Washington's desk.

"Private Barnes, I am eager to hear what your sources have told you concerning General Howe, especially if they think it likely that he will mount an offensive."

"Your Excellency, I spoke directly with Jean Paul Pierre DuBois. Given his extensive network of spies throughout Boston and his relationship with Revere, I felt that he was the only one whom I would need to contact."

"I concur with that assessment. From what I know of DuBois, he is Paul Revere's most trusted lieutenant."

"That is correct, Your Excellency. The information that Jean Paul has received to this point is that, despite what the Tories think, which is that Howe will take the initiative and attack, that is in fact highly unlikely. The word out on the street is that he wrote to the voters back home in Nottingham, England, who sent him to Parliament and told them that most Americans are really still loyal to the Crown and will give up the fight and come back into the fold."

"As crazy as that sounds," said Washington, "I am not so certain it is that far from the truth. I do know that I am struggling right now to keep this army together. The passion of our troops is on the wane."

"There is another matter, sir, that may influence General Howe's disposition."

"Oh—and what is that?"

"Apparently he has taken a loyalist's wife, Elizabeth Loring, to be his mistress."

"He has done what?" said Washington, astonished.

"Joshua Loring is a staunch loyalist, and in exchange for being named to head Boston's prisons, he agreed to the arrangement."

"It never ceases to amaze me the lengths that some men will go to for assurance of their financial security," Washington said, sadly shaking his head.

"A verse is circulating around town that pretty much sums things up, sir. I do not know the exact words, but it is something to the effect that Sir William is snug in bed like a bug, while keeping warm next to Mrs. Loring; snoring as if he had not a care in the world."

Washington and William could not suppress spontaneous chuckles at Richard's recitation. Gathering himself, Washington stood up and said, "I think I have heard enough. It seems evident that Howe is not going anywhere soon. Private Barnes, you have put my mind at ease."

"Sir," said Richard as he and William saluted the commander in chief and then turned and left.

"You did what, Becky?" Francois said to Becky as both were seated at a back table in Maggie's, partaking of the evening meal.

"I told you, Francois, I exposed Wilson for what he is, a worm, spying for those contemptible Brits. I told him good-bye."

"I am glad you are no longer seeing him, but by calling him a spy and your rationale for coming to that conclusion, you could be in danger, mon chéri."

"I am not worried. I told him that I have friends who will be keeping an eye on him, watching for any additional spying activity. He knows who my friends are, and that especially includes you and Jean Paul. He would not dare try to do anything to hurt me. He knows that if he did, everyone would know that he was ultimately responsible."

"Oui, we would know, but I want you to be especially careful until we can drive the Brits from our beloved town. I will tell Jean Paul right away about what you have done and make sure that his lieutenants keep the good doctor and you under observation."

"It will not be necessary to have them keep me under observation; I can take care of myself, and besides, Mark does not scare me."

"It is not just Mark who is my concern, Becky. He is going to tell his superiors that he has been exposed and who exposed him. They are my real concern."

"All right, but tell Jean Paul to keep his men at a distance—maintain a low profile; I do not want to be going around town with an obvious escort."

"Do not worry, my love; you will not even know they are watching over you."

17

"The chair now recognizes the Honorable Stephen Hopkins, delegate from Rhode Island," John Hancock said, in a loud clear voice. The date was October 3, 1775.

"Thank you, Mr. President and honorable delegates," Hopkins said as he rose from his seat to address the Second Continental Congress. "I have a matter that I and the Assembly of Rhode Island believe is of the utmost importance for our glorious cause. On August twenty-sixth of this year, our assembly passed a resolution instructing our delegation to this esteemed body, to introduce legislation calling, and I quote, 'for building at the Continental expense a fleet of sufficient force, for the protection of these colonies, and for employing them in such a manner and places as will most effectively annoy our enemies.'"

Almost before Hopkins could finish his sentence, the catcalls began in earnest from all corners of the room. Samuel Chase from Maryland jumped to his feet and in a loud voice proclaimed, "Are the Honorable Mr. Hopkins and the assembly of the colony of Rhode Island stark-raving mad? That may be the craziest, most outrageous proposal I have ever heard of!"

"Hear, hear, Honorable Mr. Chase," chided Hancock, while wild cheering went up, supporting Chase's proclamation. "This body will come to order." Hancock pounded his gavel. Slowly the cheers died down. "Mr. Hopkins still has the floor."

"Thank you, Mr. President. I am now making the aforesaid resolution a formal resolution for adoption by this body."

Again the room was filled with shouts of derision, mocking Hopkins and his proposal, and again Hancock pounded his gavel to bring order.

"Mr. President, if I may have a few brief words," said John Adams as he rose from his seat.

"You may, sir. The chair recognizes the Honorable John Adams, distinguished delegate from Massachusetts," Hancock said as the room suddenly became quiet to hear what the great orator had to say.

"Mr. President, esteemed delegates. If you may recall, back in September I set forth the idea to the members of this illustrious body that if we had a navy of our own, we could harass the British and perhaps even disrupt their war effort by capturing vessels for our profit, by selling some of what was captured and by supplying our army with ammunition, guns, and other materials obtained from the prizes. Gentlemen, I am not so naïve to suggest that we can compete with or defeat the British navy; that would not be the objective. However, I believe the Honorable Mr. Hopkins and his delegation are saying that it is time for us to have a serious presence on the water and that much benefit can be derived therefrom. Am I correct in that assumption, gentlemen?" Adams said, looking at Hopkins and Samuel Ward, another Rhode Island delegate.

"If I may, Mr. President," said Ward as he stood.

"You may. The chair recognizes the Honorable Samuel Ward, delegate from Rhode Island."

"Mr. President, Mr. John Adams, honorable delegates, what the Honorable Mr. John Adams has conveyed to you is, in my opinion, exactly what our assembly had in mind with this resolution. Yes, the resolution says 'for the protection of these colonies,' but it goes on to say 'and for employing them in such a manner and places as will most effectively annoy our enemies.' The emphasis is on *annoying* our enemies."

As Ward spoke, Hopkins nodded his head in complete agreement.

"While we cannot hope to take on or defeat the British fleet, and I would agree with you that such an idea would be stark-raving mad, we certainly can annoy the British—seriously annoy them all to our own profit. Gentlemen, we have to do something. The merchants of Rhode Island and other New England colonies have had their vital smuggling operations harassed and otherwise disrupted by the British navy. We must hit back at them. Therefore, I believe we need to move forward, keeping this objective, as stated by our assembly, in mind." With that, Ward sat down.

"Mr. President, may I respond?" asked Samuel Chase again, jumping to his feet.

"Now you may. The chair recognizes the Honorable Samuel Chase, delegate from Maryland."

"With all due respect to the honorable delegates from Rhode Island, who said anything about taking on or defeating the British fleet? I certainly did not have that in mind when I proclaimed the idea of purchasing a fleet of ships at this body's expense as the craziest, most outrageous proposal I have ever heard. Gentlemen, this is ludicrous. Even if we are able to annoy, do we really believe that this will provide some form of protection to our colonies? I believe the whole idea to be farfetched, a waste of time and money—and money, gentlemen, is something we can little afford to waste," Chase said as he abruptly sat down.

Hopkins was ready to stand and rebuke Chase, when Adams, who was still standing, motioned him to stay seated and again spoke.

"Mr. President, if I may have a few more words on the subject."

"Proceed, Mr. Adams."

"While I am wholeheartedly in support of the resolution as put forth by the honorable delegates from Rhode Island, in light of current opposition, I would propose to the honorable Rhode Island delegation and to the chair that the matter be tabled, for now, to possibly be considered at a later date," Adams said, again looking at Hopkins and Ward.

Hopkins then rose. "Mr. President, if I may."

"You may," said Hancock.

"The Rhode Island delegation is in agreement with the honorable delegate from Massachusetts."

"Any discussion? Hearing none, the resolution as stated by the Honorable Stephen Hopkins delegate from Rhode Island is hereby tabled."

$$\sim\!\!\mathcal{D}$$

"Congress is now back in session," President John Hancock said as he pounded the gavel on his table. The date was October 13, 1775. "The chair is in receipt of a letter from the esteemed commander in chief of our army, the Honorable General George Washington." Hancock proceeded to hand the letter to Secretary Thomson to read aloud to the body. He read the great news relayed by Washington that his army had captured a British vessel in New Hampshire. Upon the completion of the reading, John Adams rose from his seat.

"Mr. President, I request permission to address the body."

"The chair recognizes the Honorable John Adams, delegate from Massachusetts."

"Thank you, Mr. President, distinguished colleagues. In light of the letter from the esteemed commander of our army, the Honorable General George Washington, I believe it is time to take action. I am proposing that this Congress authorize the purchase of two vessels to be equipped to set sail against the British merchant ships that are supplying the British war effort."

"Is that your motion?" Hancock inquired.

"Yes, it is, Mr. President."

Before the words came out of Hancock's mouth, Stephen Hopkins rose.

"I second the motion of the Honorable John Adams," Hopkins said.

"We have a motion and a second," Hancock said. "Do we have any discussion?"

"Mr. President," said Samuel Chase as he rose from his seat.

"The chair recognizes the Honorable Samuel Chase, delegate from Maryland."

"It was only ten days ago that we were dealing with this ridiculous proposal. Fortunately the matter was tabled, as well it should have been, but now it is brought forth again. Let General Washington carry on, if he so chooses, with his own little fleet of schooners, but that has nothing to do with us. Nothing has changed."

"Mr. President," Adams interjected.

"Mr. Chase has the floor," Hancock replied.

"Mr. Adams may proceed, Mr. President," Chase said, deferring.

"Very well, proceed, Mr. Adams."

"Thank you, Mr. President. First of all, I am not proposing, at this time, that we revisit the Rhode Island proposal of purchasing a fleet of vessels; I am proposing that we purchase and properly equip two ships to engage and harass the British merchant fleet. This is a significantly different proposal. Secondly, how can you say that nothing has changed? I beg to differ, kind sir—in fact everything has changed. If our army, the Continental Army, can capture a British vessel with a refitted schooner, imagine what these two proposed ships can do! Now is the time to act, to support our army and its land efforts. We can do this with a navy and its sea efforts—not to destroy the British fleet or to attempt to directly engage the Royal Navy in battle, but 'for the protection of these colonies—and for employing them in such a manner and places as will most effectively annoy our enemies.' It is not the Royal Navy that should be the focus of our attention. It is the British merchant vessels that are supplying the British troops. If we can capture some of these ships, we can if not cripple at least impact the British war effort and provide ourselves with goods and supplies, including valuable military supplies."

⚘

"John, you did it," Jonathan Barnes said to John Adams in the courtyard following the session.

"Did what, my friend?"

"Pushed through resolutions that for all intents and purposes created a Continental Navy."

"Well, thanks go to you for your support of my proposal during the intense and lengthy debate and then for seconding my modified motion, but the real credit, the impetus for the resolutions, belongs to the Rhode Island delegation," Adams said, nodding at Hopkins and Ward as they approached.

"Yes, I would agree with that," Jonathan said, shaking the hand of first Hopkins then Ward.

"Perhaps the initial impetus was ours, but nothing could have happened without you, John. As usual, you are the one who makes things happen in this Congress," Hopkins said.

"That is the truth," Jonathan added.

"Gentlemen, you flatter me with your words, but it takes more than one to get the job done, and while this is a beginning, there is much yet to do."

"Our resolution for a fleet?" Ward asked.

"Precisely. Two ships are hardly a navy, but with several we can begin to break the suffocating control that the British have over our smuggling trade. With a dozen ships or more, we can begin to *annoy our enemies*, and nothing would give me more pleasure than to annoy them as much as possible. We need do the groundwork to convince our colleagues that a fleet is needed. The sooner the better."

"John, what can I do to help?" Jonathan asked.

"Jonathan," Adams said, "with the relationship you have developed with General Washington, you have connections and standing with the Virginia delegation."

"I will talk with the Virginia delegates and with Benjamin Franklin to see if he would be willing to assist us in getting delegates on our side," Jonathan replied.

"And I will lobby the other Maryland delegates and those from the southern colonies other than Virginia and from the mid-Atlantic region. Gentlemen," he said to Hopkins and Ward, "please secure our base in the northeast."

"Will do," said Hopkins.

"We will get right to it," Ward concurred.

Dear Mr. President,

    I come to you, sir, with the most urgent request. I fear our situation here is most desperate. With expiring enlistments, the army is crumbling before my very eyes. I have pleaded and pleaded with them, appealing to their patriotic duty and the great and glorious cause on which they and our nation are now embarked, but all appears to be for naught. I beg you and the Congress, which you so ably lead, to give me all the troops you may be able to muster along with the necessary supplies to support them. The situation is dire, sir; I assure you that I would not make such a plea if it were not so. I thank you for any assistance that you will provide.

Your most humble servant,

G. Washington

Congress decided to appoint a committee to meet with Washington and his staff to attempt to forge a policy to meet military needs without abridging the very personal liberties for which the war was being waged. Franklin was chosen to head the committee, with Thomas Lynch of South Carolina, Benjamin Harrison of Virginia, and rounding it out with a New Englander, Jonathan Barnes of Massachusetts. James McDonnell asked Jonathan if he could accompany him and Lydia so that James could see William again and meet Annabelle and Victoria Finch and Eleanor, Richard, Margaret, and James Barnes. Jonathan was delighted to have James along and was very pleased with the development of the relationship between him and Lydia.

It had been an amazing summer for Lydia and James. Though initially there was little work for her with John and Betsy Ross and their new upholstery business, it did not take long for the workload to increase. Lydia was so thrilled to be in Philadelphia at this time in her life and the life of her new country that she could hardly believe it. She was literally in the epicenter of the dawn of American history! What could possibly surpass that? Well, James McDonnell could! The handsome, debonair, yet very hardworking, ambitious young man had totally captured Lydia's heart. A quick wit, a wry smile, a flair for the romantic, yet with his feet firmly planted on the ground, made him irresistible to Lydia and almost too good to be true. For James, Lydia was just *so* beautiful, yet not at all pretentious. She had sparkling eyes that seemed to dance with delight at his sense of humor, which brought a chill to his spine and goose bumps on his arms. And perhaps best of all, behind the beautiful face and lovely figure was a warm, genuine heart and a bright inquisitive mind. They spent as much time together as was possible, considering their work schedules and Jonathan's commitments to Congress. They took full advantage of all that the growing, bustling, fascinating city of Philadelphia had to offer, from plays to picnics in the park to art galleries to concerts to wonderful suppers and evenings with the great Dr. Benjamin Franklin and his family. It was as if they were living in a fantasy world they hoped would never end—yet both were only too aware of the monumental, dynamic days in which they were living. The war, and with it winds of change, loomed large over them and their relationship. They were determined to make the most of each moment they were given. Thus, when the chance came for James to travel with Jonathan and her, Lydia was thrilled that James initiated it. James could not wait to meet Lydia's mother and sister, and he also very much wanted to meet the wife and children of the man whom he had come to greatly admire and respect, Jonathan Barnes.

"Henry, that is a job well done. I commend you and the men," Washington said, at his headquarters, to Henry Knox after surveying the fortifications with his servant, Billie Lee, and Knox. "I know that it is boring work, but it is absolutely vital. Even if it is unlikely that Howe will make a frontal attack, we must be ready."

"Thank you, Excellency," the smiling, rotund Knox said, "but I must confess that much of the credit must go to Captain Finch."

"You made a very good choice with him. His work is excellent as is his relationship with the troops. They have the proper respect for him, and he is attuned to their needs, wants, problems, and concerns. The upcoming meetings with the congressional delegation will be crucial for us, and I want my best to be a part of these proceedings. Thus, I am adding Captain Finch to the staff for the purpose of joining us in the negotiations."

"I concur, Excellency, and I believe Captain Finch would be a valuable asset in those meetings."

Franklin and the rest of the committee, including Jonathan, James, and Lydia, arrived in Cambridge and settled into the home that Washington had rejected as his headquarters—Samuel Langdon's home, president of Harvard. Langdon graciously offered the home to the committee for the week of the meetings.

Prior to the meetings getting underway, Lydia and James met with William.

"Mr. McDonnell, it is so good to see you again. So glad that you were able to come with Jonathan and Lydia to Massachusetts," said William as he firmly shook the hand of the handsome young man.

"Mr. Finch, it is so good to see you again, sir. I am excited to be here and look forward to meeting your family and the family of Mr. Barnes."

"The feeling is mutual. Annabelle and Eleanor Barnes are most eager to meet you for the first time. They heard about you from me upon my return from Philadelphia, and they heard or, shall I more appropriately say, read much about you from Lydia and Jonathan, and all of it good—very good."

"Thank you for that kind assessment."

"You are most welcome, but my observations to the ladies pale in comparison to those of my daughter in letters written to her mother."

"Sir, I assure you that I thank her every day in every way that I can for allowing me to be in her company. She is the most beautiful, intelligent, charming, exciting—I could go on and on with superlatives—woman I have ever met," James said as he looked into the adoring eyes of Lydia.

"Father, do you now understand why I love this man?" Lydia said, looking at her proud father.

"I am beginning to understand," William said, grinning. Looking back at James, William said, "Well, Mr. McDonnell..."

"Please call me James, sir."

"Well, James, welcome to Massachusetts. I am certain that I speak for Lydia's mother, whom you will be meeting shortly, when I say that we are grateful for the respect that you have shown our daughter. We are so glad that we allowed Lydia to remain in Philadelphia and of the resultant growth in your relationship. And her mother and I have decided to let her return to Philadelphia."

"Oh, Father, thank you and Mother!" said Lydia as she threw her arms around William.

"And I too am very grateful to you and Mrs. Finch, sir, for your decision."

"So Lydia, when are you going to Lexington?" asked William, as he pulled her back from their embrace.

"We leave first thing tomorrow morning."

"And how will you get there?"

"Mr. Barnes has graciously agreed to loan us his carriage while he is in meetings with the rest of the committee."

"That is quite generous of Jonathan."

"James offered to rent one from the local townspeople here in Cambridge, but Mr. Barnes would have none of it."

"That sounds just like something Jonathan would do."

"Have you seen him since we arrived?" Lydia inquired of her father.

"No, not yet, but I plan on getting together with him as soon as possible."

Lydia and James arrived in Lexington to a very warm reception. Annabelle and Eleanor were thrilled to see them.

"Mother, Mrs. Barnes, Judah," said Lydia as Judah helped her down from the carriage.

"Miss Lydia," said Judah.

"Lydia...Lydia," said Annabelle as she hugged her daughter with a force that nearly took Lydia's breath away and then planted several kisses on her right cheek. "Lydia, I am so happy to see you!" said Annabelle as she pulled her head back and looked into the now-moist eyes of her daughter.

"And I to see you, Mother," said Lydia, catching her breath.

"I am sorry I squeezed you so hard, my dear."

"It is quite all right, Mother. I loved it. Mother, this, I am sure you know, is Mr. James McDonnell."

"Mr. McDonnell, we are very happy to meet you," said Annabelle, shaking his hand.

"Yes, we are," agreed Eleanor, who shook his hand when Annabelle was done.

"And I feel the same. It is wonderful to be here. I truly feel as if I am the luckiest man in the world. Your daughter, Mrs. Finch, is the most beautiful, exciting, wonderful woman I have ever known," James said, beaming as he again gazed at Lydia.

Annabelle and Eleanor looked at each other with an acknowledgment on their faces that young love and its promise were in their presence.

"Mother," Lydia said as she continued gazing into James's eyes, "as I said to Father, do you understand why I love this man?"

"Yes, dear, I understand; I understand," Annabelle said, nodding her head, looking first at Lydia and then at Eleanor, whose mouth reflected a slight grin.

"Mother, thank you and Father so much for allowing me to return to Philadelphia!"

"We came to the conclusion, based on your letters and Jonathan's to Eleanor," Annabelle said, while Eleanor nodded her head. "And Jonathan's responses to your father's letters about the relationship and Jonathan's willingness to continue chaperoning you when you are with Mr. McDonnell."

Judah helped James unload the carriage, and soon James met Margaret and James Barnes and Victoria Finch. After meeting Eleanor's parents, the Williamses, James and Lydia settled in with them and then gathered Margaret, James Barnes, and Victoria and recounted stories of Philadelphia, including meeting the great George Washington. The Barnes children were held in rapt attention, and Victoria was at her inquisitive best. Not only did she ask several questions about Washington but she was also especially intrigued about the maneuverings that took place in Congress.

"Yes, it is fascinating how they compromise positions to reach solutions," said Lydia. "Mr. Barnes has told me that frequently agreements are reached out in the State House yard behind the State House or in taverns about town during breaks or after congressional sessions. I have personally witnessed some of the political bargaining while in the taverns with Father or Mr. Barnes. Mr. Barnes informed me that a delegate might get up during a session and take a strong position on a matter. Then after a break or following a reconvening, the same delegate stands up and now takes a very different, sometimes entirely different, position to the amazement of all. It is usually the product of a compromise struck in the courtyard or in the back of a tavern."

"So it basically is a game of give-and-take," Victoria interjected. "I will help you with this issue, if you will help me with this other issue I have now or may have in the future."

"That seems to be the universal game of politics," said James McDonnell, nodding in agreement. "I will scratch your back if you will scratch mine."

"Well, in a sense, everyone wins," added Victoria. "You do not get everything you want, but you try to get the most important things while conceding the less important points. Those may be the most important points for someone else."

"I think you understand the process," said James.

"It is fascinating, but I think it seems to be the only feasible approach; after all, each has his own personal agenda or the agenda of the colony he serves. The only way to broker your agenda with others is to compromise."

"That is the way the system works, or perhaps I should say that is the way it is supposed to work, if anything is to get done," Lydia said as she smiled and nodded in agreement with Victoria.

"I must have a standing army if we have any hope of defeating the Regulars. They are professionals. What do I have? Militia who have a serious independent streak, and their length of service is generally so short that no sooner are they trained than they leave. This simply is unacceptable," Washington said very forcefully to the committee. "Then there are those who are temporaries. It seems that they are constantly leaving the army to do their jobs or to deal with their farms and crops. And I am supposed to win a war with this group? What am I going to do when we get in the heat of battle, instead of this interminable standoff?"

"Gentlemen, I must agree with His Excellency. We cannot possibly hope to compete with a professional army, once the battle is joined. We must have regular men we can train and discipline and who we can count on to be there in the tough times. I understand the concerns that you have about a standing army, and those concerns are certainly legitimate," Nathanael Greene interposed, "but without a standing army, I assure you, we will have no freedoms to be worried about." William, who was sitting next to Henry Knox and across from Jonathan Barnes, was taking everything in, very pleased to now be directly taking part in these vital discussions. It was fascinating to hear these great men and the passion they brought to their arguments.

"There are several areas that must be addressed; perhaps primary among them is discipline," Washington said, addressing the committee. "I am trying everything I can think of to increase discipline and instill a sense of pride in the troops and especially in the officers. This is essential if this army has any hope of winning. I must say there have been successes in this area. Captain Finch, who graciously agreed to join our committee, has embraced the attitude that I am seeking in my officers and troops. He has done a marvelous job of conveying that attitude to all in my army. However, and I think that the captain would be the first to concur with this statement, gentlemen, I need violations of my discipline code to have consequences, not just be empty threats."

"Yes, Your Excellency, I have already seen violations that go unpunished, and that includes some that were serious. Unfortunately, when the troops see other troops committing breaches of conduct that go unpunished, that has a debilitating effect on the discipline we are attempting to instill in them and troop morale, as you all can well imagine," William responded as he looked around the group and conveyed his message.

"Certainly, discipline is vital," Franklin agreed, "and a code of behavior is only as good as the ability to enforce the same."

"Stern measures need to be brought to bear for serious breaches," Jonathan added.

"Such as mutiny or inciting mutiny?" Franklin asked.

"Yes, there cannot be much more serious breaches than that, can there, Your Excellency?"

"No, there cannot, Delegate Barnes. I need to be able to inflict the ultimate penalty for those most serious breaches."

"Death?" Franklin interjected.

"Yes, death. It must be unmistakably understood by all that this behavior cannot and will not be tolerated. While I must have the power to commute, I must have the power to execute any of those who would commit such vile acts. I believe this is critical to any discipline code."

"Privateers and privateering is not on the top of my list of matters to be addressed," Washington said at another session of the committee. "Nevertheless, it is something that needs to be dealt with, like it or not. My greatest concern is what has already happened in the area of recruitment and retention of troops directly owing to privateering. Truthfully—the army cannot hope to compete monetarily with privateering. The potential money to be had from that endeavor far exceeds anything that we can offer a recruit. However, I believe we can lessen the negative impact of privateering and increase the positive if the proper rules, regulations, and procedures regarding the same are put in place and then into practice. Also, I need to be able to implement procedures regarding disposition of prizes that we are fortunate enough to capture."

"I believe I speak for the committee," Franklin responded, looking at Jonathan and then fellow committee members, "when I say that this is a reasonable request. Would you agree, gentlemen, that we should give His Excellency the authority to make whatever arrangements he deems necessary regarding privateering and selling or disposing of enemy ships captured by ships outfitted at government expense?"

All the committee members gave their assent.

"Another matter that needs to be addressed, gentlemen, is strategy. While I would dearly love to strike the enemy with a frontal attack before winter, I have concluded, with insight from my council of war, that it would be impractical. However, I do need guidance on another important strategy matter, and that is an artillery bombardment of Boston. I believe it could have a significant impact, even a demoralizing effect, on the Brits, but obviously it could result in substantial damage to the city."

"General Washington, the committee appreciates your position on a possible artillery bombardment, but this is a matter that Congress must decide," Franklin said, after the committee had met briefly to consider Washington's request. "We will submit this matter forthwith upon our return."

"Very well, I understand. Now, there is one other matter I must bring up over and over, and that is the money be constantly sent, as well as regularly sent. I simply cannot emphasize this enough to you. We must have money. How can we expect to pay and keep soldiers and run an army without money? The answer is obvious: we cannot. I implore you to urge Congress to make this a top priority. Thank you, gentlemen, for your kind attention to our concerns."

"I must say that was a very informative series of meetings," Franklin said to the committee. "While I sympathize with the general's plight, my personal observations made over the course of our week here in Cambridge are that the dire reports of this army are overblown. It appears to me that the key need for this army is substantial improvement in its officers. Jonathan, I would say that from all that I have heard and observed, your friend William Finch is a fine officer. Unfortunately, he is clearly more the exception than the rule. What this army needs most is for the officers to embrace their role as leaders rather than attempting to curry the enlisted men's favor by acting as if they are no different than the men they command. General Washington himself said that there needs to be adequate separation. It just must be put into practice far more often than has been the case to date."

Franklin, William, and Jonathan headed to Lexington in Franklin's carriage to join James and Lydia, who had been there for nearly a full week. Arriving just in time for supper, the entourage received a very enthusiastic welcome.

"Jonathan!" Eleanor exclaimed to her loving husband as he disembarked from the carriage.

"Eleanor!" Jonathan exclaimed as he ran into her arms.

The two simply embraced for several seconds without saying a thing—they did not need to. The bond between them was strong.

William and Annabelle also shared a warm embrace, and then the Finch children joined them in a family hug, followed by a hearty introduction of Franklin to all.

Finally the bags were unloaded, and everyone gathered for supper.

It was a special time around the table as stories were shared, lasting well into the night.

All in the Finch and Barnes clan were very impressed with James McDonnell, and Franklin lauded the praises of the young printer.

Franklin was in his glory, sensing and feeling the adoration of all in the room. Victoria was enthralled to have a living legend in her midst, a virtual historical encyclopedia. She took advantage of the situation.

"Dr. Franklin, do you think there is any realistic possibility of reconciliation with the British?"

"No, not at all, not after what happened here at Lexington and at Concord. Then there was Bunker Hill. But to be truthful with you, I do not believe there was ever any realistic possibility of reconciliation. The king and his Parliament made their intentions known regarding the colonies when they refused to lift the hated tea tax and then imposed the draconian Boston Port Act after the destruction of the tea. Despite some weak-kneed members of my home delegation who simply cannot tolerate the thought of a break with the motherland, reconciliation will not happen. I know your John Adams is itching for the colonies to declare independence, but unfortunately, the time is not quite ripe. However, it will soon be, and then a clean break will finally occur."

"Yes, but when it does, can we win the war that will validate declaring our independence from the Brits?" Victoria posited the question with a furrowed brow.

"That, young lady, is—the great question of our time. If I had the answer to that question..." his voice drifted off, his eyes a blank stare. Then suddenly he forcefully declared to the amazement of all in the room, "Of course we will win! We must win for ourselves and for generations to come. Liberty, no matter what the cost, is worth the price, and we must pay that price—and no doubt we will. The cause is just. General Washington is a great man. He will find a way; we will find a way—defeat is not an option," Franklin said, with an air of decisiveness.

The room had been so quiet, as all were hanging on every word of the great elder statesman, that they could have heard a proverbial pin drop. Then simultaneously the room was filled with cheers coming from every throat. All gathered around Franklin and patted him on the back and shook his hand. Franklin's face broke out in a big smile as William said, "Benjamin, you said what we wanted *and* needed to hear."

"Yes," added Jonathan, with an air of resolve, "the cause is a great cause and a just one. The cost of liberty may be very steep, but we must pay the price—indeed, we are *already* paying a huge price—but it is worth it. We must and will prevail."

Franklin nodded and then said, "It has been a wonderful evening, but it is now time for this old man to say good-night. We have a long journey ahead of us tomorrow."

Grace and her fellow servants outdid themselves in preparing the breakfast meal. Pancakes, eggs, biscuits, ham, hard cider, and coffee were in abundance, and everyone ate their fill. Jonathan, Lydia, James, and Franklin then headed out for Philadelphia amid emotional good-byes from all. It had been a memorable evening filled with many stories covering the past several months, including the great hardships faced by the Finches, Barneses, and Williamses in Lexington and finishing with Franklin's rousing answer to Victoria's most pertinent question. All parties were nearly exhausted, but it was imperative for Jonathan and Franklin to get back to Philadelphia and Congress. They loaded the carriages and quietly slipped out of Lexington before anyone seemed to be stirring in the village, where the shot heard round the world was fired just months before. A hard frost on the grass sparkled in the first light of the new day.

18

The going was hard and seemingly getting harder day by day. Though the wilderness was beautiful, it was virtually impassable. Joshua and Jeremiah assisted in carrying the leaky boats around fast-moving rapids and waterfalls, far too many to count. Not only were the boats half-waterlogged, awkward, and heavy but there were also often no passageways to carry them through. Pathways had to be hacked through dense forest and underbrush; the trek was slow going.

October 20 arrived, and the sky was ominous. The winds began blowing early, the treetops bending under the assault. By afternoon it was howling with such ferocity that trees were being knocked over. The men attempted in vain to put up tents.

"Jeremiah," screamed Joshua at the top of his lungs, "it is no use. Put the tent away immediately, or we will lose it."

"Help me, or it will blow away," said a desperate Jeremiah. Joshua scrambled to get around the tent and put his body in a position to block the tent and enable Jeremiah to gain control. After considerable time and effort, Jeremiah wrestled the tent to the ground and managed, with Joshua's help, to fold it up. Soaked to the bone, the two friends huddled together on the sopping-wet tent in what underbrush they could find, shivering and shaking mightily, not knowing if they would survive the long night with this fierce October gale.

Joshua fell asleep, thinking about what Colonel Arnold told him before agreeing to take him into his regiment: *This is not going to be a picnic or a summer vacation.* Those words now constituted the greatest understatement Joshua had ever heard.

"Wake up! Wake up!" Arnold shouted to his men in the middle of the black, howling night. "Get to the top of that hill over there, now!" he said, pointing to it.

"Jeremiah, Jeremiah, wake up—we have to move, and we have to move now. No time to lose; the water is rising and fast," Joshua said to his young friend as he shook him back and forth. Startled, Jeremiah snapped awake.

"Joshua, where are we?" Jeremiah said in a fog-like daze.

"No time to talk. Grab the tent with me; we have to get to that hill and get there right away."

Jeremiah hesitated.

"Now!" Joshua yelled, and Jeremiah grabbed one end of the tent, and Joshua the other.

They reached the base of the little hill just as a river of water came crashing down in torrents over their old campsite. Scrambling to the top with the other men, they looked down and were amazed to see the place where they had just been sleeping engulfed in fast-moving brown water, which seemed to consume everything in its path. They looked at each other in silent disbelief, slowly put the tent down, huddled up together, and went back to sleep, exhausted.

The next morning dawned bright and clear, but the results of the storm were abundantly obvious. The camp was a total shambles. Equipment was scattered everywhere; branches and trees lay throughout. There were injuries, but luckily no one was killed. Dozens of barrels of flour and pork, as well as equipment and other supplies, were carried away by flooding ponds. An already depleted food supply was now nearly gone, with winter yet to arrive. The effect on morale was very evident to Arnold. It was time to rally the troops, or all would be lost.

"Jeremiah, are you all right?" Joshua said as he gently shook his younger friend.

"What...what is happening?" said a startled, groggy Jeremiah as he awoke.

"It is daybreak—we survived the terrible storm, but just barely."

"What do you mean?"

"You saw what happened as we reached the top of this hill. The storm wreaked havoc—it practically destroyed the camp."

"It what?" said Jeremiah as he sat up.

"Come on, get up and see for yourself. This place is a disaster."

Joshua helped a cold and shaken Jeremiah to his feet and into the middle of what used to be the camp. Water was everywhere, and men were wandering about as if a huge explosion had occurred—and in essence, one had.

Jeremiah was in shock as he took in the incredible scene.

"Perhaps the worst is I have heard that dozens of barrels of pork and flour were carried away when the ponds were flooded," said Joshua.

"Our food...nearly all gone...what are we going to do?"

"We will have to do whatever Colonel Arnold orders us to do."

"But what has he done for us? Has he led us into to this terrible place just to die? I mean, I thought we were supposed to be at the gates of Quebec by now. It seems that not much has gone according to plan."

"We must have faith in God and in our leaders," Joshua said firmly.

"You may need to have faith for both of us, because I am almost ready to head home."

"You are not alone. I understand that many are ready to abandon the mission, but please do not be too hasty."

"My men are exhausted and out of patience," Lieutenant Colonel Roger Enos said to other divisional leaders in a council of war called by him, following Arnold's departure with a small party. With growing dissension, especially in the last two divisions, Arnold had called a council of war, arguing for them to continue until they reached the nearest French settlement. He set off, promising to meet the rest of the troops between where he left and the settlement. "We have had a series of disasters on this expedition, and now we suffered through this cataclysmic storm. We should be near Quebec or at least Canada by now, according to the plan that was given to all of us at the beginning of this expedition. It is apparent that we are completely lost in the middle of a vast unchartered wilderness, probably nowhere near our destination, with winter fast approaching."

"Colonel Enos," said Lieutenant Colonel Christopher Greene in an abrupt, harsh tone, "you have no authority to call this council of war. It is totally inappropriate and insubordinate without Colonel Arnold here, as you are aware."

"Colonel, my captains have been clamoring to me to turn back while there still is time to do so, so what was I to do?"

"Lead, Colonel, that is what you are supposed to do; lead the men. You are their superior officer; show some backbone."

"Colonel Greene, I will overlook your comments. This is no time for pettiness. Let this council make a decision by putting the matter to a vote."

"Very well, Colonel," Greene said. "All those in favor of following Colonel Arnold's orders and continuing on with the expedition, say aye, and all those against following Colonel Arnold's orders, say nay."

The vote was taken, and it ended in a tie. Surprisingly, the tie-breaking vote to follow Arnold's orders and continue with the expedition was cast by none other than Colonel Enos himself. Following adjournment, Enos met with his captains and returned to meet with Greene.

"Colonel, I am glad to see that you exhibited some backbone after all," Greene said as Enos approached.

"This is not about my backbone or lack thereof, Colonel," Enos said. "It is about the safety and welfare of the men. Let us be honest with one another; we have all been led down the primrose path by Colonel Arnold and his so-called map. I know it, and you know it."

"And your point is, Colonel?"

"My point is, Colonel," Enos said, with a hint of sarcasm, "my captains met with me immediately following the council, and they unanimously voted to turn back. I have no choice as commander of my men but to follow their wishes."

"Turn back?" said Greene, with fire in his eyes. "You are supposed to be their leader, not their follower. Why, you *are* a deserter, a coward—I should have you and your men shot on the spot for desertion."

"You will have to shoot us in the back, Colonel, because we are leaving right after my men give your men some of what precious few supplies we have left."

"Captain Morgan, Major Meigs, are you going to desert too?"

"No, Colonel, my men are not cowards. We have a mission to fulfill. I say let these deserters leave us and be done with it and let us move on," Captain Daniel Morgan said, with conviction.

"We are with you too, Colonel," said Major Return Jonathan Meigs, "and I completely agree with the captain."

"Captain, Major, I sincerely appreciate your dedication and loyalty and that of your men, and so will Colonel Arnold. We move out without Colonel Enos and his men as soon as the supplies change hands."

After the supplies were given to Greene's men, Enos gathered his men, much to the anger and dismay of the remaining troops.

"Enos and his three hundred men are leaving, Jeremiah. If you are serious about turning back, now is your opportunity," Joshua said to his younger friend.

"I cannot do it; I cannot leave you or the others—as much as I would like to," said a scared but determined Jeremiah. "I am in it to the end."

Joshua, a thin smile slightly turning up the corners of his mouth, patted Jeremiah on the back and said, "So am I, my friend—so am I."

In front of a dwindling fire, Jeremiah, now rail thin, whose clothes hung upon him like those upon a stick scarecrow, exclaimed, "Joshua, I am so weak!" Dinner consisted of wild berries and leaves.

"I know. I am rather weak myself," said a cold, trembling Joshua as he rubbed his hands over the fire, despair gripping him, but he attempted to maintain a strong front for his young friend.

"Joshua, are we going to make it?" Jeremiah asked, looking longingly up at his friend.

"Sure, kid, we are going to make it," said Joshua with conviction, though if truth be known, he was no longer certain of it himself. For the first time, he had serious doubts of what lay ahead, but he could not let on to his young buddy, whose life depended on him being strong. "Colonel Arnold will not let us down. Now let us get some rest. We need it to keep our strength up."

Jeremiah quickly fell asleep, trusting in his older friend's judgment; it was all he had left in the world. Joshua, on the other hand, struggled mightily to find the sleep he so desperately needed. Had he led his young friend astray? Should he have insisted that Jeremiah turn back? Was this his great contribution to the glorious cause, the pursuit of liberty, and would it end almost before it began? Would Colonel Arnold really bring them out of this nightmare, or was his faith in the colonel misplaced? Finally, after worrying himself into exhaustion, he fell into a deep, welcomed sleep.

"Captain," Arnold said to Captain Thomas Hudson, who was from Arnold's home state of Connecticut, "now that we have reached Lake Mègantic, we must get word back to the others immediately. Get me Private Gordon." It was October 27, and Arnold knew that time was running out for him.

"Yes, sir," Hudson said, saluting Arnold. Within minutes Private Arthur Gordon was brought to Arnold.

"Private Arthur Gordon reporting, sir," Gordon said, snapping off a crisp salute to his commander.

"Private, you are to go back to the trailing battalions and give them these instructions on how they are to negotiate the swamp lands above this lake," Arnold ordered. Little did he realize that the instructions he was giving came from more faulty maps. "We will be moving on above the lake following the Chaudière River northward, you and the battalions can catch up with us upriver."

"Sir, I will leave forthwith," Gordon said, after receiving the instructions.

꩜

"Joshua, Private Gordon is back in camp!"

"So I have heard, Jeremiah. That is a good sign."

"I'll say a very good sign! Colonel Arnold must have found his way out of this mess of a wilderness."

"I am certain he did, as I knew he would."

"You always knew he would find a way."

"Gentlemen, we are moving out right now; gather your supplies," Captain Morgan said to Joshua and Jeremiah as he passed by them on his way around the camp.

Jeremiah seemed to be frozen, hearing those words.

"Jeremiah, you heard the captain. Grab your bag and get moving," Joshua said as he jostled his young friend, who seemed to be in a catatonic state.

"We are going to make it—we are actually going to make it, Joshua! I wanted to believe it," Jeremiah said, looking wide eyed at Joshua.

"We are going to make it," Joshua said as he patted Jeremiah on the shoulder, "but only if you get moving."

"I am coming; I am coming!" Jeremiah replied, grabbing his bag and tossing it on his shoulder.

"Joshua, we are completely lost, and if that is not bad enough, we are lost in swampy bogs," Jeremiah said, with a disgusted look as he and his fellow battalion members tramped around in the messy, brackish bogs. It was early morning, a couple of days following the return of Private Gordon.

"They are awful," Joshua replied. "I am going to talk with Private Gordon to see what the problem seems to be."

"Please do. I am beginning to get depressed again, Joshua, and I and these men," he said, gesturing toward the soldiers behind hit, "are nearly starved to death. We must find our way out of this, and soon."

"We will…we will. Do not quit now when we are so close."

Joshua approached Private Gordon, who was conferring with Colonel Greene.

"Colonel Greene, Private Gordon," Joshua said as he saluted.

"Private Finch, you came to find out where we are, correct?"

"Yes, sir, and how we get out of this forsaken place. The men are getting very anxious."

"Yes, I know. I am not sure what has gone wrong. I have followed Colonel Arnold's instructions to the letter."

"Sir, perhaps Colonel Arnold got his information on negotiating these swamps from another faulty map."

"Possibly—that could explain how we got here. I firmly believe we are close, very close, to Lake Mègantic."

"Colonel, Private, may I make a suggestion?"

"By all means, Private," Greene said, "we are listening."

"Send Jeremiah and me in the direction you, Private Gordon, are most certain will lead to the lake. We will be back by nightfall, whether we succeed or not."

"Are you sure you want to do this, Private?" Greene asked. "You and Private Greenman could get permanently lost and separated from all of us."

"I want to do this, sir. The men are passed the limits of endurance, and begging your pardon, sir, but we cannot get more lost than we are already."

"Very well then, you have my permission to proceed," Greene said, placing his hand on Joshua's shoulder. "Godspeed."

Joshua conferred immediately with Gordon and then set out to get Jeremiah.

"Joshua, there is the lake!" Jeremiah yelled excitedly, pointing his right index finger straight ahead of him as he ran ahead.

"Where?" Joshua, who had been lagging behind his younger friend, asked as he now picked up the pace. "All I see are trees."

"Keep coming; a bit more, and you will see it!"

Joshua, with heavy breathing, slowed down as he approached the grinning Jeremiah.

"Now do you see it?"

Peering around a large stand of evergreens, Joshua finally saw Lake Mègantic.

"Yes, I see it! I must say it looks more beautiful than any body of water I have ever laid my eyes on!" Joshua said as he excitedly hugged Jeremiah.

The two men took a few minutes to rest and to let the magnanimity of the moment sink in, and then Joshua proclaimed, "Jeremiah, we have got to get moving right now. We should be able to arrive back to the battalions before nightfall. Then we can all set out together early tomorrow morning and be back here by early tomorrow afternoon. How are you feeling?"

"I am starving and weak, but finding this lake has given me more energy than I have had in a very long time. I am ready to start back."

Joshua and Jeremiah arrived back in camp just as the sun was setting in the west, to the gratitude of all the men. Their hands were shaken, and their backs were slapped to the point they were almost sorer from the heartfelt thanks lavished upon them than from the trek through the swampland. After a meager meal, they and the rest of the men retired early, anticipating the morning and knowing that this nightmare would soon be behind them. Joshua and Jeremiah fell asleep immediately and slept more soundly than since the first few days of the expedition.

"Colonel Greene, thank God, you made it!" Arnold said as Greene and his battalions met up with Arnold and his advance contingency near the falls on the upper Chaudière River. It had been four days since Arnold sent Gordon back to the battalions.

"Thank God and Privates Gordon, Finch, and Greenman. Without them we would still be wandering in that swampland near Mègantic."

"Please tell me about what happened, Colonel," Arnold said.

"Be glad to, sir, but first, I and my men are famished."

"Of course. I have spoken with a local farmer and procured several cattle. We will have more butchered immediately."

"Chief Natanis, I am much indebted to you for the assistance you have provided to me and my men by removing trees in our pathway, and I now know that the information I had received about you alerting the British of our coming was not true. I am still in need of your help," Arnold said, to the chief of the Abernaki Indians, before departing from Satitgan. "There is much to be done on the journey that yet lies ahead of us. I am willing to have you join with us in moving on to Quebec, and I will pay you and any of your tribesmen who join us the same wage that I am paying my men. I will add bonus pay. And your warriors will be allowed to choose their own officers to lead them."

"That is a most gracious offer, Colonel Arnold. I will address my people and will soon give you our reply."

"Jeremiah, what a difference a few days of good food has made in your appearance!" excitedly exclaimed Joshua. "I must admit I was beginning to worry for a while if you were going to survive. You were fading away before my eyes!"

"Yes, I was worried myself. I am not certain that I would have made it another week."

"Let us go thank Colonel Arnold for his perseverance and leader-ship," Joshua said.

"Colonel Arnold," said Joshua, saluting Arnold as they approached him standing outside of his tent.

"Privates Finch and Greenman, welcome. How may I help you?"

"Sir, we came to thank you for your strength and perseverance that brought us out of the wilderness. I knew we could count on you, sir."

"This is interesting. I was just preparing to write to General Schuyler, praising you men for *your* strength and perseverance, which in my opinion brought us through when others deserted. And Colonel Greene sang your praises, along with Private Gordon's, to me, crediting you men with getting the battalions out of the swampy bogs. We made it this far, but we still have a ways to go. The Saint Lawrence should soon be in our sights, and from there we can follow it up to the gates of Quebec City. We now are well fed, and we should have plenty of food and supplies for the remainder of our mission. I just received a great supply of flour from the manager of the local gristmill here in town."

"Wonderful—a plentiful supply of flour!" Joshua excitedly remarked.

"Yes, it fascinating how something that we normally take for granted, like flour, can now bring us such excitement."

"I will never again take food for granted, Colonel Arnold," said Jeremiah, in somber tones as he gently shook his head.

"Nor will I, Private—nor will I," Arnold agreed.

"While I was famished, sir, Private Greenman almost starved to death. He was literally skin and bones."

"He was not alone, Private Finch, but the good news is it is behind us now, and we can and must move forward. Food will not be an issue, but with desertions and death, we need help. Therefore, I have approached the French Canadians and the Abernaki Indians for them to join us. I await their answer."

"We could definitely use more help, Colonel. It is time for us to take our leave," Joshua said as he and Jeremiah saluted Arnold and left.

"Dark Eagle—he is a great warrior," Natanis said, addressing his warriors, referring to Arnold. "He is willing to give us the same pay as his own troops in the Continental Army, including bonuses, if we will accompany him to Quebec City and help him take control of it from the British."

"How can we know this white man will not cheat us?"

"For him to make such a gesture tells me he speaks truth, but the Great Spirit has impressed upon me that he will fly like an eagle to great heights, but then he will fall to the depths. We shall be with him on his assent."

⚬

"Excellency, there are several cannons at Fort Ticonderoga that could be very helpful to our cause," said Henry Knox to Washington after being approached by the commander in chief in November, regarding the need for artillery around Boston.

"Yes, Henry, what is your point?"

"My point, Excellency, is that if you provide me with some men and supplies, I will go personally and bring them back myself."

"Henry, it is a couple of hundred miles over rugged terrain, and who knows what the weather conditions will be. How are you going to be able to accomplish this seemingly impossible task, in the period of time that would be useful to us?"

"What would be the period of time, Excellency?"

"By the beginning of next year. I want—no, I need this artillery by early 1776."

"That will be a challenge, but we cannot let a perfectly good resource go to waste. Honestly, I do not know where else I could locate the artillery you need in such a short time. And while the terrain is rugged and poses difficulties for such an endeavor, the weather at this time of the year could be beneficial to us. I am depending on 'bad weather.' I must have a deep freeze to cross the Hudson with those heavy cannons. And I want plenty of snow. Besides, I know that I can do this with the help of a good team."

"Plenty of snow? Do you know what you are saying?"

"Our only hope is for enough of it throughout our entire trek so that I can pull the cannons with sleds. If there is no snow or not enough of it, I would be reduced to using wagons, and that could be very problematic. If the ground is not frozen and covered, muddy conditions could make the journey almost impossible, and if the ground is frozen and not covered, pulling wagons on rutty frozen ground, especially through the mountains, would be arduous. No, the best hope is plenty of firm, freshly fallen snow. That would be ideal for sleds through almost any terrain that we would encounter."

"Well, I think it may be foolhardy, but I appreciate your attitude. And I need something—anything to help the cause. I am facing the end of enlistments, winter looming and patriotism at low ebb. Though the council voted down General Ward's recommendation of taking Dorchester Heights, I have given that matter serious consideration and am in agreement with him. That is the something I have in mind, the something that I believe has to happen early next year. Put those cannons on the heights, with some supporting troops, and perhaps they could end this stalemate."

"I thoroughly respect everyone on the council, Excellency, but that is precisely the conclusion I have come to. The Brits would have to try to take the heights or risk a devastating bombardment. I believe they would realize the futility of such an attempt and abandon the city."

"Yes…" Washington said, musing about the possibilities. "It is bold, and we need a bold initiative. Very well, it is settled then. I am putting you in charge. Get whatever men and supplies you need."

"Thank you, Excellency. I plan on recruiting my brother William, Captain Finch, and Private Richard Barnes to accompany me."

"All fine men. Will three be enough?"

"Yes. I do not want too many men for this task. Too many could bog the operation down, but if necessary, I am certain we will be able to receive assistance from the locals."

"With you and Captain Finch gone, who will be in charge of fortifications? Not that I think Howe is going to be making any moves soon, but we must remain prepared and vigilant."

"I understand and agree, Excellency. I will take care of the matter before we leave."

"Very well, Henry, you have my blessing."

"Excellency, you will not be disappointed."

"Private Barnes, I have a proposal for you."

"Yes, sir. What is it?"

"There are several cannons located at Fort Ticonderoga. Now that the fort is ours, we must avail ourselves of them. His Excellency informed me of his need for artillery, and I suggested to him that the cannons be retrieved from the fort and transported to Cambridge. After some discussion, he agreed. This could be a tough task, but I believe that these cannons could be critical to our cause. Indeed, His Excellency has a plan for their use that could change everything. I would be most appreciative if you join me, my brother William, and Captain Finch on this major undertaking. My brother has agreed, and I plan on speaking with Captain Finch as soon as we are finished. You are a good man, and you are young and able bodied. Will you join us?"

"When do we leave?"

Knox grinned at Richard's prompt positive reply.

"That is what I was hoping you would say. Early next week, if Captain Finch agrees."

"Do you wish for me to accompany you?"

"Absolutely! You know him much better than I do. Is there something you must tend to just now?"

"No, sir."

"Then let us locate Captain Finch!"

"Captain, the plan is to retrieve the cannons from the fort and transport them over the Hudson and across the Berkshires, to be delivered to His Excellency by no later than early next year. His Excellency has a plan in place for the use of these cannons that I am in complete concurrence with; it could change everything with regard to our current stalemate with the Brits," Knox said enthusiastically to a rather skeptical William Finch. "My brother William has agreed to join me, and so has Private Barnes. We will leave early next week. Though this is short notice to you, I must have your answer, now."

"Let me understand. You are proposing to take several-ton cannons out of Fort Ticonderoga, put them on sleds, transport them across Lake George, drag them across what you hope to be a frozen Hudson River, and then take them by sled up and over the Berkshires and deliver them here within a month and a half to two months' time?" said William, with a you-cannot-really-be-serious look on his face.

"Precisely," Knox said, his enthusiasm not dampened in the slightest by William's reply.

"Have you lost possession of your faculties, Colonel? Do you realize that this expedition is completely dependent upon the most unpredictable aspect of this planet—the weather?"

"Winter has already arrived, Captain. One must have faith. We must act, now. His Excellency has a plan, and it depends upon these cannons. Our cause, our great cause, may depend on what we do."

"And you agree with the colonel, Richard?"

"I do, sir. Admittedly, I would do almost anything to get out of digging trenches, but I concur with the colonel. The enlistments of many men are soon going to expire. This stalemate is wearing on everyone. I know much depends on unpredictable weather, but it is likely that conditions are going to be bad, and that is good. We already have had our usual freezing weather and snow. General Washington has a plan for the use of the cannons that could change everything. I want to be a part of making that happen."

"I understand," William said, gently nodding his head. "I think you both may be a bit daft, but I must concur that we must take some sort of affirmative action to terminate this stalemate. Though I do not share your obvious effervescence about this—indeed, I am still highly skeptical—I will join the team and give you my full effort in this endeavor."

"We know that you will. Thank you, Captain. I am confident with your help we will succeed," Knox said.

As they were leaving, Knox said to Richard, "Private, I am so glad I brought you along. You convinced him, not me. Your logic and great relationship carried the day. His Excellency would be most pleased to know of this, and he will in time. Captain Finch is a vital cog to our operation. I am not certain we could succeed without him."

"I am happy to have been of assistance, sir."

19

"Captain Finch, this is truly a test of endurance," said Richard as he rowed along with hired men, taking turns in shifts with others in the boat. It was early November, just a few days after Arnold's troops reached the Saint Lawrence River. After rendezvousing with Knox and his brother at Fort Ticonderoga, Richard and the two Williams, along with hired men and local soldiers, completed the strenuous task of loading cannons and mortar on boats to be transported down Lake George some thirty miles south to Fort George, where Knox had arranged for sleds and oxen to be delivered.

"It is, Private Barnes—it is more of a test than even I could ever have imagined when we started. However, as skeptical as I was before this journey began, I am now certain of a positive outcome. I have never seen anyone more determined to succeed in an endeavor than Colonel Knox."

"You are quite right about that," said Richard as he strained in pulling the oar up to his chest. "It just seems…" Richard said, struggling for air. "It just seems that we are not making any progress."

"Agreed, especially when we have to cut through ice, but we are making progress."

That night, upon reaching shore, Richard sat down and wrote a letter to Victoria:

> My dearest Victoria,
>
> I cannot tell you the challenges we have already faced and overcome during this difficult mission. Carrying these guns in boats, it seems every day we are backing up against a very strong headwind. We just finished our fourth day on the lake, and Fort George, our first destination, is nowhere in sight. And once we do make Fort George, it is only the beginning. Without snow, we will never be able to transport the guns across the mountains. Pray for us, my darling. I hope to see you soon.
>
> All my love, your beloved,
> Richard

"Colonel Knox, with all due respect, sir, I am pleading with you not to attempt this on your own," said a distraught Captain William Finch upon learning that Knox was planning on leaving Fort George for Albany alone, following a Christmas blizzard that brought three feet of snow, along with brutal cold conditions.

"Brother, Captain Finch is quite right. The current situation is far too dangerous for one man to go alone. You must let me come with you."

"I also concur, Colonel Knox, sir, but rather than your brother, please take me. I am the youngest here and I believe the best able to assist you," Richard added.

"Gentlemen, thank you all for your concern, but I am perfectly able to proceed on my own. I must get to the Hudson River, immediately, to cut holes in the ice. The refreezing of water seeping through the ice to strengthen it is vital to our success. I need all of you here, to guide and direct the hired men in moving these cannons out, shortly after my departure."

"But, Colonel," William Finch said.

"The matter is closed, gentlemen. I am leaving in the morning. I will see you all in Albany."

"John, Sam—great news!" Jonathan Barnes said as he rapidly approached John and Sam Adams, who were chatting in the State House courtyard.

"Jonathan!" said a startled John Adams, waiting for Jonathan to catch his breath.

"What is it?" Sam Adams blurted out. "What is this great news?"

"My apologies, gentlemen…I need to gather myself."

"Quite all right, Jonathan. How do you feel?" John asked.

"I am fine, thank you, very fine. John Manley, appointed captain of the schooner *Lee* by General Washington, just captured the British brigantine *Nancy*."

"The *Nancy*—are you sure about this?" Sam asked.

"Positive, Sam. A letter from General Washington was just delivered to President Hancock."

"Jonathan, that is great news!" John said, grabbing Jonathan by the shoulders and gently shaking him. "That is wonderful news!" John said, with a wide smile on his face as he continued to shake Jonathan, staring at him.

"Yes—maybe now Congress will approve the fleet that the Rhode Island delegation wanted and we have all been lobbying for these past months."

"The fleet…" said John, as he let go of Jonathan, thinking about what this meant to the cause.

"John?" Jonathan inquired, looking at his musing friend.

"Sorry—it just suddenly occurred to me that with a fleet we would actually have an authentic navy."

"That would—I should say *will*—be awesome!" Jonathan concurred.

"How did it happen, and what did Manley actually get from the *Nancy*? Was there any information about that?" Sam asked, bringing the group back to the present.

"It appears that *Nancy* was coming into Boston Harbor and thought that *Lee* was a British pilot boat that would bring them in to dock. Manley played along, carrying out the ruse, and sent a small boat of men with concealed arms over to the ship, and when they boarded, they drew their weapons on the stunned crew, and the captain surrendered without a shot being fired."

"Absolutely amazing!" said John with rapt attention.

"Some two thousand muskets were captured, tons of ammunition, including flints, musket balls, solid shot, and even a thirteen-inch cannon, all along with numerous other supplies."

"Just wait until those supplies are hauled to Cambridge," said Sam.

"They will create quite a stir, let me tell you," Jonathan added. "After going to Cambridge last month and hearing General Washington's pleas for supplies from the Congress, this will be a most welcome bonus."

"Yes, they will!" John said joyfully. "Gentlemen, I believe our cause now has momentum. We just passed an act authorizing the capture of British vessels, which included the issuing of commissions to captains of privateer vessels, which was sorely needed, I might add. Then we passed rules and regulations for the navy a few days ago, and now this news. I will talk to Ward and Hopkins about revisiting the motion for the fleet."

"I agree, John," Jonathan exclaimed. "Now is the time to move forward."

"Momentum does seem to be on our side on this matter," Sam concurred.

"Yes, and we must seize the opportunity it presents," John said. "Now let us get back to the session!"

※

"Maggie," Jean Paul said as he entered Maggie's and planted a big smooch on the cheek of Maggie Mae. "I must see Francois right away. May I *borrow* him for a few minutes and *borrow* that office of yours?"

"Bribery like that," said Maggie, gently touching the side of her face just graced by her lover's lips, "will get you everywhere. You may, but please be quick about it; as you can see, we are very busy," Maggie said as she gestured to the crowded tavern.

"Oui, you are jumpin' tonight, and that is so good to see. I promise I will not be long with him."

"Then be my guest, my dear! I will get him for you."

"Merci, my love."

A couple of minutes later, Maggie returned with Francois.

"Francois!" Jean Paul said as they embraced. "I promised Maggie that I would not take up too much of your time. This is a very busy evening for you," Jean Paul said as he led his son to the back of the tavern toward Maggie's office.

"What is this about, Father? Could it not have waited until the weekend was gone? This, as you know and can see, is our busiest night of the week."

"It is JP's busiest night too, as you are well aware. I will explain in a minute," he said as he entered open door to the office, with Francois following close behind.

After Francois closed the door, Jean Paul took Maggie's seat behind her desk, and Francois sat down in front of it.

"The reason I came tonight is that I am scheduled to meet tomorrow morning with Monsieur Braun about a business endeavor."

"Becky's father? About a business endeavor? What kind of a business endeavor?"

"Privateering."

"Privateering?"

"Oui. General Washington has given his blessing to privateering, and the Congress will as well. But we are already well behind in this matter. People are making fortunes. With the capture of the *Nancy*, though that was done by one of Washington's ships, it proves that there is a treasure trove to be had for those who are willing to take some risks, while helping support our country and its glorious cause."

"And you are going to get involved with Becky's father?"

"Oui, and you. I need your assistance."

"Me? Father, I do not have the money to put into such an expensive undertaking. And what about you? Despite all your smuggling efforts, the blockade has crippled your merchant business, and though JP's is doing reasonably well, it is not covering your shortcomings from the mercantile trade. How can you afford another business endeavor?"

"I do not want your money. And it is precisely because of the blockade and its effects on my merchant business that I want—no *must* get involved. As I already said, a treasure trove is to be had in privateering, and perhaps, just as important, we can strike a blow at the Brits where they have hurt us, in the arena of supplies, capturing the ships that bring supplies to the troops and selling those supplies to our troops and compatriots. I want to propose to Monsieur Braun that he and I put up the money and that you find some candidates for captain and present them to us. The three of us will interview them and pick one for the job."

"While I know something about the merchant business, I am no expert on seafaring captains, especially as to who would be the right choice for this undertaking."

"Not to worry. I have several friends who can assist you in coming up with a list, the best of whom is Reginald Tolbert. Reginald knows virtually all the captains in New England, and he has an eye for those who handle their crews well. You know who he is, do you not, Francois?"

"Ole Reggie? Sure, I know him. Ole Reggie Tolbert, the great shipping magnate. He was a captain himself at one time, correct?"

"Oui, he was one of the best, which is part of the reason I believe he would be a top choice to begin your inquiry. He knows exactly what it takes to be a captain, and while he never commanded a privateering expedition, he knows all about what it takes to lead a crew. That is what is really important, regardless of whether the objective is fishing, transporting goods or people, engaging the enemy in warfare, or attempting to commandeer a vessel for its supplies."

"I would agree with you, Father. So how do I benefit from this business, if I may so inquire? You and Monsieur Braun would be partners, correct?"

"Monsieur Braun, you, and me, Francois. That is to be my proposal to him."

"I would be an equal partner with the two of you, though I would not be involved in the financing?"

"Picking the correct captain may be everything in this undertaking. Once he is chosen, you will be his overseer. He will be reporting directly to you regarding all the details of his operation. You, Monsieur Braun, and I will meet monthly to discuss how things are progressing, though we will meet much more frequently in the beginning until this operation gets firmly established."

"So basically, I am going to be his manager."

"Oui."

"I am not sure that I have the time to do that, Father, let alone the expertise."

"As far as the experience is concerned, you have learned more than you think, first from me and my merchant business, from Monsieur Finch and his business, and also by your own involvement in my mercantile business. You have had considerable contact with merchant-ship captains. You have seen how they operate and think. And do not discount the experience at JP's and Maggie's. While it is not seafaring experience, it is business experience, which is invaluable and is the same regardless of the business. I am certain that Monsieur Tolbert will be more than happy to advise you as to what to do in overseeing a captain and his work. As far as time is concerned, if it gets to be too much, then we will hire an assistant who can take over most of your day-to-day duties."

"So you really think I can do this?"

"Oui. If I did not think that, I would not be asking you. I want you to join us, son. I think it is a wonderful opportunity for all of us and, as I said, can benefit our great cause."

"Is Monsieur Braun as enthusiastic as you about this?"

"While I have not sketched out the details for him, he is excited about the prospects."

"Does he know about your plans regarding me? And do you think he is willing to trust me with all this responsibility?"

"He does not know about you specifically, though he knows I am planning on hiring someone to find a captain and manage him, but I think he will be willing to trust you."

"How do you think he will react when he knows it is me, the one who loves his daughter?"

"I think he will be very happy. Why not join us tomorrow?"

"I cannot. I am committed to be here at Maggie's all day."

"I understand. I will let you know the outcome as soon as I am able."

"I will be very interested to hear what Monsieur Braun has to say."

"Francois!" Jean Paul said as he nearly ran to hug his son, who had come through the back door of JP's looking for his father.

"Father!" Francois said. "How was your meeting with Monsieur Braun?"

"Come join me in my office. Do you have a few minutes to talk?"

"Oui. I came to hear what happened at the meeting."

The two entered the office and sat down, Jean Paul with a big grin on his face.

"From your expression I presume the meeting went well."

"Oui, I would say that is a bit of an understatement. Monsieur Braun was thrilled to hear my plans for you. He thought it a wonderful idea that the three of us would be partners in a new privateering company named Braun, DuBois, and DuBois."

"That is truly astonishing!" Francois said, shaking his head. "So please explain to me the actual workings of this business partnership. I understand that the two of you will pay the upfront expenses."

"Correct. Monsieur Braun and I will provide the initial capital to acquire a schooner, and if and when the partnership is dissolved, that capital expense will be reimbursed to us. Then any debt that may exist will be paid, and the balance split three ways. He and I will pay for the ongoing expenses, and then when we capture a prize, those expenses will be paid back to me and Monsieur Braun off the top, and then the balance, less a possible agreed-upon capital reserve, will be split three ways."

"What if...what if we do not capture any prizes, or if we do, they do not have enough goods to cover the expenses, not counting the capital investment? Am I going to be required to reimburse you and Monsieur Braun in that scenario?"

"Good question, but no. He and I will bear the burden and take the risk."

"And what about the paperwork?"

"His lawyer should be done drafting the paperwork this week."

"May I look at it with you when you receive it?"

"Certainly. He is going to have three made so each of us will have one. I am going to have my lawyer review mine."

"And I would like to have my lawyer review mine."

"You should."

"Did he have any thoughts about whom I should talk with about prospective captains?"

"He agreed that Reginald Tolbert would be the best person to start the inquiry."

"Then there is unanimity. Ole Reggie it is. I will contact him as soon as the partnership agreement is signed by everyone."

"Wonderful. I am excited, Francois. I think this is going to be a very profitable venture for all of us," Jean Paul said as he stood up, grinning, and embraced his son as they headed out the door.

"I must say that I am getting excited about it also, Father, though I am not certain that I yet share your optimism about the monetary prospects," Francois said as they moved into the crowded tavern.

"You will in time, Francois—trust me. Now, let us have a beer in celebration of our future venture together!"

"Becky, Becky!" Francois said as he greeted her with a hug and kiss on the cheek as she entered Maggie's to join him for supper. "I am going to be in partnership with your father and my father in a privateering venture. They want me to pick a captain for the vessel and then oversee the captain and his activities."

"So I have heard," Becky Braun said as she looked lovingly and proudly into the eyes of Francois.

"Becky, I am excited, but I have to admit I am also a bit scared," Francois said, his face now reflecting his changed mood.

"Scared? You, Francois? Scared of what?"

"Scared that I will not be able to do the job, nor have the time to devote to it. I am young, and I have not had any direct seafaring experience."

"True, but you have had business dealings and managerial experience that you have proved to be quite adept at, and besides, if your father and my father believe you can handle it, then there is no doubt that you can."

"Oui—I suppose you are right."

"I know I am right, Francois, and I know that I am feeling very hungry right now."

"Then let us eat!"

The resolution calling for the construction of thirteen frigates, after some additional debate, passed the Congress on December 13, for a total cost of just under $900,000 for the entire fleet.

John Adams and Jonathan Barnes left Congress together in late December to spend some time with their wives. Riding along together through the Massachusetts countryside, Adams reflected about his wife.

"Jonathan, I cannot wait to be with Abigail. I am certain that we will have serious discussions about a range of topics. She will not hesitate to express her opinions."

"She is an incredible woman, John."

"Yes, she is my compass. I periodically need to consult with her to make sure I am on course."

"I understand. Eleanor is a solid rock for me. She is level headed and full of common sense. I can always count on her to set me straight if I get a bit off base."

"You are a very fortunate man yourself, my friend. She is the salt of the earth, and I dare say she stays abreast of all manner of current affairs."

"She always seems to. I am very interested to hear her views on everything, just as you are with Abigail, and to see how closely aligned our spouses are on all that is transpiring. We will have to compare notes about our wives' thoughts and opinions when we ride back next week."

Adams laughed. "Congress, I am sure, is not ready for what our better halves have to say."

"I surmise you are correct." Jonathan nodded in agreement.

"Indeed." Adams was headed east to Braintree, and Barnes west to Lexington. "I will see you back here next week," Adams said as they waved good-bye to each other.

20

"Gentlemen, I have been contacted by a man who I am certain is an emissary of the French crown, though he claims to be a merchant from Antwerp, with friends in high places in Europe," Franklin said to a meeting of the Committee of Secret Correspondence, a committee that included Jonathan Barnes, John Jay, and other distinguished delegates, formed for the express purposes of reaching out to sympathizers in other parts of the world, particularly Europe. "The contact has been made through Francis Daymon, who is well known to all of you. The man's name is Chevalier Julien-Alexandre Achard de Bonvouloir. He conveyed to Daymon that he is here to assure us of the goodwill of his country, though he would not give details as to his purpose for being here."

"Benjamin, the man might actually be working for the Brits. What better way to gain access to the inner workings of Congress than to gain the confidence of Benjamin Franklin?" said committee member Thomas Johnson of Maryland.

"I had my suspicions when Mr. Daymon approached me about the matter. That this man might be a spy had occurred to me, but given the current circumstances we are facing in the war effort, I believe it is worth the risk."

"Ben, I agree," Jonathan Barnes said, gently nodding his head. "I believe the potential benefit from pursuing a connection with France outweighs the risks involved in meeting with him."

"That is my feeling exactly. Gentlemen, we need all the help we can obtain. Despite Bonvouloir's disavowals, it seems quite apparent that he is indeed working for the French crown."

"We must be very careful," John Jay interposed. "If we are too open with this man, we could all be hanged."

"Quite right, but if we lose this war, we will all be hanged anyway," Jonathan said.

"Benjamin," said John Dickinson, "I agree we need to meet with this man, but it needs to be discreet, very quiet. I recommend that only a couple of members of this committee accompany you when you meet with him."

"In keeping with John's point, what about conducting the meetings at night?" asked Benjamin Harrison.

"Those are excellent suggestions, gentlemen," Franklin replied. "With the blessing of the committee, I will take John Jay and Jonathan Barnes with me, and we will meet with Bonvouloir and Daymon, who will serve as a translator, at Carpenters' Hall in the evening. We will all arrive separately, by different routes, in the event there are spies out and about. If we need additional meetings, we will follow the same basic procedure. Is this satisfactory to all?"

"It is satisfactory to me," Thomas Johnson said. "You have my blessing, and I believe that of the committee."

"Are we all in agreement?" Franklin asked, looking at each member as all nodded affirmatively. "Very well. I will inform Mr. Daymon at once of our plans. Thank you, gentlemen, for your insights and support. This meeting stands adjourned."

"Ben, now that you have arrived, we are all here," Jonathan said, greeting Franklin as he entered Carpenters' Hall.

"Excellent," Franklin replied, shaking Jonathan's hand. "Mr. Daymon, would you please introduce us to your acquaintance and then lead us upstairs so that we may get on with the business at hand?"

"It would be my pleasure," Daymon said as he briefly introduced the three committee members to Bonvouloir. "Follow me." Daymon, being the curator of the Library Company's books, was very familiar with all aspects of the building. He made sure that all shutters were pulled in and properly fastened so that no light would shine outside. He led the group by candlelight up the stairs to the east room on the second floor, which contained the books. Bonvouloir in a disguise, posing as a much older man than his actual age, was addressed immediately by Franklin.

"Tell us plainly: Is France with us and our efforts to break the bonds with Britain? Can we count on your country to assist us in this great endeavor?"

"Monsieur, I do not know. I cannot answer the question. I am only a private citizen."

"With all due respect, sir, we know better than that," Jonathan opined. "You would not have gone to all this trouble to have Mr. Daymon contact us and arrange this meeting if you were just a 'private citizen.'"

Bonvouloir hesitated.

"Does France favor us?" John Jay said firmly, as he stared directly into the eyes of the now-defensive French agent.

"Oui...yes, but of course, messieurs," the agent said cautiously. "France favors you and your cause." Small beads of sweat appeared on his brow.

"Monsieur, we need more than good favor from your country; we need your help. Will France lend us two military engineers?" Franklin queried.

"Monsieur, I do not know, but I will pass along the request immediately upon my return."

"Military supplies, particularly armaments, are needed, but our money is in short supply. If your government will supply us with the arms and ammunition we need, we will pay in commercial goods, which we have in abundance," Franklin said.

"The government would not be involved in such transactions, messieurs, but there are private merchants I am familiar with who may be willing to supply you."

"Your Majesté," French Foreign Minister Charles Gravier Comte de Vergennes said, bowing as he approached King Louis XVI. It was Comte de Vergennes who commissioned Bonvouloir to go to America and learn about military and political matters and express French sympathies toward the American cause against the British. "I have received a report from Chevalier Bonvouloir, who had several meetings with Dr. Benjamin Franklin and members of a committee of the American Congress. Bonvouloir says that there are upward of fifty thousand troops in the Continental Army, they are well paid, clothed, and armed, and they have great eagerness and have capable leadership. He says that, in his opinion, independence is certain for next year."

"Comte Vergennes, is this to be believed?" the king asked skeptically.

"I believe that it is, Majesté. Bonvouloir was very enthusiastic in his report; his impressions of the rebels were very favorable. I believe it is time that we assist them with additional arms and ammunition."

"We are already in a serious financial position, as you know, Vergennes, and I loathe the silly notion of personal liberty, but it would give me great satisfaction to see the Americans defeat the British," the king said, with a slight smile crossing his face at the thought.

"Ah—it would indeed," Vergennes intoned, nodding in agreement. "I would suggest that we set up a dummy corporation to pass supplies, along with arms and ammunition, to our friends in America.

Additionally, I feel certain that I can persuade Spain to join in this endeavor."

"A dummy corporation—and Spain joining—good ideas," the king said, warming to the possibilities. "All right, Vergennes, let us put this plan into action."

"As you wish, Majesté," said Vergennes, bowing low again and backing away from the king. "I will see to it."

"Father," Francois said as he approached Jean Paul, who was in the back of JP's, chatting with a customer.

"Francois!" Jean Paul said as he looked up and then embraced his son. "Monsieur Stearns, this is my son, Francois. Francois, this is Monsieur Jacob Stearns, one of the finest silversmiths in Boston and a good friend of Monsieur Revere."

"Pleased to make your acquaintance, Monsieur Stearns. Any friend of Monsieur Revere is a friend of mine," Francois said as he heartily shook the strong hand of Jacob Stearns, a short, stout, muscular man of about forty years of age.

"Thank you, kind sir, the pleasure is mine."

"I would to very pleased to stay and converse, but, Father, I need to speak with you for a few moments—in the office."

"But of course. Monsieur Stearns, will you excuse us for a few minutes?"

"Certainly, gentlemen, take all the time you need," Stearns said as he took a drink from his mug of beer.

"Merci," Francois said.

Father and son entered in the office, and Jean Paul said, "You bring good news?"

"Oui, I met with Monsieur Tolbert this morning," Francois said excitedly.

"How is Monsieur Tolbert?"

"He is excellent. Ole Reggie sends his best greetings to you, Father."

"That is very nice of him."

"I explained to him what we were doing, and he agreed with your assessment that we were a bit late in getting involved, that many fine captains are spoken for, but he did say that there were two captains still available, one from Marblehead and one who fishes out of Gloucester."

"Their names?"

"Jonas Bartholomew from Marblehead and Phineas Stoll from Gloucester. Monsieur Tolbert says these captains know the New England waters like the backs of their hands. They have excellent crews who have been with them for some time, and both are highly regarded in the seafaring community."

"But would they be willing to give up, at least for a while, their fishing business for a risky but potentially very profitable enterprise?"

"I guess that is the great question. Monsieur Tolbert seems to think that they would be willing to do so."

"Jonas Bartholomew sounds familiar to me—I know that name."

"I hope that means in a good way," Francois said, somewhat concerned.

"Oh yes, in a good way, I am sure."

"Then I will speak with him first. Any progress on locating a vessel for our captain?"

"I have a few possibilities, though nothing definite yet."

"I will get back to you after I meet with Monsieur Bartholomew."

"It was an incredible time of fellowship," said John Adams as he again met up with Jonathan to ride back to Philadelphia and Congress. "How was your stay, Jonathan?"

"Wonderful—thank you for asking. It was great to spend time with Eleanor and the children, as well as Annabelle and Victoria."

"And how was Eleanor?"

"She was fantastic and insightful, as always. She expressed concern about a tax on liquor imposed by Massachusetts."

"Interesting," said Adams as the two of them rode along at a gentle trot, side by side, "and what was the concern?"

"That it would draw trade away from Massachusetts."

"Really?" said Adams with a contemplative look on his face. "That is insightful. What else?"

"I expressed my concern about a 'leveling spirit' that seems to be appearing everywhere. You and I have discussed this at some length, and we agree that it is one thing to bring down a rung or two those who are above and quite another to allow those on the bottom rungs to spring up a notch or two. And you know what she said?"

"Let me guess," said Adams, with a wry smile. "She said, 'Remember the ladies; be more generous than your ancestors—all men would be tyrants if they could.'"

"How did you know?" said a dumbstruck Jonathan. "Those were Eleanor's exact words!"

Adams laughed loudly.

"What is so funny?"

"I am afraid our wives have formed an alliance while we have been gone. They obviously have been corresponding with one another to double up on us when we returned to drive home their agenda. You see, Abigail also had the exact same concern about the liquor tax."

"And what is their agenda?" asked a suddenly startled and shaken Jonathan.

"To abolish slavery, but perhaps more importantly, equality for women."

Jonathan's jaw dropped, his eyes wide open.

"Equality for women? Are you...they cannot be serious, can they?" Jonathan said, almost begging Adams to assuage his fears.

"Oh, I am afraid they can be, my friend, and indeed they are," said a now-almost-melancholy Adams. "You see, our smug, pharisaical, holier-than-thou talk of the grand and glorious cause—the pure and pristine pursuit of liberty against the tyrant king—has had the effect of letting the proverbial genie out of the bottle."

"We have indeed opened the door to the lower rungs for them to move up the ladder, or we in fact are hypocrites in their eyes," said Jonathan, with a now-knowing look in his eyes.

"That is it in a nutshell," acknowledged Adams, "and once the genie is out of the bottle, you cannot get him back in, unless and until he so chooses, and trust me on this; they will not so choose."

"So we must give them equality?"

"No, *no way* can we do that—at least not yet," said Adams. "As I explained to Abigail, it is imperative that we take one thing at a time, and the first thing is to be united and win the war, otherwise all strata of our society will lose everything."

"But the time will be forthcoming," said Jonathan.

"Yes, most certainly for the ladies and the slaves—mark my words. However, while they will undoubtedly make progress toward their goal, if we defeat the Brits, I do not think they will see anything resembling equality in our lifetimes."

"I certainly hope not, and by saying that, I do not mean any disrespect to Abigail and Eleanor or to Annabelle. They are extraordinary women and every bit, if I may say so myself, our intellectual equals, and I am sure William would concur with that, but I do not think I could handle it if they and other women obtain equality—it just does not seem right. And after all, *there is* a natural order of things."

"I could not agree with you more, and I could not have said it better myself."

"And you were worried that you were not up to the job," said Jean Paul, grinning, as he, Francois, and Becky sat at the "finest table in all Boston" at the back of JP's, for a delectable meal in celebration of their new privateering successes.

"But, Father, that was just picking the captain, not managing him. That was the easy part. Besides, you gave me the lead," Francois said rather sheepishly.

"As I told you before, son, picking the captain is the most important part of this whole endeavor because, if you have the right one, he will practically manage the operation himself. I did some follow-up with ole Reggie, and he said both the captains he recommended to you were excellent, but Jonas Bartholomew was definitely his first choice. Not only that, but you did a marvelous job of negotiating with him—holding the line on the cut he would take, even when he knew that there were not many excellent captains left and he figured he could work a deal with a young negotiator. He knows the incredible profits being made by other captains, and he desperately wanted in."

"Father, I just applied what I learned in the merchant business," Francois said.

"That is what I was trying to tell you when you were not sure that you were up to the job," Jean Paul pointed out. "Hopefully this will give you confidence. You should not question your ability to handle this anymore."

"Thank you, Father, I guess you are right," Francois said, nodding his head.

"Of course he is right," Becky added. "You did a wonderful job, and I know my father will be thrilled."

"He will especially be thrilled to know that we have not only a captain but also a boat, thanks to your efforts, Father. And by the way, that is a wonderful boat."

"Well, I must say that it should be adequate for our needs," Jean Paul said, feigning modesty.

"Adequate! That is the nicest privateering boat in all Massachusetts!" Francois said, with enthusiasm.

A big smile creased Jean Paul's face as he stood with a glass of wine in his hand.

"A toast to the great privateering adventure of Braun, DuBois, and DuBois."

"Hear, hear," said Francois as he and Becky stood, grinning, and clanked their wine glasses together with Jean Paul.

§

General Montgomery had come up from Montreal to join forces with Arnold outside Quebec City.

"Colonel Arnold," Montgomery said, greeting and saluting Arnold.

"General Montgomery, am I glad to see you!" Arnold said, saluting, then smiling and giving Montgomery a firm handshake.

"I am sure you are. I understand that you had quite an ordeal getting here."

"You have no idea what my men endured. If not for their great strength of character and courage, all would have been lost. I am afraid I gravely miscalculated the distance and dangers of this expedition. Thank God Almighty that He saw us through."

"Colonel, I understand that your determination had much to do with it, but yes, it is evident that God's hand was upon you and He brought you through, in spite of all the perils you faced."

"I must say that thus far I have been very disappointed in the Canadians, not in the aid and succor that they provided as our ragtag troops emerged from the wilderness—for that I am most grateful—it is just that I do not understand why they have not risen up and supported our cause against the Brits."

"I too am disappointed. I also naïvely believed that all we had to do was show up in Canada, and they would immediately join us in our illustrious cause of liberty. I was wrong, very wrong. With regard to Quebec City, I recommend a short siege followed by a storming of the walls," said Montgomery.

"General, no disrespect, but do you really think we have enough troops for a siege? When I started this expedition, I had some one thousand men, but due to death and desertion, I am left with six hundred seventy-five or so of my original number, along with fifty

Abernaki Indians who were kind enough to join us. I do not know if that number coupled with yours is enough for a siege."

"You may be correct, Colonel, but I am not certain we have much of a choice."

"You said it would be short?"

"Yes," said Montgomery.

"Good. Most of the troop enlistments are over by the end of the year."

"I know; I face the same problem. That is why I said it would— *must*—be short."

"Jeremiah, keep your head up and eyes focused on the tops of the walls. We must shoot some of their marksmen perched up there. We are far too vulnerable in this setting," Joshua said to his young friend. The siege had been attempted and then abandoned, proving to be ineffective. In a blinding blizzard, the troops inched forward into the walled city, on narrow roads, making them easy targets for the Brits.

No sooner had Joshua said this than a shot rang out and a scream could be heard at the back of the troop line. The slow movement became no movement as everything ground to a halt.

Musket fire poured down from the walls and ramparts with deadly force. Joshua and Jeremiah were in a company that made it into Quebec City's lower town.

"Joshua," Jeremiah practically shouted over the noise of the blizzard and gunfire, "this place gives me the creeps."

"Me too, Jeremiah," Joshua said as they crept along in the near-blinding snow. Joshua continuously looked left and right, up and down.

"I just have a feeling that things are not right," Jeremiah responded as his hands gripped tightly around his musket.

"I have the same feeling," said an increasingly nervous Joshua.

Visibility was continuing to drop as they turned a corner to the right in the tightly walled quarters of the lower town.

"Joshua!" said an excited Jeremiah. "I see them—there they are! Oh no—we are surrounded!"

EPILOGUE

The year 1776 was a pivotal, monumental year in American history. Arguably, it could be said that it was the single most important year in our history. The audacious step of declaring independence from the mother country was taken while war was raging, and the chances of prevailing were slim at best. Washington's army was on the ropes in New York, and it seemed that only a miracle(s) could save the American experiment in liberty, before it could really get underway. Follow me as we go back in time to that fateful year and witness the cost that was paid and the part that was played by the cast of characters in *The Cost of Liberty*, as they came alongside some of the great men and women of American history, in forging liberty in the crucible of a war that would test every aspect of their resolve to be free. Would the year end with victory, preserving the quest, at least for the time being, or would it end in ignominious defeat and thus squelch the last vestiges of the great and glorious cause? Those questions and more will be answered in the next edition of the Cost of Liberty series, *Victory or Death*!

ABOUT THE AUTHOR

David Ross Cornish is a lawyer who spent twenty years practicing law in Xenia and Fairborn, Ohio. He moved to Venice, Florida, and has been engaged in a solo practice, concentrating in the areas of estate planning, probate, and trust administration. He attended the University of Florida and The Ohio State University where he received his bachelor's degree. He received his law degree from Ohio Northern University Pettit College of Law.

He is married to Diane Cornish with whom he has a daughter, Lindsay.

David is a member of the Bridge Church, Venice Area Chamber of Commerce, Venice Sunrise Rotary Club, and Venice Civil War Round Table. He serves on the board for the United Way of South Sarasota County Foundation and is vice chair of the Salvation Army of Venice, Advisory Board. He enjoys making presentations to organizations on various historical topics and he is an avid golfer.

93691479R00207

Made in the USA
Columbia, SC
13 April 2018